THE HELPER

Also by David Jackson

Pariah

THE
HELPER

DAVID
JACKSON

MACMILLAN

First published 2012 by Macmillan
an imprint of Pan Macmillan, a division of Macmillan Publishers Limited
Pan Macmillan, 20 New Wharf Road, London N1 9RR
Basingstoke and Oxford
Associated companies throughout the world
www.panmacmillan.com

ISBN 978-0-230-76048-6

1 3 5 7 9 8 6 4 2

A CIP catalogue record for this book is available from
the British Library.

Typeset by CPI Typesetting
Printed and bound by CPI Group (UK) Ltd, Croydon, CR0 4YY

Visit **www.panmacmillan.com** to read more about all our books
and to buy them. You will also find features, author interviews and
news of any author events, and you can sign up for e-newsletters
so that you're always first to hear about our new releases.

Acknowledgements

I'd like to thank all of my family and friends who have supported and encouraged me in my writing. I think I have surprised them, and many of them in a good way! I'd also like to thank the staff at Pan Macmillan for their incredible work. In particular, though, I will be eternally grateful to Will Atkins, the man who gave me my first break as a novelist, who offered me my subsequent contract, and who has played an invaluable part in making my books what they are.

This one is just for Lisa

ONE

She doesn't know it yet, but she needs his help.

The special kind of assistance only he can provide.

He's in a used bookstore, pretending to browse. She's behind the counter, pretending she hasn't noticed that her favorite customer has graced her with his presence. Which would be difficult, seeing as he's the only customer here. He was the sole customer here last time, too. And the time before that.

He wonders how the hell this place manages to stay in business.

It's called Brownlow's Book Emporium, which makes it sound like something straight out of a Dickens novel. Not that Mr Fuzzypubes or Ebenezer Scrotum or whoever would seem out of place in an antiquated dump like this. Listen carefully and you'll swear you can hear the scratching of ink-dipped quills on parchment.

The tiny store is squeezed incongruously between a Laundromat and a massage parlor, here on East Tenth Street. Farther along the street there's a place offering tarot reading. The owner of Brownlow's might be well advised to drop in there for a quick peek into his future. Alternatively, he could compare the present with the past by turning the corner onto Fourth Avenue. The stretch running from Astor Place up to Union Square was once known as Book Row. In its heyday it offered a home to something like four dozen bookstores. Now they're all gone, which says something about the book trade. And when even the big players like Borders are struggling with the recession, how the hell does the owner of Brownlow's Book Emporium even manage to pay the staff?

The man wonders if there is something about the book-buying business of which he remains blissfully ignorant. Some special time of day when a plague of frantic bookworms descends and purchases every dusty volume on the shelves. Maybe he should ask the girl.

She's looking at him.

Even when she's not looking at him, she's looking at him. She's one of those people who can keep their head in a fixed position while their eyeballs roam around and take in the surroundings. Like a gecko or chameleon or some other creepy reptile.

Not that she's repulsive. She wouldn't shatter a camera lens. But on the other hand she'll always be a stranger to the catwalk. For one thing, she has no bone structure. Her contours are buried beneath a thick layer of pallid flesh. And a million freckles congregate around the bridge of her nose like they've come to hear the sermon on the mount.

These things he could overlook. He could easily while away a few hours talking to a girl whose primary drawback is a spherical dotted head.

But the sniffing, no. Not the sniffing.

She does it every few seconds. She does it so often it's a wonder she isn't dizzy with oxygen overload. It's probably the reason her face looks so inflated.

Stop the sniffing, girl. Let some of that air out so we can see your cheekbones.

He guesses she's not aware of the habit. That it has never occurred to her that her frequent snorting just might be a source of intense irritation to others. That maybe it's one of the reasons she's stuck behind the counter of this dingy little bookstore in the East Village.

Nonchalantly, he reaches at random for a book. *Moby Dick*, it's called, and it's not even pornographic. Although it could be called obscene. Heading out to sea to kill a big whale just because it's, well, big. And things aren't much different now either, the way those so-called 'research' programs involve hunting down those innocent blubbery creatures.

Speaking of which . . .

No, that's too cruel. She's not fat. Not even especially over-weight, in fact, although she could do with a little more muscle tone. She should try hefting a few of these books around instead of sitting there scribbling in her little notebook all day.

He opens the first page of his book and reads. *Call me Ishmael.* Well sure, if that's your name. Pleased to meet you, Ishmael. My name's . . .

What is my name today?

It needs to be something with a hint of mystery, an undercur-rent of danger. A name a spy might have. Or the hero in a cowboy movie. Something like John Rambo or James Bond.

Hi. The name's Gordon. Flash Gordon. Wanna see why I'm called Flash?

He feels her eyes on him.

They're her redeeming feature, those eyes. Huge and wide and wet, they make Bambi look shifty in comparison. She doesn't realize what an asset those peepers are. She should use them to her advantage a little more often.

Her tits too. That's quite a rack she's got there. If she unfas-tened a couple of buttons she'd have guys eating out of her hand and drooling into her cleavage.

He looks across at her and she bows her head even further.

3

She brings pen to paper, pokes out her tongue in mock concentration. But he knows that in another few seconds her head will tilt slightly upwards and her eyes will roll around in their sockets until they can lock onto him again.

She's smitten, is what she is.

He's not surprised by this, and he acknowledges it without arrogance. Girls go for him. They find him attractive. Years ago he went to live in Paris, France. The only thing he was good at was languages – science and technology just never interested him – so moving somewhere where his forte might actually come in useful seemed a potentially fruitful idea at the time. He ended up teaching English at a girls' school.

Now *that* was an experience.

It began with the suggestive remarks. Passages of text would be deliberately mistranslated to give them lewd overtones. Some of the girls would exploit any opportunity to sit next to him, sidling up close and sucking on their pencils, one too many buttons unfastened on their virginal white blouses. Others would jockey for position at the front of the classroom, affording them an optimal view of the shadowy region beneath his desk. They would sit there, whispering and giggling and constructing their fantasies.

He let it all pass him by. He knew what they were doing, but was never tempted to succumb. He saw them initially as childish, later as faintly ridiculous, later still as irritating and even despicable. They held no attraction for him.

Not those girls, anyway.

There were others, however. The less than beautiful ones. The quiet ones. The girls who would sit at the back of the class, hiding their faces and their fears and their very presence. The vulnerable ones. They were the ones who fascinated him. He would go out of his way to talk to those girls, much to the chagrin of their more assertive and voluptuous classmates. When he could do so without inviting criticism of his motives, he would chat to them in private. And what he quickly discovered was that he had a talent for getting them to open up to him. It was as if he possessed a magic key which, when he turned it, released a flood of emotions and tales of personal woe. His secret was to listen intently, with an interest that was never feigned, and he knew that they relished the attention from this dashingly handsome teacher. This was when he first became aware of his ability to help life's unfortunates.

Like the bookstore girl.

He decides it's time.

He tucks the book under his arm, picks up his sports bag and starts toward her. She continues her pretense of being unaware, but he knows that his every footfall is the first beat of a whole bar in her fluttering heart.

When he reaches the counter, and any further denial of his presence would be so obvious as to be rude, she looks up at him and blinks myopically.

Those big eyes.

She gets off her chair, smoothes down her skirt, affixes a warm smile. He notices how round-shouldered she is. Throw 'em back, he thinks. Stick that chest out. You wanna shift some of this paper, then give the public a reason to come through the door.

'Hi,' she says. 'Found something you like?'

He wonders if this is meant as a *double entendre*, whether she has spent the last few minutes slaving over that opening line. If so, it's a stinker.

He drops his bag, holds the book up so that she can see the cover. 'I'm trying to work my way through all the books I should have read when I was younger.'

'That's a worthy ambition. You shouldn't speed-read them, though.'

'Excuse me?'

'*The Grapes of Wrath*. You finish it already?'

The book he bought the last time he was in here. Two days ago. Obviously he made an impression.

'You remember.'

She reddens as she wrestles with her answer. 'I, uh, I have an excellent memory when it comes to books.'

Good recovery, he thinks. Now my turn for a plausible response.

'My mother took the Steinbeck. Saw it in my hands and thought it was a gift. Yanked it from me so fast I got paper cuts.'

He laughs and she joins in. Which makes it even funnier to him because she doesn't appreciate the real joke. Not yet, anyhow.

'Maybe you should put on gloves next time you visit your mom,' she says, trying to continue the humor.

He stops laughing. That's not funny. It's just stupid. It's such a lame riposte that he finds himself feeling embarrassed for her.

She looks confused now, out of her depth, so he gestures toward her spiral-bound notebook.

'You mind me asking what you're writing there? You seemed really lost in it.'

'This? Oh, it's nothing. Just a little poetry. Helps pass the time.'

'Poetry? Really? I love poems. Could I hear some?'

He doesn't want to hear any. He suspects they're shit. But when people need your help you sometimes have to make sacrifices.

She grabs up the notebook, clutches it to her ample chest, flutters her eyelids at him, sniffs a couple of times. 'Oh no, I couldn't possibly. It's way too personal.'

He finds it hard to maintain a smile. He knows what she wants him to do. She wants him to plead to see her outpourings. She wants him to keep on asking so that she can keep on saying no, no, no, until he just wants to rip the fucking pages from her hand.

But he manages to hold on to his civility. 'What, you mean it's hot stuff?'

She looks shocked. 'No. What do you . . . No.'

'I'll bet it is. I bet I'd never be able to look you in the eye again once I'd found out what goes on in that head of yours.'

'Well, you're just going to have to keep on wondering, aren't you?'

He studies her. Watches the way she tilts her head to one side while she beams her wouldn't-you-like-to-know smile.

'Tell you what. If I guess your birthday, you have to let me read your poetry.'

She considers this. 'My birthday? The exact day of the year?'

'Give me a sporting chance. Allow me two days either way.'

'All right. You're on.'

He folds his arms, looks her up and down. She seems to enjoy the scrutiny. Probably the most rigorous inspection she's had in a long time.

'First of all, I'd say you're a Pisces. Am I right?'

'That's pretty good. How'd you figure that one out?'

'Pisces people are creative and imaginative. You'd need that for the poetry.'

They're also weak-willed and gullible, he thinks.

'Okay,' she says, intrigued now. 'Go on.'

'I'd say . . .' He pauses for effect. David Blaine, eat your heart out. 'I'd say March rather than February.'

She's shifting from foot to foot now, like she's about to pee herself.

'The tail end of the star sign,' he intones. 'Yeah, right toward the end.'

She lets out a tiny squeal of excitement. He thinks she's easily entertained. He thinks that if he gets this right, she's going to have an orgasm.

'March the . . . the seventeenth.'

Anti-climax. She lets out a puff of air in disappointment. Her face says, *Don't worry about it, it happens to all guys at one time or another.*

'Close,' she says, holding her finger and thumb apart like she's commenting on his manhood. 'It's the twentieth. That was pretty impressive, though.'

He smiles. Not at the compliment, but at how far a deliberately wrong guess can get you.

'So I suppose I don't get to see your poems then?'

'No. Not this time.'

Oh? A hint of opportunities yet to come? How daring of you, young lady.

'In that case,' he says, 'you don't get to see mine.'

'Your what?'

'My writing.'

Her eyes bulge. 'You write? Poetry?'

'Fiction, actually. Short stories mostly, although I'm trying my hand at a novel. It doesn't come easy to me, though. You know what somebody once said about writing? All you have to do is sit at a typewriter and open up a vein. That's kind of how I'm finding it.'

'I know what you mean,' she says dreamily, like he's her new-found soulmate. She doesn't know he hasn't written a single line of fiction since he graduated from school.

She sucks up another deep lungful of the musty air. 'Maybe we could do a trade. One of your stories for one of my poems. Next time you drop in.'

Here we go . . .

'Or sooner.'

She blinks. 'What?'

'I'm not in this area too often. I live upstate. But maybe . . . well, I was just thinking . . . if I could call you or something . . .'

Her mouth opens and closes like she's a landed trout. 'I . . . I'm not sure . . .'

'That's okay. I understand. Why would you give your number out to a perfect stranger? Tell you what: I'll give you my number. If you want to call me, that's fantastic. If not, then, well, I understand.'

He fishes a pen from his inside pocket, makes a show of looking for a piece of blank paper. Before she can find one he points to her arm. She's wearing a woolen sweater with sleeves that reach only to the elbow. Perfect.

'Give me your arm. Come on, that way I know you won't lose it.'

She hesitates, but only for a second. Smiling, she lays her arm on the counter. What harm can it do, right?

He clicks his biro, scribbles a number in blue ink across the inside of her wrist.

'No washing until you call me, okay?'

She laughs as she glances at the number, then follows this up with a frown.

'What?' he asks.

'I, uh, I don't even know your name.'

He motions for her to surrender her arm again. 'Close your eyes,' he says. 'No peeking. You can look at it when I'm gone.'

'Why? Is it that bad?'

'It's . . . unusual.'

She sighs, then sniffs, then does as she has been asked.

He looks down at the column of white flesh with its network of blue-green veins. Like marble.

It's the moment. His plan has worked. He's surprised at how easy it's been. Perhaps it's because, even though she's not conscious of it, her soul is crying out for help.

It's okay, he wants to tell her. I'm here now.

'What's taking you so long?' she asks with a giggle.

He does it then. One swift motion.

Her eyes pop open. He sees the total lack of comprehension in them as her brain struggles to switch context, to make sense of this unexpected phenomenon.

Because what she sees is a geyser of blood spurting from her wrist.

And when the pain strikes home and her brain realizes that something is seriously wrong here and she opens her mouth to scream, he tightens his grip on her wrist and strikes again with his scalpel. And again, and again, moving higher and higher up her bare arm.

And when her hand becomes so slick with her hot blood that she is able to wrench it out of his grasp, he steps around the counter and continues his methodical onslaught. The screams continue as he slashes at her face and neck, at her full, ripe breasts, and when she finally spins away he stands and watches as she whirls and crashes into walls and bookshelves, the blood spraying from her body onto all those books, all those words.

When her heart has almost nothing left to pump and her brain has decided the fight is over, she collapses in a corner of the room. The blood leaks more slowly now from the gaping mouths in her flesh.

He walks over to her, looks down at her twitching figure.

Paper cuts, he thinks. It was a hint.

Sit at a typewriter and open up a vein. Another hint.

Hell, I practically told you why I came here.

He knows the precise moment when life leaves her. He's

witnessed it before. It's as if every cell of the body sighs with the lifting of its burden of coping with the world.

For a couple of minutes he absorbs the peace of it all, allows the calm to percolate through his system.

He surveys the scene. Messy, very messy. But it had to be this way.

He's drenched in her blood. It's on his face, his hands, all down his nice white shirt. A drop of it trickles down his cheek and onto his lips. He licks it away.

He walks over to the front of the store, his shoes squelching on the carpet. He turns the lock on the door, flips the sign to 'Closed', then moves back to the counter and retrieves his bag. Carrying it into the small office at the rear, he strips, washes himself down at the sink, then changes into the clean clothes he brought with him. He puts the blood-soaked garments into the bag and retraces his path to the front door.

When the street seems momentarily clear, he unlocks the door, steps outside and walks without hurry to his car.

As he fires up the engine he takes a last look at the bookstore. It looks so small, so dull, so lacking in energy and adventure. So absent of life.

God knows how they stay in business, he thinks.

TWO

Detective Second Grade Callum Doyle tilts his face an inch toward the grimy window of the squadroom, allowing the slender fingers of sunlight to caress his face. Spring is calling him. He could so easily follow that call right now. It wouldn't have to be a long trip – we're not talking a vacation in New England here. Maybe just a short stroll along the street to Tompkins Square Park. Somewhere where there are flowers and trees and kids playing and young couples enjoying the sap rising. On a day like today he feels certain he could ignore the occasional drunken bum sleeping it off on a bench, the drifting odor of canine and human feces, the mentally imbalanced having heated arguments with themselves, the clattering of skateboards, the junkies looking to score, the childless women talking to their dogs as though they were babies. Sure he could overlook all those things, on a day like today. Anything has to be better than continuing to listen to the interminable life story of Mrs Sachs.

She has told him about how she came to New York at the age of three, her father wanting to put his tailoring skills to good use in the garment district. Naturally enough she became a dress-maker herself, but gave it up to go to drama school. It was one night after singing her heart out despite a strained throat that she met and fell in love with Bernard, a jeweler by profession and doing very well for himself, thank you very much. They married, he continued to prosper. Twenty years ago they had amassed enough riches to buy a townhouse on Stuyvesant Street. Six months later Bernard died when he stepped out in front of a car. Doyle is not sure whether he is supposed to laugh or not when she tells him that, ironically, the car that killed him was an Opel.

'You have beautiful eyes,' Mrs Sachs croaks at Doyle. 'In the sunlight they're like jewels. Emeralds. Did anybody ever tell you that before?'

He looks across the desk. Mrs Sachs's own eyes are milky. It's hard to tell what color they are behind the film. She has to be ninety if she's a day. And now she's hitting on him?

'My *wife*,' he says with emphasis. 'Sometimes I think it's the only reason she married me.'

Mrs Sachs sneaks out a hint of a smile. 'Is she what brought you to America?'

Doyle feels the hurt, although he knows he shouldn't. When he was whisked across the Atlantic at the age of eight, he made it one of his most urgent tasks to shed the Irish accent that most of the natives here found impenetrable and some used as an excuse for beating the crap out of him. It comes as a shock to discover he hasn't been as successful as he has always believed, and he finds his tone suddenly becoming less accommodating.

'Mrs Sachs—'

'Olivia,' she interrupts. 'Please, call me Olivia.'

'Olivia,' he says, although he intends it to be the last time he gets so familiar, 'you mind if we cut to the chase here? I'm still not sure why exactly you felt the need to speak with a detective.'

'My daughter has eyes like yours,' she says, and now Doyle wants to pick up his stapler and fire its contents into those orbs of his that she finds so remarkable. For Christ's sake, he thinks, what did I do to deserve this, on a beautiful spring day like today?

'Not green,' continues the old lady – and she is certainly old:

13

a hundred if she's a day. 'Blue, actually. But stunning to look at. Like a wolf's eyes. Or a husky. Have you ever seen a husky's eyes?'

Doyle suppresses a sigh and tries again. He has patience – he has been trained to have patience – but sometimes . . .

'Mrs Sachs—'

'She worked in the South Tower.'

And now the spell is cast. She has him. Doyle is a cop, and like every other cop in this city, anything connected with the World Trade Center has a direct line to his very core. 9/11. Nine-One-One. The mother of all emergency calls. The mere mention of that day is enough to bring a lump to his throat. He can almost taste the dust.

He looks more intently at the woman opposite, and she suddenly seems so frail, so in need of human support. Her beige coat – an expensive one with a fur trim – seems baggy on her now, as if she has shrunk. She has to be a hundred and twenty years old if she's a day.

'Her name is Patricia,' she says, and Doyle notices her use of the present tense. 'She worked for Hadlow-Jones. You know it? The insurance company? She was doing so well there.'

Doyle remains silent. Spring is put aside while he awaits her story.

'She called me that day. On her cellphone. Twice, actually. The first time to tell me she was planning to come see me after work. The second time to tell me she thought she was about to die.'

She pauses for a moment while she turns her own gaze toward the window. Doyle guesses that she is traveling back in time, that she is hearing her daughter's words all over again. Moments like that, they never leave you.

'She told me she didn't think she would be able to make it to my house after all. A slight change of plan, she called it. She kept apologizing, because she felt she was letting me down. But the fire . . . She didn't think she would be able to make it through the flames.'

Mrs Sachs faces Doyle again. 'In the background I could hear people screaming. Have you ever heard the sound of a roomful of people all screaming for their lives? You don't want to, believe me. It's the worst sound on earth. A sound like that tears your heart out. It made me say a prayer. You want to know what I prayed for at that moment? I said to God, let it be me in that building. I'm old, I've had a good life, let it be me who has to walk into that wall of fire. Anything to save my baby.'

Doyle has been here before. Many times, with the relatives of many victims. Usually he will toss them a crumb of condolence: 'I'm sorry for your loss,' or some equally pat phrase that has been robbed of all sincerity through overuse. But Mrs Sachs has stepped over a threshold and touched him. She deserves more. And so he offers her his patience and his silence.

'They never found her. Not a trace. Not a hair, not a finger-nail, nothing. But still they offered me money. She was insured with Hadlow-Jones themselves, and they offered me a lot of money. You think I needed money? My husband, God rest his soul, was a very successful man. I told them if they wanted to give me something useful, they could give me proof that my daughter was dead. I'm still waiting for them to get back to me.'

'You're not alone, Mrs Sachs. There are many, many victims who still haven't been identified. In a lot of cases it's simply that the technology isn't advanced enough yet. Maybe one day soon you'll get the closure you need. I hope so.'

She looks at him for a moment, and he wonders if that's all she came to hear. A splinter of hope to take back to her empty townhouse.

She reaches for the leather purse on her lap and unsnaps the silver clasp, then reaches in and slips out a buff-colored envelope. She passes it across the desk to Doyle.

He opens the envelope and slides out a grainy black-and-white photograph. It shows a city street scene. Crowds of people hurtling along a sidewalk. One woman in particular stands out because she is not looking where she is going. Instead, her head is twisted toward the camera and she is smiling. The woman is smartly dressed but not attractive. Her smile seems forced somehow.

'Your daughter?' Doyle asks. He wonders why she didn't bring a better photograph than this. When Mrs Sachs doesn't answer he says, 'When was this taken?'

'Last month,' she answers.

Doyle stares at her, but finds no trace of mischief hidden in her lined features. 'Last month? So she's alive?'

'Yes.' A pause. 'I don't know. I think so. I mean, it looks like Patricia. But it's so hard to tell. The photo, it's so grainy. I . . . I don't know what to think anymore.'

'Please, don't get upset. Can I ask who took the picture?'

'A man by the name of Travis Repp. Well, actually, somebody who works for Mr Repp.'

'And Mr Repp is?'

'A private detective.'

'What made you go to him? Someone recommend him to you?'

'Actually, he contacted me. He just called me on the telephone one day, about two years ago. He told me he'd done a lot of work on the 9/11 victims. Mainly on behalf of relatives, insurance companies, the firms that were in the Towers, like that. He said he wanted to talk with me about my daughter. About Patricia. I told him there was nothing to discuss. She was gone.

She was killed on that day. I had no reason to talk with him about it. And then he said maybe there was a reason. He said he had learned something about Patricia. Something *curious*, was the word he used.'

'Did he say what it was?'

'Not at first. He suggested a meeting. He even said he would come over to my house to discuss it.'

'And did you have the meeting?'

'Of course. Why would I not? Look, Detective Doyle, I know what you're thinking. I may be old, but I'm not senile. He is a real private detective with a real office. It's on Thirty-third Street. Close to Third Avenue. I've been there myself on several occasions.'

'So what did he tell you?'

'The first thing he said was that he didn't usually approach people out of the blue like this. He said that if I wanted nothing more to do with him after our meeting, then that was fine by him. He just felt it was his duty to tell me what he'd learned.'

'Which was?'

'That there was a chance my Patricia was still alive.'

'Uh-huh. And did he explain how he reached this conclusion?'

'He said it was luck more than anything. Back in 2001 he was asked to investigate a list of people from the Towers. You know, the missing ones. Patricia was one of the people on his list. He didn't find her. Not alive, not dead. And nobody else who could say she was alive or dead. 'Course, he wasn't the only one looking. None of the experts could find anything either. But because Patricia had been seen at work that day, they said she must have perished. Officially, she was declared deceased, and that was that.'

She goes silent for a moment, seemingly gathering her thoughts.

'Two years ago, Mr Repp took on another client. A totally unrelated case. But this client also worked in insurance. Anyhow, they got talking, and the topic of 9/11 cropped up. The client told Mr Repp that he knew a lot of people who died that day, and he mentioned a few firms. One of the firms he mentioned was Hadlow-Jones. So when he said this, Mr Repp dug out his old list and started reading out the names. And then he got to Patricia.'

'He recognized her name?'

She nods. 'He wanted to know what the list was. So Mr Repp told him it was the employees of Hadlow-Jones who lost their lives. And this client, you know what he said? He said, "Not if Patricia Sachs is on there, it isn't. When I saw her a couple weeks after the attack, she couldn't have been any healthier."'

Doyle stops her with a raised finger. 'Wait a minute. This guy saw Patricia *after* 9/11?'

'Yes, after. At the Port Authority Bus Terminal. She was getting aboard a Greyhound.'

Doyle sees a gleam somewhere behind the dim surface of her eyes. He tries to imagine how overwhelmed Mrs Sachs must have felt when confronted with the possibility that her daughter was still on this earth. With a rope like that dangling before her, she would have been willing to be led anywhere.

'What else did Repp tell you?'

'Not much. Not at that meeting, anyhow. He simply gave me his card and said that if I wanted him to look into it further, he would be only too happy to help.'

'For a fee, of course.'

'Yes. For a fee. But money is not the issue here. Not if my daughter is still out there somewhere. Alive.'

Doyle would like to differ over the money issue. In his opinion, financial considerations are probably very much at the center of what's going on here. But, for now, he keeps it to himself.

'So you hired Repp?'

She shoots him a sharp look intended to remind him of her mental acuity. 'Not immediately. I told him I wanted to speak with the man who said he saw Patricia.'

'Did Repp set that up?'

'Yes, he did. The man's name is Pinter. He used to work for Invar Insurance. I have his business card somewhere. The meeting we had didn't take long. He didn't know Patricia very well, but he'd met her on a few occasions, and he was pretty sure it was her he saw at the Bus Terminal. He said he even called her name, and she glanced his way, but then she jumped on the bus like she was afraid of something.'

'Did Pinter seem genuine enough?'

'Absolutely he seemed genuine. Even if he was mistaken about seeing Patricia, I think he truly believed it was her.'

'Did he explain why he hadn't spoken up about this before?'

'You think I didn't ask him that? I asked him. He said he didn't even know that Patricia was supposed to be dead. He hadn't worked with the Hadlow-Jones people in a long time, and so the first time he heard Patricia's name again was when Mr Repp mentioned her.'

'So then you hired Repp?'

'I did. You wanna call me a fool, then call me a fool. I don't care. I would give everything I own in the world to see my Patricia again.'

Doyle rests his index finger on the photograph. 'And he came up with this?'

'Amongst other things, yes.'

'Did he say where the picture was taken?'

'Boston.'

'Boston? Is there any reason why your daughter would go there?'

'None that I know of.'

'Mrs Sachs, how old is your daughter?'

'I'm eighty-three now. I didn't have Patricia until late in life. I was forty at the time.'

Doyle studies the photograph again. It's not the sharpest of snaps. The woman could be forty-three, but she could also be somewhere around thirty.

'You get anything else from Repp?'

'Several more sightings. The last one in Chicago.'

Doyle sighs. It's all so neat, so convenient.

'Mrs Sachs, when people disappear like this, just dropping off the edge of the world, it's not on a whim. They have reasons. Big reasons. They're throwing away a life, usually because they're so sick of it they need to start a new one. Was it like that for Patricia? Did things get so bad?'

Mrs Sachs shifts in her chair. She's uncomfortable, and Doyle knows it's not because of the seat. This is deep, personal shit he's asking her now, but it has to be put out there.

'Patricia made a big mistake. The man she married was a bum, a parasite. He was also a control freak. She didn't talk to me about it much, but I knew Joe made her life miserable. One time, I saw a bottle of anti-depressants in her bag. I think . . . I think he even beat her sometimes. If she wanted out, then who could blame her? So what Mr Repp was suggesting, about her running away from it all, it didn't seem so crazy.'

'Did you speak with her husband about the disappearance?'

'Not in any depth. Joe doesn't do depth. Far as he's concerned, Patricia is dead. He got a lot of money from it, and he's happy with that. It tells you everything about him you need to know.'

Doyle hesitates before voicing his next words. Dashing the hopes of desperate mothers is not his favorite pastime.

'Okay, let's suppose that Patricia did survive somehow, that nobody she knew saw her leave the WTC, and that she then decided to use it as the ideal opportunity to change her life forever. She would then have to go into hiding. She couldn't go home, couldn't pack a bag, couldn't go anywhere she might be recognized, couldn't take any money from an ATM. She would have to go it alone, using only what she had on her. That's a tough stunt to pull off.'

Mrs Sachs nods all through this, as if to say, *Yes, yes, don't you think I haven't already considered all this?*

'But not impossible,' she says. 'People disappear all the time, don't they? They fake their deaths and just go. They leave everything behind them.'

Doyle hears the touch of agony in her last sentence, and he knows he has to reach out for it.

'I think that's why you came to see me today, isn't it, Mrs Sachs? If Patricia is still alive, if she has run away from her past life, then she has run away from you too. She has left you behind, left you with all the hurt of believing your daughter has suffered a tragic death. Do you really think she could do that to you, to her own mother?'

Mrs Sachs raises her face and catches some of that spring sunshine herself. It glints off the wetness in her eyes.

'I'm not very well, you know, Detective. I have diabetes and high blood pressure and an enlarged heart. I don't know how much longer I have to live. I have few friends and no family, unless Patricia is alive. When Mr Repp came to see me I was overjoyed. I was filled with hope. But you know what? You're right. The pain of believing that Patricia could abandon me in this way, without a word or a message of some kind – well, that's come to hurt even more than believing she died on that awful day, along with all those other poor souls. So now I need the pain to end. If she's alive, then maybe she can tell me why she did this. If not, well . . . Either way, I need to know the truth. It's all I have left.'

Doyle taps the photograph a few times. 'I'll look into it,' he says. 'You mind if I keep this for a while?'

When she shakes her head, he reaches for the envelope. Before he can withdraw his hand, Mrs Sachs takes hold of it.

'Thank you.' Then she gets up from her chair and shuffles away.

Doyle looks with sadness at the retreating form. And even when she has disappeared from view, he continues to stare for several minutes.

He jumps when he hears the booming voice.

'We got a homicide. And it's messy.'

THREE

For the briefest of moments Doyle experiences a surge of excitement. This city isn't the murder hot-spot it once was. In fact it's become pretty tame lately. A homicide landing on one's desk these days is almost a cause for celebration for an NYPD detective.

So when he looks up and finds the square-jawed face of Lieutenant Cesario pointed decidedly in the direction of the only other two detectives in the room, his disappointment is almost enough to make him cram his gold shield into his mouth and swallow it.

He knows he shouldn't be surprised. It has been like this for months. Ever since the events of last Christmas. Cops died then. Other people died too, but the cops are what matter most to the members of this squad. They lost colleagues, friends, partners. Doyle himself lost his partner. He went through hell that Christmas. It almost seemed worth it when he came out of it to a hero's welcome. But of course it didn't last. Questions started to get asked about his involvement in the case. Even the cops who had at first applauded Doyle started to wonder about his integrity, especially when there were certain officers who had never been slow to spread poison about him. All the media attention he was getting didn't help matters either. For some, this was pure jealousy: they had worked their asses off for twenty years and still never seen their faces on Fox News.

In his logical moments, Doyle realizes he can't blame the other cops. Not really. He tries putting himself in their shoes. He tries picturing a cop who is a relative newcomer to a precinct, who arrived with a prior history involving the death of a female partner, and who has now just been at the epicenter of a series of events that has taken out several more cops. Whatever that officer does to redeem himself, whatever explanations he provides, he will always be remembered as the man associated with members of service losing their lives. Death taints in that way.

I wouldn't work with me if I were them, he thinks.

He hopes it will all blow away eventually. With that in mind, he has tried to stay below the radar. His superiors haven't argued with that. The new lieutenant hasn't really known what to make of Doyle, and so the man has played safe. All the low-key cases have come Doyle's way. Cases nobody else can be bothered to spend any time on. Cases like that of Mrs Sachs.

So, for now, he puts aside his hopes and turns his attention to his current DD5 report, trying to remember how to spell 'pseudonym' and then giving up and changing it to 'alias', trying to ignore the voice of Cesario as he summarizes what little he knows, trying to block his mind to the detectives behind him tugging on their coats and moving toward the door, trying to convince himself that it will be a crap case that he wouldn't want anyway.

Out of the corner of his eye he sees the legs of Cesario as they turn and propel him back toward his office. But then they stop. Cesario's shiny shoes twist around to point at Doyle.

Doyle's gaze moves up from the shoes. Over the sharp gray suit. Onto the dazzling teeth set into a tanned face beneath a fringe of perfectly sculpted gloss-black hair.

He wonders what the man's flaws are. Nobody is that perfect. He looks too much like a movie star playing the part of a cop. Maybe if I yell 'Cut!' Doyle thinks, he'll relax into his normal self.

He'll start calling everyone darling before mincing off to adjust his make-up.

And who the hell has a tan this time of year, anyway?

'Go after them,' Cesario says.

Well now you're just being too nice, Doyle thinks. You can't even do me the courtesy of allowing me to hate you. What kind of spiteful behavior is that?

'Go,' Cesario urges. 'The more bodies we have on this, the quicker we get it off the books.'

Doyle almost smiles. Cesario is throwing him a bone. But he's also trying to come across as not being a soft touch. This is purely an operational decision, he's saying; don't go getting all teary-eyed on me now.

Doyle takes it. It's the best he's going to get. And who knows? Maybe this is the start of something. Maybe this isn't a homicide at all, but a subtle way of getting him to a surprise party where the police commissioner will jump out of a cake and welcome him back into the fold.

Yeah, right, Doyle thinks as he grabs his coat.

It's messy, all right.

Blood everywhere. It never ceases to amaze Doyle how much blood there is in the human body, and how far it will travel once someone opens the faucet. It's on the floor, it's on the books, and – yep – it's even on the ceiling. And the source of all this mayhem? The pale crumpled form of a young girl. She looks small and unreal – a mutilated mannequin.

Doyle stares at her for a good while. It's something he always does at a murder scene, and he doesn't know why. It's like he's trying to make some kind of connection, as though simply look-ing at her will give him an insight into what kind of life she lived, and therefore why that life was taken away from her.

He is slow to become fully aware of the other people in the bookstore. Gradually he notices the glances, picks up the muttered remarks and the muted snickers.

'Long time no see, Doyle,' says a Homicide South detective called Kravitz. The correct name for his outfit is the Manhattan South Homicide Task Force, but Doyle and most of the other people gathered here know it as Homicide South.

Doyle shifts his gaze to the man. He is thin and tall – at least six and a half feet. His hands are buried in the pockets of a black overcoat. Behind him, almost hidden in his shadow, is another Homicide dick called Folger. He is short, squat and balding, and he is grinning idiotically at the barbed humor lurking in Kravitz's greeting.

'Well, well,' says Doyle. 'If it ain't Lurch and Uncle Fester. How you doing, fellas?'

This gets a laugh from everyone except the Homicide boys. The amusement in Folger's smile drops away, to be replaced by something more menacing.

His words are a lot more direct than those of Kravitz: 'They let you out finally? What, you finished putting all the case files in alphabetical order? You painted the station house walls already?'

'Yeah, all that,' Doyle answers. 'I still got the ladders in the car outside, you want to borrow them to reach something. You must get sick of looking up your partner's nostrils all day. Say, are you still using a kiddie seat in that car of yours?'

Folger tries to maintain his smile, but it's clear his muscles are struggling. His mouth twitches on one side.

'Well, now that you're here, Doyle, let me explain something to you. This here is what we call a homicide. You see the girl there, all cut up like that?' Folger slaps a hand to his forehead. 'Oh, but wait. I'm forgetting. You know all about homicides, don't you? In fact, they kind of follow you around. You remember that movie,

The Sixth Sense? You should get one of those *I See Dead People* T-shirts, the number of DOAs you get to see in your life.'

The laughing has stopped now. Everyone in the room has lapsed into an embarrassed silence. This has become too personal. Doyle knows that people are expecting him either to start a fight or back off.

Doyle adopts a pained expression. 'Hold on here. Maybe I overstepped the mark. Am I right in thinking you ain't happy?'

Folger glares at him, still angry but also looking somewhat surprised. 'Yeah, you could say that.'

'Uh-huh,' says Doyle. 'So which one are you? Bashful? Dopey?'

The place erupts. Even Kravitz cannot suppress a smirk. And while he smiles, he takes the furious Folger by the shoulders and holds him in check. Both of the Homicide detectives, as well as everybody else in this room, know that Doyle would kick Folger's ass into his skull if things became physical.

Doyle strolls over to where one of the uniforms is relaying what he knows to the other detectives. The Hispanic officer glances briefly at Doyle, then returns to his notebook.

'DOA's name is Cindy Mellish. Twenty years old. She works here at weekends and in college vacations. The owner often leaves her to mind the store – it's not the busiest of places. Owner's name is Simon Brownlow. He opened up this morning, stayed for about an hour, then left. He didn't get back till after two-thirty. He's sitting in one of the RMPs outside, you wanna talk to him. He's pretty shaken up, though.'

Doyle listens in silence. He has a million questions he wants to put to Mr Brownlow, but this isn't his case. Cesario made that clear. The other squad detectives know their job. They'll get round to interviewing Brownlow, and they'll do it just as thoroughly as he would.

He drifts away again, itching to get more involved. Soon enough he'll be given a task. The door-to-door, probably. Maybe later poring over the store's paperwork for customer details so he can call them up. All necessary work. But tedious background stuff mostly. Not where it's really at.

He goes back for another look at the girl. The Medical Examiner, a Chinese guy called Norman Chin, is working on her now. Checking out her wounds. Speaking his findings quietly into a voice recorder.

What's she telling you, Norm? he wonders. Those cuts whispering secrets to you? They giving you any clues about the psycho who did this? Tell me, Norm, because I want this son of a bitch.

He realizes then that he is already starting to make the case his own. Bad idea, but he can't help it. This girl needs him. She is staring at him and pleading for his help, and he is going to find it oh so hard to take a back seat on this investigation.

He moves away again, trying to shake the girl's empty stare from his mind. He sees the door ahead of him. Starts heading toward it, thinking about the cool spring air outside.

'Got something for you,' Chin says.

Doyle is not being addressed directly, but he stops in his tracks. He has to hear this. He turns slowly, sees the backs of all the cops leaning in to hear what profound wisdom Chin is about to impart.

'First of all, the cuts here, they look pretty random, right? A frenzied attack, cuts here, there and everywhere, right?'

He pauses until he elicits a couple of nods from his audience.

'Wrong! Not random. At least not at first. See the wounds on this arm?'

Intrigued, Doyle pushes through the group for a better look. Norman Chin is staring wide-eyed at the surrounding cops. Actually, he cannot do anything but stare wide-eyed, given the intense magnifying effect of the spectacles he has to wear. On a sunny day, he could laser a hole through steel with those babies, Doyle thinks.

The glasses, together with the black toilet-brush hair, lend Chin the look of a mad scientist – someone who could quite happily experiment with trying to bring corpses like this back to life. But what all the cops here know is that Chin is one of the best in his field. You got a DOA on your hands, then you want Chin involved.

Chin points to the girl's left forearm with his pencil, and waits for more nods. He's in his element here.

'Defense wounds?' some brave cop ventures.

'Not defense wounds. These first few cuts are too regular, too parallel. Not like the other cuts. See?' He indicates other areas of sliced flesh. 'See how they've been done in wide angular sweeps? They're not as deep as the first ones, neither. Besides, this is her left arm. Most of the defense wounds are on the other arm, being as she's right-handed.'

He pauses and surveys his class. Waits for the question which doesn't come. The seasoned detectives here know Chin's routine only too well.

'Ask me how I know,' Chin says. 'About her being right-handed. Go on, ask me.'

Clearly a glutton for punishment, the same cop plays along.

'Okay, so how do you know she's right-handed?'

Chin points again with his pencil. 'Ink on the fingers. Plus, I sent someone out to ask the bookstore owner.'

He gets a laugh, and revels in it. The cop who posed the question gets jostled playfully by his colleagues.

'Next question,' says Chin.

The cops go quiet. Nobody wants to run the risk of asking a dumb-ass question, or even to be made by Chin to look a dumb-ass when posing a perfectly sensible question.

'Come on, come on. There's something obvious you should be asking me here.'

When the silence continues, Doyle offers his two cents.

'The cuts on the forearm. You said they were done first. How do you know the order?'

Chin jabs his pencil toward Doyle. 'Correctimundo! Excellent question. Give that man a banana.'

Gingerly, Chin takes hold of the girl's left arm and raises it. 'There are pressure marks here, right around the wrist, like it's been held onto, tightly. Also, these smears here are where the blood has been dragged down and over the hand. I'd say that the perp grabbed her wrist while he made the first few cuts, and then she managed to pull her arm away. After that, he just hacked at her any way he could.'

Like every other cop in the room, Doyle is thinking this through, building the picture. The killer didn't just pull out a knife and start slashing. He grabbed her arm and held on tight while he severed the veins in her wrist. Why did he do that?

Deep in thought, Doyle and the others start to turn away. There is work to be done.

'Wait a minute!' Chin calls. 'You hear me say class dismissed? No, you did not. You want me to earn out the lousy small change the city pays me for this job, you need to listen some more. I was just getting to the interesting part.'

Doyle cannot help but smile as he focuses on Chin again. You gotta love the guy, he thinks. What a showman.

Chin picks up a small flashlight and shines it on the inside of the girl's wrist. 'There's something written here in pen. Looks like a telephone number. Before I tell you what it is, you need to know it was written *before* the girl was killed.'

A snort of laughter from the audience. 'Be a neat trick if she did it after she was dead. Unless she's a ghost writer.'

Chin whirls. He shines the flashlight directly into the eyes of the joker. Doyle almost expects Chin to send the guy to the principal for detention.

'Who says it was written by the girl?'

'Well, wasn't it? I write stuff on my arm all the time.'

'My opinion, it's a wonder you can write at all. Now listen and learn, knucklehead. Some of the blood has run down over the numbers. If the writing had been done after the attack, the killer would have had to wipe the blood away first, and there's no sign of that.'

The cop persists. 'That still doesn't say the girl didn't write it.'

'Upside down?'

'What?'

'When you write things on your arm, do you do it so *you* can read them, or so that other people can read them?'

Now the cop goes quiet.

Chin continues: 'This number was written by someone facing the girl, and it's right next to the site of what I think was the first incision. I'm not saying it was put there by the killer, but my guess is that the girl probably didn't get out of bed with this on her arm, and she probably hasn't met a substantial proportion of the city's population working in a place like this. Maybe it's important, maybe it's not. If you want to check it out, here it is. Notebooks at the ready, guys, because I don't think your meager brains are capable of retaining something as complicated as a phone number.'

As Doyle listens to the sound of pages being flipped, his mind is racing ahead with possibilities. Did the killer write that number? If she let him, that means she trusted him. And that means either she knew him, or she had a thing for him. Was he hitting on her? Did he offer to give her his number? And if she was willing to allow a perfect stranger to write on her skin, to invade her personal space so intimately, what does that say about someone who could charm her in that way?

'All right,' says Chin, examining the girl's wrist with his flashlight again. 'Area code is three-five-three.'

The cops look at each other.

'Anybody know where that is?' asks Kravitz.

He gets shrugs and headshakes.

'Next,' says Chin, 'we have three, six, and I think it's a two.'

Coincidence, thinks Doyle.

'And finally – check your lottery tickets – we got . . .'

The first of the remaining four digits reaches Doyle's ears. Then the second. No, he thinks. Surely not. Coincidence is one thing, but this . . .

When the third digit falls neatly into place, Doyle just knows what's coming next. A four. It has to be a four.

'A six,' says Chin.

Doyle blows air. Jesus. For a minute there—

'Scratch that,' says Chin. 'It's a four. Definitely a four.'

What? WHAT?

For a moment, Doyle sees the funny side. 'Hey, guys,' he wants to say, 'replace that area code with two-one-two and you got my home number. How fucking freaky is that?'

But he keeps quiet. There's something else about that number. Something that tells him this isn't entirely coincidental.

Chin is still talking, breaking into his thoughts.

'Now ask me how tall our killer is.'

The area code, Doyle thinks. It's familiar. Have I dialed it before?

'All right, Norm. What's his height?'

Shit! I know this. I have definitely used this area code.

'How the fuck should I know? You're the detectives. Do some fucking detecting!'

The audience breaks up, streams around Doyle. He stays rooted, staring at the body of the girl but not seeing it.

And then he gets it. He dialed it not so long ago when his great-uncle died. Three-five-three. Not an area code. At least not that he knows of. It's a country code. The number you dial to specify a foreign country when you're making an international call.

Three-five-three is the country code for Ireland, the place of his birth.

It could still be coincidence, he tells himself. But his inner voice is weak and lacking in conviction.

A few minutes ago he was wishing he could play more of a role in this case. Now he's beginning to fear that he could be center stage.

Be careful what you wish for, Doyle.

FOUR

Doyle in the squadroom. Not relaxed. Not relaxed at all. A part of him still wanting a bigger piece of this investigation. Needing to be out there, talking to people. Trying to find out what possible connection there could be between a butchered girl in a bookstore and his telephone number.

And yet he also has the feeling that he wants nothing to do with it. He wants to sit here at his desk, shuffling papers and staying the hell away from whatever dark things might be swimming in the depths of this case.

He tells himself to relax. If there was a link to him, they'd have found it by now. Wouldn't they? Yes, of course they would. They're good detectives. They'd have found it.

So it must be a coincidence. And anyway it's not *really* his number. Not exactly. Only the last seven digits are his. The area code is way off, and just happens to be the country code for Ireland. Surely you can take any string of numerals and read meaning into it that isn't really there? People do it all the time. They do things like adding up the positions of the letters in the name 'Adolf Hitler' and coming up with 666. They find codes hidden in passages of the Bible that tell them when the world will end. It's all hooey.

Yeah, but . . . seven digits? *Seven?*

A couple of times he's picked up the phone. Actually started to dial the number. Then he's put it down again. He's not sure he wants to know.

Be careful what you wish for.

The squadroom door opens, and the two lead detectives on the case walk in. The youngest is a blond-haired cop named Tommy LeBlanc. His gold shield is still fresh in his pocket, and Doyle hasn't yet made his mind up whether or not he likes the guy. For one thing, thinks Doyle, he's too fashion-conscious. Cops should look like slobs. Even when they're wearing smart suits they should look like slobs. At the very least, they should dress traditionally and soberly. Lieutenant Cesario just about gets away with that. But junior here – well, look at him. Shoes so pointy you could pick a lock with them, and garish designer spectacles that seem to change with the weather. Probably doesn't even have a problem with his eyesight.

The other detective is called Jay Holden. A truck-sized black man with a shaven head that reveals a puckered circular scar above his left ear. Rumor has it that the scar is the result of a gunshot wound inflicted when he ran with gangs in his teenage years. What Doyle likes about Holden is that he is his own man, with his own thoughts and opinions, most of which he keeps to himself. When he occasionally does come down on one side of a debate, you can be sure that he has given it considerable deliberation beforehand.

Doyle waits for the detectives to settle themselves in, then wanders over to Holden's desk.

'Hey, Jay.'

Holden looks up. His expression remains fixed.

'Cal.'

'You anywhere with the girl?'

Holden shrugs his linebacker shoulders. 'We talked to the mother. She didn't really know nothing. No enemies, no fights, no jealous boyfriends, no stalkers. Nothing useful.'

'No boyfriends at all?'

'Last one finished with her a year ago. The mother says she was devastated. Wouldn't talk about it, wouldn't eat – all the usual teenage angst stuff.'

'You talk to the guy?'

'Yeah. He's just a kid too. Shacked up with another girl now. He seemed shocked enough when I told him about Cindy. Says he dumped her when she got too possessive, but there was no way he wanted anything bad to happen to her. My opinion, he's telling the truth.'

'You think this is just a nut-job?'

Holden leans back in his chair while he ponders. The chair groans in complaint.

'Too early to say. It looks like it, the way he cut her up like that. On the other hand, he's been real careful. Crime Scene haven't come up with anything yet, and I'm not convinced they will.'

'What about that number on her arm? Who does that belong to?'

Doyle tries to make it sound like a natural follow-on question, and hopes his anxiety doesn't show.

Holden shakes his head. 'Garbage. That area code ain't in use. Looks like the ME was right. Killer offers to give his number, writes down some crap, then does his thing while he's holding her arm.'

So they're dismissing the number, thinks Doyle. Which means that nobody has looked at what you get if you ignore the area code and treat the remainder as a local number. If they had, they'd be all over him now.

He decides he's not going to be the one to suggest it.

'So what's next?' he asks.

'I was hoping you could tell *me*. Maybe find something in that customer list you got. A name like Jack T Ripper, something like that.'

'I'll keep looking.'

He moves back to his own desk, relieved that the issue of the telephone number has been pushed into the background, at least as far as the squad is concerned. Maybe he should do the same. Maybe it's okay for him to forget about it now.

Maybe.

It's always the same. Delight and resentment, intermingled. Every time he enters this building.

It's a beautiful brownstone on West 87th Street. It has history and character and solidity. It has stone lions above the entrance. It has real wood floors. It has a tree-lined sidewalk that takes you to Central Park at one end, and Riverside Drive and the Hudson at the other. But best of all, it has his apartment. The place where he lives. His home.

Except – and this is where the resentment creeps in – it's not his home, is it? Not really. He didn't buy it with his own money. Because he is only a New York City detective, and second grade at that. He can't afford this. He should be living in a crappy tenement, or a place in the outer boroughs.

But we know who *can* afford this, don't we? That's right: Rachel's parents. They have the money to buy this many times over with whatever's currently in their wallets. And they'll never let you forget it, either. And they'll especially never let you forget that they only bought this for their daughter's sake rather than yours. And they'll also never let you forget that they don't like cops, and they don't like the fact that their daughter married a cop, and they don't like you in particular.

As always, Doyle's unease dissolves once he enters the apartment and shuts himself off from the world outside. The family photographs on the walls welcome him in. And in the living room, the real thing. His wife, Rachel, twisting away from the computer, sending him a smile that explains to him why life is worth living. There is music playing in the background that makes this feel like he's in a scene from a movie.

He goes over to Rachel, puts his arms around her neck, kisses her, breathes in her perfume and shampoo. Squeezes her until she squeaks.

'What's the music?' he asks.

'Coldplay.'

'I should have known. You ever play anything that's not Britpop?'

'I thought you'd like it, you being a Brit and all.'

He shows her a fist that's backed up by a smile. It's a running joke between them: Rachel referring to him as a Brit just to get a rise out of him. His father, wherever he is now, would have become apoplectic at the very mention of the word.

'How's Amy?' he asks.

Rachel shuts off the music. 'Exhausted. I took her over to Ellie's house this afternoon. You know what those two are like together – thick as thieves. God knows what they find to talk about, considering they see each other at school every day. And you know what? Soon as I got her home she was on Skype, talking to Ellie again.'

'She in bed now?'

'Yeah. She wanted to stay up to see you, but she couldn't make it. Fell asleep on the couch in the end.'

'I'll make it up to her tomorrow.' He nods toward the computer screen. It's displaying an image of a wrinkled old black guy sitting on a stoop. 'What you working on?'

'Just some touching up. I've got some gallery space at that exhibition in the Rennie Building next month.'

'Yeah? That's fantastic. You need a model to pose for you?' He puts the tips of his fingers to his chin, adopts a wistful expression and flutters his eyelashes at her.

Rachel grimaces. 'Uhm, no, that's okay. I don't think the world is ready for that just yet.'

He chin-points at the screen. 'You got much more to do?'

'Plenty, but that's not what you're asking, is it? What you really want to know is when your dinner's ready.'

Doyle smiles. 'How come you can always see through me?'

'You're a man, and men are transparent to us women. You like to think you're impenetrable and enigmatic. What you don't know is you're all glass vases. Big, round, see-through and empty.'

'The only thing empty about me is my stomach. Now get in that kitchen, wench, and rustle me up some food.'

She gets off her chair and slides past him. 'About this vase. Did I mention that it was antiquated yet worthless?'

He sends her toward the kitchen with a smack on the ass, then watches the wiggle in her walk.

Without turning round, she calls back to him, 'And I should also add that only women know how to make them and break them. So watch your step, mister.'

When she's out of sight, he looks again at the image of the old man on the stoop. He's tempted to use the software to draw a mustache on the man, or maybe something pornographic. Only he knows next to nothing about computers, and is afraid he might do something irreversible. Now *that* would cause a real fight.

He met Rachel when she was working for her father as a realtor. She was showing him an apartment in Washington Heights. He knew as soon as he walked into it that he hated it, but he pretended to like it just so he could spend longer in her company.

She could read him way back then too. When she asked him

what he thought of the apartment and he said it was okay, she said 'Bullshit.' In the next few minutes she managed to discover a multitude of facts about him, from where he was born to his current status as a single man, all apparently without asking him about those things directly. And later, when she told him he could do a lot better than his current situation, it wasn't just a place to live she was talking about.

She gave up the realty business after they got married. She wanted to follow her real passion: photography. Her parents blame Doyle for that too.

Sometimes Doyle wonders what he would have to do to get in the good books of his in-laws. He believes that even becoming President wouldn't cut it.

Sighing, he shucks off his coat, slings it onto the back of the sofa, then collapses into the cushions. Rachel walks back in a minute later.

'Lasagna okay? It just needs reheating.'

'Sure.'

She curls up next to him on the sofa and studies his face. 'So are you going to tell me what the big case is?'

The question doesn't surprise him. For months now he's been coming home directly after his shift. Tonight he was hours late.

'A homicide.'

She smiles, then punches him on the bicep. 'Hoo hoo. Way to go, Detective! They letting you play with the big boys again?'

'Don't you start. I get enough of that at work.'

'But still – a real honest-to-goodness homicide. Somebody must think you deserve another chance. Is it a juicy case?'

Doyle narrows his eyes at her. Juicy isn't a word he would normally use for something like this.

'A girl working in a used bookstore on Tenth. Someone came in and cut her up.'

'My God. You got any leads?'

'Nothing much. No motive we can find. Nothing in the girl's personal life. Who knows? Could be some psycho who wanted a book they didn't have in stock.'

Doyle doesn't mention the phone number. Why should he? It's not important. It's totally irrelevant.

'What else?'

Rachel reading him yet again.

'Huh? Nothing. It's just been a weird day.'

'Weird how?'

She's not letting this drop. But let's not bring the number into this. Let's not freak her out. Not that it *should* freak her out, of course, it being one of those funny coincidences that happens to all of us from time to time.

'A different case,' he lies, and hopes it sneaks past his wife's bullshit detector. 'A sweet little old lady called Mrs Sachs. She lost her daughter in 9/11. She got a phone call from her in the South Tower, just before it came down. Mrs Sachs said something to me. She said that she would have given anything at that moment to swap places with her daughter. She would have walked straight into the wall of flames in front of her if it meant her girl could live.'

He can see the tears already building in Rachel's eyes. He knows she's a sucker for human interest stories like this, and now he feels guilty as hell for using such diversionary tactics.

'Tell me about it,' she says. So he does. And once he gets into it, he's glad of the distraction himself.

When the phone rings and Rachel gets up to answer it, still sniffing and talking about how unfair life can be, Doyle offers silent thanks to Mrs Sachs.

'It's for you,' Rachel says, handing him the phone. 'I'll go fix you a side-salad.'

He takes the phone and she walks away.

'Hello.'

'Hello, Doyle. No, let me start that again. Hello, Cal. It's okay to call you Cal, isn't it? A little more friendly that way.'

Doyle doesn't recognize the male voice. It's deep, quiet and well-spoken. Loud music is playing in the background, almost drowning him out.

'Who is this?'

'Forgive me. We haven't met, although I hope we will one day. I know a lot about you, though. About you and Rachel and Amy. About your apartment on West 87th Street. About your work as a detective in the Eighth Precinct. You're a fascinating man, Cal. That's why I picked you.'

'Picked me for what? Who the hell is this?'

'Picked you to receive my help. Didn't you get the message I left for you?'

'Message? No. What message?'

'Your phone number, of course. On the girl's arm.'

The world vanishes. There is no Rachel, no living room, no apartment. There is only this man's voice, this man's words.

'I don't know what you're talking about.'

'Did you like the little twist I gave it? The Irish touch? Your birthplace, I believe. To be more exact, County Kerry, wasn't it?'

For a moment Doyle cannot speak. The music blares in his ear. U2. An Irish band. Ha, ha, very funny.

But there is no humor in Doyle's thoughts. Only anger. And, yes, fear. If this man knows so much about him, about his family . . .

'You want any dressing on this salad?'

It's Rachel, calling from the kitchen. Doyle gets off the sofa and moves to the kitchen doorway. He makes some hand signals to indicate that he doesn't want dressing, and that he needs to continue this call. When she nods that she understands, he walks into the bedroom and closes the door.

'Hey, Cal, are you still there, buddy?'

'I'm here.'

'Was that Rachel I heard just then? Nice find, Cal. I saw her picking up Amy from her friend Ellie's house today. Those tight black slacks really show off her curves, don't you think?'

He's been watching me and my family, thinks Doyle. Stalking us. Finding out everything he can about us.

He heads for the window, looks down onto the street below. The traffic is light. Plenty of cars parked up, but no sign of anyone monitoring the building. Nothing that he can see in the windows of the buildings across the street, either.

'Listen to me, you son of a bitch. If you're thinking about making some kind of threat to me or my family, then you better think again. I don't respond lightly to threats.'

'Whoa, steady there, Cal. I said I wanted to help you, didn't I? I'm not threatening you. That's the last thing on my mind.'

Doyle concentrates on the voice again. There's a slight inflection to his accent that makes it sound mid-Atlantic. Doyle tries to match it with any of the faces he's encountered before, but fails.

'Help me how?'

'With the investigation. The bookstore girl.'

'That's not my case.'

'Don't lie to me, Cal. I saw you there. At the bookstore.'

He was watching me? Where was he? Did I see him?

'I mean I didn't catch the case. I was just helping out.'

'Well now I'm helping you out too. Let's all help each other. Make the world a friendlier place, huh, Cal?'

'You wanna be friends, you should give me your name.'

'I'm just a good Samaritan, Cal. You know what the good

Samaritan's name was? No, neither do I. Doesn't make him less good though, does it?'

'You feeling so charitable, go give some money to a dogs' home.'

'Now, now, Cal. That's hardly the spirit. I know how they've been treating you at the precinct. The way you've been sidelined. Wouldn't you like the chance to prove to them what you can really do when given the chance?'

'I don't need you or anybody else to help me do that. Now say what you gotta say, then get the fuck off my phone.'

'Oh but I think you do need me, Cal. So here's what I'm of-fering. The chance to solve the case. The opportunity to catch the killer. Single-handed. Don't you think the NYPD would be impressed with that?'

'Why would you do that? Why would you want me to catch you? This is bullshit.'

'No, Cal, it's genuine. You'll find that out for yourself. If you're willing to hear me out, you'll discover that everything I tell you is true. Of course, I'm not going to come right out and give you names. That would be too easy. But I'll give you clues. All you have to do is use your brain and follow the leads I give you.'

'What's the catch? What do you get out of this?'

'Satisfaction. Helping people is all I live for, Cal. Those other clowns in your squad don't have a chance in hell of solving this. They got any leads yet? Okay, I know you can't answer that, but you and I both know the answer.'

The chorus of the song breaks through, and Doyle realizes it's I Still Haven't Found What I'm Looking For. Ha, ha, very funny again.

There is a knock on the door. It opens, and Rachel pops her head round.

'Cal, this food's going cold again.'

He waves her away too brusquely, and he doesn't blame her when she closes the door much harder than she needs to.

'So you're willing to act as an anonymous informant. For nothing in return except your own spiritual improvement. No financial considerations. No trade-off on legal charges. Nothing.'

'That's correct. Although there are certain . . . conditions I will have to impose.'

'Uh-huh. Why did I think it wasn't as simple as you laid it out?'

'I have to protect myself, Cal. You can't blame me for that. So here's the deal. I will help you, but in return for my help you must tell no one. Not your boss, not your friends, not even your wife. No one. Do you understand? The minute you reveal to anybody what I'm doing for you, my assistance will cease. Permanently. You must also promise not to attempt to trace my calls to you. And believe me when I tell you that I will know about it if you try to cheat on me.'

'Forget it. No way can I agree to that. I'm a cop. We have rules. If I keep information like that to myself, I'm breaking the law. I could get prison time for that. Is that what this is about? Are you trying to jam me up?'

'My, my, Cal. What a suspicious mind you have. No, this is not about setting you up. With what I know about you, I could have done that a long time ago. By the way, Cal, how are the nightmares these days? About you and . . . oh, what's her name? Lorna? No, Laura.'

Doyle goes cold. Laura Marino. She was his partner in his previous precinct. She took a blast from a shotgun when Doyle sent her the wrong way in an apartment bust. It was an honest mistake, but some people suggested there was more to it. There were rumors of an affair that Doyle wanted to end and she didn't. And there were rumors that Doyle did terminate it when the opportunity presented itself in that apartment.

It was a mistake, and he paid for it. With the subsequent investigation and scandal that almost wrecked his career and his marriage. And with the nightmares that still plague him.

The death of Laura became public knowledge. Anyone could read about that in the papers. But the nightmares? Who knows about them? Rachel, of course – she's had to put up with her sweat-soaked husband jumping out of bed in the middle of the night – but even then he has given her only the scantest of details. How the hell does this guy know about the nightmares?

But maybe it's just a bluff. Any cop who went through what Doyle experienced would have nightmares about it. Maybe it's not such a hard jump to make. Maybe that's this guy's skill. Throw in some facts that are easy to discover, mix in a few educated guesses, and you end up with someone who appears to know you intimately. Is that what this guy is doing? If so, he'd make an excellent poker player.

Or is this someone I really have met before?

'I sleep fine. And I'll sleep even better when we catch you, you sick son of a bitch. Now take your assistance and shove it up your ass, because you don't have long before I come over there and do it for you.'

There's a pause, and then a faint sigh, and then a note of disappointment in the caller's voice. 'That's a pity, Cal. A real shame. I thought you were made of sterner stuff. Someone I could really think of as one of New York's finest. Just think of what you're throwing away here. The chance to bring Cindy Mellish's killer to justice. The chance to save all those lives.'

He leaves the final words hanging there. *All those lives.* They drip with the terror of promised carnage.

'What do you mean? What lives?'

The disappointment turns to amusement. He's proud of his little twist. 'Oh, didn't I say? Cindy is merely the first. The first of many. In fact, you may be interested to know that the second life will be taken tonight.'

Doyle feels his grip tighten on the phone. He had been on the point of hanging up, but now he knows that's impossible. Refusing information on a past crime is one thing, but how can he reject the opportunity to save someone's life?

The caller presses home his advantage. 'Still there, Cal? Interested now, are we? Perhaps just a little bit? I can help you, Cal. I can help you solve the murder of Cindy Mellish, and I can help you to prevent another murder that is scheduled to take place tonight. What's it to be? Do we have a deal?'

Doyle considers it, but not for long. He needs to hear what this man has to offer, but whether it turns out to be bogus or not, he has no intention of sticking to any agreement with this douche bag.

'All right. Deal.'

'So you won't tell anyone about me, or try to trace my calls?'

'I said deal, didn't I?'

There is a slight pause, and when the man comes back on there is an excited energy in his voice. It's as though he can't quite believe his luck at getting this far, and is not quite sure what to say next.

'Good. Excellent. Then listen carefully, Cal. On the Cindy Mellish case, you need to find her diary. There will be clues in there.'

'Her diary. Are you sure?'

'Certain. Find the girl's diary, and you'll know what to do next.'

'Okay. And what about the other victim? The one who's supposed to die tonight?'

'That's up to you, Cal. What actions you take will determine whether the second person dies or just ends up somewhere like Bellevue.'

'What do you mean, the actions I take? I don't know what I'm supposed to do.'

'That's all I can tell you. Take it from here.'

'That's it? That's all you're giving me? The next one dies or ends up in hospital, and I'm supposed to affect that somehow? What kind of help is that?'

'Follow my advice, Cal. Think about what you've heard. Forget about what your heart tells you to do. It's the brain that's important here. You don't need anything more than that.'

Doyle is ready to unleash a torrent of abuse, but before the first expletive escapes his lips, there is a click and the phone goes dead.

He stares at the handset. What the fuck was that? Did I just dream that conversation?

He tosses the phone onto the bed as though he's just noticed that it's crawling with insects. He continues to stare at it.

Someone is going to get hurt tonight, maybe even killed. And I can make it go one way or the other. I don't know who the intended victim is. I don't know their name, where they live, what they look like, where they work, nothing.

And yet I have the power to save them.

So what do I do now?

What the fuck am I supposed to do now?

FIVE

I should call it in, he thinks.

I should call the station house, let them know I just had this phone conversation. Let them decide what to do about it. Then I'm in the clear. I don't have to worry about it. I can go back to thinking about what to do for poor old Mrs Sachs. They can go look for the stupid diary and solve the case and get all the glory.

But on the other hand . . .

What can I tell them? I know nothing about the person who is supposed to get whacked tonight, so telling them that isn't going to make any difference. I suppose I can mention the diary. If there *is* a diary. And if it contains any clues. Which it probably won't, because this guy is probably just a complete flake who gets off by getting cops to dance for him. And anyway I can check out for myself whether this diary exists.

Shit! Why does my life have to be one huge fucking dilemma?

Doyle opens the bedroom door and re-enters the living room. Rachel is watching the television with the volume turned up – something she often does when she's annoyed and she wants to shut out everything and everyone else.

First things first, he thinks. So he goes over to her and sits next to her on the sofa and asks her what she's watching and waits for her gruff reply and then tells her he's sorry.

'I was just trying to let you know . . .' she begins.

'I know, I know. I'm sorry. I didn't mean it. It was just one of those calls.'

'I don't know what "one of those calls" is. We don't have calls like that. We don't have secrets that have to be whispered to other people in other rooms. Do we?'

'Uhm, not usually, no. This one was different. Sensitive. You know? Sometimes there are things happening that I can't even tell you about. Sometimes it's better for you and Amy if you don't know what's going on.'

She searches his face with worried eyes. 'Are you in danger?'

'No. But sometimes there are things connected with the job that I can't discuss in front of you. I know it hasn't happened very often in the past, but occasionally something crops up.'

'What, does Mrs Sachs actually work for the CIA or something?'

'Something like that.' He gives her a chance to mull it over. 'We still friends?'

She answers him with a kiss. 'Now go eat your freezing cold lasagna. You'll have to pick out the broken glass yourself.'

He returns the kiss, then moves to the table.

Why didn't I tell her? he wonders. What was it about that particular call which made me unable even to tell my own wife about it? Okay, the guy knows a lot of things, but surely even he can't find out if I talked to Rachel.

Deep down, he knows the answer, and it tears him apart. He's kept things from her before. About the things he's had to do. About the actions he's had to take in order to keep his life together. It wasn't difficult for another little lie like this to trip off the tongue.

And he hates himself for it.

He pushes his food around the plate and stares at the back of Rachel's head, and he tells himself that if she turns around now he will burst into tears and he will open up his soul to her and she will be able to decide for herself whether he is a monster or just a frail human being, just like everybody else on this planet.

But she doesn't turn and he doesn't speak. He just pushes the food around and tries to convince himself that he is doing the right thing. That maybe, just maybe, his silence will save lives.

All is confusion.

She thinks at first that she is in her own bedroom. Which would mean that there wasn't this stupid oversized nightstand on which she's just smacked her skull. And it would mean she wouldn't have wasted time fumbling around for the damned light switch so that she could see where she was going instead of slamming into other items of cumbersome furniture. Why does a single guy need so much storage space, anyhow? Especially a guy who seems to have only about three changes of clothing?

She gets to her cellphone just before it cuts to voicemail. Stabs at the receive button as she tries to blink away the blurriness from her vision.

She attempts a hello, but it gets choked away. She clears her throat, tries again. A voice she doesn't recognize says her name.

'Yes, that's me. Who is this?'

'This is Detective Doyle, Eighth Precinct. I'm sorry to call you so late like this . . .'

'What? What is it?' She's wide awake now. A call from the police at – what time is it? Four o'clock on a Sunday morning – has that effect.

The figure in the bed stirs. A groggy face squints at her. 'Whassamatter? Whoozaonphone?'

She raises a finger to silence Alex while she listens to the caller.

'It's nothing to get alarmed about, Miss. It's about your husband.'

'Gary? What about him?'

'Like I say, it's nothing to get too worried about. Your husband was brought into the precinct station house a couple of hours ago. He was drunk and he'd been in a fight.'

'A fight? Oh, Jesus!'

'He's not badly hurt. A few cuts and bruises is all, although he seems to have lost his keys and his phone. We normally let people like this sleep it off in the cells, but it being a Saturday night they're all full. At the moment he's asleep in one of our interview rooms, but he can't stay there. So we were wondering if you could come over and take him off our hands. We couldn't get much sense out of your husband, but he did manage to tell us where you work, so I know you're only a few minutes away. We found your phone numbers in his address book. I tried your work number but they said you'd gone out on a break, so I hope you don't mind me calling you on this number.'

'No, that's fine. I'll come right over.'

'You know where we are?'

'I think so. By Tompkins, right?'

'That's it. Just ask for Detective Doyle at the desk.'

She ends the call. 'Shit!'

In the bed, Alex is sitting up. 'Who was that?'

She starts searching for her clothes. They got thrown in all different directions not long after she got here.

'Some detective called Doyle at the Eighth Precinct. Gary's there. Drunk and beat-up. They want me to go get him.'

Alex lets out a snort of laughter. She picks up one of his socks and throws it at him.

'It's not funny. You know, one of these days we're going to get caught doing this. The cops even tried calling me at work tonight. I think Bella must have covered for me. But what if Gary calls one night when I'm supposed to be working? What if it's not

Bella who answers, but someone who doesn't know I'm supposed to be at work when really I'm over here getting my brains banged out?'

'Yeah, well if Gary did a little more brain-banging himself, maybe you wouldn't have to put yourself through all this.'

'Shut up, Alex. You're really not helping.'

She's cheating on Gary. She accepts this. Mostly she tries not to think about it. When she can't avoid it, she tries to justify it to herself. Unreasonable behavior on his part. Lack of attentiveness to her womanly needs. Her conjugal rights. Whatever. But when others attack him, as Alex just did and frequently does, she feels compelled to leap to his defense. Gary has issues. After what they went through they both had issues, but she got over it and he didn't. It's sad, but there it is. He's not a bad man, she thinks, and he doesn't really deserve what I'm doing to him.

As she starts to dress, Alex relaxes back into the pillows and watches her.

'Couldn't you spend just another few minutes here?'

'No, I couldn't. The cops believe I'm practically on their doorstep. They don't know I have to drive all the way downtown to get there.'

'This time of night, it shouldn't take too long.'

She ignores him, continues dressing. When she passes the bed on her way to the door, he lunges forward and grabs her by the arm.

'Come on. Just a little longer. I'll be quick, I promise.'

'No change there, then.'

He pulls her closer to the bed. 'Well, if that's what you think, I'll just have to prove how wrong you are.'

She yanks herself free. 'No, Alex. No. Okay?'

She picks up her bag from a chair by the door, then gives him one last look. In response, Alex pulls back the sheets and shows her what he's got.

You don't have a clue, Alex, she thinks. Not a clue.

Shaking her head, she opens the door and leaves.

The apartment is way up on West 107th Street, near Amsterdam Avenue. She knows that what Alex likes about it is its proximity to Columbia University, where he works as a lab technician, and the karate school where he gets paid as an instructor. The only thing she likes about it is that she can usually get a parking spot on this block. She's not so sure she would bother to drive all the way here if she had to leave the car a couple of blocks away and come traipsing along these streets at the unearthly hours she often arrives.

Actually, she's not so sure how much longer she will continue this anyway. Alex is fun, he's got a great body, the sex is terrific. But there's a staleness to it now. The novelty has gone. What's worse, the guilt hasn't gone. She thought it might after a while. She thought she would become so accustomed to doing this that she would eventually become deaf to the admonishments of that little angel on her shoulder. But it hasn't worked out that way. If anything, the angel has taken to using a loudhailer. Tonight's little episode has just made things worse. Gary's a mess. He needs her help. Maybe she should try harder.

She steps out onto the dark street, glancing both ways before closing the door behind her. Directly opposite is a Jehovah's Witness building – another reminder of her sinful ways. She sometimes expects that she will step out of Alex's apartment building one night and the young men in dark suits will all be grouped there, pushing the Watchtower into her hands as they castigate her for her adulterous behavior.

She hurries along the sidewalk to where her Toyota is parked next to a school soccer field. Hearing a noise coming from beyond the graffiti-adorned wall across the street, she hurriedly unlocks the car door, throws her bag onto the passenger seat, and climbs in.

Only then does she see the note tucked under her windshield wiper.

She opens the door again and reaches round to retrieve the note. She unfolds it and reads the hastily scribbled words.

Sorry about the damage to the rear of your car. I accidentally clipped it when I drove off. Sorry!

What the . . . ?

She reads it again, to make sure she fully comprehends it. He smashed into my car? And he didn't even have the decency to leave a name or contact number? What a bastard! And what's the fucking point of leaving a fucking note just to say how fucking sorry you are?

She clambers out again, thinking what a shitty night this is turning out to be. Thinking that maybe she's getting what she deserves, that her shoulder-borne angel has really gone hardcore now.

She steps around to the rear of her car, her fear replaced by indignation. Wondering how much this is going to cost her.

The car looks fine.

I mean, it's really dark here, but even so . . .

She squats. Stands up again. Runs her hand over the bodywork. What the hell is the writer of this note talking about?

She unfolds the sheet of paper again, starts to read it through.

A few yards behind her, a car engine roars into life. She jumps, startled, and glances around. She catches a glimpse of a dark hulking shape – some kind of SUV – before its headlights flare on, blinding her.

Ignore it, she tells herself. Let them go on their way.

She turns back to her own car. The bright light from the SUV gives her an opportunity to get a good look. There's nothing here she can see. Not a dent, a scratch, nothing.

She is mystified. But now she is also a little afraid again. Something isn't right. Something about this whole setup . . .

The SUV is on her in an instant. She hears a squeal of tires, a blast of engine noise, and she barely has time to turn toward it before those intense lights fill her vision and their leviathan owner rams into her, crushing her against her own car.

At first she screams. It's automatic, driven by the pain and the shock. And then confusion takes over. She loses the ability to make sense of the world. She cannot understand what has just happened to her. Why can't she move? Why won't her legs obey her orders to take her away from here?

She looks down, sees only bent, twisted metal from her hips downwards. And still her brain cannot fully grasp its significance. She opens her mouth to cry out again, stops when she sees she is not alone.

The SUV's door is open. Its driver is standing alongside her, looking at her. Studying her, in fact, his head cocked to one side like a curious puppy. He is tall and well-groomed. Could be considered good-looking in other circumstances. And yet there is an absence of empathy in his face that is intensely disturbing.

'P-Please,' she says to him through quivering lips. It should be enough. It should tell anyone all they need to know about the predicament of the fellow human being in front of them.

'Sorry,' the man says.

It makes no sense to her. It's a word that doesn't seem to fit the situation, as though it has been chosen at random.

In explanation, the man reaches toward her and plucks out the note still clutched between her fingers.

'Like I said in the note. I'm sorry. About the damage I've

done to your car.' He waves the paper at her and smiles. 'I like to apologize in advance for these things.'

She tells herself it's the shock. He cannot really be saying all this. She blinks and fights the shaking that is growing in intensity in her body. She feels cold. So cold. Why doesn't he do something?

'Please,' she repeats. 'Help me.'

The man drops his smile. At last he seems to appreciate the seriousness of what he has done.

'Yes,' he says. 'Of course. Help. You need my help.'

He gets back into his car and closes the door. She looks directly into his eyes through the windshield. She sees the slight jerk of his shoulder as he shifts the vehicle into reverse.

She braces herself and closes her eyes. She hears the pinging of metal and the tinkling of glass and her own cries as the cars separate.

And then she falls.

She knows she has fallen. She knows she has hit the ground. She knows she is alive. Reality is flooding back again.

She opens her eyes but does not look down. She is afraid of what she might see. Her legs must be a mess. Flattened useless ribbons of flesh and bone. She will never walk again. She understands that now and accepts it. But at least she is alive. On the edge of death, sure. But there's hope.

Good one, angel, she thinks. You really told me this time. Are you done with me now?

She can almost swear she hears a tiny voice tell her that she should be so lucky.

And so it's really no big surprise when the SUV comes thundering toward her one last time.

SIX

The first thing Doyle does on Sunday morning is break his promise.

What was that he said to Rachel last night? Something about making it up to Amy, wasn't it? And is he making it up to Amy? No. Because while Amy is trying to tell him all about what life is like in her small world, mixing with all kinds of small people doing small things that seem oh so immense to her, her father is just grunting at her while he tries to concentrate on the local news stories on the television. Grunting so often, in fact, that she eventually gets the message and gives up and requests the cartoon channel for its greater intellectual challenge.

The news programs continue to demand his attention on the journey to work too. Early Sunday morning is the one time of the week when driving to the precinct station house is a comparative breeze, and so he knows when he finally gets there that he has listened closely to every local story deemed noteworthy enough to be broadcast without listeners wondering what the fuck they are being told this for. And guess what? A murder in Manhattan did not figure among them. A councilman fracturing his toe – that made it in. A woman suing her cosmetic surgeon for botching an enhancement job on her buttocks – that made it in too. But homicide? Uh-uh. Not in this city, buddy.

At his desk he reflects on this. What does it mean? Either

butt-jobs have leaped ahead of homicides on the scale of what matters most to people these days, or else there was no killing last night. The caller got it wrong. And if he got that wrong, then the stuff about the diary is probably bullshit too. In fact, Doyle thinks he can probably disregard everything that was said by that cuckoo and get back to worrying about poor old Mrs Sachs.

There is, of course, one other possibility . . .

The call comes through at ten-forty.

'Detective Doyle. Eighth Precinct.'

'Hey, Doyle. This is Lopez up at the Two-Seven. Sorry to bother you, but we caught a weird one here, and your name came up.'

Doyle feels his insides drop into his shoes. Even without the details, he knows this is his worst fears coming true.

'My name? Why? What's the case?'

'Homicide. A woman crushed between two cars on West 107th Street.'

'You sure? That it's a homicide, I mean? Not some kind of freaky accident?'

'Nah, it was deliberate all right. According to the ME, she was rammed twice.'

'Jesus, what a way to go. You got any wits?'

He's thinking there has to be a witness. Surely you can't make a vehicle sandwich on the streets of New York like that without somebody seeing something?

'Nope. Nobody that's come forward so far, anyhow. There are no occupied buildings near where it happened, and it was four o'clock in the morning.'

'Four a.m.? There was nothing on the news about it.'

'Body wasn't discovered until seven-thirty. A woman jogging back from Central Park stopped for a rest and saw a foot underneath one of the vehicles. Then she took a closer look and found the foot-bone was connected to the leg-bone, and she heard the word of the Lord. Thing is, she'd already passed it on her way to the park and thought nothing of it. Just two mashed-up cars, looked like. My guess is other people walked past it too and thought the same thing. Who's gonna call the cops for something like that, right?'

Doyle finds himself nodding in agreement. He knows that many people wouldn't have called the cops even *after* they'd discovered the body.

'I still don't get how it went down. What was this woman doing out on the street at four in the morning?'

'Yeah, that got us too. Especially when we find the woman's wallet and learn she lives over in Brooklyn and works on the East Side. We contact the husband, deliver the bad news, wait for the crying to stop, then ask him the same question. Only he has absolutely no idea what she was doing there either. So we start knocking on doors, and eventually we find a guy in one of the apartment buildings farther along the street. Turns out she's having an affair with him. A regular thing, apparently. She tells her husband she's pulling a double shift, then goes and pulls something else over at this younger dude's place.'

'Still doesn't explain how she ended up getting squashed.'

'No. That's where you come in.'

'Me? How?'

'Reason we know she was killed at four was that she got a call on her cellphone when she was in the apartment. She told the boyfriend about it. He says it was a cop, or someone pretending to be a cop, telling her that her husband had been locked up for drunkenness, and could she come take him home. The boyfriend thinks the cop called himself Boyle, or maybe Doyle, at the Eighth Precinct.'

Doyle finds himself shaking his head. The sheer deviousness of that bastard.

'Shit, Lopez. I don't know what I can tell you.'

'That's okay. I didn't expect nothing. Whoever did this probably just picked your name at random off a list. I just needed to check it out, okay? You know, tick the boxes.'

'Sure, no problem. You look at the husband for this?'

He asks because it's an obvious question. Cuckolded husband doing away with his cheating bitch of a wife – it's one of the oldest reasons under the sun. But deep in his gut, Doyle knows it's not the story here.

'Natch. The boyfriend too. Both of them look safe right now, but we're digging. CSU are checking out the SUV used in the hit. It's stolen, but maybe we'll get some useful forensics. Anyways, Doyle, thanks for the input. Now I've crossed you off I can get on with something useful.'

A thought occurs to Doyle. A question. He's not sure he wants the answer, but it tumbles out of his mouth nevertheless.

'Anything you can give me on the DOA?' Then, so as not to seem as though he has a pressing need for this, he adds, 'Just so I can make sure I don't have a connection to her.'

There's a pause, during which Doyle thinks he's been rumbled. But then Lopez comes back at him.

'Her name is Lorna Bonnow. She's a nurse at Bellevue. That strum any chords with you?'

And now Doyle really is wishing he hadn't asked that question. Because yes, there is a huge fucking orchestra in his skull right now. His mind is pouncing on Lopez's words, tearing at them for meaning, and they're telling him what a complete fucking idiot he has been.

'Doyle? You still there, man?'

'Uh, yeah, sorry – there's somebody else trying to talk to me here. No, I never heard of her.'

'Okay. For a minute there I thought you were going to tell me it was you who aced her. Catch you later, Doyle.'

He hangs up. Doyle puts the phone down without knowing he's doing it.

Shit.

Shit!

What was it his anonymous little helper said to him?

What actions you take will determine whether the second person dies or just ends up somewhere like Bellevue.

Doyle had taken that to mean the victim would end up either dead or severely hurt. But it didn't mean that. Not at all. It meant: if you act on this information in time, the target will make it back into Bellevue.

Because that's where she works, you dick!

It was all there in the phone conversation, wasn't it?

By the way, Cal, how are the nightmares these days? About you and . . . oh, what's her name? Lorna? No, Laura.

That was no slip of the tongue. He's too clever for that. No, he was giving out her first name. Lorna.

And the surname? That was the cleverest thing of all, you sneaky bastard.

Bonnow. Sounds like Bono. Lead singer of U2. Playing loud and clear in the background during the call.

Lorna Bonnow who works in Bellevue. I had all the information I needed to save her, thinks Doyle. I just didn't know it. And so she died.

Follow my advice, Cal. Think about what you've heard. Forget about what your heart tells you to do. It's the brain that's important here. You don't need anything more than that.

Shit!

And it gets worse. Because now I'm the only person other than the killer who knows there's a link between these two deaths. And I can't say anything. It's too late for that.

What, do I go to the boss and say, 'Hey, Lou, you know that

homicide up in the Two-Seven? Well, that was done by the same guy who whacked the bookstore girl. How do I know this? He told me he was going to do it. Practically gave me her name and everything. Thought you might want to know that. How about you put me in for that promotion now?'

Sure, that'll work.

And if I say nothing? If other detectives don't figure out the link?

Can I stand by and let that happen?

Shit and double shit.

This all feels a little underhand. Coming here like this without telling Holden or anyone else involved in the case. But he has to know. He has to find out.

Cindy Mellish's mother lives in a three-story walk-up above a women's clothing store on Thompson Street. What they call a mixed-use building. When she opens the door she looks like she has cried several years' worth of tears. The life has gone from her – from her bloodshot eyes, her body, and even her hair. She's an empty shell. When Doyle flashes the tin, she doesn't even bother to look at it. She just pushes the door open wide, then turns and walks back into the apartment.

When Doyle follows her into the living room, he notices how clean and tidy the place is. He bets there isn't a speck of dirt or dust left in here. He pictures her moving from room to room, cloth in hand, trying to distract herself with work while the tears run down her face.

'Mrs Mellish,' he begins. 'I'm sorry to bother you. This won't take long. There's just a coupla questions—'

'I haven't seen you before,' she says.

Doyle wonders if she's heard any of his words.

'No. You haven't. I'm just helping out on the case. Do you mind if—'

'What was your name again?'

He had given it at the door, but he obliges nonetheless.

'Doyle. Detective Callum Doyle. I just need a little information from you. Would that be okay?'

Silence. For what seems to Doyle like a full minute. He is beginning to think it was a mistake coming here, intruding into her grief. It's too early. She needs more time.

But he needs to know.

'Will you catch them?' she says finally. 'Whoever did this to my daughter. Will you catch them?'

'I'm sure we will,' Doyle answers. 'We'll do everything we can, I promise you.'

She gives a slight nod, then stares at the carpet. Doyle waits what he thinks is a decent length of time before he tries again.

'Mrs Mellish, do you know—'

'Why?'

For a second, Doyle is flummoxed.

'Excuse me?' he says.

'Why do you think he did it? Killing her in the way he did. So savagely, I mean. Why would he do that to her? I keep asking myself that question. What sort of bad thing could Cindy have done to anyone that would make them think she deserved this in return?'

Doyle shakes his head. 'Cindy didn't deserve it. It just . . . happened. She was in the wrong place at the wrong time, that's all. Please don't go thinking this was any fault of Cindy's. The only person to blame here is her murderer.'

She nods again and returns her gaze to the carpet. Doyle knows she is trying to make sense of something which defies reason. We all do it, he thinks. When something terrible happens in our lives, we want to know why. Sometimes it can be hard to accept that there are no answers.

When he begins his question again, he half expects another interruption, and so he pushes his words out in one fast burst: 'Mrs Mellish, do you know if Cindy kept a diary?'

She raises her head, and Doyle is convinced he sees a flicker of puzzlement and interest in her eyes.

'I . . . A diary? I don't think so. No.'

No. So that's it, then. The caller was wrong. There is no diary. What a fucking waste of time and effort this little trip has turned out to be. And from the looks of her, it hasn't done Mrs Mellish any favors either.

'Why?' she asks.

For a moment Doyle thinks she is continuing her quest for philosophical answers he is not equipped to supply, but then she adds, 'Why do you ask about a diary?'

He realizes now that he has stirred all kinds of possibilities in her mind. Perhaps even jostled some expectations to the surface. A detective schlepping all the way over here to ask about something as specific as a diary? That has to be important, right? That has to signify a lead of some kind, right?

I should get outta here, thinks Doyle. This is wrong.

'Girls this age, sometimes they keep journals. Sometimes they put stuff in there they might not tell anybody else about, you know? Thoughts they've had, people they've met, things that have happened to them. It can help us build a picture.'

And now he can see a light returning to those sad eyes. She is latching onto this. Making it into something more than the nothing it probably is. Perhaps there are answers here, she is thinking. Perhaps there is meaning.

'You think this was done by somebody she *knew*?' she asks.

He catches the incredulity infused into that last word, and he knows he has to move quickly to stop her joining dots which aren't in sequence.

'No. I'm not saying that at all. We don't know if she met her killer before or not. All I want to do right now is learn a little more about Cindy. Maybe it'll help.'

He hates the fact that he's hiding things from her, that he's pretending this is all on his own initiative. Hates it even more that he's leading this woman down paths she has no reason to navigate.

Can it, Doyle. Shut the fuck up and leave now.

He says, 'But if you say there's no diary, then . . .'

'I . . .' she starts, and Doyle catches her glance at one of the doors. Unlike the other doors, this one is firmly shut.

Cindy's bedroom, he realizes. She probably can't bear to go back in there. She has cleaned every nook and cranny in this apartment. But not in there. Opening that door breaks the spell. Shatters the illusion that Cindy is still in there, listening to music or reading a book. Or just being alive.

'She writes,' says Mrs Mellish. '*Wrote*. A lot. Ever since she was little. Always scribbling in her notebooks. Poetry mostly. Some stories. But a diary . . .'

Doyle waits. Part of him wants to ask if he can search the room. Another part insists this is bullshit. This is all a part of the killer's sick game: sending him here to push this poor woman to her breaking point.

'If you want to take a look,' she says, 'it'd be okay. If you think it'll help. Just . . . don't mess it up, okay?'

He nods. 'I'll be careful.'

When he moves toward the room she doesn't follow him. When he opens the door, he hears her footsteps moving away. She doesn't want to look in here. Not yet.

It's a cozy, welcoming room. Tidy but full. The bed is made, and a baby-pink dressing gown lies along the bottom of it. A white bra hangs from one of the bedposts. There is a table with a mirror and a large array of make-up items. On one side of the room is a line of cheap white storage units. They comprise a tall closet and a row of low-level units interrupted by a recess with a chair pushed into it. The counter running above these units supports a music system and speakers, racks of CDs and DVDs, lots of cuddly toys, a hairdryer, straightening tongs, a stack of magazines, an electric fan. On the wall above are several posters of actors and pop stars. On the other side of the room is a row of bookcases. Cindy Mellish read a lot of books.

Doyle takes a deep breath. He can smell perfume. He wonders why it's familiar, then realizes it hung on the air in the bookstore too.

He moves closer to the bookcases. Fiction, poetry and biography mostly. Nothing trashy. No bodice-rippers for this girl. On the bottom shelves are Cindy's notebooks. All different sizes, different colors. Doyle sits cross-legged on the thickly carpeted floor, pulls out the first book, and turns the cover.

What he sees on that first page is a poem entitled 'Life Without End'. He starts to read it, but gives up after six lines. He turns the page, finds another poem called 'Nobody Hears Me'. Doesn't bother to read this one. He flicks through the rest of the book, finds more of the same. Occasionally a doodle leaps out at him, but to Doyle's eye the artistry is as bad as the poetry. He wonders whether it's him just not getting this arty stuff, then decides no, it really is that amateurish.

He moves on to the next book, then the next, and the next. More poetry, more doodles. He chances across a short story called 'Freud's Ghost', reads the whole thing through and decides that either it wasn't finished, or else it was finished and the point of it has totally escaped him.

He speeds up his search then. Pull out a book, riffle through its pages, put it back. He gets all the way to the end of the shelf.

Nothing. No diary. Nothing whatsoever about the events of her life save for what may be lurking in the depths of her prose and poetry. And he's already decided it's beyond his ability to tease that out.

He gets to his feet. He scans the spines of every book on the shelves, just to make sure he hasn't missed anything. He goes to the storage units and opens each one. He finds clothes, bags, shoes, more cuddly toys, but no diary. He tries all the drawers of the make-up table. Hair pins, jewelry, perfume bottles, tissues, shopping receipts, tampons.

But no fucking diary.

Doyle takes another look around. He tries the not-so-obvious places. Under the pillow, under the mattress, under the bed. Behind drawers. Inside bags and purses. Slipped behind other books.

Nothing.

And now he's pissed off. Now he feels like he's being jerked around.

He leaves the bedroom. Mrs Mellish is sitting at a table, doing nothing. She stands when she sees Doyle.

'I think you were right,' he tells her. 'I can't find a diary.'

He is convinced he sees disappointment on her face. When he abandons her in this apartment she will have nothing but her grief again. He starts to reach into his jacket for a card with his number on it. 'I tell you what—'

The phone rings then. Mrs Mellish says, 'Excuse me a moment,' and goes to answer it. Her conversation is brief, and then she turns to Doyle.

'It's for you.'

'For me?'

'Yes. A man. He says he's got that help you wanted from him.'

SEVEN

When he takes the phone he tries to remain calm. He wants to scream obscenities into the mouthpiece, but he also doesn't want to alarm Mrs Mellish. He turns away from her, tries to keep his voice low.

'Doyle.'

'Hello, Cal. How's the search for the diary going?'

'How'd you know I was here?'

'Actually, I didn't. But it seemed like a good bet. I thought once you heard about what happened to that nurse last night, you'd be keen to check out the diary. You're starting to trust me now, isn't that right, Cal?'

'I don't trust you as far as I can piss. How'd you get this number?'

'Have you ever heard of the phone book, Cal? It's a way of finding out somebody's phone number. So have you found the diary yet?'

'There is no diary. I looked everywhere. It's not here.'

'You're not looking hard enough. It's there, all right. Use your eyes, and think about what you see.'

'I looked. It's not here. You made a mistake.'

A sigh of exasperation. Then: 'Do I have to lead you by the hand, Cal? Are you really that helpless? Come on, then – back into the bedroom.'

He says this as though he's indulging a young child. Doyle bites down on his bottom lip. He wants so much to tell this sonof-abitch to shove his phone up his ass.

He lowers the phone, looks across at Mrs Mellish.

'I'm sorry, Mrs Mellish, but my colleague has just given me a few more ideas about where I might search for the diary. You mind if I take one more quick look?'

He can tell she's unsettled now. And he can't blame her. He's not acting like a cop should. She's probably wondering if he even *is* a cop.

'I . . . all right.'

He flashes her his most comforting smile and heads back into the bedroom. He pushes the door to but doesn't close it. That would be just too suspicious.

'Okay,' he says into the phone. 'I'm in the bedroom.'

'Well done, Cal. At least you've managed to find something. Now all you need is the diary.'

'I told you, I've looked. It's not here. I've looked on every shelf and in every drawer and closet.'

'You are so behind the times, Cal. Think like a teenager. The answer's right there in the open.'

Doyle scans the room. What the hell is this freak talking about? How can it be right here in front of me? I've looked every-where. What could I have missed?

His eyes alight on each group of objects again. The make-up. The cuddly toys. The CDs and DVDs. The magazines. The . . .

Wait a minute. Rewind.

He steps toward the row of cabinets. The counter they support is covered in items. Every square inch is occupied by something. Except . . .

Except where the chair is, pushed into the recess. In front of the chair is the only space in the clutter. Just a couple of square feet, but a space nonetheless. Doyle tries to imagine Cindy sitting on this chair. She would reach for those pens and pencils just on the right here. This is where she would make all those jottings in her notebooks. And to her left . . .

Doyle slides the chair out and bends down to look into the recess. That's when he understands.

He hears what sounds like the faint buzzing of an insect, and realizes that it's the voice emanating from the phone that's now down at his side. He raises the phone to his ear, but doesn't wait to hear what's being said.

'The space,' says Doyle.

'What?'

'The space. In front of the chair. Where Cindy worked and studied. There's an empty space there. The only clear space in the room.'

Silence. Like maybe he has just surprised the guy.

'Okay, there's a space. So what?'

'If she had a diary, this is where she would have written it. But not necessarily in one of these notebooks, right?'

A faint chuckle. 'Way to go, Columbo. I'll be in touch soon.'

There's a click, and the line goes dead. Doyle goes back into the living room. Mrs Mellish is standing exactly where he left her, still looking uneasy. He goes over to her and hands the phone back. She is wary when she takes it, almost as if she expects him to grab her arm.

'What's going on?' she asks. 'Who was that man on the phone?'

Doyle knows he needs to get her back on his side. 'Mrs Mellish, I'm sorry. There are things I can't tell you right now. Things that have cropped up in our investigation. One of our sources has told us that Cindy had a diary, and that it might be important.

That man who just called was giving me some further information to help me locate it.'

'But you looked. You said there isn't a diary in her room.'

Okay, thinks Doyle, here goes.

'Mrs Mellish, did Cindy have a computer?'

She stares at him. Either she's not sure whether to tell him the
truth, or else she's trying to figure out how he knows this.

'The DVDs,' he explains. 'She has lots of DVDs but no
player, no TV. Underneath the counter where she sat and worked
there's a power socket and cables.'

She stares some more. Finally gives the faintest of nods.

'A laptop. I bought it for her two years ago. For her birthday,
and to help in her studies. It's usually in her bedroom, but I
asked her if I could borrow it for a while. I've been on the Web,
looking for new jobs.'

'Do you think it's possible Cindy might have kept her diary
on that computer?'

'I . . . I guess it's possible. Maybe.'

'Mrs Mellish, do you think I could borrow that computer?
Just for a day or two, so I can get it looked at?'

He watches her body language. Sees the defenses going up.

'I don't know. Is this . . . normal? I mean, do the police usually do things like this?'

'There's no such thing as normal. Every situation is different. In this case, it's just possible there may be something
useful on Cindy's computer. I just want the experts to take a
look. They won't damage it, and I'll get it straight back to you,
I promise.'

'But you can't say why you think there's a diary?'

He thinks, I want to tell her. I want to let her know there's
a psycho running around out there who has already killed two
people and may be about to kill again, and the reason I know

about the diary is that he's been phoning me up and taunting me, and when I catch this cocksucker I'm gonna make him wish he'd never been born. I'm gonna do that for you, Mrs Mellish. For you and for Cindy.

'It's a possibility, that's all,' he says, not really answering her question. 'But if we find anything, you'll be the first to know.'

She looks into his eyes, and he hopes that his determination to get justice for her shines more brightly than his lack of candor. Eventually she turns and walks through one of the open doors into her own bedroom. She comes back a minute later with a laptop in her hands.

'Please, be careful with it. I know it's just a lump of metal and plastic, but, well . . . it was Cindy's.'

Doyle takes the computer and smiles his gratitude. As he leaves the apartment, he makes a promise to himself that the laptop is not the only thing he will bring back to this woman.

Sometimes they have to be called in.

It's nice to know they're there. Sitting in the background, acting as insurance. For when you really need help. You don't want to use them frivolously – that would be a waste. They are far too valuable.

But sometimes cashing them in is the right thing to do.

This particular favor is owed to Doyle by a man called Lonnie Adelman. Detective Lonnie Adelman. Doyle was at the Police Academy with him, and although they don't see as much of each other as they used to, they still get together socially now and then. It's a relationship which, in itself, could probably act as enough of a basis for Doyle to approach him for help. But Doyle has additional leverage. Four years ago, he was involved in the arrest of a group of teenagers for possession of cocaine. One of those teenagers turned out to be Adelman's son. Following Adelman's representation and a promise that he would keep the boy on the straight and narrow, Doyle kicked the kid out and kept his name out of the paperwork.

Now it's payback time. Because what makes Adelman especially valuable to Doyle is that he is a member of CCS, which used to be called CITU, cops loving abbreviations the way they do. CCS is the Computer Crimes Squad, while CITU stood for Computer Investigation and Technology Unit. Whatever the hell it's called, the key thing to Doyle about both of those titles is the word *computer*. It means that Adelman knows all about that technology stuff, whereas to Doyle computers are little more than glorified typewriters that never want to do what he asks of them. It's the reason Doyle called on Adelman when he wanted to buy a new computer system for Rachel, and it's the reason he calls upon him whenever that system goes wrong.

It's also the reason why Doyle now finds himself in the NYPD headquarters at One Police Plaza, the building known fondly to cops as the Puzzle Palace, the Big House, or – to use yet another abbreviation – simply 1PP.

Adelman looks delighted to see Doyle when he enters his office, but he also looks like a man who is late for an appointment. To Doyle he always looks that way, even when he's supposed to be relaxing. His flushed face says that there just aren't enough hours in the day. Doyle figures he's an ideal candidate for an early heart attack.

'Hey, Cal,' says Adelman. He grabs Doyle's hand, slaps his shoulder. He's a big man, a couple of inches taller and broader than Doyle, and Doyle is no waif himself. 'How's it going, man?'

Doyle shrugs. 'Still sliding down the razor blade of life.'

Adelman laughs. 'Yeah, I know what you mean. I read about you in the papers. You been busy, dude.'

'Life's never dull. What about you and those cyber-crooks?

You arrested that Super Mario guy yet? Mustache like that, he's gotta be on the wanted lists, right?'

Another hearty laugh. 'Can't catch him. Boy drives like a motherfucker. '

They chat for another few minutes, catching up. So as not to seem too pointed, Doyle waits until the topic of family crops up in the conversation before he asks about Luke, the son he arrested.

'Still straight,' Adelman says. 'No doubt about that. He's a man now. Even got himself a girl. Subject of drugs comes up, he just talks about how stupid he was back then.'

Doyle nods. 'Good to hear. He's a great kid.'

In the silence which follows, Doyle catches Adelman sliding his eyes toward his wristwatch.

'Listen, Cal, it's been great seeing you and all, and we should definitely get together properly soon, but I gotta shoot to a meeting in five minutes. Are you gonna ask me about that computer under your arm, or have you forgotten it's there?'

Doyle looks down. 'Hey, whaddya know? There *is* a computer here. And since you're asking . . .'

'Go ahead. You wanna hide that trail of porn sites you been visiting?'

'This doesn't belong to me. I need you to search it for me.'

'Search it? For what?'

'A diary. I just been sitting in Starbucks for the last hour, looking through this thing, and I can't find it. But then I don't know what the hell I'm doing, and I don't want to screw up the system. You think you could—'

'Whoa, buddy. What diary? Whose computer is this?'

Doyle senses this isn't going as smoothly as he hoped.

'It's connected with a case I'm working. My information says there's a diary on here. If that's so, I'd like to know what's in it.'

Adelman looks at him. 'A case, huh?'

It's no surprise to Doyle that Adelman knows something is fishy. This isn't how it works. It should go through official channels. The precinct detective squad investigating the case makes a formal approach for assistance to the CCS, which in turn allocates whatever resources it deems appropriate. Sometimes that may mean getting held up in a queue. What it certainly means is that there's an official record of the request. A lowly detective strolling in here without an appointment and with a computer tucked under his arm is making such a blatant attempt to circumvent NYPD red tape it's laughable. It's so suspicious it stinks. Even given their friendship, even given the fact that he saved the ass of Adelman's son, Doyle fully expects to be thrown out of here in the next five seconds. Put him in Adelman's shoes and he's not sure he would do any different, especially given the rep he has now after all the media coverage.

When Adelman stands abruptly, Doyle says, 'Lonnie, let me explain . . .'

Adelman holds up his hand. 'No details. I don't want to hear details. Come with me.'

He heads for the door, Doyle trailing.

'Where are we going?'

'I investigate cyber crime. What I don't do is spend all my time poking around inside computers.'

Shit, thinks Doyle. He's getting rid of me.

But then Adelman adds, 'We have whiz kids for doing that kind of thing.'

He leads Doyle along to the end of the corridor, then opens a door without knocking.

'Meet our resident genius,' he says.

Doyle walks through the doorway. He sees a room that looks like the aftermath of an explosion. There are computers and bits of computers everywhere. He hears the whirring of fans and the chatter of disk drives. Behind a long desk, facing away from Doyle, a young man sits staring intently at a bank of monitors. On one of the screens, text scrolls upwards so quickly it must be impossible to read, and yet the man's gaze remains fixed on it. His feet are up on the desk and he's eating from a bag of corn chips on his lap. He wears a huge pair of headphones, playing heavy metal music so loud that Doyle can hear it clearly.

'Hey, Gonzo!' says Adelman.

Doyle's eyes widen. *Gonzo?*

Oblivious to his visitors, Gonzo continues to nod his head in time to the music.

'GONZO!'

The guy nearly falls off his chair. Corn chips spill onto the floor. Gonzo powers off the music and yanks the headphones away, knocking his glasses off his face. He pushes them back into place as he struggles to look calm and collected.

Adelman says, 'Detective Doyle, meet Gonzo.'

Gonzo gives him a goofy smile and a meek wave.

Adelman continues, 'Tell him what you need, and he'll work his magic. If what you want is on that machine, he'll find it. I gotta go. Nice seeing you again, Cal.'

They shake hands, and Adelman leaves them alone. Doyle approaches the desk while Gonzo watches his every move. Doyle looks down at the chair, which has a jacket crumpled in a ball on the seat.

'You mind if I sit?'

Gonzo shakes his head, but makes no attempt to move.

'This your jacket?'

Gonzo nods, puts some more chips in his mouth. Still doesn't move.

Doyle picks up the jacket. He looks for somewhere to hang it, but can't find anywhere, so he hands it across to Gonzo. Still munching, Gonzo takes the jacket, holds it for a few seconds, then tosses it onto the floor.

As Doyle lowers himself onto the chair, he takes a closer look at his host. Gonzo's hair is red and curly and thinning at the temples, even though he looks to be in his early twenties. His thick-framed glasses are supported by a beak of a nose. His body is thin and wiry. On the window ledge to the side of the desk is an inhaler of the type that asthmatics use.

'You want a Dorito?'

The shock is threefold. It surprises Doyle that Gonzo can speak at all; he is surprised by the spray of food fragments that hits him in the face; and he is surprised by the voice, which is a high-pitched squawk that sounds like it belongs to Homer Simpson's wife.

Jesus, thinks Doyle. The offspring of Woody Allen and Marge Simpson. What a set of genes that is.

'They're my favorite,' Gonzo continues. 'Give me some Doritos and a salsa dip, and I'm your friend for life.'

'Yeah,' says Doyle, not sure how to progress that topic. 'Anyways, I got this computer here . . .'

He hands it across to Gonzo, who gives it the once-over before dumping it unceremoniously on his desk.

'You like Lugzz?'

'Are they anything like Doritos?'

Gonzo stares at him, then taps a finger on his headphones. 'The band. Music. You wanna listen?'

'Uh, actually I thought we might talk about the computer.'

'Oh. Okay,' says Gonzo, seemingly amazed that Doyle is willing to pass up such a golden opportunity. 'What about it?'

'Well, I'm trying to find something on it.'

'Have you tried switching it on?'

Doyle looks across to check whether Gonzo is yanking his chain, but he seems serious enough.

'Yes, I've switched it on. I just can't find the file I want.'

'The file being?'

'A diary.'

'A diary?'

'Yeah. You know. A journal. A record of events in some-body's life.'

Gonzo stares again. He pushes another fistful of chips into his mouth.

'You sure you don't want some of these? I got lots. Six more bags.'

Doyle is starting to wonder what planet this kid is on.

'No. Thank you. Now, the diary. You think you can find it for me?'

'Sure. If it's on there, I'll find it.'

The very words Adelman used. But Doyle is starting to find it hard to believe that this kid is capable of anything other than ingesting corn chips to a four-four beat.

'Great. How long?'

'How long is what?'

Jesus, thinks Doyle. Do I have to spell everything out?

'How long will it take you to find the file?'

'Depends on how well it's hidden. Plus I got a whole load of other stuff I need to get done first.'

'So how long?'

'Give me till tomorrow. I'll call you. What precinct are you at?'

Doyle reaches into his pocket and pulls out a card and a pen.

'I'm putting my cellphone number on the back of this card. That's the only number you call me on, okay? *Not* the precinct number.'

Just to be sure, Doyle crosses out the precinct telephone number.

Gonzo narrows his myopic eyes at him. 'You don't want me to phone you at the precinct?'

'That's what I said.'

'Does Lonnie know about this?'

'He knows,' says Doyle, which isn't strictly true. But then Lonnie doesn't want to know.

Gonzo nods unconvincingly.

'I gotta go,' says Doyle. He gets up and walks across this computer junkyard of an office. Just before he leaves he adds, 'Call me tomorrow.' Because genius that this kid is supposed to be, he seems like someone who could forget everything, including his own name, as soon as Doyle walks out the door.

For the rest of Doyle's working day, nothing much happens. Which is not such a good thing. Because what he hoped was that someone would make a connection between the Mellish murder and the Bonnow murder. And nobody has. As far as the NYPD is concerned, these two killings are related only by the fact that they remain unsolved. They have different MOs, they were in different precincts, and there is nothing so far to suggest that the two women even knew each other. So why should anyone even conceive of a link between these two? Hell, it's not as if there's anyone calling up cops to suggest such a thing, now is there?

Officially, he's still helping out on the Cindy Mellish case. Unofficially, he's just going through the motions. He continues to chase up bookstore customers. He continues to call up people that might have known Cindy. He continues to feel guilt over his knowledge that it's probably all such a waste of time and manpower.

He is so glad to get home. Away from other cops. Away from eyes that seem to dare him to reveal what he knows. For a few hours he can put all that to the back of his mind. He can enjoy a roast dinner with his family, a bicycle ride in Central Park, bath time with Amy, a glass of wine with Rachel. And when he finally goes to bed and melts into the warmth of his wife, he is almost convinced that there is nothing to worry about, that it will all work out in the end.

The call comes at midnight precisely.

When he blinks at the clock and the pale fuzzy light gradually forms into recognizable numerals and he sees 12:00 written in front of him, he knows the time has been chosen as a signal that this is no ordinary call. It's the witching hour. Expect to be scared.

He hears the music before the phone even reaches his ear. It's purely instrumental. An Irish jig.

'Hello, Cal,' says the smooth-talking sonofabitch.

Doyle climbs out of bed and staggers out of the bedroom, the phone clamped to his ear.

'What do you want?'

'I was just wondering how your day went. Did you find the diary?'

'I'm working on it.'

'You're too slow, Cal. You're wasting time.'

'Time for what?'

'For saving lives. Speaking of which, it's a shame about poor nurse Bonnow, don't you think? You didn't save her. Despite all the help I gave you, you didn't do anything about it.'

Now in the living room, Doyle listens again to the song. He doesn't recognize it, doesn't know what it's called.

'You're enjoying this, aren't you?'

'I enjoy helping people, if that's what you mean. That's why I'm calling now. To offer my assistance again.'

'Why me? Of all the cops in this city, why pick me?'

'Oh, I don't know. Why does anyone donate to certain charities and not others? Let's just say I think you're a particularly worthy cause. I like to give where it's most needed.'

'Thanks, but I think you've done enough. I'm already overwhelmed by your benevolence. I'm sure they'll put up a statue in your memory once you're dead. Which I hope won't be much longer.'

A low chuckle. 'Do you like the music, Cal? Remind you of home? Making you thirsty for a drop of the black stuff?'

'Not really. This time of night, I'm more of a milk and cookies kinda guy.'

'Really? Cops do like a drink, though, don't they? Even guys who aren't cops themselves but who are the sons of cops have been known to find themselves in the company of drink. Like it's passed down in the genes or something. Your father wasn't a drunk, was he, Cal? You have other reasons for detesting him.'

Doyle decides he's not getting into this. He's not giving this guy the pleasure of screwing with his mind.

'Get to the point, asshole. I got a warm bed waiting for me.'

'Okay, Cal. Get back to your bed. But I don't think you'll get much sleep. You've got work to do. And you've got less than twenty-four hours to do it in. Midnight precisely. That's when it will happen. That's when somebody else will die.'

'That's it? That's all you're going to tell me?'

'I've told you all you need to know, Cal. Like I said before. Use your brain. Use your senses. Use what you've heard. Show me what a brilliant detective you are. Oh, and one other thing about the person who has just started their last day on this earth.'

'What's that?'

'It's somebody you know, Cal. Somebody you know pretty well.'

EIGHT

The caller was right about one thing. Doyle doesn't get much sleep that night. He spends most of his time replaying the conversation in his mind. Over and over. Desperately trying to pick it apart for meaning. Looking for clues. Anything that will help him prevent another death.

Not for the first time he wishes he had asked for a trace on his phone, despite the warnings to the contrary he was given. But the only way he can do that is by making an official request to the Police Department, which is a sure way of alerting them to the cozy chats he's been having with the killer.

He gets into work for six-thirty – an hour and a half before his shift is officially due to start. The desk sergeant tosses a joke at him about his wife throwing him out of bed. Doyle laughs it off and trudges upstairs to the squadroom. He spends the next hour reading through the DD5 reports – the fives – and all the other notes that have been made on the Cindy Mellish case.

And gets nowhere.

Interviews with dozens of people, but not a whiff of a solid lead. Doyle realizes he's not going to find the killer this way. Not in the short time he's got left.

People say goodbye and leave. New faces arrive and say hello. Doyle is largely unaware of the transitions taking place around him. His midnight chat is back on his mind. He flips to a fresh page on his notepad and starts making notes on all he can remember of the conversation. Trying to decide what's relevant and what's just filler. Looking for hidden meanings and subtle hints. Making connections, most of which he crosses out again as being absurd. But he has to consider all the possibilities, no matter how ludicrous they might seem. He can't afford to get this wrong.

When he's done that, he thinks about the only other possible pointer to the killer. The diary. If in fact it exists. And if Gonzo the wonder boy can find it. And if it does indeed contain some useful information, instead of being a pile of crap that's going to be used to jerk him around some more.

All big ifs.

And time is ticking away, my friend.

The address has been used by many wishing to mock the New York accent. *Toidy-toid and Toid.* Meaning: Thirty-third and Third.

The premises are situated above a nail salon. It has never entered Doyle's head to consider getting a manicure, and he is surprised at how many people are not of like mind. He imagines that they do pedicures there too, then quickly blots out the thought. He's seen quite a few corpses in his time, in various states of putrefaction, but the one thing guaranteed to turn his stomach is the idea of working on other people's feet.

Upstairs, he knocks on a glass-paneled door and enters. The room's sole occupant – a young girl hiding her beauty beneath too much make-up – sits behind a desk uncluttered with any signs of work. She slides a metal file along her own highly polished fingernails. Doyle wonders if she's getting in some practice to apply for a job downstairs, because this place is dead.

Alongside her desk, another door leads to an inner office.

It's half open, and Doyle can hear a man's voice, presumably in the middle of a telephone conversation. He's saying, 'What the fuck, Marty? You can't twist their arms a little? I'm offering them bottom-dollar here. Where else they gonna get peace of mind for a price like that? Jesus.'

Doyle approaches the girl's desk. She presents him with a bright smile but nothing more.

'I'd like to speak with Mr Repp.'

'Do you have an appointment?'

Doyle displays his gold shield, and the girl responds by arching a perfectly plucked eyebrow. Through the door, the voice is saying, 'Let me speak to him, Marty . . . No, just put him on the goddamned phone, will ya?'

The girl tilts her nail file toward the door and states the obvious: 'He's on the phone just now.'

'No problem,' says Doyle, and heads into Repp's office.

Travis Repp is lounging back in his executive chair, trying to look executive. Sharp blue suit and skinny tie. Gold rings on his fingers. Big flashy wristwatch. Blond hair flopping low over his forehead. He gives Doyle the once-over, but seems uninterested. He raises a finger, instructing Doyle to wait while he continues his phone call. Doesn't even offer him a seat.

'Mr Uterus . . . I'm sorry, Mr Yurtis. I misheard my colleague . . . Yes, I know what you told him, but I assure you that we can offer a better service than any of our competitors . . .'

Doyle sighs and flashes the tin again. Repp glances at it, gives Doyle a look that says, *So what?* Then resumes his conversation.

'Yes, Mr Yurtis . . . Manpower? Of course we do. I have a whole team of investigators here that I can call on if necessary . . .'

Doyle looks around the empty office and wonders where they're all hiding. He decides he's had enough of this, and that

Mr Yurtis could probably do with a break too. He leans forward and announces his presence like he's about to raid the joint.

'Detective Doyle, Eighth Precinct.'

Repp clamps his hand over the mouthpiece. 'Jesus! What do you think you're doing? You wanna put me out of business here?' He speaks into the phone again. 'Mr Yurtis, I'm sorry about . . . Hello? Mr Yurtis?'

He slams the handset down and glares at Doyle. 'Great. You know you probably just cost me that gig? What is it with you?'

'Something we need to discuss.' Doyle gestures toward a chair. 'You mind?'

'Make yourself at home, why don't you?' He makes a show of looking at his watch. 'Is this gonna take long? Because I'm kinda busy.'

'Yeah, I saw the long line of people waiting outside. But I guess if you share them out among all your other investigators here . . .'

'Hey! This is business. This is how you do things when you gotta fight tooth and nail for every buck, instead of just sitting there waiting for your share of the taxpayers' money to land in your account every month. Now don't you got criminals to catch or something?'

'Is why I'm here,' says Doyle. He doesn't like Repp. He came here thinking he might be able to reason with the man. His inclination now is to take the secretary's nail file and rasp this prick's fingers down to the bone.

'Meaning what?' Repp asks.

'You have a client. Mrs Sachs.'

'Who?'

'Mrs Sachs. A sweet old lady who lost her daughter on 9/11.'

Repp moves his jaw from side to side. 'So?'

Doyle can see that he's already rattled.

'I need you to tell her the truth. I need you to tell her that her daughter's dead.'

'You're obviously a very needy person, Detective . . .'

'Doyle.'

'Detective Doyle. But I have to act in the best interests of my client. I can't go making shit up just to please you. What is this, anyhow? Is this an official police investigation, or is it personal? Could it be you got the hots for Mrs Sachs?'

Doyle sighs again. 'How much have you fleeced her for, so far?'

'I haven't fleeced nobody. Mrs Sachs is a client. She's paying me for a service. A service I think I do pretty damn well, as it happens. I'm a licensed private investigator with an impeccable record. You want to start casting aspersions, take it up with my lawyers.'

'I'm taking it up with you, Travis. Patricia Sachs is dead. I know it and you know it, and now her mother needs to know it too. And you're the one who has to break it to her.'

Repp waves his arms wildly like he's about to have an epileptic fit. 'Who says she's dead? Do you know that? Do you know it for certain? No, you don't. Have you busted your ass investigating this case? No you haven't. That would be me. And all the evidence tells me that Patricia Sachs may in fact be alive and well. And that's what I've told her mother. No more, no less.'

Doyle pulls Mrs Sachs's photograph from his pocket and slaps it down on the desk. 'This your evidence?'

Repp glances at it, says nothing.

'How long did it take you to fake that?'

'What are you talking about?'

'It's a phony, Travis. Dozens of people all walking in the same direction, all looking where they're going. All, that is, except one. How come she's the only one who finds your photographer so interesting?'

Repp waggles his jaw again. 'We have ways. Tricks to attract attention. Anyhow, I didn't take this; it was one of my operatives.'

'Neat trick, singling out one member of a crowd to look your way. Do Penn and Teller know about you? Where'd you get the headshot, Travis? From a corporate brochure? That looks to me like the face of somebody posing for a portrait. Neat cut and paste job, though, making it all grainy like that just to add the right element of doubt.'

Repp is quiet for a good ten seconds. 'You finished? Because like I say, I got work to do.'

Doyle takes back the photo and stands up. 'Finish it, Travis. Tell Mrs Sachs what she needs to hear about her daughter, and then leave her be. I don't want to have to come back, and I'm sure you don't want me back either.'

On the way out, Doyle receives a smile from the secretary. He gets the impression she really enjoyed listening to her boss being told what to do.

The worry returns with a vengeance once Doyle is back at his desk. The visit to Repp was a nice distraction, but it hasn't gotten him any nearer to catching the killer that only he knows is of the serial variety. The weight on his mind is so intense it feels as though his brain is about to burst.

An hour later he sees Cesario heading toward his office. Cesario glances across, as if to say, *Ready when you are, Doyle. Whenever you feel like unburdening yourself* . . .

Doyle starts to rise from his chair, ready to pursue Cesario. He hasn't rehearsed this. Doesn't know exactly what he's going to say. The only thing he does know is that he's about to be crucified for revealing the truth at such a late stage. But it has to be worth it. If it might improve the chances of saving somebody's life, does he really have any alternative?

The phone on his desk rings. He looks at it, trying to decide whether to answer it or to follow through with his decision to see Cesario. Out of the corner of his eye he notices another cop looking at him, wondering why he's hesitating.

He sits down again, answers the phone.

'Doyle.'

'Cal? It's Marcus, downstairs. I got someone here says he wants to see you. Won't say what his business is, though. Won't give his name neither.'

Marcus Wilson is the desk sergeant. The station house's huge black gatekeeper. Three months after Doyle arrived at the Eighth, Wilson took over the desk from the previous sergeant – a man named Hanrahan. Whereas Hanrahan didn't even notice half the people who walked past him, Wilson rapidly gained a reputation as a man who was not beyond making visitors strip naked if he thought it was necessary to get them to prove they were harmless.

'What's he look like?' Doyle asks.

'Geeky-looking kid with red hair and a squeaky voice. Acts like something's missing upstairs, if you know what I mean.'

Shit, thinks Doyle. What the . . .

'Keep him there. I'll be right down.'

Doyle ends the call and heads for the stairs. Cesario will have to wait.

When he gets down to the first floor, Wilson looks at him, then directs his gaze toward the waiting zone opposite his desk. Gonzo is sitting between two doped-up hookers and looking petrified that he's about to have his virginity snatched away from him. He holds a black cloth bag firmly on his lap, as though using it as a groin shield.

Doyle beckons him over with his finger. As Gonzo gets up, one of the hookers pinches his ass, and he scampers across for Doyle's protection.

'Outside,' says Doyle.

'But—'

'Outside.'

They exit through the large double doors of the station house, Gonzo now clutching the bag tightly under one arm. Doyle takes him by the sleeve and drags him along the street.

'What are you doing here?' Doyle demands.

'What do you mean? And where are we going?'

'I said not to come here. I said to call me on my cell.'

'No. No you didn't. You said your cell number was the only one I should use if I wanted to phone you, but that I shouldn't phone you on the precinct number. You didn't say anything about making personal visits. I have a good memory for things like that.'

Doyle stops and spins Gonzo to face him.

'Did you have to take it so literally? Wasn't there a small part of that gargantuan brain of yours that said, Hey, maybe that means he wants to keep this under wraps?'

Gonzo blinks at him. 'Why would you want to keep it quiet? This is a homicide investigation. You never said it was a homicide. Does Lonnie know about this?'

Doyle stares back at Gonzo for several seconds. He brings his hand out of his pocket in a sudden move that causes Gonzo to flinch. In his hand is the key to his car.

'Get in.'

Doyle opens up the car, and they both clamber inside. Doyle doesn't start the engine.

He says, 'How do you know it's a homicide?'

'This computer belongs to Cindy Mellish. Her name is in lots of her files on here. She's the same Cindy Mellish who worked in that bookstore, right?'

'Maybe,' says Doyle. He thinks about it for a while. Realizes he has to admit at least something if this conversation is to go anywhere. 'Okay, yes. The computer belongs to the homicide victim from the bookstore. Happy now?'

Gonzo pushes his glasses up his nose. 'I don't get it.'

'Get what?'

'This. The cloak and dagger stuff. I mean, it's really cool and everything, but—'

'Wait! Wait a minute. Cool? Why is it cool?'

'Well . . . it's exciting. Working with you like this. I don't normally get to—'

'Gonzo! Hold on. We are not working together, okay? I'm not looking to set up some kind of long-term relationship here. I just asked you to do a little job for me. That's it. End of story.'

Gonzo looks crestfallen. Like he's just had his favorite toy snatched away.

Doyle adopts a more mellow tone. 'Look, it's complicated. Don't ask me to explain. There are things happening on this case that I can't tell anyone about. It'll all come out eventually, but right now it has to be kept quiet.'

'A secret,' Gonzo says.

'Yes.'

'Just between us.'

'Yes.'

'I won't tell anyone.'

'Good.'

'Does Lonnie know?'

'No, not even Lonnie knows about this.'

'Just you and me.'

'Yes.'

'Wow.'

Gonzo sits there nodding and smiling and staring into space. This is the high point in his week. Maybe even in his whole sad life. It almost pains Doyle to break the spell.

'So . . .' he prompts.

Gonzo raises his face. 'What?'

'Did you find anything?'

'Where?'

Jesus, thinks Doyle, not for the first time.

'On the computer?'

It's as if Gonzo suddenly realizes where he is and what he's doing here.

'Oh. Oh! The diary. What you asked me to look for.'

'Yes. Did you find the diary?'

Gonzo unzips his bag and starts rummaging around inside. 'You are gonna love this. You are so gonna . . .'

'Gonzo.'

'. . . love this. I mean, when you see what . . .'

'Gonzo!'

'. . . I found on this baby, you will just . . .'

'GONZO! Did you find the freakin' diary?'

Gonzo pulls out a sheaf of paper and holds it up triumphantly. 'I found it. It was hidden in her pictures folder and it was encrypted.'

'It was what?'

'Encrypted. It was in code. That's what took me so long to get back to you. I had to break the encryption.'

Doyle reaches out for the paper. 'That's fantastic, Gonzo. Good job.'

Gonzo makes no attempt to hand over his document. 'Don't you want to know what's in it?'

'Well, I thought I'd just read it through and—'

'It's mostly crap. Girly stuff, you know?' He gives Doyle a knowing wink, as if to lay claim to being a man of the world who knows all about girly stuff. 'Most of it was written a while back, when she was with her boyfriend. What she thought about him. All that lovey-dovey stuff that makes you want to puke, you know?'

'Okay, Gonzo. That's great. So if I could just—'

'And of course then he goes and dumps her, doesn't he? That's when she gets really emotional, and her whole universe is falling around her ears, and nobody loves her any more, and life isn't worth living. I mean, puh-lease!'

Doyle puts his fingers on the papers. 'Maybe if I was to take a look at—'

'But then there's the therapist. And that's when it gets interesting.'

They both fall quiet. Each studies the other.

Doyle lets his fingers drop from the printout. 'Therapist? What therapist?'

'A certain Dr Andrew Vasey. Likes to be called Andy, apparently. She gets depressed about her boyfriend, goes to see this guy, and—'

'Wait a minute. She goes to see a shrink? She's a college student. Her mom doesn't look like she ever earned much. How the hell does she afford to see a shrink?'

'She can't. It's a favor. Cindy gets introduced to him by a friend at NYU. She gets talking to him, tells him her woes. Next thing you know, he's offering to let her lie on his couch. He says it won't cost her a cent. What he doesn't tell her is that he's got a different form of payment in mind.'

'What do you mean?'

Gonzo slaps the sheaf of paper. 'It's all in here. Guy was a lech. Kept asking her all sorts of weird sexual things. Then he sat real close to her and put his hand on her knee. She got out of there fast. It really freaked her out.'

Doyle thinks about it. It's strange, totally unprofessional

behavior, all right, and he needs to check it out. But all the same, could this really be a precursor to murder?

'Is that it?'

'That, and the visit.'

'What visit?'

'When he came to see her. Ask me where.'

Doyle is reminded of the way Norman Chin engages his audience. He wonders if all scientists have such an annoying habit.

'Where?'

Gonzo practically sings the next bit, which in his voice sounds comical. 'In the bookstore.'

Doyle finds himself sitting up straighter. 'He saw her at the bookstore?'

'Yup. Told her he was crazy about her. When she told him she wasn't interested, he started getting frisky again. He even touched her on the . . .' Gonzo drops his voice to a whisper and circles a finger in the air close to his chest, '. . . in the thoracic region.'

'He fondled her breast?'

Looking a little embarrassed, Gonzo clears his throat. 'She slapped him then, and when he left he was really pissed. He told her she'd be seeing him again.'

'When was this?'

'Last November.'

Doyle stares through the windshield for a minute, thinking that this changes everything. Vasey coming on strong, showing up at the bookstore, making inappropriate comments, then getting his face slapped and threatening a return encounter – well, that's a disturbing progression if ever there was one.

'Okay, Gonzo. You done good. Thanks.'

'So this Vasey. We need to go see him, right? I mean, the way he's been acting—'

'Whoa! Did you say *we*?'

'I looked him up. His practice is on Fifty-second and Fifth. I thought we—'

'Gonzo! Watch my lips. It's the same message I already gave you. I ain't looking to do a duet with you.'

'But if you're working alone—'

'Who says I'm working alone?'

'Well, aren't you? If you're trying to keep this so quiet for whatever reason, then I guess—'

'Yes, okay, I'm working solo. But for now it has to stay that way, all right? You did a great job, kid, but you're not a cop. Your contribution ends here.'

The disappointment on Gonzo's face is so unmistakable it almost breaks Doyle's heart.

'Here,' says Gonzo, pushing the printout toward Doyle. 'You better take this.'

Doyle accepts the document in silence. He has the feeling that anything he adds will only make Gonzo feel worse.

'I better get back,' says Gonzo. 'I'm supposed to be on my lunch break.'

Doyle watches him get out of the car. Before Gonzo closes the door, Doyle says to him, 'Uhm, you forget something?'

Gonzo peers into the car interior, then gives Doyle a blank look.

'The computer?'

'Oh. Oh yeah.'

Gonzo digs the laptop out from his bag and passes it across to Doyle.

'See you around,' says Gonzo. 'Good luck with the case.'

'Yeah. Take it easy, kid.'

Doyle watches in his rearview mirror as the nerdy young man heads down the street with a gait that makes it look as though his shoelaces are tied together.

NINE

Gonzo was right.

The one thing which stands out from all the other entries in Cindy Mellish's digital diary is the description of her encounters with Dr Andrew Vasey. Prior to that, the text is mostly made up of long flowery transcriptions of her thoughts about the beautiful, delectable, incredible Josh, followed by a series of interminably depressing passages about her longing for the now-absent hero.

Doyle finds himself deciding that his own daughter will not go through this kind of turmoil when she reaches her teens. He's not going to allow it to happen. Just to be sure, he makes the further decision that Amy will not go out with boys until she is of sufficient emotional maturity to deal with any unfortunate circumstances. Which, in Doyle's estimation, means no earlier than her twenty-fifth birthday.

The first mention of Vasey is in mid-September of last year:

September 17

I haven't written here for a while. This summer was so bad. It just wasn't the same without Josh. Mom kept trying to cheer me up, but it just didn't do it for me. I needed Josh. He was all I could think about every day.

I'm glad to be back at college. It helps to take my mind

off things. Plus it's great to see M again. She's so nice to me. She can see how upset I still am. Last night she gave me a business card for this therapist friend of her dad's. His name is Dr Andrew Vasey. She said he's amazing, and that he could really help me get myself together again. She said he would even do a session for free. I don't think I'll call him, but it was a kind thought.

Nothing much happens for the next few days. Then:

September 26

I've been a wreck this week. It's been months since Josh and I split up, and I know I should be over him by now. But it doesn't work like that. Not for me, anyway. I always thought he was the one.

M has made a decision for me. She's booked me in with that therapist. I don't really want to go, but she's insistent. Maybe it'll help. What the hell. It can't get any worse.

There is another tedious interlude, but then it really kicks off:

October 8

Oh. My. God.

It still seems unreal. I'm not even sure I can write about this, but here goes . . .

I saw Vasey today. It should have been a good day. It should have helped me. It should have been a lot of things it wasn't.

Here's what happened.

The session started off OK. He told me to call him Andy, which I did in the session. Now, though, it just seems way too familiar, and that's the last place I want to go.

He asked me what was going on in my life, what was bothering me. It didn't take long for me to get onto the subject of Josh. I mean, what else do I ever think about? He asked me more questions about why we split up and how it affected me. I started crying, just like I always do when I talk about Josh. But this time it was different somehow. I really felt like a weight was being lifted off my shoulders. It was so good to talk to someone who I felt could understand and help me.

But then the questions started to get weird. I mean really weird. I suppose I expected some intimate questions, because that's what these people do, right? They get inside your mind. But not like this. I can't even bring myself to write down the exact words he used. He wanted to know how Josh and I were when we were together. Sexually, I mean. What positions we liked, how I liked to be touched by him, whether we ever had oral sex. I mean, Jesus!

I asked Vasey if it was all right for him to ask me those things. He said that he needed to appreciate in detail how our relationship worked. I told him I wasn't comfortable with that. He said all of his clients feel that way at first, but they soon get used to it. I didn't know what to believe or what to say. He's the professional, right? What do I know?

But then he did something which made me reach a decision pretty damn quickly.

He put his hand on my knee.

I mean, hello! This is not what doctors do, right? Questions are one thing, even when they get so personal. But touching?? I don't think so.

So I was out of there. I muttered something about this not really helping, I grabbed my coat and I left.

Sitting here now, writing all this down, it feels like I

imagined it. Like I'm telling somebody else's story. But I know it happened. I'm just not sure how I feel about it. Later, I'll probably get real upset. Or angry. Or both. Right now I'm just too stunned for words.

And what will I tell M? This is a close friend of her dad's. Would it upset her? Would she fall out with me? I don't know what to do.

Other than revealing that she decides not to say anything to M, whoever that is, Cindy doesn't refer to the incident again until November of last year, a month after her consultation with Vasey.

November 10

Unbelievable.

He came back. Vasey. He came to see me at the bookstore today. He tried to apologize. He said he got carried away in the session, and that he wasn't normally like that. I said it was OK, and that we should just leave it at that. I didn't really want to speak to him.

But he wouldn't go away. He kept saying that I'd had a huge effect on him. He said he couldn't stop thinking about me. I wasn't interested. I mean, jeez, the guy is at least thirty-five! And after the way he behaved, did he really think he could sweet-talk me?

And then guess what? He did it again. He touched me. On the breast this time.

So I slapped him.

I mean, I am not one for confrontation. I hate violence of any kind. But this was a reflex action. I didn't even think about it. I just slapped him real hard across the face and yelled at him to get out.

He told me I was making a big mistake, and that

nobody treats him like that. I don't know what I said back. I just kept screaming at him. I may have even used some swear words, which isn't like me.

But he went. I got him out of the store. He said he was going to come back again, but I don't think he will.

And you know what? I feel proud. I stood up for myself. Maybe it's the new me. Maybe I'm a lot stronger now.

Maybe my visit to Vasey did me some good after all.

When he's finished reading, Doyle gets out of the car. He puts the laptop and the printout in the trunk, then locks them away. Before he goes back into the station house, he checks his watch. It's a few minutes after two.

Less than ten hours before somebody gets what is possibly their final chance to hear the clocks chime twelve.

He realizes something is wrong as soon as he enters the squad-room. Jay Holden is giving him a stare he usually reserves for perps and people who have riled him. You don't want to be on the receiving end of a stare like that.

Doyle starts toward his desk. He tenses when Holden stands up and intercepts him.

'Can we talk?' Holden says.

Doyle looks into Holden's eyes and tries to find whatever's bugging the man.

'Sure.'

The two men find a room where they can be alone. It's a room they use for interviewing suspects. It contains the obligatory wooden table and some plastic chairs, but also too many file cabinets that don't really belong here.

Doyle leans against a radiator and folds his arms.

'What's up, Jay?'

Holden doesn't take up a relaxed pose. He clenches and un-clenches his fists, which in Doyle's experience is not a promising start to any discussion.

'S'pose you tell me, Cal. What *is* up?'

Doyle waits for elaboration. Doesn't get any.

'Look, man, I don't know what's on your mind, but whatever it is—'

'I took a phone call while you were out at lunch.'

Uh-oh, thinks Doyle. If this was from my little helper . . .

'From Mrs Mellish. Cindy Mellish's mother.'

Doyle almost breathes a sigh of relief, but it sticks in his chest. The lesser of two evils maybe, but still not good news.

'Okay. And?'

'She asked about the computer. 'Course, this being my case, and me knowing everything about it, I asked her what the fuck she was talking about. "You know," she said. "The computer. The one Detective Doyle borrowed from me."'

Ah, thinks Doyle. This cat is definitely out of its bag.

'Yeah, I guess I shoulda told you about that.'

'You *guess*? Man, what the fuck is going on?'

Doyle holds off for as long as he dares before Holden can guess that he's desperately trying to come up with something plausible.

'Look, I got tired of being the office boy, all right? So I went to speak with Mrs Mellish. I'm assigned to the case too, remem-ber? I thought maybe it would help. Maybe she could give me something useful. We got talking, and she told me about how Cindy liked to write. All kinds of personal shit about her life. It sounded like there was a chance something might be in her bedroom, so I asked to see it. I couldn't find anything in her notebooks, but then it got mentioned that she also wrote on her computer, so I asked if I could borrow it so I could take a look at that too. If there was nothing on the computer, I was just going to hand it back and that would be it.'

Doyle pauses, partly because he knows that people who ramble on too long often do so because they're trying to hide something, which he is, but also because he wants to check whether Holden appears convinced with the story so far. Holden continues to glare at him, but when he speaks, there is a slight softening of his tone.

'You shoulda brought it to me, Cal. Even just a mention. Something.'

'You're right. I should have. I apologize.'

Holden nods. A sign it's over. They can forget about it. Unless there's a next time.

Doyle considers this. He wasn't intending to say anything more about the diary. His plan was to go see Vasey himself and hope it led somewhere. But he's wondering if this hasn't changed things. Didn't Holden ask him about the computer? Isn't this a prime opportunity to bring his colleagues into it without breaking the terms of his contract with the mysterious phone caller?

He adds, 'But maybe it paid off.'

Holden narrows his eyes at him. 'In what way?'

'I found something on the computer. A diary.'

Holden is clearly interested now. 'Go on.'

'When Cindy broke up with her boyfriend she went to see a shrink. A friend of a friend. He came on to her. She rejected him. This was last October. A month later he tracked her down. In the bookstore, no less. He tried it on again. This time she slapped him.'

There are questions written all over Holden's face.

'Hold up. The shrink tried to hit on her? During a consultation? And then he went to see her at her place of work?'

Doyle frowns. When you put it like that . . .

'Yeah. Crazy, huh? But worth a look, wouldn't you say?'

Holden stares again. Doyle imagines that there are all sorts of doubts and queries jockeying for position in his brain.

Finally, Holden shakes his head, turns away, and takes the few short paces across the room. At the door, he pauses and faces Doyle again.

'You coming, or what?'

Vasey's practice is situated on the twentieth floor of an office building on Fifth Avenue at Fifty-second Street. Doyle finds himself comparing it with the office of Travis Repp. It's like comparing a prize Arabian stallion with a three-legged mule.

Instead of an indifferent girl with a nail fixation, the receptionist here is a model of clinical efficiency and professionalism. She smiles appreciatively at the two hunky policemen in front of her, offers them a seat and coffee while she puts through a call announcing their presence. The cops relax on a tan leather sofa and leaf through magazines that are crisp and current instead of the curled specimens dating from the previous century that are normally on display in waiting rooms. When they're done with the magazines, the detectives while away their time observing the tropical fish in the tank set into the wall. Cynic that he is, Doyle wonders if all this is designed to lull clients into a false sense of security and calm before the shrink pounces on their brains and dissects their thoughts.

As if timing everything to perfection, the glossy-haired receptionist waits until Doyle drains his coffee cup before crooning that they can enter the inner sanctum. Doyle is almost reluctant to abandon the comfort and service that would better that of most hotels.

Vasey's office is as big as the Eighth Precinct squadroom. It has a small seating area with comfy-looking chairs and a coffee table, a long bookcase housing weighty tomes on psychology, and a display cabinet exhibiting a softly lit collection of fossils. At the far end of the room, framed by the vast window behind him, Vasey sits at a pale wooden desk. As his visitors enter, he finishes typing at his computer and stands to greet them. He appears to Doyle to be over six feet tall and in his early forties. He also looks tanned, well-groomed, healthy, self-assured, and not short of a few bucks. Some people always end up grabbing the shitty end of the stick, thinks Doyle.

'Gentlemen,' says Vasey. 'Come on in.'

He shakes their hands, waves them into chairs, then retakes his own seat behind the vast desk.

'What can I do for you?'

Doyle is happy to let Holden lead the questioning. Partly as an acknowledgement of Holden's role as primary investigator on this case, but also because he hates talking to psychologists, psychotherapists, psychoanalysts and anybody else who has 'psycho' as the first part of their profession. They make him feel uncomfortable. He always thinks they are capable of seeing meaning beyond what he actually intends to impart – that every word he utters reveals clues to his psyche, rendering him transparent. He finds himself being overly cautious in what he says, for fear that he is being analyzed and labeled as exhibiting all kinds of neuroses and psychoses. He doesn't know where this unease originated. Perhaps a traumatic event in his childhood. He should probably ask a shrink.

'Just some routine questions,' says Holden. 'Your name came up in a case we're investigating, so we have to check it out.'

Vasey glances at Doyle, who gives him nothing, then back to Holden.

'May I ask what the case is?'

'Do you know the name Cindy Mellish?'

Vasey thinks for a moment. 'It doesn't ring any bells. Should it?'

'She was the girl murdered in the East Village bookstore on Saturday.'

'Her? God! Then this is serious.'

'It's serious, all right.'

'And my name came up? How?'

'Miss Mellish kept a diary. Your name was in it. She said she came to see you. Here, at your office.'

'Really? Just a minute.' Vasey's fingers fly over his keyboard. 'No. I've never had a client by that name. Are you sure about this?'

Holden looks across to Doyle, who takes the reins. 'It's possible she was never an official client. According to the diary, Cindy's appointment with you was made by a student friend of hers. Apparently, you're a close buddy of the friend's father.'

'What's the man's name?'

'We don't know. The student friend is only referred to in the diary by the letter M.'

'M? And I'm a friend of her father's? And a consultation was arranged with me because of this relationship? I'm sorry, fellas, but I have no idea what you're talking about. When was this session with me supposed to have taken place?'

'At the beginning of last October.'

Vasey thinks some more. 'No. I don't recall anything like that. Not in October or any other month last year for that matter.'

'Do you ever do consultations for friends and people they pass on to you?'

'Sometimes. But I prefer not to work that way.'

'Why is that?'

'Because it can be difficult to remain detached. Sometimes

it's hard to reveal painful truths to friends. They might not remain friends very long.'

Holden speaks up again. 'Dr Vasey, how did you hear about the murder of Cindy Mellish?'

'I can't remember. I think it was on the radio.'

'So you haven't seen a picture of her?'

'No. At least I don't think so. Maybe there was something in the newspaper, but I don't recall it.'

Holden reaches into his pocket and takes out a photograph.

'Take a look, please, Dr Vasey. Do you recognize her?'

Vasey picks up the photograph, studies it for several seconds, then slides it back across the desk.

'I've never seen this girl in my life.'

'Are you sure? Take another look.'

'I don't need another look. I have never seen this girl before, and certainly not as a client. Now, I'm sorry, gentlemen, but—'

'Why would she lie?' says Doyle.

Vasey turns on him. 'What?'

'This is a young woman's private diary. Nobody else is likely to see it except her. Why would she make something up like that?'

'And why would *I* lie, Detective? What possible reason could I have for lying about something as inconsequential as a therapy session?'

'Who says it was inconsequential?'

'What do you mean?'

'According to Cindy Mellish, her session with you wasn't all that innocent. She says you came on to her.'

Vasey's eyes are blazing now. 'I did *what*? Are you serious? Are you actually accusing me—'

'She says you asked her inappropriate questions. Questions of a sexual nature.'

Vasey shakes his head, an expression of disbelief and revulsion on his face.

'This is too much. Now you have really gone too far. I don't know what—' He stops himself in mid-sentence. Something has dawned on him. His mouth twists into a humorless smile. 'Oh, no. No you don't. You're trying to make me a suspect, aren't you? That's what this is about. You're getting nowhere with your murder case, and so you're frantically trying to find someone to pin it on. Well, I'm sorry, gentlemen, but it's not going to work. Not with me.'

Doyle presses on. 'Dr Vasey, did you go to see Cindy Mellish at the bookstore where she worked? Did you make sexual advances to her, and did she slap you in the face?'

Vasey just sits there shaking his head slowly, as if in pity for his poor desperate interrogator.

'Give it up, Detective. It's not working. I don't know what really brought you here, and frankly I don't care. My guess is that you came across my name in some totally innocent context, drew some very tenuous and fanciful conclusions, and then concocted this whole charade to see if you could get me to blab. Well, tough. It was a nice attempt, but I'm afraid it was always doomed to fail. To be frank, even if I'd been guilty I would have seen that pathetic ruse for what it was. It doesn't take a degree in psychology to realize what you're doing. Now if you'll forgive me, I have clients to see. Genuine ones.'

Doyle doesn't want to leave. He thinks that Vasey is too smug, too smart. But Doyle also knows that, for the moment at least, he doesn't have enough ammunition to continue this battle.

Before he departs, he warns Vasey not to leave the city.

Says Vasey, 'I don't plan to go anywhere, Detective. I'm innocent of any crime. Why would I need to abscond?'

In the corridor outside the office, Doyle says nothing. He

remains mute as they wait for the elevator. Continues with the silent act as he pounds the button to descend.

'He could be lying,' says Holden. 'He's a shrink. He knows about lying, body language, all that shit. Right now, though, it's just a he-said-she-said. We need more.'

Doyle is thinking the same thing. He needs more. And that need is making him furious. The diary was supposed to provide answers. It was supposed to lead him to the killer.

Did it do that? Could Vasey possibly be their man?

Maybe.

But *maybe* isn't good enough.

Not when someone's life is about to run out.

TEN

Doyle's shift officially finishes at four o'clock, but it's after five before he gets out of the station house. He walks along Seventh Street, his mind buzzing. Less than seven hours to go now, and he's not convinced he can stop what's coming.

He arrives at his car, takes out his keys. He is so preoccupied he doesn't hear the footsteps until the figure is within striking distance. Doyle whirls, his hand reaching for his gun.

'Hey, Detective!'

Doyle blows air. 'Jesus Christ, Gonzo. What are you trying to do, get yourself shot? Don't sneak up on me like that.'

Gonzo puts on the sad puppy-dog eyes. 'You said not to come into the station house. So I didn't. I waited for you outside. You know, to keep our little secret.'

'All right, Gonzo, all right. What are you doing here, anyhow?'

'I thought maybe I could catch up on the case. Find out what happened. Shall we get a coffee?'

'No, Gonzo. No coffee.'

'Well, then . . . How about the park? It's a nice evening. We could sit in the park while we chat.'

'Gonzo, it's been a long day. I'm tired. I need to go home.'

'Oh, okay. But what about Vasey? Did you speak with him? What did he say about the girl? Did he own up to it? Did you have to get a little rough with him? I bet you did. I bet he refused to say anything, so you had to roll up your sleeves and swear at him. Did you hit him? Because that's okay with me. I mean, not that generally I think violence is the answer, because I don't, but when—'

Doyle feels like employing a little violence right now, but makes do with a hand clamped over Gonzo's mouth.

'Kid, listen to me for a minute, okay?'

Gonzo nods, his eyes wide. Doyle takes his hand away slowly.

'Let's get something straight. I'm a cop, and you're a lab technician. Those two things, they're not the same. I'm sure you're a very clever guy, and you do all kinds of valuable things for the PD. You must have helped put a lot of bad guys behind bars. You should be proud of that. I couldn't do what you do. I don't have the brains. Most of what I do is fill out forms and answer phones and talk to people. So don't go thinking it's glamorous, because it ain't. Stick with what you're doing, and don't go looking to mess with the shit I have to deal with. Believe me, you're better off.'

Gonzo appears unconvinced. 'Yeah, but . . . You said it was a secret. Just me and you. How can you handle a case like this all by yourself? I thought maybe I could—'

'No! You hear me? No!' Doyle feels like he's talking to a young child who wants to help out in the kitchen. Like he has to be told in no uncertain terms that while it's okay to fill a kettle, the sharp knives and the stove are definitely out of bounds. 'It's not safe. And anyway, things have changed. I got somebody else working with me now.'

Gonzo blinks at him. He looks as though he's just been jilted at the altar.

'Somebody else?'

'Yes.'

'But you can't have. You said it was complicated, and you couldn't tell anybody except me.'

'I think I also made it clear it was a temporary situation. It's different now. When I went to see Vasey, it was with a partner.'

'A partner.'

'Yeah. Another detective.'

Gonzo looks down at his worn-out sneakers. 'So you don't need me anymore?'

'Not at the moment. But the next time I get a case involving computers, you're the first guy I'll come looking for.'

Gonzo scrapes one of his feet on the sidewalk. 'Okay.'

Doyle bends at the knees to get a look at Gonzo's downturned face. 'Okay?'

'Yeah.'

Doyle straightens up and slaps Gonzo on the shoulder. 'Go home, kid. Give that brain of yours a rest.'

For a few moments, Doyle isn't sure he's been heard. Gonzo stands rooted to the spot. Eventually he turns and shuffles away, still studying the ground.

Watching him go, Doyle shakes his head and wonders how somebody like that manages to get around in this city without being devoured by it.

'Why do dogs walk so fast?'

Doyle stops stroking his daughter's hair.

'What?'

'Why do dogs walk so fast? When I see dogs on the street or in the park, they always walk really, really fast. They're always in a hurry. They never walk at the same speed as people. Even when they're on a leash they try to pull the person along.'

Doyle tucks in Amy's bed covers while he mulls over his reply. It's not a question that's ever crossed his mind before, but he can tell from the earnestness on Amy's face that a considered answer is required.

'Well, what you have to remember, hon, is that dogs have twice as many legs as people.'

'Oh,' says Amy. 'Yes.'

Doyle stands up. 'Shall I put the light out now?'

'Well, what about cats then? They have the same amount of legs as dogs, but they don't walk very fast. They only go fast when they're chasing something. And tortoises. They have four legs too, and they go really, really slow. So it can't just be the number of legs, can it?'

You got me there, Doyle thinks. Then he wonders how the hell he's going to worm his way out of her seemingly inescapable logic.

'No. Obviously it's not *just* the number of legs. But the other thing about dogs is that they have a very good sense of smell.'

'What's that got to do with it?'

Doyle doesn't know. It was the first thing that came into his head.

'Well, they can smell things we can't. So they're always rushing toward those smells. Just like you might come running if I said I had some chocolate.'

'Yes, and dogs like chocolate too, don't they?'

'Yes they do. So that must be the answer. And now I think you need to get some sleep.'

'All right, Daddy.'

He wishes her goodnight and beats a hasty retreat before she can bombard him with more baffling questions.

In the living room, Rachel is working on her photographs again. Deciding to leave her in peace, Doyle picks up a newspaper and flops onto an armchair. He skim-reads it for all of five minutes before breaking the silence.

'I have to go out later.'

Rachel continues to peer at her computer screen. 'Out?' she says distractedly. 'Where?'

'A stakeout. I'll only be gone a coupla hours.'

'All right,' she says. 'Stay safe.'

Another minute's silence. Then Rachel turns in her chair.

'Are you okay?' she asks.

'Yeah, fine,' he says. 'Why?'

'I dunno. You've been acting a little distracted lately. You sure you're okay?'

He thinks about telling her then. Telling her that somebody is due to die in a few hours, and that only he can prevent it. Telling her that he's the only person who knows there's a serial killer out there. Telling her that only he knows of the link between Cindy Mellish and Lorna Bonnow.

Telling her that, in effect, he's been withholding the truth from his wife, as well as his colleagues.

'I'm fine,' he says. 'Really.'

He leaves the apartment shortly after ten o'clock. He kisses Rachel, tells her not to wait up.

There is a heaviness in his step as he descends the building staircase. Halfway down, he pauses. He takes out his Glock, checks that the magazine is fully loaded and that there's a round in the chamber, then re-holsters it.

Outside, he breathes deeply of the night air. There's a sweet aroma to it that he can't quite place. He moves to his car, unlocks it, and climbs behind the wheel. He inserts his key in the ignition, goes to turn it.

His cellphone rings.

He takes it from his pocket and thumbs the call answer button.

'Doyle.'

'Hey, Cal. Tonight's the night. Are you getting excited?'

It's him. Of course it is. That deep, mellow voice has become unmistakable. And if it were not, that Irish jig in the background would give it away. The bastard is calling because he wants to squeeze every ounce of self-gratification out of this.

Doyle says, 'So you know my cellphone number too.'

'There are a million things I know about you, Cal. Don't get complacent. Don't start thinking you can say or do things without me finding out.'

Doyle checks in his mirrors, then twists in his seat to get a good look around him. Am I being watched right now? he wonders.

'What do you want?'

'Just a courtesy call. You have less than two hours now. You do know that, don't you? I hope you followed my advice and that you're doing something about it.'

'Your advice ain't worth shit.'

'That's a bit unfair, Cal. I told you about the diary, didn't I?'

'Like I said, your advice is worthless.'

'Or perhaps it's just that you don't know how to interpret things correctly. I'm helping you, Cal. Showing you how to be a better detective. Training you to use your mind like a good investigator should.'

'Yeah? Well, here's me using my mouth in a more productive way: Get out of my fucking life, you sick fuck!'

He ends the call. Stares at the phone for several seconds. As he goes to replace it in his pocket, it rings again. He stabs the answer button so hard his finger almost pokes a hole in the casing.

'Didn't you hear what I said, jerkoff? I ain't playing this game no more. I'd tell you to go fuck yourself, but you're probably doing that already. That's if you can find that tiny dick of yours.'

'Uhm, Detective?'

Doyle groans inwardly.

'Gonzo? Is that you?'

'Uhm, yeah. Is this a bad time?'

'How the fuck did you get my cellphone number?'

'You gave it to me. You wrote it on your card. Remember?'

'Oh. Yeah. Sorry, Gonzo. I thought you were somebody else. Ignore what I said. I don't really think you're playing with yourself. What do you want?'

'I'm not sure I should tell you.'

'Gonzo, you *called* me. Why would you call me to let me know you don't want to tell me what you're calling about?'

'Promise you won't get mad?'

'I am getting madder by the second. Now what the fuck is it?'

'I'm doing surveillance. On Vasey. I thought you should know.'

Doyle wonders if his ears are playing tricks on him.

'Surveillance? What are you talking about?'

'I've been watching Vasey for you. I'm outside his apartment building now.'

'Gonzo, you're not making any sense. How do you know where he lives? How do you even know what he looks like?'

'I told you. I looked him up. He's in the phone book. He lives in a fancy apartment building here on Sixty-first and Third. And he has a website with his photo on it. I watched him go into his building two hours ago. I made notes and everything. "8:04: Vasey enters apartment building." Did I do right? What should I do now?'

Doyle sighs. The kid's a tryer, he thinks. You have to give him that.

'Go home, is what you should do. Isn't there something on TV you could be watching?'

'Nah. They're all re-runs. This is much more exciting.'

'Believe me, it gets stale pretty fast. When you've been sitting there for five hours or whatever, you'll wish you hadn't bothered. Now go home, Gonzo.'

'But—'

'Gonzo, were you listening to anything I said to you before about what cops do and what lab technicians do, and about them being totally different things?'

'Sure, but . . . well, Vasey's a suspect, isn't he? And I bet you don't have the time to watch him constantly. Even if you do have a *partner*.'

Doyle smiles at the emphasis on the final word, intended to show him how hurt Gonzo feels. Gonzo is right, of course. The squad doesn't have the resources to watch Vasey around the clock, and Doyle isn't sure how profitable it would be anyhow. But tonight . . . well, maybe Gonzo could be of some use after all.

Doyle checks his watch. 'All right, Gonzo. Here's what we'll do. Are you prepared to sit on Vasey until midnight?'

'You mean it? Absolutely. I'll stay here all night if you—'

'No, midnight's fine. If Vasey leaves his apartment before then, I want you to call me, okay? Don't do anything. Don't approach him, don't go in the building, don't do anything except watch the place. Is that understood?'

'Perfectly. I will monitor and report. Don't worry, Detective, I won't let you down. I've got a flask of coffee here to keep me awake.'

He needs caffeine to keep him awake until midnight, thinks Doyle. Jesus.

'Nice to hear you're fully equipped. Speak to you later.'

He ends the call. He is almost surprised to realize there is a smile on his face. Gonzo's childish enthusiasm has just brightened his night.

But it quickly fades when the enormity of what may happen next reasserts itself in his thoughts.

ELEVEN

When the cops from the Eighth Precinct say they're heading over to the Island, they don't always mean Staten Island. Or Long Island. Or Roosevelt Island, Governors Island, Liberty Island, Randall's Island, or even Riker's Island, for that matter. Quite often, what they are referring to is a drinking den more properly known as Gilligan's. Which isn't an island at all, except in the poetic sense of being a place to escape from life's hustle, bustle and trouble. Television has a lot to answer for.

Gilligan's is situated on Avenue A, and has been for a long time, even back in the days before all the other bars and restaurants sprang up in this area – back when Alphabet City was not as friendly an area as its preschool-sounding name might suggest (although it was certainly capable of giving visitors an education they would never forget). What has always made the Island a safe watering hole is the fact that, on an average night, you probably have more chance of finding a cop here than in the Eighth Precinct station house.

Doyle guesses the place hasn't changed much since those fun-filled days of yore. It has always been styled as an Irish pub, but unlike more recent pretenders to that title it manages to pull it off. As soon as Doyle opens the door, the Irish music draws him inside. Admittedly, it's emanating from a music system rather than a live ceilidh band, but he always knows that as soon as he knocks back some of that smooth Guinness and tunes in to the Irish lilt of the garrulous bartender, he is able to transport himself back to the land of his childhood. Or at least to a censored and somewhat romanticized version of what he recalls of those bygone days.

Except that tonight he cannot drink alcohol. He must remain as sober as a judge on antibiotics. Someone's life may depend on it.

For the hundredth time, he thinks back on what he was told over the phone.

Do you like the music, Cal? Remind you of home? Making you thirsty for a drop of the black stuff?

Irish music – check. Drink – check. Guinness – check.

He approaches the bar, more alert than he has ever been before in this place. He tries to perceive and absorb every detail. As he walks, he notices for the first time how loud his footsteps seem on the wood-planked floor. He scans faces. Many are familiar. He receives smiles, nods, a couple of handshakes, one or two slaps on the shoulder. He is aware that his responses are muted to the point of being rude, but he knows he cannot afford to narrow his focus. His eyes search every corner of the room, on the lookout for anything unusual, anything suspicious, anything warranting further scrutiny.

'A late start for you tonight, Cal.'

This from the bartender. He is also the owner of this bar, and his name is Patrick Gilligan, although most know him as Paddy. The previous owner was Paddy's father, another Patrick Gilligan. He died of cirrhosis of the liver, but before he succumbed to the devil that is drink, before he took ownership of the pub, he was a cop. Paddy here never became a cop, but he should have been, in Doyle's opinion. Doyle has seen him defuse many a potentially explosive situation simply by walking up to the offenders and telling them how things are going to be. He is one of those people whose mere presence demands respect, even among those who wear a badge.

Cops do like a drink, though, don't they? Even guys who aren't cops themselves but who are the sons of cops have been known to find themselves in the company of drink.

Not a cop – check. Son of a cop who drank – check. In the company of drink now – check.

It all fits.

Doyle looks into the eyes of the big man behind the counter – eyes as blue as his own are green – and thinks, If I get this wrong, Paddy, if I fuck this up, then you are a dead man.

'Cal?' says Paddy. He already has a glass in one hand and the other on the Guinness pump-handle.

'Yeah, sure,' says Doyle, nodding for Paddy to pour him one out. He has no plans to drink it, but he also knows that he can't sit there with an orange juice in front of him unless he wants to draw attention to himself.

Says Paddy, 'You come straight from the House?'

Even talks like a cop, thinks Doyle.

'Yeah,' says Doyle. 'There was some OT on offer. And with my daughter's birthday coming up . . .'

'I know what you mean. Grab it while you can. You never know what's around the corner.'

Well, *you* certainly don't, thinks Doyle.

They pass a few more pleasantries back and forth while the ancient art of Guinness-pouring is carried out in the proper leisurely fashion. Then Doyle says, 'You got a newspaper back there, Paddy? I need some downtime.'

Paddy finds a *New York Post* and hands it across. 'You find any good news in there, let me know.'

'You'll be the first,' says Doyle, hoping that tomorrow's

edition won't have Paddy's face splashed all over it. Hoping even more that Paddy's face doesn't get splashed all over anything tonight.

Doyle carries his drink and his newspaper to a quiet spot at the end of the bar. Somewhere he can get a good view of anyone who comes near Paddy. He opens the newspaper, puts his hand up to the side of his face so that nobody can see what his eyes are really doing, and waits.

It's the most awkward he has ever felt in a bar. Not drinking, but with a beautiful tall glass of black and white just demanding to be poured down his gullet. Not reading, but with an expanse of images and headlines tugging at his eyeballs for attention. And all this while trying to appear to be just another harmless customer winding down after a hard day at the office.

When Paddy looks across and catches his eye, Doyle hastily picks up his glass, raises it in a salute, and pushes his lips into the creamy foam. He takes the tiniest of sips, and when Paddy looks away, he puts the glass down again. The taste of the beverage on his tongue is sheer torture. He's starting to think he should have ordered an OJ after all.

He is also thinking that maybe he should just let Paddy know what's going on. Tell him to leave the bar now, go upstairs, and lock himself away in a room until midnight has come and gone. Until another day is here and Paddy is free to enjoy it and all the other days that will follow.

Except that he knows it won't solve a thing. Because, despite what the caller said about midnight being the deadline, the killer could just try again later. Or maybe another night entirely. And Doyle can't spend the rest of his midnights coming to Gilligan's, even if he could permit himself to drink the beer. His only chance to catch the perp is to let him think he has a chance of completing his mission tonight. Which means that Paddy has to be kept out of the picture. He has to be unaware that his hours – or rather his minutes now – may be numbered.

It's not an easy choice for Doyle. And he's not sure that Paddy will ever forgive him.

He checks his watch. Eleven-fifteen. Only forty-five minutes to go.

Doyle allows his attention to wander from the bar. His gaze skips from table to table, from booth to booth. Everyone chilling. Alcohol-emboldened guys eyeing up girls. Girls discreetly flicking their own eyes toward their admirers. Cops exchanging stories about the job. Dirty jokes. Laughter. Nobody alone. Nobody looking like they have an appointment with death tonight. It's all good.

It occurs to Doyle that this is a weird choice of location for a hit. Most of the cops he knows carry guns when they are off-duty. Even those who don't take their service sidearms usually carry a smaller, lighter weapon. That's potentially a lot of muzzles pointing at anyone who starts trouble in here.

Doyle slips a hand under his jacket. His fingers find the reassuring cold metal of his own Glock 19.

How the hell is he going to get away with it? he wonders. Does he even expect to survive?

But then this killer is one clever son of a bitch. He's already proved that.

'You sick or something?'

Doyle realizes that Paddy is talking to him. He doesn't understand the question until he sees Paddy nod his head toward Doyle's full glass.

'It's my second,' says Doyle. 'Terry just poured me one.'

Paddy stands there looking unconvinced. 'Still not up to your usual standard. How am I going to turn a profit with you drinking at that rate?'

Doyle laughs, but when Paddy doesn't turn away, he's glad for the ring of his cellphone. He answers it and gives his name.

'It's me, Detective.'

'Gonzo?'

'Yeah. I'm still outside the apartment building, like you asked. Only I thought you should know: Dr Vasey has just come out the front door.'

Doyle glances at his watch again. Eleven-twenty.

'He's leaving? Which way's he going?'

'Heading west on Sixty-first.'

That's not toward here, Doyle thinks. Where the hell's he going?

'He's staying on foot?'

'Yeah. I'm going to follow him.'

'Gonzo . . .' He wants to stop him, but he also wants to know what Vasey is up to. 'All right. Stay with him. When he gets where he's going, give me another call. And be careful, okay?'

'Don't you worry about me, Detective. I can do this. I'm watching him like a hawk, and he doesn't suspect a thing.'

Doyle rings off. He doesn't like this. Vasey leaving his apartment at this time of night is just too much of a coincidence. He starts to wonder if he did the right thing in sending Gonzo after him. He worries about it until his phone rings again barely ten minutes later.

'Detective, it's me. Gonzo. I, uhm, I lost Vasey.'

'You lost him? You've only been tailing him for a few minutes. What did he do, jump in a taxi?'

'Maybe. I don't know. We got as far as Sixty-second and Park, and then he just disappeared. I've been looking everywhere. There's no sign of him.'

Doyle sighs. He realizes there's no point blaming the kid.

'All right, Gonzo. You did your best.'

'I'm sorry, Detective. What should I do now?'

'Go home. Vasey could be anywhere. It might be hours before he gets back. Go home.'

This time, there's no protest. 'All right. I'm really sorry. I'll make it up to you, I promise.'

'No need, Gonzo. Take it easy.'

He ends the call. Despite his quirks, Gonzo is a good kid. Not detective material, but a good kid nonetheless.

So, he thinks, Vasey's on the prowl. Whatever happens tonight, he's got some explaining to do.

Doyle continues his vigil. He can feel his adrenalin level increasing with every minute that passes by. While everybody else is getting more drunk, more relaxed, Doyle is becoming increasingly wired. His whole body feels so tight it could snap.

At eleven-forty-five a middle-aged man staggers over and takes the barstool closest to Doyle. Doyle gives him the once-over. He's in a suit, but his tie has been dragged away from his neck with such force that it has created a tiny knot that looks impossible to unpick, and his top shirt-button is unfastened. His movements are unsteady, his eyes unfocused. He has a tumbler of what looks like whiskey in his hand.

'I think women are wonderful,' he slurs. 'Don't you? Women? Wonderful?'

'Sure,' Doyle answers.

'Especially,' the man says, '*younger* women. They have a certain . . .' his eyes roll around in his skull as he searches for his next words, '. . . a certain . . . *firmness*. Wouldn't you agree? Firm. Not saggy. I don't like women who flop around all over the place. They're so . . . untidy. What do you think?'

'I think I'd like to read my newspaper,' Doyle says.

'Take my wife,' the man continues. 'Please. Take her.' He laughs uproariously at the old joke, then suddenly switches back into serious mode. 'A terrific lady, my wife. But no longer of the desired level of springiness, if you know what I mean. She has become yet another victim of gravity. Yes, my friend, gravity.'

Doyle tunes him out. While the drunk prattles on, Doyle's antennae lock on to Paddy. As time ticks by, the bar becomes busier. Doyle recognizes a few of the newly arrived faces – cops who have just come off their tour. Others he has never seen before, and they are probably the ones he needs to worry about. They mill around the bar, waiting for their turn to be served. Paddy deals with them one by one. He is unconcerned by anything except his customers. Doyle watches them all. Watches where their hands go, the expressions on their faces, the way they move.

The drunk is saying something about whiskey now. For some reason, Doyle finds his attention pulled back to the man. He watches him toss back the rest of his drink.

'One for the road,' the man says.

He slips gracelessly from his barstool and zigzags toward Paddy.

Doyle takes a quick peek at his watch. Two minutes before midnight. Just two more minutes.

He gets down from his own stool. Prepares himself to spring into action. His eyes are fixed on Paddy and those in front of him. He begins to move closer to the throng.

From this new position he can see the clock behind the bar. Its large hand edges ever closer to the vertical. Doyle stares at the group of men at the counter. They wait patiently. They don't seem nervy, don't look as if they're about to blow somebody's brains out. The drunk is among them now. Again Doyle's eyes are drawn to him, and he doesn't know why.

He thinks about it.

And it all seems so wrong.

This man hasn't been here for the whole night. Doyle would

have noticed him. So he's been somewhere else, happily throwing back whiskey. Then why the sudden switch to this bar? Why sit by Doyle, not drinking except to knock back that one tumbler? Was there really alcohol in that glass? Did he have to choose a time so close to midnight to make his way over to Paddy? And why the rush to head over there anyhow? Why not just stay where he was and wait to be served?

Doyle is certain something is about to go down. He edges closer to those at the bar. His senses seem to sharpen. He is attuned to every sound, every movement.

The clock behind the bar begins to chime twelve. Doyle never even knew this clock had a chime.

The drunk pushes closer to the counter. He is no longer swaying. He pulls open his jacket, slips his hand inside. Doyle reaches under his own jacket. Closes his fingers around the butt of his Glock. The clock chime seems pounding now. Midnight is here. The drunk pulls out his hand. Doyle starts to draw his gun. It's happening.

And then it isn't happening.

The dark shape in the drunk's hand is a wallet. The man opens it up, peers inside, begins to sway again.

Doyle slowly eases his Glock back into his holster, but keeps his hand on the weapon.

His eyes flick over the other people grouped here. No unexpected moves. No reaching for guns. No diving across the counter to get at Paddy.

The clock is silent again.

Paddy continues to take orders and pour drinks. The customers walk away happy. The drunk's turn comes. He orders a double Jim Beam. As he turns and walks past Doyle, he burps, and Doyle smells the stench of the alcohol on his breath. He really is intoxicated.

So what the hell?

What the fuck is going on?

'Cal? What can I get you?'

Doyle blinks at Paddy, almost surprised that the man is still able to talk to him.

Why aren't you dead, Paddy?

Doyle checks the clock. Four minutes into the new day, and Patrick Gilligan is standing there, as hale and hearty as ever.

'Uhm . . . It's okay. I'm good.'

'Well, if that's good, I'd hate to see you when you're feeling unwell. You're a strange one tonight, Cal.'

Doyle forces out a smile, then goes back to his spot at the end of the counter. He climbs onto his barstool and pulls his glass into his chest. He stares at Paddy and fails to comprehend.

He decides to give it a few more minutes. Ten past twelve, that should do it. Then there can be no mistake, no more leeway for a slow watch or whatever. But inside he knows it's over. His adrenalin is already leaking away. There'll be no floor show tonight, folks.

So he waits until ten past. Waits and watches in the knowledge that it's a waste of time. And then he picks up that glass of Guinness, tips it to his mouth and begins to chug it back, thinking as he swallows that he's never waited so long to down a drink in his life.

He doesn't want to think any more about the information he was given over the phone. He is too tired for any kind of analysis. Something has gone wrong, and he doesn't want to know what it is. Because it will be bad. He wants to get drunk instead, so he can forget.

But he doesn't get let off that lightly.

He thinks at first that it's his mind teasing him cruelly. Reminding him of the phone call. Haunting him with that Irish jig.

When he realizes that it's real – that the music is actually being played here in Gilligan's – he almost chokes on his beer.

He slams the glass down. Guinness splashes out of it and onto his sleeve. He looks at Paddy again, sees that the man is innocently polishing a wineglass. But over to his left is the other bartender, Terry. And Terry is standing over the CD player.

Doyle jumps from his stool and races to the other end of the bar counter.

'Cal?' says Paddy. 'What's wrong with you, man?'

Doyle ignores him. He gets to where Terry is standing.

'Terry! TERRY!'

Terry looks round, raises his eyebrows when he recognizes Doyle.

'The music, Terry. Why are you playing that music?'

Terry waves the plastic CD container that's in his hand.

'This? A guy came in earlier. Asked me to play it right after midnight. Gave me twenty bucks for it. He said it was for senti-mental reasons. I'm a little late, so I hope he's okay about it. Nice tune, huh? Catchy.'

'This guy. What did he look like?'

Terry shrugs. 'Tall. White. I don't really remember. I was busy.'

'What color hair?'

'I don't know. He was wearing a baseball cap. Why are you asking?'

'Gimme the case, Terry.'

Terry walks over and hands the CD case to Doyle. Doyle looks at the cover, then turns it over. He reads the title of the first track.

And then he gets it.

Shit.

He drops the case on the counter and runs for the door. He

knows people will be watching him, wondering what the hell's biting his ass, but he doesn't care.

He crashes through the door, keeps running to the next block where his car is parked. He gets in the car, fires it up. He takes it up to Fourteenth Street, then aims it west, desperately trying to remember the address. He knows it's in the West Village, but he can't remember the street. He hits the gas pedal.

Cops do like a drink, though, don't they? Even guys who aren't cops themselves but who are the sons of cops have been known to find themselves in the company of drink.

A clue, yes. But also meant to throw him. Sean Hanrahan isn't a cop, and he is the son of a cop. And he's also too fond of the booze.

But here's the thing: Hanrahan *used* to be a cop. That's why Doyle discounted him.

Hanrahan was the desk sergeant at the Eighth when Doyle arrived. Being an Irishman himself, he took Doyle under his wing. Showed him the ropes. Introduced him to the other cops. Made him feel at home. He also wasn't swayed by the baggage that Doyle carried with him from his previous precinct, following the death of Doyle's female partner.

Yet Hanrahan was weighed down with baggage of his own. When he was on patrol he was involved in a shootout in which his partner was killed. Hanrahan received a flesh wound in the leg, but his damage went deeper than that. He moved to the desk job, but he also moved to the bottle. Three months after Doyle arrived, Hanrahan retired from the force. The other cops threw a 'racket' – a party – for him, and Doyle landed the job of seeing him home. Doyle gave him the usual parting invitation to call in at the station house any time, but even then he had a feeling he would never see Hanrahan again.

Now – unless he is mistaken – that could well be the case.

Doyle takes a left onto Seventh Avenue. He looks at the street names at each intersection. When he sees Charles Street, he knows it's the one. He hangs a right, praying that it's all a mistake. I've got it wrong, he thinks. Hanrahan's okay.

He can't remember the number of the building, but it doesn't matter. The flashing roof lights of the police patrol cars give it away. And in that moment Doyle knows there's no error. He slows as he passes the cars, and a uniformed officer on the stoop of the apartment building glances toward him. He steps on the gas again. Being spotted here would raise too many questions.

He continues down the narrow tree-lined street, takes the next left onto Bleecker. The sight of more white-and-blue police vehicles parked here reminds him that he's too close for comfort to the Sixth Precinct station house, so he keeps on driving. Seeing Seventh Avenue ahead of him again, he takes a right onto Barrow Street, then parks the car in a quiet spot opposite the Greenwich House Music School.

And then he lets it out.

He gives out a long roar of pain and anger while he pounds his fists on the steering wheel and slams his elbow into the door and smashes his heels into the footwell. And even when he is spent, even when all he has left are the tears streaming down his face, he can still hear that stupid Irish jig. He will probably be unable to get it out of his head for a long time to come.

The song called 'Hanrahan's Last'.

TWELVE

He has to act like the rest of them.

When he arrives at work that next morning and they say to him things like, 'You hear what happened to Hanrahan last night?' he has to pretend that he's only just heard the news himself. He has to appear convincingly shocked and appalled. He has to look them in the eyes when he enquires about what they might have heard on the grapevine about the death of their former sergeant. When they tell him about an unknown perp entering Hanrahan's apartment and blowing his face off with a shotgun he has to react with the expected level of disbelief and horror. And he has to do all this without sounding like he's a member of the local amateur dramatics society.

Because yes, this is theater. Doyle is an actor. Delivering lines already written in his mental script. And it has to be the most convincing portrayal of his life. Otherwise his audience will see him for what he really is and their faith will be gone.

But it's difficult. Reality keeps wanting to intrude. It wants to point a huge finger at Doyle and say, 'See this guy here? Well, he had information relating to the death of Hanrahan. Truth be known, he possessed it way before Hanrahan was killed. And you know what? He didn't want to share it with any of you. He didn't want to give any of you the chance to prevent the murder of your big old friendly desk sergeant. What do you think of that?'

He tries doing what he did previously: telling himself that it would have made no difference if he had revealed his inside information. But this time the assurances ring hollow. This time he knows he made a huge error of judgment. He had an Irish tune sounding loud and clear in his head, and he didn't follow it up. He could have gone into a record store or called up a music society or a relative in Ireland and he could have hummed or whistled it to them, and maybe they would have known what it was. And if they had said, 'Yeah, I know that tune; it's called "Hanrahan's Last",' then he wouldn't have spent fruitless hours sitting in a bar on the wrong side of the city. So maybe a difference *could* have been made. If he'd told somebody. Or even if he'd just tried a little bit fucking harder, for Christ's sake. So what if Hanrahan used to be a cop? Wouldn't a little more pondering about it have made Doyle say, 'Okay, he used to be a cop, but he's not now, so maybe this guy fits the clues.' Shouldn't he have done all this? Shouldn't he have opened up the possibility for others to do this? Shouldn't he have gone just that extra fucking inch?

Of course he should. He is painfully aware of this. It's excruciating. It's why he is exasperated and despondent and furious.

And it's why he's bringing this to an end. Initiating divorce proceedings. No more relationship with the mysterious helper.

He can't bear the awful pressure.

He can't live with knowing.

It means becoming a cop again. No inside knowledge means he has to do what other detectives do. He has to rely on shoe leather and his dialing finger and his wits and his questioning skills to get at the truth. Just as he would normally do in an investigation.

Jesus, what a relief that is.

Except that it's not so simple. He wants to talk to Gary Bonnow, husband of the murdered nurse. Only he lives in

Brooklyn, and Doyle doesn't have a good excuse to go driving over to Brooklyn and back right now. So he decides to call him on the phone. Only he can't make the call from the squadroom for fear of somebody overhearing and wondering what the hell he's doing posing questions concerning a case that has nothing to do with him. So he goes for a short stroll to grab a coffee, and on his way back he gets into his car and makes the call from his cellphone. And as he dials he thinks back on the talk he had when Gonzo turned up unannounced at the station house, and he wonders how many more times he will use this car for clandestine conversations like this. So much for becoming Detective Normal again.

The voice that answers the phone sounds weary. Doyle figures that this man has probably spent a lot of time on the phone these past few days.

'Mr Bonnow? This is Detective Doyle at the Eighth Precinct. We haven't met, but I hope you don't mind if I ask you a coupla questions relating to your wife. Would that be okay?'

'Well, ya know, I'm not so sure. I don't know if there's anything more I can tell you guys. I don't really know anything. Do we have to do this now?'

'I'll be real quick, I promise. Just a coupla things I'm sure my colleagues haven't asked you yet.'

Doyle gets a long silence, followed by a sigh. 'Okay, shoot.'

'Mr Bonnow, do you know if your wife kept a diary?'

'A diary?'

Doyle can hear the surprise in the man's voice. He was expecting a question he's already been asked a million times, and for a change he didn't get one.

Bonnow repeats himself: 'A diary?'

'Yes, a diary. A journal. Or maybe just a notebook she liked to write in. Did she have anything like that?'

'No. Lorna wasn't a big writer. She was never even sure what to put in birthday cards, ya know?'

'Okay. Here's my other question. Did Lorna own a computer?'

'A computer?' Again, the question has thrown him. 'No. She hated computers. Technology was never her thing. She always came to me just to work the DVD player.'

'Okay, thank you, Mr Bonnow. That's all I wanted to know.'

'That's all? I don't get it. Those questions are kinda strange. I mean, a diary and a computer? I don't get it.'

'Don't worry about it, Mr Bonnow. Sometimes we hear things and we have to follow them up, and it can all seem a little weird. You might get a few more weird questions as the investigation proceeds. It just means we're doing our job.'

'Oh. Well, okay then. It's just . . . well, I loved her, ya know? Even though she went with that other guy . . . I kind of understand why she did that. So, I was . . . well, I was hoping for a little *more*.'

'I understand. Give us time. We'll catch him.'

Doyle rings off. He too was hoping for a little more. He wanted a connection. A pattern. If the nurse had kept a diary or owned a computer, just as Cindy Mellish did, then that could have meant something. As it is, it's just another dead end.

But there has to be a link of some kind. The killer has gone to far too much trouble for the victims to have been selected purely at random. There is a thread of some kind tying these three murdered people together.

Doyle just can't see what it is.

Doyle waits until his lunch break before making his next excursion. When he arrives at the apartment building on Charles Street, he first of all checks that there are no parked cars that look like they might belong to the NYPD. Satisfied, he goes looking for the wife of Sean Hanrahan. He doesn't find her, but the building superintendent tells him that she is staying with her daughter on Jones Street, just a few blocks away.

Doyle drives down to the address. It's a low-rise Greek Revival rowhouse situated between a café and a record store with a stone-cladding fascia that makes Doyle queasy just to look at it.

A woman aged about thirty opens the door of the first-floor apartment and directs a gaze filled with suspicion at Doyle.

'Yes?'

'I, uh, I'm looking for Mrs Hanrahan.'

'Are you a police officer?'

'Yes, but I was also a friend of Sergeant Hanrahan. Was he . . . was he your father?'

'Look, this is not a good time, okay? My mother, she's not in the best of health. She's tired, she's upset, and right now she could do with a rest. So if this isn't urgent—'

'I'll only take a few minutes of her time. Please.'

He sees her wavering. This is a lawman at her door, and as a good law-abiding citizen she wants to do what's right. But as a grieving daughter she also wants to tell him to fuck off and leave them alone. And Doyle understands that perfectly. He wonders what she would do if he told her how he failed to save her father's life last night.

'Who is it, dear?'

The voice comes from inside the apartment. Its owner comes into view. Doyle sees a flash of recognition in the woman's eyes.

'We've met before,' she says. 'Detective . . .'

'Doyle,' he says. 'Cal Doyle. Hello, Mrs Hanrahan.'

'Please, come in.'

She beckons him inside. With reluctance, and wearing an expression of annoyance, the daughter opens the door wide to admit him. Doyle nods his gratitude and his apology as he enters.

It's a light, airy apartment. The furnishings are modern and tasteful. On the walls are numerous photographs of two young children. An upright piano sits in one corner of the room, and supports yet more photos.

'I'll leave you two alone,' says the daughter. 'I need to get some air.'

She grabs a coat from a peg near the door, then shoots Doyle another look of anger as she leaves.

Doyle turns back to Mary Hanrahan. He knows that she is somewhere in her mid-fifties, but thinks she looks a dozen years older. He remembers Sean telling him that she used to own a bakery store but had to sell up because of problems with her circulation. He notices now how ruddy her complexion is, and how her breathing seems somewhat labored.

'You'll have to forgive Fiona,' she says. 'She's been through a lot.'

Doyle smiles at her. 'Nothing to forgive. I know how difficult this must be for both of you. I was really sorry to hear about what happened to Sean.'

She nods slowly, her eyes glistening. For an awful moment Doyle thinks she's going to break down, but then she recovers her composure.

'Please,' she says. 'Take a seat.'

They sit at opposite ends of a long cream-colored sofa.

'How did you find me?' she asks.

'The super at your building directed me here. I hope you don't mind.'

'I can't be at our apartment. I don't know if I can ever go back to our apartment. Even if they can clean it up, I'm not sure that, well . . .'

Doyle makes a show of looking around the living room. Anything to change the subject.

'This is a nice place.'

She gives him a matronly smile. 'Fiona and Brett have done well for themselves. They both have good jobs. They work hard. They deserve a break every now and then, but it's difficult with two young children. Do you have children, Cal?'

He holds up a finger. 'One. A girl.'

'Then you know. I mean, how hard it is to get time to yourselves. That's why I came here last night. To look after the children while Fiona and Brett had a night out. That's why I wasn't at home.'

Doyle gets what she's saying. She wasn't at home last night. When her husband was killed. She wasn't there with him, and she regrets it bitterly. Doyle can hear the self-recrimination in her voice.

She continues: 'You see, last night was their wedding anniversary. I couldn't say no, could I? I couldn't let them down. The reason we moved to the Village was to be near our children and grandchildren. I love to see them. Why would I say no to helping them out? I can walk here in just a few minutes. And it's good for me too. I have problems with my circulation, you know.'

'I'm sure you're a wonderful parent and grandparent. It's nothing to beat yourself up about.'

She looks at him, seemingly grateful that he understands. He imagines she has spent the whole morning talking to people who are concerned with *just the facts, ma'am*. The whos, whats, whys and whens. And when she answered their questions, perhaps nobody picked up on her subtext. Perhaps they failed to see what was happening to her inside.

'They won't make me see him, will they?' she asks. 'For identification purposes, I mean. They say that he's . . . well, that he's not what he was. I don't want to see him like that. I want to remember him as he used to be.'

Doyle has seen bodies with shotgun wounds to the face. It's not a pretty spectacle. Uncomfortable even for cops who have seen all kinds of terrible sights.

'No, don't worry. The NYPD has his fingerprints on file. You won't need to identify him.'

She nods again. Doyle is glad that he has been able to lift one small weight from her shoulders. Not much, but something.

She says, 'You probably know more about this than I do, but the police were very interested in hearing about our friends. People we know well. People we trust. Is it possible, do you think? That someone we know might have done this?'

Another worry. It's bad enough when an act of extreme violence is perpetrated on you or your family, but the thought that it could have been done by somebody you know, somebody you might meet again very soon, can be almost impossible to accept.

Doyle hesitates before answering. She is looking to him for help, and by God he owes it to her to clear this fear from her mind. But he has to be careful. What he knows and what he can say are not necessarily the same.

He says, 'My guess is that there were no signs of a break-in, no signs of a struggle?'

'No. The police said there was nothing like that.'

'Then it's understandable that they would want to talk to everyone who Sean might have allowed into the apartment. In most cases that would mean friends, family, people the victim knew pretty well.'

'Oh my God.'

'But that's not always the case. It could be somebody pretending to be something they're not. An authority figure, maybe. It could be someone Sean never met before in his life.'

She looks at him like it's a ridiculous suggestion. Which, he has to admit, is exactly how it sounds. A complete stranger who is such a smooth talker that he can get close enough to an ex-cop to pull out a shotgun and obliterate the man's features before they can even register surprise. The funny thing is, Doyle is pretty sure that it's almost exactly how it went down. The killer, whoever it is, has this magic ability to inveigle his way into the homes of his victims. Into their lives. And once he's there . . .

'But if it's somebody he never met before,' Mrs Hanrahan is saying, 'why on earth would they want to kill him? And why would they go to such lengths? If they hated him that much, why not just gun him down on the street?'

Why indeed? Because maybe it's not about hate. Maybe it's about power. Maybe he's doing it simply to prove he can. And that makes him so much more dangerous than a killer who is blindly driven by something as basic and primitive as raw hatred.

'I don't know. I think it's too early to say. But we'll catch him. That's one thing I'm sure of.'

'We?'

'Excuse me?'

'You said, "We'll catch him." Are you working Sean's case?'

He hears a note of hope in her question. She wants someone who knew Sean personally to be taking care of things for him.

'I meant the police. But I'll do everything I can.'

He notes the look of disappointment. She was a cop's wife for God knows how many years. She knows how these things work. She knows that unless there's a break in the case in the first forty-eight hours, then it's unlikely the perp will ever be caught. And that means she wants every resource at the NYPD's disposal to be allocated to the search for her husband's murderer. Doyle has promised her that he will play his part, and he intends to keep that promise.

'I suppose the detectives asked you all the usual questions

about whether Sean had any enemies, anyone that may have threatened him recently.'

'Yes, they did. My answer was no. Nobody that I know of.'

'Anything bothering him recently? Any financial worries, that kind of thing?'

She hesitates before answering. 'Sean was a very troubled man, Cal. It started a long time before last night. But as for anything specific happening more recently, the answer is no again.'

Now it's Doyle's turn to pause. He tries to slip the next question in with as much nonchalance as he can muster.

'I don't suppose that Sean was the type of guy who might have put his troubles down on paper? In a diary or a notebook maybe?'

She gives him a quizzical look. 'No. That wasn't Sean. He needed an outlet, all right, but writing wouldn't have done it for him.'

'What about a computer? You have one of those at home? Maybe Sean made a connection with the wrong people on the Internet.'

Now her brow is furrowed in suspicion. 'No, we've never seen the attraction. I guess that Sean and I have always been old-fashioned in that way.'

Give it up, Doyle tells himself. The diary, the computer – there's nothing there. That's not the way you're gonna find the killer. So what is? What possible link can there be between this woman's husband, a young girl who worked in a bookstore, and a nurse who was having an affair? What am I missing?

'Cal,' she says. 'Why did you come here?'

Just when he thought he'd gotten away with it.

'I . . . I'm not sure what you mean.'

'Sean and I were married to each other for thirty-one years. In all that time I hardly ever asked him about his police work.

Not because I wasn't interested, but because I was frightened. I didn't want to hear about the drug addicts and the murderers and the rapists he had to clean off our streets. I didn't want to know that Sean was putting himself in dangerous situations each day, that he was putting his life on the line. Closing myself off to those things somehow helped me not to worry that he might not come home one day. But I still managed to learn a few things. I know, for example, that investigations are usually carried out by the squad controlling the precinct in which the crime takes place. You're in the Eighth Precinct, Cal. That's east side. It's not here in the Village. Now a minute ago you told me that you're not working Sean's case. Fine. Except that you're asking some damn strange questions for someone who's not officially involved. What's going on, Cal?'

Go ahead, he thinks. Worm your way out of that one.

'I don't know if you read about it – maybe Sean told you about it – but just before Christmas I was involved in a big case. Some cops died. People thought I had something to do with it. Some still do. Anyway, after it was all over, the Department wanted to make sure the fire didn't start up again, so they made sure I went nowhere near the matches. They started giving me the cases nobody else wanted. If there was a dumpster to be searched, I was your man.'

'That must have been tough on you.'

'It was okay at first. But now I'm starting to get kinda sick of it. So I'm looking for a way out, a way to redeem myself in the eyes of the Department. If it means working cases in my spare time, then that's what I'll do. You're right, I'm not officially on Sean's case, and the PD would go nuts if they found out I was working it. But the answer I have to give you is that I *am* looking for Sean's killer, and some of the reasons for doing that are selfish ones.'

He waits for her to yell, 'Liar, liar, pants on fire!' After the plate of horseshit he just served to her, it's the least he deserves. But instead she lets it ride. It seems to Doyle that she senses it's wise not to pursue this too closely. She is giving him her trust, on the assumption that he will repay it when he is able. And although he is grateful, he doesn't feel too bad about himself. Because his real reasons are not at all selfish. He wants to get to this killer so that he can stop him. That's it, pure and simple. Nothing to do with improving his image. He couldn't give a rat's ass about what others might think of him. Lies or no lies, he feels he can hold his head high, and he guesses that Mrs Hanrahan detects that too.

Her smile is a knowing one. 'All right, Cal. Then I wish you well. Whatever your reasons, I hope you get whoever did this. Perhaps even my daughter would find some forgiveness in her heart if the NYPD could catch her father's killer.'

'Forgiveness?'

She pauses, but only briefly. 'As I said before, Sean was a troubled man. I'm sure you already know that he was a drunk. He was probably drunk last night. If he hadn't been, maybe his guard wouldn't have been down. But that's beside the point. Sean turned to drink after his partner was killed. He blamed himself, even though it wasn't his fault. I believe that's a very common reaction in your job.'

Oh yeah, thinks Doyle. Been there, done that, still wearing the scars.

She says, 'His whole character changed. I'm not saying he became violent or anything, but he wasn't the same man. Fiona in particular couldn't come to terms with it. Even though she was a grown woman when this happened, one minute Sean was her daddy, and the next he wasn't. She took it hard, and she blamed Sean's job. Not for the shooting itself, but for the lack of support which followed. She felt that the NYPD were never really there for him. And when it just got worse, we started to worry that Sean might . . . well, that he might harm himself. To be honest, when I heard the news that Sean had been shot in our apartment, my first thought was that he'd done it himself.'

'The job has counselors for this kind of thing. Didn't Sean go to see any of them?'

She shakes her head. 'I think he was afraid that word would get around, and that it would be seen as a sign of weakness. It took me long enough to get him to see a private counselor, but Sean couldn't stick with that either, even though Fiona and Brett were willing to keep paying. He only went to two sessions with Dr Vasey before he gave up, and then—'

'I'm sorry,' says Doyle. 'Who did you say he went to see?'

'Dr Vasey,' she answers. 'Dr Andrew Vasey.'

THIRTEEN

Bingo!

A connection.

Cindy Mellish and Sean Hanrahan were clients of the same therapist. Dr Andrew Vasey. Vasey is the missing link.

Okay, Lorna Bonnow hasn't been tied into this yet, but maybe that'll come. Maybe she too was a client of Vasey's.

To Doyle, spring seems instantly sunnier and warmer. He almost feels like singing as he races back to the station house. Finally he has something to work with.

All he has to do now is convince the squad to go with him on this.

Yeah, sure. That'll be easy. It'll be just what they've been waiting for. Doyle coming in and saying, 'Hey guys. Drop what you're doing. Forget everything you did for the last few days. Here's what we need to do next. Yes, I know that these are not my cases, but that's okay. There's no need to thank me.'

Should be a breeze.

When he gets to the House, he decides to start small. From little acorns and all that. No point in getting everybody excited all at once. So he takes Jay Holden aside and invites him once again into the interview room crowded with too many file cabinets.

Holden says, 'Why do I get the feeling you're about to tell me something I don't wanna hear?'

'Maybe it's because I'm about to tell you something you don't wanna hear.'

Holden looks up at the ceiling. 'Shit.'

There's nothing Doyle can do now but spit it out. 'I just came back from seeing Sean Hanrahan's wife.'

Holden looks at him. 'Please tell me it was a personal visit. Please tell me you weren't looking to work that case.'

'She told me something.'

Holden raises his arms and lets them drop back to his sides with a slap. 'Shit. I knew it. Why did I even agree to come in here and listen to this? I think it's time for me to leave now.'

'No. Listen. It's important. You know how Hanrahan went to pieces after his partner bought it? Well, his wife made him seek professional help. Psychological help. Given to him by a shrink called Andrew Vasey.'

For a few seconds Holden doesn't move. He just stares at Doyle in stunned silence.

'Okay, now I am definitely outta here.'

He turns and heads for the door. Stops when he's within an arm's length of the door handle.

'All right, now why would you have to go and do that? Why'd you have to go and ruin a perfectly good day? What the fuck is it with you that you can never leave things nice and simple?'

Doyle shrugs. 'I can't help it. I was born like this. When I was a kid I tied my shoelaces with such a complicated knot that my mother had to cut them off with scissors.'

Holden marches back toward Doyle. 'What the fuck were you thinking, going to see Hanrahan's wife like that? It's not your case, Cal. Watch my lips: Not. Your. Case. Not my case neither. Not even this fucking precinct's case. Jesus!'

'Good job I went, though, huh?'

Holden wags a finger in front of his face. 'Uh-uh. No. Not

good. Simple is good. Straightforward is good. This is complicated. This piece of information that you had no right uncovering
connects my DOA with a completely different DOA, whereas
what I would prefer is if the two DOAs were completely unrelated. That's what I would like 'stead of this heart-attack item of
news you feel you have to land on me.'

Doyle waits patiently. Then: 'So what do you want to do
about Vasey?'

Holden looks back at him.

'Let's haul that motherfucker's ass in here.'

Vasey doesn't take kindly to having his ass hauled anywhere.
He doesn't like having to cancel his afternoon consultations at
such short notice. He objects to being marched past his secretary
and out of his office building like a common criminal. And he
especially resents being cooped up for ages in a cramped uncomfortable room with only file cabinets for company.

In retaliation, he lawyers up.

It has to be said that cops don't like it when suspects bring
in their lawyers, even though the participants on both sides are,
ostensibly, engaged in the search for truth insofar as it can be
established in law. The problem is not so much that it prevents
the boys in blue from judicious employment of the rubber hose or
the nightstick, although there are some who still lament the pass-
ing of those more robust techniques of yesteryear. It's more that
experienced lawyers know every trick in the book when it comes
to eliciting, cajoling and conning information out of interviewees.
They will leap on every question that smacks of an attempt to
smear their client with the perfume of guilt, and will advise the
client to claim the Fifth in response to any question for which the
answer has not already been rehearsed. A good lawyer can cause
an interview to degenerate into little more than a mud-slinging

DAVID JACKSON

match between the lawyer and the cops, with the suspect silently twiddling his thumbs and waiting to go home.

Anna Friedrich is a good lawyer.

At least, that's Doyle's impression of her, even before the interview has properly begun. There is an air of professionalism, efficiency and punctiliousness about her. From her perfectly sculpted bob of black hair to her Jimmy Choo high-heeled shoes, she exudes confidence and authority. Doyle knows she will accept no nonsense, brook no challenge to her legal standing. She is going to be one tough bitch.

Doyle finds Anna Friedrich sexy as hell.

At least he would if he wasn't happily married. But since he is, such thoughts would never enter his head. He is certain that Holden is attracted to her, though. Holden is a single, red-blooded male. He will be imagining that beneath that clinging red sweater and that tight, short skirt, Anna Friedrich is wearing a brassiere-and-garter matched set. In black. With decorative flame-red stitching. Holden will be picturing her in the bedroom, still in those heels, and with all manner of instruments of discipline hidden in her closet. He will be guessing that any man who enters her boudoir leaves as a quivering shadow of his former self, but wearing the biggest fucking smile he's ever had.

Holden's mind will be working like this because he is unattached. Whereas Doyle is married. Happily. Yes-sireee.

A curse on Holden for not keeping his mind on the job. Doesn't he realize there's important work to be done here? To wit, getting Vasey to admit his guilt.

It occurs to Doyle that asking a doctor to cough is a nice reversal of the usual run of things.

They get the preliminaries over with, and then Doyle kicks off the Q&A.

'Dr Vasey, the last time we met, we asked you about a patient of yours named—'

He stops because Anna Friedrich has raised a finger. Already. Before Doyle has even finished his first question. She has erected a slim index finger with a perfectly manicured nail painted in red.

'Client,' she says.

'Excuse me?'

'Client. Dr Vasey would prefer it if you would refer to them as clients, not patients.'

'Is there a difference?'

'It's a nuance. In the same way you prefer to call this an interview rather than an interrogation.'

Doyle glares at her. She reflects it right back at him.

'All right, then. Dr Vasey, we asked you about a *client* of yours named Cindy Mellish. Do you—'

There it is again. The finger. At this rate, Vasey will die of old age before they finish the fucking interview. Doyle is tempted to show a finger of his own, and it's not the index finger.

'No,' says Friedrich, 'you did not ask Dr Vasey about a client of his. You asked him about a woman named Cindy Mellish. She was never his client.'

'We have information to the contrary.'

'And my horoscope this morning told me I was going to meet a highly intelligent man today. Go figure.'

Doyle shuffles in his seat and tries again. 'All right, let me give you another name. Sean Hanrahan. Does that ring any bells?'

Vasey looks to his lawyer before answering, and only opens his mouth once she gives him the nod.

Great, thinks Doyle. A ventriloquist act.

'I don't recall that name,' says Vasey.

'No? Before he retired, Sean Hanrahan was a sergeant with

the NYPD. When he was on patrol his partner was killed in a liquor store holdup that went wrong. Still not remember him?'

Vasey hesitates and clears his throat. 'Now that you have supplied the additional details, he does sound familiar.'

'So was he a client of yours?'

'Possibly.'

'Possibly? What does that mean, Doctor? Was Sean Hanrahan a client of yours, yes or no?'

'If it's the man I'm thinking of, then yes, he was a client. For a short while.'

'How short?'

'I'd have to check. One or two sessions at the most.'

'And when's the last time you saw him?'

'The consultations? I believe they were over a year ago.'

'And since the consultations?'

'I . . . I don't know what you mean.'

'When was the last time you saw Sean Hanrahan *after* the consultations?'

'I don't understand. I've never seen him since then. What is this?'

'Yes, Detective,' says Friedrich. 'Where exactly are you going with this?'

Doyle looks at her. Sees her half-open mouth with its glossy lipstick. Flame-red again.

'Sean Hanrahan was killed last night in his apartment. Someone took his face off with a shotgun.'

She blinks. Once. Twice. Then, without further breaks in her eye contact with Doyle she says, 'All right, Andrew, let's go. This meeting is over.'

Doyle turns his gaze on Vasey. 'You can go if you want, Doctor, but if you want my advice, you should stay. This isn't looking good for you at the moment. Two people are dead, and you're the only thing we can find that connects them. Maybe it's just coincidence. Maybe somebody's trying to set you up. Who knows? But if you're innocent, then I'm sure you'll want to get to the bottom of this as much as we do. This is your chance to do that.'

Friedrich now also turns to Vasey. 'Andrew, the only people trying to set you up here are the police. That means any advice they offer you is less than worthless. If they had anything on you, they would have charged you by now. Let's get out of here.'

She waits. Doyle and Holden wait. Vasey wavers, his mouth opening and closing.

'I'll stay,' he says.

Friedrich stares at him in disbelief. When she twists back in her chair, she folds her arms in what seems a petulant gesture, the action pushing up her breasts.

'So,' says Doyle, 'do you still want to deny that you ever met Cindy Mellish in your office, whether she was officially registered as a client or not?'

'I never met that girl,' says Vasey. 'And I also want to put on record that I have never acted in anything other than a professional manner in my consultations. The idea that I would physically assault somebody is . . . it's abhorrent.'

Doyle thinks the good doctor is starting to sound a little melodramatic. He wants to ramp up the pressure. In particular, he wants to ask about Lorna Bonnow, but he knows that if he throws that in he'll have a lot of explaining to do to Holden.

'What would you say if I asked you to open up your client files to us, Dr Vasey?'

It's Friedrich who answers. 'He'd tell you to take a hike. Those files are confidential. A psychologist's reputation is built on trust. A lot of people tell Andrew a lot of things. Very intimate things. They do so in the knowledge that he won't go divulging their personal details to everybody that asks for them. Next question.'

'We could get a court order.'

'You think? On what grounds? That one of Dr Vasey's former clients was murdered? Big deal.'

'On the grounds that Dr Vasey is the common factor in two homicide cases currently under investigation.'

'Hello? Didn't we cover this already? You've got one guy who Andrew saw twice, and you've got a woman he never met even once, despite your continued insistence that he did. What kind of common factor is that? I bet I could find two dead people who both ate at Katz's at some point in their lives. Wouldn't mean that the owner poisoned them. But if you think you can get a lame duck like that to fly in front of a judge, then good luck to you, Detective.'

Doyle is starting to feel more than a little pissed now. Not least because he knows that she is correct. He tries to appear as though she hasn't rattled him, although he suspects she already scents triumph.

'Doctor, where were you last night, around midnight?'

'Here we go,' Friedrich mutters.

Vasey says, 'I was at home. Where else would I be?'

'At home. Are you sure?'

'What do you mean, am I sure? Of course I'm sure.'

'And what were you doing?'

'At midnight? I was in bed.'

'You were in bed.'

Doyle goes silent then. He gives Vasey his best withering stare. Any second now, he thinks. The beads of sweat, the loosening of the collar, and then he'll break.

'All right, Detective,' says Friedrich. 'Now that we've established my client's nocturnal habits and found them to be completely mundane, can we bring this interview to a close? Dr

Vasey is a very busy man, and I am sure you are too when you're not going on fishing expeditions like this one.'

Any second now.

'Dr Vasey, would you like to reconsider your previous answer?'

All eyes are on Doyle now, and he knows they're all wondering what's gotten into him. He figures that Holden in particular will think he's flipped.

'I, uhm . . . I went out. For a short while.'

Gotcha, thinks Doyle. But now he knows the others are all trying to work out what made him push it.

'You went out. At what time?'

'I'm not sure exactly. Eleven-fifteen. Eleven-thirty. In there somewhere.'

'And what time did you get back to the apartment?'

'About two.'

'Two o'clock in the morning. You were out of your apartment from eleven-fifteen or thereabouts until two o'clock.'

'I think so. Yes.'

'Did you go out in your car?'

'No. I walked.'

'You don't mind me saying, that's a strange time to be going for a stroll. Where did you go?'

'Park Avenue.'

'Where on Park Avenue?'

'Corner of Sixty-second Street.'

Exactly where Gonzo lost him, thinks Doyle.

'And what was so fascinating about that location that made you schlep all the way over there so late in the day?'

'It's not so far. Just a couple of blocks.'

'Dr Vasey, I don't care if you only went as far as your closet.

What I want to know is why you felt the sudden urge to go there at that time of night.'

He looks to Friedrich again. She gives him the green light.

'I, uhm, I got a call.'

'A call? You mean on the telephone? Who from?'

'Well, the thing is, I'm not sure any longer. It was kind of weird.'

Doyle feels something inside his abdomen do a back-flip. Oh shit, he thinks. I know what's coming.

For the first time in the interview, Holden puts a question. Because he's intrigued, whereas Doyle's interest has suddenly waned.

'Weird how?'

'The guy on the phone said his name was Waxman, and that he was a neighbor of my ex-wife's. She's the one who lives at the Park Avenue address, by the way. Now, I happen to know that her neighbor *is* called Waxman, so I had no reason to doubt him. He told me that he'd heard some weird noises and then a scream coming from her apartment, and that he'd been ringing her doorbell for the past fifteen minutes and couldn't get an answer. He also told me he couldn't get hold of the building superintendent to open her door, so that's why he was calling me, to see if I had a key.'

Doyle nods along with Holden. Trying to pretend that this is a weird one, all right. Preparing himself to look suitably surprised when the punchline gets delivered.

Holden says, 'So you went over there. What happened next?'

'Nothing. I mean, it was business as usual. The doorman had no idea what I was talking about, and when I got upstairs there was no sign of Waxman. The hallway was empty. No signs of any problems whatsoever. So I rang my ex's doorbell. A minute later she opened the door. She was fine. Said she also had no idea what was going on.'

Doyle sees how puzzled Holden looks, and he can imagine the thought processes going on in his mind. The story is too crazy not to be believed. And yet why would anyone choose to pull a stunt like that? If they were trying to set Vasey up, why not just leave him in bed, with no alibi for the time Hanrahan was being murdered, instead of moving him somewhere where presumably his location could be verified?

Because, my dear Watson, Doyle wants to say, the caller somehow knew that Vasey was being watched, and saw his opportunity to add a little more fun to his game. He was playing me. Again.

Holden says, 'Do you know anyone who would make a prank call like that?'

'No. I'd never heard this voice before. It sounded almost British. A little like that actor, whatshisname . . .'

Cary Grant, thinks Doyle.

'Cary Grant,' says Vasey.

Holden rubs his hand across his chin. 'With all due respect, Doctor, don't you think this sounds too convenient? My guess is that the doorman at your apartment building saw you leave at around eleven-fifteen. You don't come back until two. Between those times, Mr Hanrahan, a previous client of yours, is murdered. And then you come up with this story about a mystery phone call that caused you to go over to your ex-wife's place. Can you see how that might sound to us, Dr Vasey?'

Vasey leans across the table. Doyle thinks he's starting to look a little flustered now.

'Yes, I can see that. But it's exactly what happened, I swear to you. My ex-wife will confirm it.'

'She might confirm you came knocking on her door at about eleven-thirty, maybe a few minutes earlier. That says nothing about what you did after that. Doesn't say why you didn't get home until two.'

'I . . . I . . . Look, if you must know, she invited me in. She was touched that I seemed so concerned for her welfare. She . . . she was *grateful*.'

There is a huge nod and a wink contained in that emphasis, and everybody understands it for what it is. Even Anna Friedrich is looking up at the ceiling for distractions.

'You mean you had sex?'

'Uhm, yes.'

'Until what time?' Holden asks. Then, seeing the expression on Vasey's face, he says, 'Scratch that. What time did you leave your ex-wife's apartment?'

'Just before two. Then I went straight home.'

Holden sighs. 'If that's so, why didn't you just give it up a coupla minutes ago? Why did you lie when Detective Doyle asked you where you were around midnight?'

'Because . . . because for one thing I didn't think it was necessary. I thought you were trying to pin the murder of Mr Hanrahan on me, and I didn't see the point in giving you extra ammunition to do just that.'

'But you just said that your ex-wife could give you an alibi. Why not say that from the start and save yourself all this trouble?'

'Because . . . she has a boyfriend now. A very rich and very powerful boyfriend. I was trying to protect her.'

Holden sighs again. 'All right, Dr Vasey. We'll still have to talk to her. Don't worry, we'll be discreet.' He flips open a note-pad. 'What's her name and full address?'

Vasey checks in with his lawyer again. This time she doesn't nod. Doesn't give him a word or a gesture.

'Dr Vasey?'

The lawyer turns her beautiful dark eyes on the detectives.

'Her name is Anna Friedrich,' she says. 'I reverted to my maiden name.'

FOURTEEN

Bitch.

Is what Doyle thinks.

His view is that she was planning to spring this on them all along. That story about covering up her infidelity was a crock of shit. She wanted to watch the detectives dig themselves into a hole and then, at the last possible moment, she would bury them under a truckload of dirt.

And now she's the one who's acting as the injured party. Un-fucking-believable.

'Where did that come from?' she demands of the detectives when Vasey is out of earshot. They have left the interview room, and Vasey has walked ahead of them.

'What?' says Doyle.

'That question about where Andrew was at midnight.'

Doyle shrugs. 'It was routine.'

'Oh no. Not the way you asked it. Not the way you kept pressing him to alter his answer. You knew something.'

'I know a lot of things. Most of all, I know when someone is lying to me or holding back. My spidey sense told me your hubby was holding back.'

'Uh-uh. You were too confident. You were in no doubt he left his apartment last night. That tells me you had him under surveil-lance. I know better than anybody that Andrew can be an asshole

– that's why I'm no longer a Vasey. But I also know that basically he's a stand-up guy. He's not the man you're looking for. So call off the dogs or I'll fire a harassment suit at you so fast you won't have time to duck.'

She turns on her heel and click-clacks down the hallway, leaving the detectives with an indelible memory of her rear view.

'Is she right?' Holden asks Doyle.

'Right about what?'

'That your intuition couldn't be that good. That you had more to go on than a hunch.'

'You really wanna know?'

Holden stands there for a moment while he weighs up the pros and cons.

'Maybe it's better if I don't.'

He starts to walk away. Doyle trails after him.

'Because if you're really interested, I'd be happy to tell you.'

Holden speeds up his pace to get away.

'All right,' says Doyle, 'if you're gonna drag it out of me, it was like this . . .'

But by now Holden has his fingers in his ears and is singing loudly.

The call comes just as Doyle pulls up outside his apartment. He knows from the absence of any caller ID who this is going to be, and he's ready for him. He presses the answer button, but says nothing.

'Cal?'

'Don't say another word,' Doyle tells him. 'Not one fucking word. No stupid clues. No music. Nothing. I don't just mean now, either. I mean forever. I don't need your help no more, get me? That man you killed last night was a cop and a friend. That makes you my enemy. That puts you top of my list of people

I need to take off the streets. And if it was my decision, I'd reinstate the death penalty just for you. In fact, I would stick the fucking spike in your arm myself and watch you die, you sick fuck. Do you understand?'

'Ten-four, Detective. Message received loud and clear. No clues. I get it. But to be honest, I wasn't calling to give you clues. You know why? Because you already have them.'

And then he ends the call.

Just like that.

Leaving Doyle staring at his phone and wondering how it could have gone so awry. This wasn't how it was meant to happen. He was supposed to deliver his rant and then come away feeling good about himself, satisfied that he'd put both himself and the caller in neat little labeled boxes. The hunter and the hunted. The investigator and the criminal. But yet again he has been left with blurred vision, unable to make out the boundaries between right and wrong. Feeling somehow sullied by that simple brief reply.

You already have them.

What do I have?

What the fuck do I have?

It bothers him the whole evening.

For one thing he is furious with himself. He should have said what he had to say and then ended the call. Goodbye. So long. See ya, wouldn't wanna be ya.

But you had to hang on for those extra few seconds, didn't you, Doyle? You had to go and let yourself hear those words. The words that now seem to be the only things in your stupid brainless head, you dumb prick.

Because now it's too late. The words won't go. They won't be ignored. They insist on flashing themselves in front of his eyes like they're written in neon, or tapping on his skull like his own personal woodpecker from hell.

You already have them.

The clues.

And that's the other thing. Because he really has no idea what that means. What clues does he have? There was the U2 song and the Irish jig. So does that mean the next victim will be Irish? Or is he not meant to look at the clues that have already been used to point to victims? Is there something else that has been said? Something he's overlooked?

He is tempted to sit down with a notepad and pen and do what he did before: jotting down everything he remembers of the phone calls and trying to read something into them. But that didn't help Hanrahan, did it?

At the dinner table, Amy asks him something he doesn't even hear. When he doesn't answer, Rachel has to prod him.

'Honey, Amy's asking you a question. A very important question.'

'Huh?' He comes awake and looks at his daughter. 'What is it, Amy?'

'I said, which is more spiky – a hedgehog or a porkie-pine?'

'Oh. Definitely a porkie-pine. No doubt about that.'

'Good. Because that's what I said to Ellie, and she said I was a doofus. I'm not a doofus, are I?'

Doyle smiles at her misuse of the English language. She has developed a habit of saying 'are I' instead of 'am I' and he doesn't have the heart to correct her.

'No, you're not.'

Not like your dad, he thinks. I graduated *summa cum laude* from the School of Doofus.

And my ignorance is going to get someone killed.

★

Andrew Vasey sits motionless in his typist's chair in his apartment, staring straight ahead. Looking out through his floor-to-ceiling window at all those lights. All those sparkling, twinkling, colored lights. The city at night. Millions of people. Perhaps someone is looking back at him now. Wondering.

He breathes, and the air seems to shudder as it gets dragged into his lungs. His body vibrates with the effort. His eyes sting.

He wants to cry out to all those people. Look at me. LOOK AT ME!

It is not time yet. It will be soon. Seconds away, surely. A few pulse-beats of time remaining.

He has accomplished many things, he feels. Helped many people. He is a good man. Not everyone can see that. But he doesn't deserve this.

He thinks about last night. With Anna. It was unplanned and perfect. The irony is that he knows whom to thank for it now. But that's not important. He must latch onto that moment. Hold it tightly. Remember her warmth, her passion, and yes, her love. Because there was still something there. He is sure of it. And that is what he will take with him.

It is time.

The movement begins.

Slow at first, then gathering speed. Until that huge window is rushing at him at what seems like fifty miles per hour. Filling his vision with all those lights. Those bright twinkling stars.

He closes his eyes at the last possible moment. He feels the massive impact, hears the incredible noise. It is the universe breaking apart, and when he opens his eyes all he can see are the stars it contains. The wind rushing past his ears seems primordial to him. As it was at the beginning, so is it at the end. The cosmos is taking him back.

He wants to cry out. Something profound. Something befitting the moment.

But even if he had the words, he does not have the ability to broadcast them.

And so he remains silent. Watching the world rush up to meet him. Feeling that his heart is about to burst open. Listening to the roaring in his ears. Trying to rise above the absurdity of it all.

A man bound to a typist's chair with duct tape. His mouth also sealed with tape. Plummeting from the twenty-eighth floor of his apartment building.

Falling, falling.

Until the rope around his neck becomes taut, and the man's head is ripped from his shoulders, while body and chair smash onto the roof of the adjacent brownstone.

The man who has just wheeled Andrew Vasey across his hardwood floor and through his own window moves quickly now. He steps over broken glass, smoothes down his hair that has been ruffled by the cool air now blowing into the open-plan living area.

He leaves the apartment and walks swiftly along the hallway. He summons the elevator, which arrives almost immediately, then gets in and presses the button for the lobby. When the doors eventually swish open again, he steps out and looks around. The place is deserted. He glances toward the door of the small back office where the doorman keeps his possessions, makes himself the occasional cup of coffee, that kind of thing. He can be found there now. Dead, of course.

The man regrets the death of the doorman. He didn't need helping. Not to the man's knowledge, anyway. But Vasey *did* need help. And getting to Vasey meant removing the doorman. It was a matter of expediency, pure and simple. Poor guy.

He steps out onto the street. Starts walking toward his car. Casually. Without too much haste that might attract attention. He looks around him, expecting to see very little out of the ordinary. A window breaking twenty-eight stories up is just a tinkle when set against the background noise and frenzy of a city like New York. Even a subsequent thud five stories up is difficult to pinpoint and identify, especially when most of the passers-by at this time of night are comfortably ensconced in cars. Now if Vasey had come crashing down onto the sidewalk here, chair and headless body flattening and splattering across the slabs, then that might have been noticed. That might have caused one or two citizens to break stride for a moment, to be a little delayed in taking the next bite out of their Big Macs.

But as it was, the presence of the brownstone directly below Vasey's window proved hugely convenient. An ideal landing pad for a decapitated body flying a typist's chair. Not that it was fortuitous, of course. Things like that cannot be left to chance. It was all in the plan. All factored into the scenario. And everything went just as it was supposed to.

Except . . .

That guy.

Across the street. Looking up at the hole left by Vasey in his window. Talking animatedly into his cellphone.

Now *he* is noteworthy.

Not just because he is aware of what just happened way up there. There was always the possibility that somebody might see or hear something. That was anticipated. It was accounted for.

No, this man is significant for other reasons.

Turning his face away in case the man should look across and see him, the killer quickens his pace toward the corner of the block.

What bothers him is that he has seen that onlooker before. And at almost exactly the same spot.

A nerdy-looking redhead like that is not easily forgotten.

Doyle is beginning to wish he never had a cellphone. It seems that almost every time it rings it brings him trouble. He expects this call to be no exception.

'D-Detective. It's m-me. Oh my gosh. Oh my g-g-gosh.'

'Steady, Gonzo. Calm down. What is it?'

'I'm here again. I was trying to help. I just thought I could keep watch for you. You know, like I said. Because of you not having the m-manpower. And so I came here. But now I don't know what to—'

'Gonzo! Take a deep breath. Okay? Now, nice and slow, where are you?'

'Outside Vasey's building. Watching him for you.'

Doyle rolls his eyes. Oh brother, he thinks. What is it with him?

'All right, Gonzo. You don't need to watch him every night, okay? Now what's got you so worked up?'

'I think . . . I think . . .'

Doyle can hear his rasping breath. He sounds like he's on the verge of an asthma attack.

'What do you think?'

'I think he's dead.'

Tired though he is, Doyle is instantly alert. He is glad that Rachel is in the shower, so that he doesn't have to sneak off to the bedroom again to continue his conversation.

'Who? Vasey? Are you talking about Vasey? What makes you think he's dead?'

'I . . . I just saw him. At least I think it was him. Oh my God.'

'Gonzo, where did you see Vasey? Outside his apartment building?'

'No. Well, yes. But not in the way you mean. I think it was him . . . but I'm not sure. Maybe it wasn't him. I couldn't see too well. It's dark, and it was high up. I dunno. Maybe I'm wrong. But it was somebody. It was definitely somebody—'

'Gonzo! For Pete's sake, tell me what the hell is going on!'

There is a pause. Gonzo trying to compose himself, presumably.

'He came out of the window. Whoever it was. But I think it was Vasey because he lives in apartment 28A, and this looks about the right height to me. He came out of the window. Smashed right through it. And he was tied to a chair. And then . . . and then . . .'

Doyle puts his free hand to his forehead. He feels sick.

'Go on, Gonzo.'

'There was a rope. Around his neck. I think . . . I think his head came off. Oh, God.'

Doyle says nothing for a long while.

'D-Detective? Are you there?'

'I'm here, Gonzo.'

'What should I do? I don't know what to do.'

Doyle chews his lip. 'Listen to me, Gonzo. Are the cops there yet?'

'No, not yet.'

'Is there a big crowd around the body?'

'No. The body landed on a roof. It's on a brownstone next to Vasey's apartment building.'

'So did anybody else see this?'

'No, I don't think so.'

'Look up at the apartment building, Gonzo. Is anyone looking out onto the roof of the brownstone?'

A pause. Then: 'Yes. I can see figures at some of the windows. I think maybe they heard something.'

'All right, Gonzo. Now go home.'

Another pause. 'Go home? What do you mean? I'm a witness. I saw a murder. What do you mean, go home?'

'Just do what I say. You saw a crime. You reported it to me, a police officer. You've done all you can. I'll get some cops to come over there.'

'If you're sure . . .'

'I'm sure. If you stay there, you'll have a lot of explaining to do. Now leave it with me. If I need to speak with you again I'll call you on this number. Is that okay?'

'Yeah. That's fine. I'll . . . I'll go home now.'

'You do that, Gonzo.'

He ends the call. He wants to throw his cellphone through the window, the way Vasey just went through his. Jesus, what an exit.

He has no intention of calling the cops. The people in Vasey's building will see to that. And what would he say, anyhow? How would he explain Gonzo's role in all this? Especially when he's not even sure what goes through that kid's head at the best of times. Who does he think he is? Dick Tracy?

Doyle thinks he could do with someone like Dick Tracy right now. He could have figured this out. He would have known Vasey was next.

I wasn't calling to give you clues. You know why? Because you already have them.

It should have been obvious. He'd uncovered a link between Cindy Mellish and Sean Hanrahan, and he'd assumed it was a pointer to their killer. Only he was wrong. Sure, the link was there, all right. But it wasn't telling him anything about the murderer.

It was telling him who the next victim would be.

The link was the clue. And a bigger fucking clue you couldn't ask for. Doyle feels as though the caller might just as well have said, 'The next person to die will be Andrew Vasey,' and still he would have missed it. He feels that stupid.

Something else occurs to Doyle. He looks at his watch . . .

And laughs out loud.

The timing of the murder. He missed that, too, didn't he?

When Doyle delivered his tirade over the phone, and the guy responded with 'Ten-four, Detective.'

Ten-four.

Which can be cop-speak for 'message received'.

But which can equally mean four minutes past ten. The time Vasey was killed.

So he'd been told who, and he'd been told when. What more could he have asked for?

Stupid, stupid, stupid.

And just how clever is this bastard, that he can assure you he is giving you no clues when in fact he's giving out every fucking clue under the sun?

There's a severe mismatch of intelligence here, Doyle thinks.

It doesn't bode well.

FIFTEEN

'So let me get this straight . . .' says Cesario.

Doyle and Holden sit opposite the Lieutenant in his office. This is their first task of the day: to bring the boss up to speed without causing him to wet his pants over what a nightmare this is becoming.

'Both the Mellish girl and Hanrahan go to see Vasey as patients—'

'Clients,' says Doyle.

'Whatever,' says Cesario, giving Doyle a withering look. 'They're both connected to the psychologist.'

Yeah, thinks Doyle. They're shrink-linked.

'So you bring him in, he lawyers up, and you get nothing.'

Doyle looks at Holden. Holden looks at Doyle. Doyle feels they should have something to add. That word 'nothing' seems a little harsh. It sounds less than the emptiness it represents. In fact it resounds with negativity. Only he's not sure how to nudge it over the line and into the positive zone.

Cesario continues his narrative: 'And then Vasey gets whacked. Does that about sum it up?'

Doyle would have phrased it differently. He thinks it's like summarizing the movie *Jaws* as *Fish attacks bathers, sheriff kills fish.* Where's the fine detail? Where's the emotion? Where's the stuff that makes it interesting? But he shrugs nonetheless. Says, 'I guess.'

Cesario sits in silence for a while, then says, 'So where are you going with this, Detectives?'

'We think . . .' Doyle begins, emphasis on the *we*, 'we think these could all be the work of the same perp.'

Cesario sighs. 'See, that's what I thought you were gonna say. I didn't like it when I thought it and I hate it even more now. Do you understand the enormity of what you're asking me to accept?'

Holden says, 'We understand, Lou. But we have to at least consider the possibility.'

'All right, so let's consider it. Go ahead. Convince me.'

Doyle finds the ball rolling back to him again. Thanks, Holden.

'Okay. We have three DOAs, not counting Vasey's doorman, who we'll put down as collateral damage for now. Admittedly, they were all killed in different parts of the city, and with completely different MOs. A multiple stabbing, a shooting and a guy thrown through his window. On that basis alone, I agree, there's nothing there. But toss in the Vasey connection and it changes the whole picture. It's just too much of a coincidence that a shrink and two of his clients should all take hits from separate, completely independent killers. And there's something else they have in common, too.'

'Go on.'

'These murders weren't spur of the moment. There's no obvious motive for any of them. What we do know is that they were planned. These people were targeted. In each case, the killer seemed to befriend them or at least get them to trust him before he whacked them. The bookstore girl let the killer get really close to her, close enough to write a fake number on her arm. Hanrahan and Vasey allowed him into their apartments. Maybe they all knew him, or maybe he's just an excellent con artist. Whatever, to me this sounds like the work of one killer or group of killers.'

Cesario leans back in his chair and puts his arms behind his head, bringing them perilously close to two tall cactus plants flanking him. Just like his predecessor often did, thinks Doyle.

'There's a lotta supposition here, fellas,' says Cesario.

He rocks a little, ponders some more, makes a decision.

'I can't ask the Chief of D's to give us the other cases. Not on what we got so far.'

Doyle is almost out of his seat. 'Lou—'

Cesario raises a warning finger.

'But I want you to look into this. Talk to the precincts working the other cases. Talk to Homicide. You find anything more concrete that ties these DOAs together, then I'll put in that call to the Chief of D's.'

Doyle realizes it's the best they're going to get. He can't blame Cesario. After all, what they're talking about here is a possible serial killer. The task of stopping someone like that is a heavy responsibility for any squad commander to take on.

He sees Cesario reach for a file from his in-tray. He's moving on to his next job. Meaning this discussion is over. Holden starts to rise from his chair.

'Something else,' Doyle says.

Cesario raises his eyes just as Holden lowers himself back onto his seat, like they're on opposite ends of a see-saw.

Doyle says, 'If we're right, and this is a serial killer, what if it's not just these three?'

Both Cesario and Holden stare at him. 'You got somebody else in mind?' Cesario asks.

Doyle hesitates. He wonders, Is this a step too far? Maybe I should quit while I'm ahead.

'Lorna Bonnow,' he says.

'Who?'

'Lorna Bonnow. A DOA up in the Two-Seven. She was rammed by a car.'

'Uh-huh. And you single her out because . . .'

Because the same guy wasted her too. Because he told me so.

'She was also targeted. A guy called her up, told her that her husband needed her. When she got to the street, he took her out. It was clever, it was planned. Just like the others.'

'Anything that connects her with Vasey?'

'Not that I'm aware of.'

'Anything that connects her with Vasey's patients?'

Clients, thinks Doyle. He shakes his head.

'Has the Two-Seven been in touch to say they think this might be the work of a monster terrorizing New York?'

No, not that, although they did wonder why my name cropped up in their investigation.

'No.'

Cesario breathes out heavily through his nose. 'Cal, this is already bigger and badder than I would like. Please don't go roping in every unsolved DOA simply because it doesn't smell right. Work on what you got already. When you've tidied those away, I'll think about letting you loose on the rest of the city's problems. Dinner first, dessert later. Now get out of here.'

They step out of Cesario's office. Holden says, 'Lorna Bonnow? How did she get into this?'

Doyle shrugs. 'I heard about the case. It sounded like it might be the work of our man.'

Holden looks as though he doesn't know whether to laugh or cry. '*It sounded like* . . . Man, you are one seriously fucked-up individual. I am truly starting to regret agreeing to work with you.'

'I could be right, though.'

'Yeah, and maybe he shot JFK too. Maybe he sabotaged

Apollo 13. Hey, maybe he's got green hair and a permanent smile and he's about to blow up Gotham City.'

As Holden walks away, Doyle calls after him, 'Did I ever tell you I was thinking about changing my name to Bruce Wayne?'

When Doyle gets back to his desk, he finds he has a visitor. As he approaches, she affixes a welcoming smile. He could fall for a smile like that. If he were fifty years older.

'Hello, Mrs Sachs. How are you?'

'How am I? I'm alive. At my age, I don't have much else to be grateful for. If this body were a building, it would be condemned as unsafe. Not fit for human habitation. The aches and pains I have, you don't want to know. A young man like you wouldn't understand the purgatory I go through every day. And why should you? You have your whole life before you. Enjoy. Don't worry yourself about poor schmucks like me.'

Doyle smiles. 'The way I see it, you got a lot of mileage to get through yet.'

'Mileage? What I got left you can't measure in feet, let alone miles.'

Doyle laughs. 'So what can I do for you?'

'I saw Mr Repp again yesterday.'

Good, thinks Doyle. That clown finally saw the error of his ways.

'Did he put your mind at rest?'

'Well . . . not exactly.'

Uh-oh, Doyle thinks. What's the idiot done now?

'What did he say to you?'

'He told me that . . . that my Patricia isn't in Chicago.'

Oh. Okay, Travis. So maybe I misjudged you. Maybe you did the decent thing after all.

'No?'

'No. Apparently she's moved to Hawaii.'

I take that back, Travis. You're an asshole.

'Hawaii?'

'Yes. Waikiki.'

'He offer any proof?'

Mrs Sachs reaches for her purse. The same one she brought to their first meeting. The leather one with the silver clasp. Click, it's open. She dips a leathery hand inside. Takes out a photo, just as she did last time.

Doyle looks at the picture. A beach that could be any beach. A woman that could be any woman. But she has a face that presumably belonged to Patricia Sachs.

Doyle asks, 'Do you think it's her?'

'I want it to be her. It looks like her.'

'What does Repp say?'

'He's pretty sure it's Patricia. He says the man who traced her there is good at his job. But he wants to be sure, so he's offered to go out there himself.'

'Which he'll bill you for, I suppose.'

'I have no doubt of that, Detective. But as I said to you before, this isn't about money. It's about my daughter. If he's right, and Patricia is alive . . .'

Mentally, Doyle groans. He wants to take this old woman by her bony shoulders, look her in the eye and say, Mrs Sachs, your daughter is dead. It's tragic, it's upsetting, but it's true. Now cut your ties with Repp and get on with your life.

But that's the problem. Because he's not sure how much life she will have in her once she learns the truth. It's as though there's a current running from daughter to mother: switch off one and maybe the other's lights go out too. Doyle isn't sure he wants that responsibility. And if he's wrong about Repp . . . If, by some slim chance, Repp is not scamming her . . .

'What do you believe, Mrs Sachs? Deep down, what do you think? Do you believe your daughter is alive or not?'

'What I think is that I'm getting too old. My mind, it doesn't function like it used to. It's like it's given up thinking about things that are too hard or too upsetting. Now, it's just willing to believe whatever comes its way. I rely on other people now to tell me what is true and what is false. Tell me, did you go to see Mr Repp?'

'Yes, I met with him.'

'And what did you think? Does he seem reputable to you?'

Doyle's thoughts are that he wouldn't put it past Repp to take the last dime from a blind beggar, but he doesn't say so. He had hoped his little visit to Repp would have been sufficient to scare him back onto the path of the righteous, at least as far as his relationship with Mrs Sachs was concerned.

'I didn't get to know him real well. Tell you what, why don't I go see him again, see if I can offer him a little police help to track down Patricia?'

She smiles again, and this time it looks to Doyle as though her watery eyes are ready to overflow.

'Thank you, Detective. You don't know how much this means to me.'

Doyle wonders how much it will mean to her to discover that her daughter really did suffer a terrible fiery fate in the Twin Towers. He makes a mental note to advise Repp in the strongest terms that he will need to let her down gently – so gently she doesn't shatter.

He helps the old lady out of her chair and sees her out of the squadroom. Before he can retake his seat, his cellphone rings. He looks at the screen. No caller ID. He presses the button to kill the call. Fuck you, he thinks. I ain't playing. This game is over.

It reminds him that there's work to be done on the homicides.

Now that he's got the lieutenant's consent to push ahead, he can investigate properly, unfettered by a need to keep things to himself.

You're mine, you sonofabitch, he thinks. It's only a matter of time.

Not again.

This is starting to get annoying.

Doyle gets to his car, reaches for the door handle, and – surprise! – he's there again. At his side like a faithful dog welcoming home its master.

Just don't start humping my leg, he thinks.

'Gonzo, what the hell are you doing here? Did you spend your whole lunch hour just waiting out here in case I should show?'

Gonzo scratches his head and puts on a pained expression. Like he's just been asked to solve the riddle of the origin of the universe.

'Well, yeah. I needed to speak with you.'

'Why didn't you just call me on my cell?'

'I didn't want to disturb you. You know, while you're working. I know how busy you are. I know how important your cases are. I thought I'd wait until you take a lunch break.'

Doyle sighs. 'Get in the car.'

They both get into what seems to have become Doyle's makeshift private office.

'What is it, Gonzo?'

'I don't know.'

'What do you mean, you don't know? You wait outside my building for an hour, and you don't know why you want to see me?'

'I . . . I just needed to talk.'

'About what?'

'About . . .' He waves his arms wildly, causing Doyle to duck. 'About all this. I'm not used to this kind of thing, you know.'

'You need counseling? Maybe you should go see a shrink.'

Gonzo glares at him. 'That's not funny, Detective Doyle. What I witnessed last night was traumatic. It may have affected my mental stability for the rest of my life.'

You mean, Doyle wonders, it can get quirkier than this?

'What do you want me to say, Gonzo? I didn't ask you to put a constant watch on Vasey. In fact, I don't recall asking you to get involved in this at all. All I wanted was for you to find one lousy thing on a computer. How did that develop into you becoming the city's secret protector?'

'I'm not trying to be a superhero. Or even a cop. I'm just trying to help. I sit over there in 1PP, looking at computer screens day after day. Except for Lonnie and a few of the other guys, I hardly see a soul. And the only reason they talk to me is when they need me to look at a computer. I never go out of the building. When you came in and asked me to look for that diary, I thought here we go again. One more request to add to the pile. But when it became obvious that you had reasons for keeping it under wraps, I thought this was my chance to prove that I'm more than just a brainy guy who knows about computers. That's all. I was just trying to be of assistance.'

'Yeah, well, maybe I've had my fill of people trying to push help on me lately. Maybe it's more trouble than it's worth.'

'How do you mean?'

'Nothing.'

They lapse into silence. Both staring out of the car windows, watching the people walk by.

Doyle's phone rings again. He takes it out of his pocket. No caller ID, so he kills it, scowling as he does so.

He notices that Gonzo is watching him, additional puzzlement on his permanently bewildered features.

Doyle doesn't want to get into it, so he throws out a random thought: 'Why do they call you Gonzo, anyhow?'

The pained expression again.

'I forget.'

'So what's your real name?'

Gonzo thinks some more.

'I forget.'

Doyle can't help himself then. He cracks up. He knows it's probably doing untold damage to this individual's fragile mental state, but the absurdity of it all just keeps hammering the laughter out of him.

And when he looks again at Gonzo, he sees that he too is wearing a smile. At last, a point of agreement. A small meeting of minds which interpret the world in very different ways.

Says Doyle, 'What you saw last night? Try to put it out of your mind. We're working on it. We'll catch whoever did that.'

Gonzo nods, says nothing.

'You want me to drop you off at the Big House?'

'No. Thanks. I'm good.' He opens the car door. 'Do me a favor, will you, Detective? If you ever need a little job doing – I mean, nothing too dangerous or anything – do you think maybe you could consider me?'

'Sure, kid. You'll be top of my list.'

And then Gonzo closes the door and is gone. Back to his lab. Back to his computers. Back to his lonely little existence.

SIXTEEN

The office is as dead as it was last time. Doyle half expects to see tumbleweed rolling by, driven by a whistling wind. He thinks the girl here must get bored out of her skull. Although she seems to have no trouble finding things to keep herself occupied. Her own appearance, mainly. Today she has moved on from her nails and is concentrating on her hair. Maybe tomorrow she'll shave her legs. She looks sidelong into a small mirror set up on her desk while she pecks her fingers at her blond strands, teasing them into order. When she notices Doyle walk in, she shows him how perfect her teeth are.

'Hi,' she says. 'You're that cop guy, right?'

'Yeah, I'm the cop guy. Is your boss in?'

'You gonna throw him in jail?'

'Maybe.'

'Yeah, he's in. Go straight through. He's not expecting you.'

Doyle pushes open the door to the inner office. He sees Repp bent over an open drawer of a file cabinet, muttering to himself as he rifles through its contents. Doyle watches for another few seconds, until Repp pounds angrily on the cabinet and straightens up.

'Hayley, do you have any idea—'

He sees Doyle in the doorway then, and he narrows his eyes. Like he's trying to beam malevolence from his pupils.

'You again.'

'Me again.'

'Do you ever bother to make appointments?'

'Only with gynecologists. They tend to get kinda tetchy when I pop my head unannounced into their business. I thought you'd prefer the surprise. More than two people in this place must come as quite a shock.'

'Ha! Allow me to hold my sides before they bust open. You ain't heard about the recession? Things are bad all round. If there was such a thing as a cop who wasn't on the take, you'd probably notice it too.'

'My heart bleeds, Travis. Doesn't give you an excuse, though.'

'An excuse for what?'

'Scamming old ladies. In particular, Mrs Sachs.'

Repp gives him a long stare, then waves him away. 'Close the door on your way out.' He turns back to his file cabinet and opens the top drawer.

Doyle sighs and ambles over to join Repp.

'We're not done.'

Repp doesn't look at him. He continues to walk his fingers across the file dividers.

'We had this conversation already. Did you forget? Or maybe you caught Alzheimer's from banging old ladies.'

Repp's chuckle pulls a trigger in Doyle's brain, and he slams the file drawer shut before Repp can react. Before he can move a muscle. Or a finger. Such as the one that doesn't manage to escape being sandwiched between two panels of gray steel.

Repp lets out a high-pitched scream. He extracts his hand from the drawer and stares at it with bulging eyes. Spittle flies from his mouth as he yells at Doyle.

'My finger! It's bleeding! What the fuck did you do that for?'

'Sit down, Travis,' Doyle commands. To help him obey, he gives him a hand. Right in the chest. A good hard thrust. Repp stumbles backward. When the backs of his legs connect with his chair, he collapses into it.

Repp continues to protest, his voice still higher than a soprano's. 'You can't do this. You broke my fucking finger. Look at it! It's bleeding. Hayley! Get the fuck in here! Get me some bandages.'

Doyle turns to see Hayley in the doorway, her features contorted with a blend of amusement and astonishment.

'It's okay, Hayley. He's fine. I'll be outta here before he loses more than a pint or two.'

Hilarity wins out. Hayley has to put a hand to her mouth to stifle her laughter, then she disappears.

'Jesus Christ,' says Repp. 'This is my good finger, damnit! I use this finger for everything.'

'Spare me the sordid details,' says Doyle. He perches himself on the edge of Repp's desk, looming over him. 'Now, where were we? Oh, yeah – Mrs Sachs.'

'You can't do this. I'm gonna report you. Your badge is gone, mister.'

Doyle picks up a glass globe paperweight from Repp's desk and hefts it in his hand. Repp eyes him warily.

'Stop being a wuss, Travis, and talk to me. You know as well as I do that you're in deep shit here. This thing with Mrs Sachs stops now, understand?'

'No, actually. Why don't you explain it to me?'

'You're fleecing her. Your two-bit operation is falling down around your ears and you're fleecing a little old lady to make some cash. You know how despicable that is, Travis? How do you even live with yourself?'

Repp puts his finger in his mouth to suck away the blood,

then takes it out again and stares fearfully at it like it's a fatal wound.

'You're talking outta your ass. I never made any guarantees to her about her daughter. The only thing I did was put some doubt in her mind. If she doesn't want me to follow it up, she's free to tell me so.'

'Just a little doubt, huh? What about the photos?'

'What about them? They were sent over by a guy who does occasional jobs for me. We think it could be the daughter. Again, no guarantees.'

'So you won't mind if I talk to this wonderful guy you can afford to employ in this economic recession you keep reminding me about? Get his side of the story?'

'Sure. If you can find him. Last I heard he'd decided to vacation in Honolulu while he's in that neck of the woods.'

'Uh-huh. And what about Pinter?'

Repp tears his gaze away from his gashed finger and furrows his brow. 'Who?'

'Now who's the one with the memory of a goldfish? Pinter. Works for Invar Insurance? Said he saw Patricia Sachs at the Port Authority Terminal?'

'Oh! Oh, him, yeah. That was two years ago. I haven't heard from him since then. I don't think he even works for Invar anymore.'

'That's real convenient, Travis. So what this all amounts to is a couple of crappy photographs and your word, with anyone who can back it up currently unavailable for comment. That's what you have, right? That's what you think is good enough for Mrs Sachs to send you on a holiday to Hawaii?'

'I don't think anything. That's for Mrs Sachs to decide. Like I say, if she wants out, that's fine with me.' He sucks his finger again. 'You know, I think this is gonna need stitches. I'll probably need a tetanus jab too. I should sue your ass.'

Doyle shakes his head in disgust. 'How many others are there, Travis?'

Repp smiles. 'Nine. I got nine other fingers.'

Doyle slams the paperweight down on the desk, causing Repp to jump in his chair. 'Not for much longer, Travis. I'll ask you again. How many others are there like Mrs Sachs? How many schemes like this you got going?'

'All right, you got me. Thirty-seven. Last week I sold the Brooklyn Bridge to a Texan billionaire who's looking for a new water feature in his backyard. I mean, Jesus, what kind of answer do you expect from me? I'm legit, get it? Maybe I'm not rich or successful, but at least I can sleep at night. Can you? Is everything you do so lily-white that you don't hate yourself sometimes?'

Doyle doesn't want to answer that. Doesn't even want to think about it. He tells himself that this isn't about him. It's about Repp. And everything about Repp and his setup tells Doyle that this is a con. Mrs Sachs is being given false hope, with the added indignity of having to pay handsomely for the privilege.

But he can't prove it. Not without an extensive and costly investigation into Repp's background and practices. His squad isn't going to be interested, not when a bunch of serial murders has just landed on its lap, thank you very much, Detective Doyle. And the District Attorney's office and the judges he would need to approach for warrants are just going to tell him to act his age. All he can do for the moment is hope that his strong-arm tactics are enough to make Repp think twice about continuing with his foolhardy scheme.

Doyle gets up from the desk. 'Don't pack that grass skirt just yet, Travis. Think about what you're doing to that poor lady. Try imagining she's your own grandmother.'

'My grandmother is dead. And when she was alive she was a bitch.'

'Okay, so picture her coming back to haunt you. Either way, I want you out of Mrs Sachs's life, and especially out of her wallet.'

Doyle moves to the door. 'Next time, it won't be your finger in that drawer. It'll be a much smaller part of your anatomy. Take it easy, Travis.'

As he walks through the outer office, he winks at Hayley and she goes all coy and giggly.

What I take from one I give to another, thinks Doyle. It's nice to keep things in balance.

'Which would you rather be – a clown or a fish?'

'What?'

'A clown or a fish? Which one would you rather be? If you could only be one.'

Doyle considers the question with the seriousness it surely deserves. Such matters cannot be regarded lightly.

'Okay, well I think probably a clown. Because then I could take off my outfit and make-up and become a normal person.'

Amy shakes her head vigorously. 'No. You can't do that. Whatever one you choose, you have to stay like that, for the rest of your life.'

'Oh. Well, that's different. A clown or a fish?'

'Yes.'

'What about a clownfish?'

'A what?'

'A clownfish. You know, like Nemo.'

'Oh, okay. But that's still just a fish. Is that what you want to be?'

'Yes. A fish. Because clowns are scary, and I wouldn't want to scare you.'

Amy beams at him. 'That's a very good answer, and so you can have a prize.'

'A prize? For me?'

'Yes.'

She reaches for a tin box on her nightstand. She calls it her Shiny Box. Anything shiny, glittery or of perceived worth in a child-centered value scheme goes in here. The hinges creak as she lifts the lid and takes something out. She hands it to Doyle. A button. It has 'Captain Awesome' written on it in lightning-yellow letters on a pale-blue background.

'Why, thank you, Amy.' He pins it onto his shirt. 'Now I really feel important.'

'Good. You can borrow it for one week.'

A whole week. Doyle feels supremely honored.

He tucks Amy into her bed, kisses her goodnight, then goes into the living room. Rachel is there, languishing on the sofa and watching an old movie. Black and white, with lots of clipped British accents. *Brief Encounter*, maybe.

Rachel glances up at him as he enters. 'What's that?' she asks, gesturing to the same point on her own chest.

'I got a promotion. I made captain.'

'Does that mean I have to salute you now?'

'Absolutely. And you have to do everything I say, at all times.'

'Pah! In your dreams, mister.'

She turns back to the television. Doyle stands behind the sofa, watching it with her.

'Is this gonna make you cry?'

'Probably.' She points down to a cardboard box on the rug. 'I have tissues at the ready, just in case. You want to join me?'

'Does it have any car chases?'

'No.'

'Any gunfights? Explosions? Martial arts? Babes in bikinis?'

'No to all the above. Stop trying to be so stereotypically male. You know you like a good cry as much as the next woman.'

'I do not.'

'No? What about *ET*?'

'That's an exception.'

'Uh-huh? And I suppose *Free Willy* is an exception too. And that movie where all the people come out of comas.'

'*Awakenings*. All right, enough already. I admit I'm in touch with my feminine side. There, I've said it.'

He regrets it when he sees the look of amusement on her face.

'My God, Cal. Next you'll be telling me you like musicals too. Is this just the tip of the iceberg? Are you wearing my underwear?'

'Hey, I can still be tough too. You should've seen me today.'

'Why? What'd you do? Claw someone's eyes out? Pull their hair?'

'Ha! Very funny. You mind stopping with the insults now? I went to see that private investigator. You know, the one who's conning old Mrs Sachs?'

'Is he still doing that to that poor woman? I hope you smashed his kneecaps, that bastard.'

Doyle stares at her. He was about to tell her how he got his message across to Repp, but saying that he made the man's finger bleed doesn't seem to match the level of vengeance that Rachel expects.

Their conversation is interrupted by the chirrup of Doyle's cellphone. He checks the screen, sees that there is no caller ID. Kills the call.

'Who was that?' asks Rachel.

'Nobody.'

She gives him a searching look that feels to him as though it's penetrating his skull and tearing its way through his mental database.

'By *nobody* I guess you mean *somebody*, but somebody you don't want me to know about.'

'I . . . no. That is, it's not that I'm keeping it from you, it's just that it's not a call I want to take. And I don't just mean now, because you're here. I mean *ever*.'

He can see the questions scrolling across her eyes. Like a Las Vegas slot machine. Which one will come to rest there first?

She says, 'That has to be one of the biggest loads of garbage I've ever heard you speak.' She pats the seat next to her on the sofa. 'Come here, Cal. Sit down.'

He doesn't want this discussion, and it's like he's walking through treacle as he comes around the sofa and then lowers himself onto it. He feels like a kid who knows he's about to get that birds and bees lecture.

She grasps his hand in hers, but it's some time before she speaks. The earlier levity has become a fading memory.

'Cal, what's going on? You haven't been yourself for days. All these phone calls you don't want me to hear, it's driving me crazy.'

He stares into her eyes, not knowing what to say. Feeling that he wants to tell her everything, but not wanting to put her in that uncomfortable position. And the longer he sits there in silence, the more he senses her distress building.

It is left to her to break into that silence, and when she does there is a tremor to her voice and a pooling of water in her eyes that threatens to overflow and cascade down her face.

'I just want you to tell me that . . . I need to know that . . .'

He studies her face, trying to read her. Trying to finish her sentence for her.

And then it hits him. He understands. And he hates the fact that he can understand. It shouldn't be able to enter his mind. Shouldn't be able to sneak into Rachel's head either. Their relationship should be stable enough to fend it off.

But there it is, and all because of what happened with Laura Marino, his ex-partner. Or rather, the thing that didn't happen with Laura Marino but which seems to have established its own poisonous existence in their past.

He clasps Rachel's face in his hands. 'Rachel, listen to me. I know what you're thinking, and you're wrong. This has nothing to do with another woman.'

She sniffs. 'I . . . I wasn't trying to say . . .'

'It's okay, really. I understand. I've been acting kinda weird and you've been looking for explanations. But it's not a woman, okay? You've been watching too many of these old movies.'

She nods. 'All right. So what then?'

He chews on the inside of his cheek. What to tell her? He should just come clean, he thinks. Let her know exactly what's been going on. She's his wife. The woman he loves. She'll understand.

'There's stuff I haven't been able to tell you. Something going on. Nobody knows. If I tell you, you have to promise not to tell anyone else.'

He watches her as she mulls it over. He can tell she's not certain she wants to hear it.

'I promise. What is it?'

'You know that murder they brought me in on the other day?'

'The bookstore girl? What about it?'

'Turns out she's not the only one. Did you hear about the cop shot in his apartment the other night? And then the psychologist being thrown out of his apartment window? They're connected. We got a serial killer on our hands, Rach.'

'Oh my God. A serial killer? How do you know? No, wait, don't answer that. I'm asking too many questions, I know. But, well, Jesus. A serial killer?'

'Uh-huh. This isn't common knowledge, Rach. You mustn't tell anyone. It could hurt our chances of catching this guy.'

'No, I swear.' She wipes her eyes, drying them off. 'And there was me thinking it was another woman. Christ, was I way off the mark. I'm sorry, Cal.'

She pulls him into her embrace. And while he hugs her he tells himself, You don't deserve this hug. You don't deserve this woman. So, okay, you told her about the killer. But the phone calls? Your little helper friend? When did that creep into the conversation? Where was all that in your little confession?

Shame on you, Callum Doyle.

His ears should be burning.

The man who has just been the subject of discussion in the Doyle household is troubled.

He is in his living room, sitting bolt upright on a wooden chair, staring at the staircase. He does this each night, building himself up to the task ahead. It's the reason he chooses a straight-backed wooden chair. Because it's not very comfortable and he can't sit here too long. His lower back will begin to ache, even though he was told that such chairs are supposed to be good for his posture. The pain will gnaw at him and it will gradually build and then he will have to stand up, and that will prompt him to carry out his task.

He hates having to do this, but he knows it's necessary. It can't be left. Not even a day. It wouldn't be right.

So do it, goddamnit!

He pushes himself off the chair. Orders himself not to think about things as he marches upstairs, toward the bedroom door. It's okay, he tells himself. It's fine. You've done this a million times. Just do it and get it over with.

He turns the doorknob and urges himself inside, snapping on the light before dark shapes can take on unwanted forms before his eyes.

He stands in the doorway, panting. His heart batters against his ribcage.

It's okay. All okay. You can relax.

It's a small room. Not much to see. A desk. A dresser. A closet.

And the bed, of course.

He steps across the room and stands at the side of the bed. He looks it up and down and he remembers.

The bed is empty now, but in his mind it is occupied. He is reminded of why he decided to help others. It's a calling. There are people suffering out there, and they need him. Who else is going to do it?

He sets to work. He strips off the covers and the sheets and the pillowcases and piles them on the floor. Then he goes over to the closet and opens it and takes a fresh set of bed linen down from one of the shelves. He returns to the bed and makes it up again. He does this slowly, methodically and with great care. Edges tucked in neatly and tightly. All creases smoothed out. He walks around the bed, checking and rechecking his handiwork. And when he is finally able to tear himself away, he picks up the old bed things and carries them out to the bathroom and dumps them in a laundry hamper.

Tomorrow he will have to do it all over again. It's never easy. Sometimes the stress of trying to get it right is unbearable. He can be in there for hours on some nights. It's the price you pay when you care about people so much.

But tonight, at least, it's done.

And yet his unease continues.

He goes back downstairs and tries to treat himself to a more comfortable chair in front of the television. It normally does the trick. He gets lost in a program and he feels his tension slowly dissipate to the point where he feels relaxed enough to go to bed. His own bed. Not the one in that room.

But tonight there is no respite. Something niggles. He can't concentrate on the television, and that means he won't sleep and tomorrow he'll be grouchy as hell. And that's not right. It's not fair. Not when you're doing your best to help people.

He knows what the problem is. His mind keeps showing him images to remind him. Keeps stabbing a pointy little finger into his consciousness. *Look at this*, it says. *What are you going to do about it?*

It's the nerdy looking guy. The one with the red hair and the glasses.

He was there outside Vasey's apartment building, staring up at the broken window and talking to someone on his phone.

It should have meant nothing. The geek should have been just a passer-by. Someone who was just getting in or out of his car who heard a noise and happened to look up.

He would have been happy with that explanation. It would not have taken a shoehorn to fit an occurrence like that into his picture of what took place.

Except for one thing. Something that happened on the previous night.

Before helping out that drunk of a police sergeant, the killer had driven over to Vasey's place. He wanted to finalize his plans. Work out precisely how he was going to help Vasey.

He'd parked up on Sixty-first Street and sat there for a while, staring up at the building. All was well until, just yards ahead of him, he noticed the driver of another car was doing exactly the same thing. Craning his neck to look up at the building. At one point the guy got out of his car and stretched his arms.

He had red hair and glasses.

It was the same guy.

And this is what has him worried. What was the geek doing there, not once but twice? Why did he feel it necessary to watch Vasey's apartment?

The guy doesn't look remotely like a cop, but could he be one? Could the police be onto him so soon?

It's a thought that makes him shudder. He won't sleep tonight, and it's all the fault of that four-eyed fuckwit. Doesn't the prick know that there are people who are desperate for help out there?

Perhaps not. But that's not the point. Nothing must be allowed to obstruct the mission.

What makes it hard is that such people aren't in need of his help. But if they're in the way, they have to be removed. He's already proved to himself that he's capable of doing that, with the doorman at Vasey's building.

And if he could do it once, he can do it again.

SEVENTEEN

It's Friday evening. Doyle's last conversation with his helper was on Tuesday evening. Vasey was killed on Tuesday night.

That's three whole days. Of nothing.

Nothing doesn't just mean lack of progress on the investigation. It also means no murders. Not a single person murdered in this city in the past three days – whether explicable or not.

Nothing further on the calls to his cellphone either. They've stopped. Dead.

To Doyle it's almost as though his refusal to take the helper's calls has brought the killing spree to an end. As if the killer needs to feed off his little chats with Doyle in order to have the fuel to carry out his mission.

He knows it can't be that simple. The killer must be up to something. More murders will take place. He can feel it deep in his bones.

It's not a comforting sensation.

It's like knowing there's a massive spider hidden in the room with you, just waiting to jump out when you least expect it.

His guess is that the swarthy bastard behind the counter isn't genuinely Italian.

Italian-American, perhaps. He'd give him that much. A Mediterranean set of genes there somewhere, no doubt. But severely diluted over several generations. Long enough for him to have lost that accent which sounds so affected it's laughable.

The name, too, has to be fake. Peppe. Clearly he has adopted that moniker purely for the alliteration it lends to the name of this dump. *Peppe's Pizza Piazza*. A nice ring to it, sure, but a tad convenient, wouldn't you say? But then the owner's real name is probably something like Timothy, which wouldn't quite conjure up the same romantic imagery of a moonlit dinner over-looking canals with gondolas and bullet-riddled mafia victims floating by.

He's willing to bet that the guy lays claim to a stupid surname too, again for the effect. Roni, perhaps. *Ciao. My name is-a Peppe Roni. Come in and-a taste-a my spicy sausage.*

And a piazza? Hardly. San Marco in Venice is a piazza. Navona in Rome is a piazza. This is more of a . . . well, a *room*, basically. Even the use of the word 'restaurant', which also ap-pears on the signage outside, is kind of stretching the definition to breaking point. Sure, there are a few small tables and some chairs here, but you'd hardly want to spend more than the time it takes to wolf down a few slices in these surroundings. Peppe and the other pseudo-Italian who works here are probably wondering why their only sit-in customer is spending so much time over his meal.

If only they knew.

The pizza must be damn good, though. It's clearly what keeps this place going. Say what you like about the ambience, there's a steady stream of people coming in for take-out orders. They might not be willing to sit here for long, but they obviously crave the product.

He's not really in a position to judge the quality of the pizza here. He decided long ago that he couldn't really class himself as a pizza person, despite the alliteration. He would much prefer a steak, medium rare, or perhaps some nice sea bass. Throw in a bottle of Chianti or Chardonnay and mood-enhancing music and lighting – heaven! Company or no.

And so his acquaintances – he can hardly call them friends – would puzzle over why he is now sitting in front of a fourteen-inch pie, heaped high with all kinds of meat toppings.

If only they knew.

He's had one slice. It was bearable, but it took him ten minutes to get through it. But then he's not very hungry. He never is when there's work to be done.

He takes a sip from his glass of San Pellegrino and looks around. The man who calls himself Peppe (ha!) is handing change to a woman who, judging from her planetary-scale girth and acne-peppered complexion, eats nothing but junk food. He watches as she waddles out of the building, and then he catches Peppe's eye.

Peppe points across to his table. 'Is-a good?'

In response, he smiles and raises his hand, the index finger and thumb joined together in a circle to signify approval. As he does so, it occurs to him that perhaps the gesture signifies something different in Italy. Like maybe, *Suck my dick*. Not that this guy would know, impostor that he is.

He checks his watch. Seven p.m. precisely. Should be any-time . . .

A phone rings.

. . . now.

The phone is on the wall behind the counter, next to the cash register. Peppe plucks at the receiver and brings it to his ear with a flourish.

'Good-a evening. Peppe's Pizzas.'

Peppe listens for a moment, and then: 'Ah, Miss Peyton. How are-a you this evening? . . . The usual? . . . Very good. And the time? Is it at eight o'clock? . . . *Excellente*. We will-a see you then. Good-a-bye.'

Seated at his table, the man listens to all this and feels his heart rate accelerating with each word. He watches Peppe disappear behind the scenes to pass on the order, and presumes that he is doing so to avoid having to reveal his lack of mastery of the Italian language.

He finds that his mouth is suddenly dry, and he takes a gulp of his mineral water. Feels the fizz of the bubbles in his gullet.

He waits for Peppe to saunter back into the room, then waves for his attention.

'Excuse me. Could you box this up for me, please? I have to go now, but I really want to finish this later. Would that be okay?'

'Sure. Is-a no problem.'

He watches while Peppe clears the table and transfers the remaining slices into one of their branded cardboard boxes. He knows what's going through his head. Peppe is wondering how anyone could take so long to eat just one slice, as if he detests the stuff, and then want to take the rest of it home, stone cold.

If only he knew.

A smile on his face, the killer pays his tab and leaves, carrying the pizza carton before him like he's one of the wise men bearing gifts. As he goes through the door, he glances at his watch again. Ten after seven. Just as he planned.

Excellente.

For Tabitha Peyton, Friday night is usually pizza night. Usually, but not always. Hence the waiting around in Peppe's. He had to be sure. But the visit also provided him with his credentials for the next step of his mission.

He heads to his car first, parked up a block along from the pizza house here on Allen Street. He opens the trunk and takes out the other items he needs if he's to be convincing. A motorcycle helmet and a leather biker's jacket. He swaps his own jacket for the leather. Doesn't exactly make him a Hell's Angel, but it ought to be enough.

He locks up the car, dodges through the two-way traffic, then walks around the block onto Orchard Street. He stops at a five-story tenement opposite the Blue Moon, once a similar tenement until it had another three stories grafted on top when it was converted into a boutique hotel. He climbs the steep set of steps to the front entrance, then finds the buzzer labeled 'T. Peyton'. He smiles to himself. Nine times out of ten, if they put just an initial with no indication of gender, you just know it's going to be a single woman. He thumbs the buzzer and waits.

'Hello?'

'Pizza delivery.'

A pause. Then: 'Mikey?'

'No. This is Pete. I'm the new guy. You ordered a pizza, right?'

'Yeah, but you're too early. The order was for eight o'clock.'

'Eight o'clock? Oh crap. I am so gonna get it for this. Yours is the second one I got wrong tonight. My ass is fried. Sorry to bother you, miss. We'll bring the order at eight, like you asked. Looks like it's not gonna be from me, unfortunately, but you'll get it on time. Really sorry about that.'

That's it, he thinks. Lay it on thick.

'Wait!' she says, and he knows he's got her. 'I guess it won't hurt to eat a little early. Bring it on up.'

He hears the buzz and the click of the lock opening. He's in.

He takes the stairs up to the third floor, then raps on the door to her apartment. She opens it in an instant.

She's wearing a powder-blue bathrobe, belted tightly at her waist. She has removed her make-up. From somewhere behind her he hears the sound of running water.

He expects a look of mild annoyance, and he gets it. But he

also expects that it will quickly evaporate, and he gets that too. This tall handsome biker giving her his most disarming smile is causing her practically to melt into a puddle on the floor.

He says, 'Thanks for agreeing to take this now. It's really kind of you. To be honest, I don't think I'm much good at this job. I feel like I'm really in over my head, you know?'

She opens the door wider now. It's amazing how much a girl can allow her hormones to override her instinct for self-preservation.

'No problem,' she says. 'I know what it's like to be out of my depth.'

He almost laughs. You do, huh?

She continues: 'Here, let me take that off you.'

She grabs the box, then carries it into the apartment, leaving the door gaping, her back unprotected. What the hell does she think she's doing? Doesn't she know how dangerous this city can be?

She puts the pizza down on the kitchen counter, then comes back with a fistful of cash. She passes it to him. Says, 'Keep the change.'

'No way. The way I screwed this up, I should be paying you.'

'No, seriously. Keep it. Buy a beer or something.'

'Well, only if you're sure. I could do with some parts for my Harley, so it all helps.'

He waits for her eyes to widen, and is not disappointed. Suspects that he could soon have the space between her legs widening too if such was his aim.

'You have a Harley?'

He nods. 'Two, actually. Not tonight, though. I have to ride the piece-of-shit lawn mower that Peppe provides. Makes me feel such a dork. If my friends saw me on that . . .'

'I used to have a Harley.'

'Get out of here. Really?'

'Really. A 2002 Sportster.'

'That's the same as mine. Which engine? The 1200?'

'Nah, just the 883.'

'Still, that's pretty cool. You got any pictures of it?'

He sees her waver, but only for a second.

'Sure. Come on in.'

He stays put. He wants her to feel that she's making all the moves here. She has no idea he's pulling all the strings.

'No,' he says. 'That's okay. I should get back to Peppe's.'

'Come on. Two minutes, okay?'

He shrugs, walks on in. Casually closes the door behind him. Just the two of them, alone in this apartment. So fucking easy.

'Be right back,' she says. She skips off to the bedroom. When she comes back he notices that she has loosened her robe, that it is patently lower in the neckline. And when she stands next to him and holds out the picture of her pathetic hunk of shiny metal, he knows that she's doing so in such a way that he can see right down her cleavage.

'Beautiful,' he says, because that's clearly what she's hoping for: a compliment that is ambiguous enough to apply either to her or her stupid bike. He wonders if he could have been even more daring – something about massive twin carbs maybe – but he has no idea whether motorcycles even have twin carbs, let alone whether it is meaningful to talk about their size. He has limited his research strictly to what he needs to achieve his aims.

'Hell of a ride,' she says, and he realizes she's continuing the game. Leaving it to him to decide whether it's the bike or her that'll give him the biggest throb between the legs.

He shifts his gaze from the photo and sees that she is looking straight at him. Guesses that she has in fact been watching him throughout to see where his eyes rove. Right now her own eyes are wide with anticipation and excitement. She is loving this game. Getting off on the subtle foreplay.

'Can I ask you something?' he says.

She smiles knowingly. Even though she knows shit.

'Sure. What is it?'

'Are we in danger of getting a little moist here?'

Her mouth drops a little. Like she can hardly believe her ears. The nerve of this guy! The sheer temerity!

But he knows he hasn't overstepped the mark. Far as she's concerned he's just upped the stakes. Made the game even more electrifying.

'Excuse me?' she says, because she has to. Because she needs to appear to be the shocked prim virgin instead of the oily slut she really is.

'Is there a bath or something being filled back there?'

There you go, he thinks. You want *double entendre*? Beat that one.

'Huh?' she answers, her meager brain not coping well with the sudden context switch. 'Oh, yeah.' And then: 'Oh, shit!'

She races for the bathroom. He doesn't wait for an invitation to follow. The bathroom is where this was always destined to play out. And Tabitha has acted her part to perfection.

He watches her fight with the faucets. He can't see where the water level is, but a mound of foam is already several inches above the rim of the bathtub. When she finally shuts off the water and turns around, she jumps when she sees him standing in the door-way, holding the pizza box.

For the first time, he's not sure how she'll react. Is she thinking, 'Whoa, fella! Who said you could come in here?' Or is this fulfilling her most outrageous porn fantasy? The one where the handsome biker drops in on the frustrated and helpless single woman and offers to tune up her sump with his crankshaft, or whatever the hell the terminology is.

Frankly, he no longer gives a shit. The game has become tiresome. It's time to bring it to its inevitable conclusion.

'You want some of this pizza? It's cold, and there's a slice missing, but you're welcome to have some. Personally, I think it tastes like vomit.'

She tries a smile, then seems to realize it doesn't fit the circumstances and drops it again.

'I think you should go now,' she says.

He hears her nervousness. Sees her discomfort.

'You don't want me to go. You've been waiting for this for a long time.'

She folds her arms. Trying to appear strong, decisive. But he sees only her admission of vulnerability.

'Forget it, fella. Whatever you think this is, you got it wrong.' She snaps an arm out, aiming her finger toward the apartment door. 'Out!'

He doesn't budge. Of course not.

'I can't. Not before I give you what you need. I have to help you.'

He sees the confusion on her face, but he understands. Her prayers for aid have remained unanswered for so long that she finds it almost beyond belief that they have finally been answered. It must be such an assault on one's perception of how the universe works.

'I don't need your help.'

He gives her what he believes to be a beatific smile. 'You need help. You just didn't expect it to come now, and from someone delivering pizzas.' He laughs. 'But don't be fooled by appearances. Help is finally here. All you have to do is accept it.'

Her eyes dart, and he realizes she isn't going to take his

advice. Sadness overwhelms him. She is so fucked up, she is incapable of appreciating the significance of this moment.

'That's it,' she says. 'I want you the fuck out of here. Now!'

He stands his ground. Maintains his smile of serenity.

She storms toward him. 'Get the fuck out of my way.'

He sidesteps a little, creating an opening in the doorway she can squeeze through. He waits for her to increase her pace toward the escape route he has just made for her. Waits for her to come almost level with him . . .

His left hand leaves the pizza box. He brings it upwards at great speed, his palm open. He drives the V-shape formed between his thumb and his index finger hard into her throat.

She staggers back, clutching at her neck. She opens her mouth and makes sounds like a cat with a furball as she sticks out her tongue and gasps for air.

Sorry, Tabitha, he thinks. No air today.

He drops the box and closes the gap. Puts a hand to her face. Forces her backwards. Her legs connect with the edge of the bathtub and over she goes. There is a massive splash as she plunges into the water, and a huge foamy wave rolls over the sides of the tub and onto the floor.

He thrusts his hands into the water. Finds her shoulders and leans on them. But she fights him, and she is much stronger than he expected. She draws on those reserves of *in extremis* strength that only those who are fighting death itself can tap. It surprises him that she actually manages to raise her face above the suds and push her legs and buttocks over the rim of the tub. He grunts as he applies more force to her shoulders, driving her under again.

Her legs still protrude from the water. They kick wildly and with force. Her robe comes open, exposing her nakedness. Her arms flail. He has to hold his face away from those clawing fingers. Her hands scrabble for purchase, but all they find is the smoothness of the wall tiles. Her nails break as they catch on the grouting.

She takes an age to die.

When he is certain she has gone, he removes his arms from the water. Rivers gush from both sleeves of his leather jacket. He looks down at himself and sees that he is sopping wet. In hindsight, he thinks maybe this wasn't the best way to do things.

He grabs two white fluffy towels from the rail and spends a few minutes drying himself off. He knows he cannot hang around much longer because the real pizza delivery guy will be arriving soon.

He takes one last look at his handiwork. Tabitha's naked lower half still hangs over the edge of the tub, the rest of her buried beneath the bubbles.

He tried to tell her why he'd come here. *I'm really in over my head*, is what he said. But what was really ironic was the way she came back with an even better line: *I know what it's like to be out of my depth*. Priceless!

He picks up his motorcycle helmet and pizza box and heads for the apartment door. His shoes squelch with each uncomfortable step.

Great, he thinks. You try to help someone, and this is what you get.

Some people are so damned ungrateful.

EIGHTEEN

'Nice position,' says Kravitz.

'Nice,' says Folger.

The two Homicide detectives are staring thoughtfully at the visible half of the murder victim, draped over the edge of the bathtub. Around them, other cops and techs swarm like ants – busy, busy, busy. But Kravitz and Folger manage to rise above it all. They see their roles here as ones of authority. They need to be seen as calm and in control. The fulcrum of all the activity, if you will. Or the hub. Or the linchpin. In any case, the bit that doesn't waste energy flapping around like the lesser mortals here.

'I don't think I ever saw a DOA in this particular position before,' says Kravitz.

'Me either. Certainly draws the eye, don't it?'

'That it does. Quite the focal point. I'm thinking of suggesting it to my wife.'

'You are?'

'Certainly. For one thing, the height is exactly right.'

As he says this, Kravitz puts his hands out in front of him, as if imagining holding onto his wife's hips, and gently pulsates his groin. In and out. In and out.

'Yeah, the height,' says Folger with obvious distaste, since any use of the word in his presence tends to be pejorative. His own contribution to the pleasure of any woman in the position now under discussion would have to be strictly oral, unless he brought a stepladder.

'And the angle is perfect. Both for me and for her.'

'For your wife too?'

'Absolutely. She's suffered from lower back pain for years. I think this would do her the world of good. Much better than those balls she keeps rolling around the house on.'

'Your wife rolls around the house on balls?'

'Well, ball, singular. You know, one of those big-ass balloon things for exercises? I'm convinced that regular adoption of the bath-based posture being demonstrated for us by this young lady here would be much more beneficial than any amount of ball-supported locomotion.'

Folger nods with enthusiasm. 'Plus,' he says, perhaps too hastily, 'you wouldn't have to look at her face.'

Kravitz turns a stony glare on his shorter compatriot.

'What are you saying about my wife?'

Only then does Folger seem to realize what he has just said. 'Uhm, I have a thing about people looking at me while I'm doing it.'

'An audience, you mean?'

'No. I mean the female. I don't like to make eye contact. I find it puts me off my stride. For you I'm sure it's not a problem. Especially with someone as attractive as your wife.'

Kravitz maintains his stare for a while, as if unsure whether to take offense.

'You should talk to somebody about that problem. Some women, they like to see what's going on when they're in the sack. Could be the reason your relationships are always so short.'

Folger merely nods, even though he resents the return insult. Resents, too, the word 'short' being thrown at him like that.

Standing a few feet behind the two Homicide dicks, Doyle

tries to avoid being distracted by their inane drivel. He watches while Norman Chin, the Medical Examiner, performs some initial scrutiny, directs the taking of numerous photographs from various angles, and supervises the extraction of the body from its watery grave. Then he concentrates on what Chin has to say about the victim.

He listens to Chin's description of the injury to the girl's throat, the pressure marks on her shoulders, her broken nails and the scratches in the tile grouting, the bloodstained frothing in her nasal passages and in her mouth. He listens to the academic asides on oxygen deprivation, hemodilution, body chemistry disruption, diatoms, and cadaveric spasm. And he listens to Chin's tentative conclusion – *wait for the damn autopsy, goddamnit* – that death was due to forcible drowning caused by an assailant or assailants unknown. In short, ladies and gentlemen, what we have here is a murder case. Who would have guessed?

But it's not just any old run-of-the-mill murder case, is it now? Oh, no.

'Well, look who it is,' says Folger, spotting Doyle behind him. 'Thank Christ for that. We can all go home now. The case is solved.'

'How do you figure that?' says Kravitz.

'Didn't you hear? Doyle here has a theory that all homicides recently committed in this city are connected. They've all been carried out by the same killer. Whatever the precinct, whatever the MO, it don't matter. Same guy every time.'

'Is that so? Kinda like a unified field theory, huh?'

Folger looks puzzled. 'Uh, yeah.'

'Well that certainly makes our job easier. What do you think, Doyle? Is this another victim we can chalk up to your Mysterious Manhattan Murderer?'

Actually, yes, is what Doyle wants to answer. That's precisely what he thinks. He could be wrong, and he hopes he is. But what worries him about this scene is that there is no sign of forced entry to the apartment. Which suggests either that the victim knew her killer, or else she was somehow tricked into allowing him into her apartment. And lulling his victims into a false sense of security before he strikes is the thing at which Doyle's oh-so-helpful enemy excels.

Except that this time he wasn't helpful, was he? No phone calls for Doyle to reject. No phone number on the victim's arms. No pretending to be Doyle in a call to the victim. Nothing.

Not that Doyle wants any of that. He's glad to be out of it. He wanted a conventional murder case and now he's got it. He should be celebrating. He should be running around this corpse, singing and clapping.

But he's not. And he knows why. It's because a part of him is saying, Maybe you could have prevented this. If you hadn't slammed the door on your only source of information, maybe you could have listened to the clues and interpreted them correctly for once and prevented the death of this pretty young girl. For the others, the clues were there every time. You just didn't know how to read them. And now people are still dying and you have no clues at all. Is that really what you wanted?

He has no answer. He is being pulled in opposite directions simultaneously. To listen to the helper or to ignore him. He has to decide, because right now it's tearing him apart.

'Who found the body?' he asks Kravitz, ducking the homicide detective's question.

Kravitz gives him a long look, and Doyle wonders whether the man is going to give him a hard time. He is mildly surprised when he gets a straight answer.

'Roomie. Even better-looking than this one. She's in quite a state.'

'Where is she?'

'With the landlady downstairs. Apartment 1A.'

'Thanks.'

'Yeah,' says Kravitz, and it seems to Doyle that there is almost a hint of respect there. He tells himself that Kravitz must be having an off day.

After the problems he's had with Holden, it occurs to Doyle that he should at least mention to him that he intends talking to the roommate. But Holden is already engaged in conversation with a thin bald man – presumably one of the tenants.

Fuck it, thinks Doyle.

He trudges down the stairs to the first floor. When he knocks on the door of apartment 1A, it opens within seconds.

He guesses that the woman before him is about sixty, even though her over-tanned skin has the appearance of antique leather. She wears a dazzling flower-print dress that Doyle thinks is far too short for a woman of her advanced years. Her hair, sculpted into a gravity-defying beehive, has been dyed a shade of red not found in nature. Minus the hair, she'd struggle to hit the five-foot mark. She reminds Doyle of the little old lady in *Rosemary's Baby* – the one who befriends Rosemary only so that she can use her to carry the Devil's child.

'Police,' says Doyle as he shows his shield.

'Big surprise,' says the woman. 'The building is crawling with them right now. Where were you when I got burglarized last Christmas?'

'This is a little more serious than that, Mrs . . .'

'Serafinowicz. With a z.'

'With a z, huh?' says Doyle, wondering where it goes.

'Yes. And don't tell me how serious this is. I know how serious this is. There's a beautiful young girl lying dead in one of my apartments up there. You better catch the son of a bitch who did that, or else you'll have me to answer to.'

Doyle decides that answering to Mrs Serafinowicz with a z is the last thing he wants.

'That's why I'm here. I need to talk to the roommate who found the body, and I'm told she's here with you.'

'She already spoke with the other cops.'

'That's okay. I just want to make sure that we've covered everything.'

'She's upset. She can't stop crying, the poor girl. Can't you come back later?'

'Time is of the essence, ma'am, as I'm sure you appreciate.'

She studies him for a while. Listening to the demonic voices in her head, no doubt.

'All right,' she says. 'Just go easy on her.'

She opens the door wide, and Doyle steps into a room that seems to be filled with junk. Almost every available surface is covered with items that look like they've come from all corners of the globe. Swiss cuckoo clocks, bears dressed in London Beefeater outfits, Japanese fans, Mexican sombreros, Australian boomerangs – she's got them all. Doyle notices that there's even a section of a shelf devoted to all things Irish, including a bobble-headed leprechaun exactly like the one he has on his desk in the squadroom.

Sitting on a chintz sofa in the center of this organized chaos is a young woman. She has curly blond hair and is wearing a very low-cut brown top. Her eyes and nose are red from crying. She looks frightened and vulnerable.

'Hi,' says Doyle. 'My name's Cal Doyle. I'm a detective with the Eighth Precinct. You mind if I ask you a few questions?'

The girl shakes her head and wipes her nose with a tissue clutched tightly in her fist.

Doyle takes out his notebook and flips it open. 'That's great,' he says. 'Let's start with your name.'

She answers him honestly, but what Doyle doesn't yet appreciate is how significant that answer is.

'Tabitha,' she says. 'Tabitha Peyton.'

NINETEEN

'I'll make some tea,' says Mrs Whatever-with-a-z, and she toddles off to the kitchen.

Doyle is relieved to be apart from her for a short while, but at the same time he feels a little awkward. Tabitha Peyton looks like she could break down at any second, and he is not good at dealing with females who go to pieces on him. He never knows what to say or do. He wishes now that Holden or one of his other male colleagues had come down here with him, so that at least if she did start bawling he could join with the other cop in a manly show of rolling his eyes at the weakness of the female sex.

'You mind if I sit down?' he asks.

She nods, and he takes his seat.

'Your roommate,' he says. 'Helena, isn't it?'

'Yes. Helena Colquitt. I've known her a long time. I still can't believe she's . . .' She wipes her nose again.

Don't cry, thinks Doyle. Please don't cry.

'It's okay to be upset. I understand,' he says. And then he thinks, Why the hell am I saying that?

'It's just that . . . I don't know why anyone would do this to her.'

Doyle doesn't comprehend it either. The logic – if there is any – still escapes him.

'Tell me what happened here tonight.'

She stares at her hands while she casts her mind back. 'We were in the apartment together – Helena and me. I ordered a pizza and then I asked her to run a bath for me while I came down to see Bridget – Mrs Serafinowicz. She's been suffering with her arthritis lately, and so I wanted to see if there was anything I could do for her. She's been so good to me since I moved here. She's looked after me like I was her own daughter. I only intended to stay for a few minutes, but we got talking, you know? Maybe if I'd gone straight back upstairs . . .'

Her voice starts to break, and so Doyle urges her on before the floodgates can open: 'So eventually you did go back up. Did you pass anyone on the stairs? See anything unusual?'

'No. Everything was normal. I got to the apartment, I opened the door. Everything was as it should be. I didn't suspect a thing. Only there was no sign of Helena. I called her, but there was no answer. And that's when I went into the bathroom.'

The word 'bathroom' comes out as a squeak that is so high-pitched it is almost inaudible. Doyle thinks it's not going to take much more to make her lose it altogether, but he has to press on.

'Okay, you're doing great. Tell me what you saw.'

She clears her throat. 'I saw Helena. In the bathtub. In the water she'd run for me. Her head was . . . she was under the water. She wasn't moving.'

'What did you do?'

'I ran over to her. I tried to pull her out of the water. When her head came up, I could see blood all around her nose, and her eyes were wide open. I'll never forget that look she was giving me. She was dead – I just knew it – and the shock of it made me drop her back in the water. That's when I started panicking. I ran out of the apartment, screaming for help. Mr Casey, my neighbor from across the hall, came out to see what the noise was. He's pretty old now, but he used to be a cop many years ago. I don't remember what I said to him – it must have sounded complete nonsense – but he went into my apartment to check it out. I walked back into the living room, but I couldn't go any farther. I could hear the movement of water in the bathroom for a few minutes, and then Mr Casey came back out. His arms were dripping wet. He didn't have to say anything. The look on his face . . .'

The dam gives way then. She brings her hands to her face and her shoulders start to heave as she sobs.

Oh, Christ, thinks Doyle. He starts to reach out a hand to her shoulder, then pulls it back again, not sure what to do.

He is saved by the bell. Or rather the rattle of crockery announcing the return of Mrs S, now burdened with a silver tray. She takes one look at the pair on the sofa, then says, 'What did I tell you? She's too upset for this.'

She sets the tray down on a dark wooden table in front of Doyle, then tells him to move over. Doyle shuffles along the sofa to allow Mrs Serafinowicz to squeeze in and console the distraught Tabitha.

While this is going on, Doyle busies himself with jotting a few things down in his notebook. The girl's story seems entirely kosher. Casey would have been the old guy Doyle had seen talking to the detectives upstairs. As an ex-cop himself, Casey would have been equipped to confirm that the girl was dead, and he would have known to put the body back exactly as he found it.

When the sniffling has subsided, Mrs Serafinowicz moves off the sofa and starts pouring the tea. Doyle takes a cup from her out of politeness.

'I won't take up too much more of your time,' he tells Tabitha. 'Just a few more questions, okay?'

He gets a nod from Tabitha and a tut of disapproval from Mrs Serafinowicz.

'Tell me about Helena. How did you meet? How did she become your roommate?'

'I think it was, like, fate, you know? I moved to New York about a year ago, hoping to make a fresh start. See, both my parents were killed a few months before that in a car crash. I thought that maybe by making the move, taking a new job, meeting new people, I could move on with my life. Only it didn't work out like that. I was a mess. I started drinking, hanging around with guys I didn't really know. If it hadn't been for Bridget here, taking me under her wing . . .'

Doyle looks across at Mrs Serafinowicz, and for the first time sees her for what she is: a woman who genuinely cares about the people living under her roof. It's a rare thing, and Doyle is touched by it.

'It was Bridget who told me that I needed to make some real friends, that I needed companionship. So I thought about a roommate. That way, I'd have company and someone to help with the rental. Not that Bridget charges me anywhere near the rent that some places ask.'

Mrs Serafinowicz doesn't react. Doesn't appear smug or holier-than-thou. She simply looks Doyle in the eye, and he feels that he is actually starting to like this woman.

'So I started searching. On the Internet mostly, until my computer broke down. But none of the women I interviewed seemed suitable. Some were downright flaky. The rest, I just didn't see myself being able to live with them for God knows how many years. So I gave up. And then, about six weeks ago, I got a phone call. From Helena. We were at university together. Carnegie Mellon. We were best friends at the time. We dressed the same, we had the same interests. She even bought a Harley Davidson that was like mine. People used to call us the Turbo Twins. And here she was, calling me up. You know why? Because she was moving to New York and needed somewhere to stay. Just when I thought I was out of luck. See, that's what I mean by fate.' She reflects on that for a moment, then adds, 'But I guess fate can work both ways. If I hadn't asked her to move in with me . . .'

'You can't think like that,' Doyle says. 'You can keep coming up with what-ifs till you're blue in the face, but it doesn't change things. What happened is what happened. You couldn't have done anything to change that.'

'First useful thing you've said since you arrived,' says Mrs Serafinowicz.

'Helena wasn't running away from anything, was she? She didn't come to New York to get away from someone who might want to hurt her?'

'Not as far as I know. She seemed happy enough. Nothing was troubling her. I was the one who needed the emotional support.'

'What about after she arrived here? She get on the wrong side of anyone?'

'No. We went out, we shopped, we had fun. There was no trouble at any time.'

It's the answer Doyle expected, and the answer he didn't want. He hoped there would be someone else he could tag for this, or at least hang a question mark over their head. As it is, it's looking increasingly likely that Helena Colquitt is just the latest victim in a deadly sequence.

'What about a key to the apartment? You or Helena ever give it out to anyone?'

'No. Absolutely not.'

'What about you, Mrs, uhm . . .'

'Serafinowicz. Maybe you should put it in your little notebook there. And don't forget the z. But to answer your question, no, I do not give keys out to anyone but my tenants.'

Which is also the response Doyle expected and feared. What confounds him is that the only sign of a struggle was in the bathroom. How does a complete stranger manage to talk his way into the apartment of a beautiful girl who isn't even properly dressed, and then get her into the bathroom without a fight of some kind? How the hell does he do that?

Doyle is starting to think that if there has been any satanic activity going on in this building, then maybe he should be looking upstairs for signs of it.

'All right,' he says. 'Thank you. I'll leave you alone now.'

Mrs Serafinowicz looks surprised. 'That's it? You have no more questions? The other cops asked a lot more than you did.'

Doyle has plenty more questions, but he knows he isn't going to find the answers here.

'I'm sure there'll be other things we'll need to ask at a later stage, but I'm done for now.' He turns to Tabitha. 'You got somewhere to go tonight?'

It's Mrs Serafinowicz who answers. 'She's staying here. I have a furnished apartment available on the second floor. She can move in there for as long as she wants.'

Doyle wants to smile appreciatively at her and maybe even pass a compliment, but he suspects she'll find a way to use it against him. Like most people, she has appearances to maintain.

'Thanks for the tea,' he says, and leaves it at that.

When he exits the apartment he stands in the hallway alone for a while. Something is troubling him, and it takes a minute or two for him to figure out what it is.

Helena was running a bath for Tabitha, and there was a pizza on the way. That means Tabitha had every intention of returning to her apartment pretty soon. She said so herself: *I only intended to stay for a few minutes.*

So why did the killer take such a huge risk? Why did he

choose that moment and that location and that method – drowning isn't always the quickest or tidiest of deaths – to murder a woman whose roommate could come back and disturb him at any second? Didn't he care? Was he assuming that he could just as easily cope with overpowering and killing both of them?

It occurs to Doyle that this act seems a leap beyond anything the killer has done before in terms of daring. In fact it seems almost uncharacteristically rash.

Has the killer become more unhinged? Or is this simply his way of stepping up the game?

Whichever it is, there's only one man who can give Doyle the answer.

TWENTY

Ten-thirty p.m. Doyle alone in the squadroom. Typing up his DD5 reports and wishing that life could be simple.

He wants to know how the fuck he ended up playing the stooge to that joker. That guy whose idea of fun is to tell Doyle whom he's going to kill next, but in such a way that Doyle can never grasp the true meaning. It makes Doyle feel like he's in a comedy sketch – the unfortunate dimwit everyone laughs at for getting the simplest things so drastically wrong.

He also wants to know how the fuck he now finds himself almost wishing he hadn't relinquished that role. Perhaps he was always meant to play the innocent fool. Doesn't the guy you feel sorry for always win out in the end?

The thing of it is, there's too much he needs to know. It's like being a child who has been told there is something very interesting in a box, but that he must never look inside it. The temptation to open the box becomes overwhelming. Sooner or later you just know you're gonna sneak a peek.

There are things going on in the killer's life. In his mind. His patterns are changing. Doyle needs to know why. He needs to open the box.

He gets a further nudge in that direction when his cellphone squawks at him. Not a phone call, but a text message:

No clues this time. I promise. Take the call. Please.

Well, well, thinks Doyle. The scumbag's actually pleading with me.

Seconds later he hears the ring tone, almost immediately drowned out by the voice in his head:

Ignore it, you prick. You'll regret it if you answer it. You'll be right back in his pocket. Playing his stupid games and losing every time. Stick to your guns and kill the fucking call.

Sound advice. For the sake of his own sanity, he knows he would do well to heed it.

But he's never been good at doing what he's told.

He answers the call a second before it goes to voicemail. Opens the box. And already he feels like Pandora, letting out all the evils of the world.

'You better not be shitting me!' he yells into the phone. 'You give me one fucking clue, sneak one piece of bullshit information under the fence like you did last time, and I'm gone. Permanently. You understand that, motherfucker?'

There is a moment's silence, during which Doyle thinks to himself, This better be who I expected it to be.

'And a good evening to you too, Detective,' says the caller. 'It's nice to hear your calm, collected voice again. I've missed our little chats. So let me give you some reassurance. You don't need to worry anymore. I'm changing the rules.'

More changes. Not what Doyle wanted to hear.

'What rules?'

'The rules of the game. You're right. I think I was a little unfair on you. The game was always a little one-sided. The outcome was never in doubt, given your limited capabilities. And so I don't blame you for walking away.'

Doyle refuses to rise to the insult, or to be seduced into feeling any gratitude for this conciliatory approach. Allowing emotions to govern his response is the most dangerous thing he can do right now.

He says, 'So you admit this is all just a game to you. What's the problem? You got nobody else to play with? Nobody wants to be your friend anymore?'

'To be frank, life was starting to become a little dull without you. You're such a good sport, Cal. I missed you terribly. And I think you missed me too, didn't you?'

'That's right, I was devastated. I was like a goldfish without a bicycle.'

'You joke about it now, but admit it. You've been desperate for me to call, haven't you?'

'Is that what that was, going all silent on me? You trying to teach me a lesson of some kind?'

'I was trying to show you that you need me too, Cal. I need you and you need me. We have a symbiotic relationship going here.'

'Actually, I think of you more as a parasite. A tapeworm or a flea. The last thing I need is you sucking my blood the way you've been doing.'

'Really? That's the way you feel?'

'That's the way I feel.'

'Then why did you answer this call?'

Doyle hesitates before he answers, and kicks himself for it. 'Because of the text message. Because I wanted to know why you've suddenly decided to change tactics.'

'Oh. Only that,' says the voice, mocking in its disbelief. 'Not because you realize that you and the rest of the boys in blue don't have a snowball's chance in hell of stopping these killings without my help?'

'Don't underestimate us, asshole. We're closer than you think.'

'Of course you are. Well, in that case you won't be needing my assistance. But just in case you change your mind, here's how we're going to do things from now on. Each time another killing is planned, I'm going to give you the option, Cal. I'll let you decide whether you want to hear my little hints or not. I won't sneak anything in. I'll simply ask you for a yes or a no. Yes if you want my help. No if you don't. It's that simple. What do you think, Cal? Does that work for you?'

Doyle thinks, He's doing this because without me he's nothing. He needs my feedback. That's what keeps him going. This isn't a favor to me. He's trying to save himself. Without me, he's going to pieces. That's why he acted so rashly with Helena Colquitt.

'You know what? I'm gonna have to think about it. Weigh up the pros and cons. Tell you what, give me a call sometime, and I'll see if I feel like answering.'

The hesitation is on the other end of the line now, and for the first time Doyle feels like he can chalk up a minor victory. He is sure he can almost hear the clenching of fists and the gnashing of teeth as the caller seethes over the possibility that his bluff is being called.

'Don't push it, Cal. Lives are at stake here. Innocent people could die because of the decisions you take tonight. Don't treat this situation lightly. I'm offering you the help you need to save those people. The question is, can you afford to turn it down?'

'Don't try to put this on me. Those people are dead because of one person – you. I've just come back from looking at one of your victims. She was young and she was pretty. She had her whole life ahead of her. What did she ever do to you? What put her on your list of people who don't deserve to live? What gives you the right to make those decisions?'

A sigh. 'You just don't understand, do you, Cal? This whole

thing. It's not about hurting. It's about helping. We all have to help each other. That's what'll make the world a better place. Until you appreciate what's really going on here, you're not going to make any headway on this case. Look beyond the surface, Cal.'

'You're seriously fucked up, you know that? You enjoy killing, and you enjoy me failing to solve your clues. That's it. Nothing deep. It's just about you getting your kicks in about the most perverted way possible.'

'Well, you can stop the killing, Cal. I'm not saying you're right about me, because you're not, but whatever my motives are, you can stop the killing. I'm willing to give you the information you need. Only you can decide whether you want it.'

'Like I said, I'll think about it.'

'All right. But not for too long, Cal. I'll be calling you again soon, and I'll make my offer only once. Turn it down and you're on your own. If you hadn't been so stubborn, maybe you could even have prevented tonight's events. I was going to play you two tunes for this one. You want to know what they were?'

'Not especially.'

'Listen.'

Doyle thinks about hanging up, but his curiosity gets the better of him. He wants to know if he really would have had a chance of cracking this one.

The first piece of music is light-hearted and catchy, but sounds really dated. Doyle thinks he's heard it before, but isn't sure where. Maybe in a rerun of a very old TV show. It fades out, to be replaced by an orchestral piece, grander and more sweeping, but still sounding like it's from an old movie.

'You know what they are?' The caller sounds excited now. Even after he's killed, he's still finding a way to extract some entertainment value from it.

'Not a clue.'

'Jesus, Cal. You've just come from seeing the victim, and you still can't put two and two together? Am I wasting my time here?'

'Like you said, I'm a man of limited capabilities.'

'All right, look. The first one, it's from a show called *Bewitched*. You know the one? About the good-looking witch who works magic by twitching her nose?'

'I've heard of it. A little before my time, though.'

'Okay. So the witch, Samantha, has a baby. And the baby's name is . . .'

'I haven't the faintest.'

'For Christ's sake, Cal. Work with me here. All right, try the other tune. A TV soap from the sixties. A family saga. Always started with a voiceover saying, "In color, the continuing story of . . ."'

'The sixties? Just how old do you think I am?'

'I know exactly how old you are, Cal, but that's not the point. There are certain things ingrained in TV history. Besides, I'm not telling you about something that hasn't happened yet. All you have to do is put what I've just told you together with the crime scene you just visited, and you get . . .'

Doyle doesn't answer. He doesn't get this at all. He's starting to think he'll never be able to stop the killings, even with a shit-load of clues.

'Lord, give me strength,' says the voice. 'It's *Peyton* fucking *Place*, Cal. And the baby's name was Tabitha. You get it now? You see how those two things go together? Tabitha and Peyton. Tabitha Peyton. Clear now?'

No words come to Doyle. His brain is too busy dealing with what it's just heard. Turning the words over and over while it examines them for something it may have missed. What did he say? Did he say Tabitha Peyton? That can't be right.

Or was it just another clue? Another example of his deviousness? He gives out the pointers to Tabitha so that I think she's the intended victim, when in fact she's just another link in the chain to Helena. Yeah, that must be it. He would do such a thing, just like he did with Vasey.

'Cal? You there, buddy?'

'Uhm, yeah. It's late. My brain's slowing down. I think I get it. You're saying that if I'd heard those two tunes, then maybe I could have kept Tabitha Peyton alive.'

He tenses as he awaits the answer. The words that say something along the lines of, *What the fuck are you talking about? Not her, you dumbass. The roomie. Helena.*

'Exactly. Honest to God, Cal, I'm beginning to wonder if you're cut out for this. Maybe I made a bad choice here.'

Exactly.

He said, *Exactly.*

Jesus fucking Christ.

Doyle feels his hand begin to shake. He tries to keep a tremor from creeping into his voice too.

'Don't underestimate me. I'm still gonna put your ass in jail. Meantime, I'll think about your offer.'

'You do that. But like I said, don't put it on hold too long. I'll be calling you again for an answer soon.'

The line goes dead. Doyle drops the phone on his desk and exhales heavily. He tries to absorb what's just hit him.

He's made a mistake.

The man who seems to plan his murders to perfection has finally made a mistake.

He wasn't being rash when he killed Helena Colquitt. He wasn't being blasé about the possible return of Tabitha while he carried out a calculated murder. He didn't even know that two people were staying in the apartment. As far as he was concerned, there was nobody else likely to come through that door while he was there.

And because of all that, the wrong person died.

Doyle leaps to his feet, almost knocking over his chair. He grabs his leather jacket and dashes out of the squadroom.

Sooner or later, the killer is going to realize his mistake. Even if it's only through hearing the victim's name on the news, he's going to learn that he screwed up in a big way. And when that happens, he may just want to put it right.

Doyle prays that he can get to Tabitha before the killer does.

TWENTY-ONE

He's thumbing the buzzer of Apartment 2B, hoping that it's the right one, praying that he's not too late. 2B is the only one without a name against the buzzer. It has to be the vacant one that Mrs Serafinowicz was talking about.

A voice breaks in eventually. It's croaky with tiredness and all that crying.

'Quit buzzing! Who the hell is this?'

Doyle puts his mouth close to the intercom. 'It's Detective Doyle. We spoke a few hours ago? I need to see you again. Can you let me in, please?'

'Now? Do you know what time it is? Can't this wait till the morning?'

'No. Please. It's urgent. It won't take long.'

Hiss over the intercom. Then: 'All right. Keep it brief, okay?'

She admits him, and he runs up the stairs to the second floor. The door to 2B is already open. Tabitha standing there, belting up her robe. Her eyelids looking like they want to slide down to her mouth.

'Get inside,' he says.

The command seems to shock her awake. 'What? Who do you think—'

'Inside. Now!'

He pushes her into the living room and follows her.

He says, 'Get dressed. Pack a few things. You're leaving.'

'No. What are you talking about? You can't just come in here like this—'

'Tabitha, listen to me. Your life is in danger. We've had some information. The guy who killed Helena, we think he's gonna try to kill you too. You have to leave here.'

She blinks. Confused. Scared.

'No. I don't . . . I mean, I don't understand. Who wants to kill me? How do you know all this?'

Inside, Doyle twists and turns about what he can tell her. Without at least some honesty she's not going to believe him. And that means she won't save herself.

'All right, I'm gonna tell you something. Nobody else knows this. Not the press. Not the families of the other victims. Nobody.' He pauses to let this sink in. 'He calls us. The murderer. When he's killed somebody, he calls the cops to taunt us for not catching him. Tonight I took the call. He did his usual thing, making fun of us. Calling us clowns. Only this time he said we were idiots for not preventing the death of Tabitha Peyton.'

Her face seems to drain of blood. She shakes her head. 'No. What do you mean? Are you saying he made a mistake? That Helena was a *mistake*?'

Put like that, it makes Helena's death sound even more of a waste than it was already. All that Doyle can say is, 'I'm sorry.'

She pushes her hands through her hair and looks around the room, as if searching for an escape route from this bad dream she must be having.

'I can't do this. I can't take any more. Why would somebody want to kill me? I haven't done anything.'

'Please, Tabitha. We can talk about it in the car. Right now, I just have to get you somewhere safe. Go into your bedroom and get dressed. I'll be waiting right here. Hurry!'

As she walks away he wants to weep for her. She's been through enough. First her parents get ripped from her, then her best friend, and now she's in danger of losing her own life. How much disastrous luck can be crammed into such a youthful existence?

He steps to the window and parts the curtains slightly. Peers down onto the street below, even though he doesn't know what he's looking for. Then he goes over and sits on the sofa. He finds himself tapping his feet in impatience and constantly checking his watch.

He thinks, Jesus, how long is she gonna take in there? I coulda had a three course meal by now.

When she reappears she is wearing jeans, leather boots and a gray coat, belted at the waist. She carries a heavy-looking overnight bag.

'Let me get that,' says Doyle.

'Are you sure about this?' she asks. 'About the killer, I mean. That he's coming back? That he wants to hurt me?'

Doyle takes the bag from her hand, but knows that what she really wants is for him to take away her fear.

'It's a precaution, okay? Maybe he won't come back. Maybe he'll realize he made a mistake and just move on. But we can't take that chance. We have to be sure you're safe.'

She nods, but still she seems unsure. He waits while she locks up the apartment, and then they head down the staircase.

When they get to the first floor she says, 'I can't just leave like this. I need to talk to Bridget – Mrs Serafinowicz.'

'Not now. You can call her tomorrow. Right now we just need to get you outta here.'

Doyle is the first onto the front stoop. He scans the street, his hand within snatching distance of his firearm, then leads her toward his car. He continues to watch all around him while she climbs into the passenger seat, and then he throws the bag into the trunk. He gets in behind the wheel, fires up the engine and takes off, exhaling his relief to get away from this place.

And only then does he think, Where the hell am I going?

Doyle has been so preoccupied with the task of getting her out of danger that he's not given any thought as to where he's going to take her next.

His own apartment is the first location that springs to mind. It's also the first to be jettisoned with extreme force.

Hi, Rachel. Look what I brought home. No, let me explain. She's a potential victim. Yes, victims can look like this. A victim of whom? Well, that serial killer who's been talking to me in those phone calls I never explained to you.

But Rachel's objections aren't the only problem. It just wouldn't be safe. The killer knows too much about Doyle, including what he does and where he goes. Inviting Tabitha into his home would be the same as inviting the killer. And that is something he cannot bring to his family.

So where? A hotel? No. Too public. And she can't be left alone. She needs to be with someone. Someone who can keep an eye on her.

But who? He can't ask another cop – not without revealing why he's got this girl with him in the first place.

'This is crazy,' she says. 'I feel like I'm dreaming. Where are we going, anyway? Some kind of safe house?'

'Uh, yeah. Something like that.' He sees a coffee shop ahead on the right. 'Listen, you want a coffee?'

'A coffee? Now?'

'Yeah. Come on.'

Without waiting for an answer, he pulls the car over and climbs out. He goes around the car and opens the door for Tabitha. While she gets out, he scans the street again.

He thinks, What are you doing? She's safe now. He can't get to her here. Relax.

But still he finds himself standing close to her as they move toward the coffee shop, his body shielding hers, his fingers edging under his jacket.

Inside, she starts to move to a booth in the window, but Doyle takes her arm and guides her over to a table in a shadowy alcove. He sits facing the door, so that he can see anybody who might enter.

You're acting like a spy, he thinks. Stop it. The sonofabitch is good, but he's not that good. He's human. He makes mistakes. Remember that.

A waitress comes across. When she smiles, Doyle gets the impression that she thinks they're a couple. For some reason he gets the urge to tell her they're not together, before he realizes how stupid and unnecessary that would be.

Tabitha orders a skinny latte, while Doyle opts for a decaf cappuccino. He's wired enough as it is without pumping caffeine into his system.

Tabitha says, 'I suppose I should thank you.'

'It's just coffee,' says Doyle. 'It's nothing.'

'I don't mean the coffee. I mean for coming to my aid like this. For being the white knight.'

He looks into her eyes, then wishes he hadn't. 'I . . . I'm just doing my job.'

'*To protect and serve*, huh?'

'Actually, that's the LAPD. But yeah, same principle.'

'Will you be staying with me?'

'What?'

'Wherever it is we're going. Will you be staying there with me?'

'Uhm, no.'

'Pity. You make a good bodyguard. You make people trust you.'

'You'll be safe. I promise. I need to get out there and catch the bad guy.'

'Will you? Catch him, I mean?'

'Absolutely.'

'I hope so.'

She lapses into silence and looks down at the table. While she is lost in her thoughts he steals the chance to search her face, and wonders why he finds it so hard to meet her gaze. It's not attraction. Of that he's certain. She is young and beautiful and shapely – those things are undeniable. But it's not attraction.

It's what she said. It's the *trust*. When he looks into her eyes it's like looking into the eyes of Amy, his daughter. There is undiluted trust there. Faith. Belief. Tabitha believes that he is her guardian angel. The white knight, as she put it. He has rescued the damsel in distress and next he will vanquish the dragon, and they will live happily ever after. That's what she believes.

He's not sure he's ready for that responsibility. It makes him wish he wasn't so trustworthy in her eyes.

Because what if he gets it wrong?

What if, despite his constant assertions to himself and his continued reassurances to her that she is out of danger, she still comes to harm?

It's an unbearable thought. And that's why he cannot look her in the eye. Loath though he is to admit it, he needs the emotional detachment. Just in case.

But no! Fuck that sick sonofabitch! He's not going to get Tabitha Peyton. She *is* safe now.

The coffee arrives, and he's glad of the interruption to his mental wrangling. Neither of them adds sugar to their drinks. Both take careful sips from their cups of steaming liquid.

'Do you like this city?' she asks.

The question throws Doyle. Not merely for its random nature, but also because it's something which for him has a lot more depth than it might appear to possess. To Doyle, this city is far more than a collection of buildings and people and vehicles crammed into a few square miles of land. He was brought here at the age of eight from a country with vast open spaces and sheep and cows and an altogether gentler pace of life. The shock of that contrast – the excitement of it – has never left him. Yes, the city can be cruel, can even seem heartless at times, but there is a soul there which, once you recognize it and connect to it, never lets you go. You reach a point where your heart beats to the city's rhythm. And then you're a part of it.

'I love it,' he answers, and he is not exaggerating.

She nods, plays with her spoon. 'I thought I would too. Sometimes I get this close to thinking I'm happy here. And then the city goes and shows me how wrong I can be.'

'You've had a tough time.'

'Ever since I got here. That fresh start idea of mine never worked out. I pictured friends, dancing, theater, movies. What I got was loneliness and despair. Millions of people all around me, and still I felt the loneliest woman on the planet. Crazy, huh?'

Doyle says nothing. Just sips his coffee. She needs to talk, to be listened to.

She says, 'I know what you're thinking. You're thinking it's my fault, not the city's. I've noticed that about New Yorkers: they're very loyal. And maybe you're right. Maybe me and New York were never going to get along. A clash of personalities. And I can see why you love it here. It has so many wonderful things, so much to offer. But I think that sometimes, for some people, it takes instead of gives. And when you're the one it picks on, you don't have a prayer.'

Doyle sips. Waits.

'It beat me, this city. Beat me into the ground. You know how low I got? I was going to finish it all, that's how low. One night, drunk as a skunk, I actually went out to the Brooklyn Bridge with the intention of jumping into the East River.'

'What stopped you?'

She smiles then, the first smile Doyle has seen from her. And on such a serious subject.

'I picked the wrong bridge. You know how difficult it is to jump off that thing? The walkway goes right through the middle. You have to climb across the bridgework to miss the traffic below. I was so drunk that night I couldn't even climb my own front stoop.'

Her smile broadens, and for a second it lights up her face before it dims again.

She says, 'You're only the second person I've ever told that story too. See what I mean about trusting you?'

'Who was the first?'

'Mrs Serafinowicz. I never even told Helena.'

'Why not?'

'Because . . . because she was another fresh start. I didn't want her pity. I wanted her happiness. I wanted her to be the same with me as she was when we were at college. And that's what I got. For a short while.'

Doyle tries to work on what he should say. He's not good with females who cry, and he's not any better at giving advice on life. But he gives it a try.

'Tabitha, listen. This is bad. As bad as it gets. There's no way I can really understand how tough this must be for you. The only thing I do know is this: it'll get better. Not right away. It'll take time. But I know you can be happy again. You're too young to give up without a fight.'

She raises her head, and this time he cannot avoid looking into her eyes. And he tries to convince her without words that everything will be all right again. And when he sees a tear bulge from her eye and roll down her cheek he wants to catch it and he wants to take her in his arms and shield her from the terrors of the big bad city she sees out there.

And he wishes he had never met this girl.

'I have to go to the bathroom,' she says.

He guesses that she's going to cry again, and he's ashamedly relieved to let her go and do that.

It also gives him the opportunity he needed. He was planning to use the washroom excuse himself, or maybe pretend he needed to go out and fetch something from the car.

He takes out his cellphone. He finds the number he wants in his contact list and makes the call.

'It's me. Detective Doyle. I need a favor.'

TWENTY-TWO

'What kind of favor?' says Gonzo.

'I need you to look after something for me.'

'Like what?'

'A package. I can't talk about it now. I'll explain when I see you.'

A lengthy silence. 'Detective Doyle, it's really good speaking with you again, but you're being very mysterious here.'

'I know. I'm sorry. It'll all be clear when we meet. What's your address?'

'My address? You mean now? You want to deliver this package right now?'

'Is that a problem?'

'Well . . . yes it's a problem. This is Friday night, Detective. I have plans, you know?'

'What, you got a girl coming over? You hitting the clubs? What?'

'Paradoxia.'

'What?'

'Paradoxia.' He says it like the meaning should be obvious.

'Gonzo, you're talking gibberish. Is that a new nightclub or something?'

'You never heard of Paradoxia? Where have you been, Detective? Paradoxia is only the hottest online game ever invented. I'm right in the middle of an all-night session here.'

Doyle hears the whoosh of a hand-drying machine as a washroom door is opened here in the coffee shop.

'Gonzo, are you gonna help me out here or what?'

Gonzo sighs. 'All right, Detective. But only because I like you, okay?'

He reels off an address, and Doyle files it in his brain.

'I'll be right over.' He cuts the call just as Tabitha gets back to the table.

'Last minute preparations,' he explains. 'You okay?'

She nods.

'Then let's go.'

'This is it?' she says. 'This is your safe house?'

He gets the feeling she's not impressed with this address on Henry Street in the Lower East Side. He's not sure why. The signs on the store fronts are at least translated into English below the Chinese. The imposing sight of the Manhattan Bridge looming over the street is a whole block away. And the graffiti covering the front of the building they're about to enter isn't even pornographic.

Doyle buzzes and gets an immediate answering buzz. He pushes open the door and heads upstairs, Tabitha trailing cautiously behind. The air is heavy with the scent of Chinese food, and from behind one of the doors comes the sound of raised voices. It sounds heated to Doyle, but he's not au fait with the tongue or the culture. For all he knows, it could be anything ranging from a murder in progress to a discussion about the cost of noodles.

He continues up to the third story and finds the door of Apartment 32, the number Gonzo gave him. He puts down the bag and knocks heavily on the door.

When Gonzo opens up, Doyle sees that he's wearing a pair of

blue-and-white striped undershorts and a T-shirt emblazoned with the message, 'Normal service will resume as soon as possible.'

Gonzo gives Doyle one of his idiotic smiles. It fades quickly when his eyes refocus to take in the figure hidden in the gloom behind the detective.

Doyle moves to one side with the intention of introducing his companion. He sees that Gonzo and Tabitha seem to have locked eyes. Their expressions tell him it's not love at first sight.

'Uh, Tabitha Peyton, meet Gonzo . . . just Gonzo.'

The two of them continue to stand there in silence, still engaged in the staring competition. Tabitha is the first to break it off.

'Detective Doyle, can I speak with you for a moment?'

Doyle turns to Gonzo. 'She wants to speak with me.'

Gonzo nods. 'Okay.' He doesn't move.

'In private,' says Tabitha.

'In private,' Doyle repeats, like he's the world's worst translator.

Gonzo's expression suggests that he still doesn't get it, so Doyle has to motion to him to close the door.

'Oh,' says Gonzo. 'Sure.' He shuts the door gently, leaving Doyle and Tabitha in the hallway.

Tabitha's voice is a harsh whisper: 'Who the hell is that?'

'I told you. Gonzo. He's gonna look after you.'

'*Him*? Look after *me*? I don't think so. Is he a cop?'

'He works for the NYPD.'

'But not as a cop.'

'Not exactly. But he's a good guy. He's helped me a lot. I can trust him.'

'Trust him to do what? Does he have a gun? Is he Karate Kid? Was that Mr Miyagi I heard downstairs? Maybe he just *stares* people to death, is that it? What the hell is this Bonzo—'

'Gonzo.'

'Whatever. What the hell is he going to do if the killer shows up here? I think it's more likely that I'll end up protecting *him*, instead of the other way round.'

'It's not going to come to that. Nobody knows you're here, and I know Gonzo won't tell anyone. Please, give him a chance. You'll like him, I'm sure. And it's only for a day or two.'

She thinks about it.

'You trust him? He's not some kind of pervert?'

'He's totally harmless, I swear. He's a computer geek. His idea of dirty talk is binary.'

She thinks some more.

'All right. I'll stay. But any funny business and I'm outta here. *After* I've kicked his ass.'

Doyle smiles and knocks on the door again. It opens immediately, Gonzo standing in exactly the same position he occupied before.

'Yes?' he says, as if the previous encounter has been wiped totally from his mind.

'Uh, Gonzo. Here I am. Like I told you? On the phone?'

Gonzo's eyes slide to Tabitha and then back to Doyle. 'Is this okay? In front of . . .' He gives a subtle nod toward Tabitha.

'Yes, Gonzo, it's fine.'

'Okay, so did you bring the, uhm, the –' his voice drops to a whisper '– the package?'

Doyle licks his lips. How to explain this?

'Gonzo, this is Tabitha.'

Gonzo glances at her again. 'Yeah, I know. We already did this. But about the—'

He halts himself. Looks again at Tabitha. Back to Doyle.

'Detective Doyle, can we have a word?'

Jesus, thinks Doyle. Not again. Why does a simple thing have to turn out to be so fucking difficult?

'I'm not leaving her alone out here, Gonzo. Either we all come in, or else Tabitha goes in and you come out.'

Gonzo shifts from foot to foot like he wants to pee. Finally making up his mind, he opens the door wider and waves Tabitha into his abode.

She looks with uncertainty to Doyle. He nods for her to go inside. As soon as she's in, Gonzo slips out and pulls the door shut behind him.

'Detective Doyle, you lied to me. You said a package. You mentioned nothing about a person. Especially one of the female persuasion. What are you trying to do to me?'

'Gonzo, please. I need your help, okay? She's in danger. The killer I've been trying to catch? He wants to kill Tabitha too. She needs somewhere she can hide for a coupla days.'

Gonzo's voice rises a whole octave. Which, given the pitch of his natural voice, is pretty damned shrill. 'He wants to kill her? And you bring her here? To my apartment? What's wrong with your place?'

'I would if I could, Gonzo. But the killer's been watching me. He's been checking up on me. If I take her back to my apartment she won't last five minutes.'

'But you're a cop. Cops put people in protection programs all the time. What's so different about her?'

Doyle hesitates. 'I'm gonna level with you, okay? This is unofficial. The squad doesn't know about this. In fact, nobody else in the NYPD knows about this.'

'Why? I mean, why do you have to be so secretive? Why not just tell somebody?'

'It's a long story. It may come to that. For now, I need to put her with the only person I can trust. That's you, Gonzo.'

Gonzo seems taken aback. For a second, Doyle is afraid the kid's going to turn all misty-eyed. He presses home his advantage: 'You wanted to get involved in police work? Well, this is as real as it gets. Helping people is what we do. Tabitha Peyton is a vulnerable citizen who needs our help. We can't turn away someone like that.'

Pretty cheesy, he thinks. Like something straight out of a police recruitment video.

Gonzo breathes out heavily. 'I guess not. All right, Detective. She can stay.'

'Attaboy, Gonzo. You're a terrific kid, you know that? You have a good heart. I'd be proud to partner up with you anytime. Here . . .'

Doyle reaches into his pocket. Finds the button that Amy gave him. The one with 'Captain Awesome' written on it. He fastens it to Gonzo's shirt.

'Now you're officially deputized.'

Gonzo stares at the button, then faces Doyle again. This time his eyes are definitely moist.

'That's pretty cool, Detective. I'm honored. I won't let you down.'

'I know you won't. Come on, let's go inside.'

Doyle picks up the bag and follows his new apprentice into the apartment. He's not surprised to see that there are at least three different computers in here, plus some floor-standing hi-fi speakers and several piles of books and magazines. What does surprise him is that the room is also home to a large number of potted plants. He never took Gonzo for the green-fingered type.

Tabitha is standing next to the threadbare sofa, looking as if she dare not risk sitting on it.

She says, 'I, uh, I couldn't help noticing that this place has only one bedroom.'

'The sofa's comfy,' says Gonzo. 'If you stay away from that one spring near the back.'

Doyle coughs loudly into his fist, then sends thought waves over to Gonzo when he looks across. For once, Gonzo seems to receive the transmission without the need for further amplification.

'So, uh, I can take the sofa, and you can have the bed. The sheets are okay. I changed them a week or so back.'

Tabitha curls a lip in disgust, then shoots Doyle a glare that says, *What the hell have you gotten me into here?*

'Okay, good,' says Doyle breezily. 'I'm gonna leave you two to get to know each other. Before I do, I need to lay down some ground rules.'

They look at him like two teenagers being left on their own for the first time. Rules? Why do we need rules?

'First of all, you stay in this apartment at all times. You don't go out. You need food, order takeout. You need something you can't get delivered, call me and I'll pick it up for you. You see or hear anything strange, or you get any weird phone calls, you need to tell me immediately. Gonzo, you have my number. Call me anytime and I'll come right over.'

Gonzo nods with enthusiasm. Being cooped up in here with all his food being delivered is probably no different from his usual existence outside of work. But Tabitha looks aghast.

'This is worse than prison. I can't live like this.'

'It's for a weekend. You can do it for that long.'

'Can I make calls? I have to tell Mrs Serafinowicz what's going on. She'll be worried.'

'You can call her in the morning, but whatever you do, don't tell her where you are or why you've left her apartment. Tell her you're okay, but you've decided to stay with friends for a while.'

She seems to agree to this, but her expression tells Doyle that she doesn't see the need for all this secrecy. Doyle doesn't want to tell her that, in his opinion, the killer would not baulk at torturing Mrs S if it meant discovering Tabitha's location.

'Okay,' says Doyle, 'I'm outta here. When I'm gone, put all the locks on the door. I'll call you in the morning. Have fun, guys.'

He looks at Tabitha, discerns that fun is probably the last thing on her mind, and beats a hasty retreat.

'One other thing, Gonzo.'

'What's that, Detective?

'Put some pants on. There's a lady present.'

Doyle hears the sirens. He sees the convoy of screaming radio cars, their roof lights bouncing color off the buildings as they hurtle toward Gonzo's place.

And then they're gone, and Doyle is blowing a sigh of relief and wiping the perspiration from his brow.

But the trigger for all this mayhem in his mind doesn't relent. His cellphone. Practically somersaulting with urgency on his nightstand.

The fear comes crashing back. Gonzo? Is this Gonzo calling for help?

He snatches up the phone and thumbs the answer button.

'Doyle,' he says, and when he doesn't get an immediate reply: 'Hello? Hello?'

'Where is she?'

Him. He's discovered his mistake. And now he wants to put things right.

Well, think again, motherfucker. This is my show now.

'Where's who?'

'Don't be obtuse, Cal. We both know who we're talking about.'

Doyle slips out of bed, leaving Rachel making murmurs of complaint behind him, and pads softly toward the living room.

'I think you need to give me some clues. Hey, you could play some music. That might work.'

'That's very amusing, Cal. Enjoy yourself while you can. It's not going to last. I'll find her, with or without your help.'

'Maybe. Maybe not. You fucked up. In a big way. You're a big fucking disappointment. But I bet that's not the first time you've heard that. I bet your mother told you that a lot.'

Silence. Doyle just hopes it's filled with teeth-grinding anger and resentment. He hopes he's got to the sonofabitch. How does it feel not to be in control of things for once, you pathetic fuck?

'You blew it, Cal.'

It's not the response Doyle was expecting.

'Blew what? What the fuck are you talking about?'

'Your reaction. All wrong. All the help I've been giving you, and this is how you repay me. No gratitude whatsoever. Just insults. So now you have to suffer the consequences. Maybe Tabitha Peyton is safe. For now. But she's not the only one on my list. There are plenty of others. And so I think the next one will have to be something pretty spectacular to make up for Tabitha. I'm not sure I'm even going to offer you any help to work out who it is. Whoever it is, their death is on you, Cal. It's all your fault.'

Sure, thinks Doyle. Like he's going to stop if I give up Tabitha. He's just trying to make me feel bad again. It's the only way he has left to retaliate for the name-calling. It's just another attempt to mind-fuck me, and it's not even a very good one.

'Whatever, man. Do what you have to. Time's running out for you, and I am really looking forward to stringing you up. Start looking behind you, asshole. You got a cop on your tail.'

'Do what I have to? You're going to regret saying that, Cal. Someone is going to die, and it's really going to be painful. For them and for you.'

'What do you mean, painful for me? If you're thinking about going anywhere near my family—'

He's interrupted by a chuckle. 'No, not your family. I keep telling you, I'm here to help. How would their deaths be classed as helping anyone? Now enjoy your day, Cal. I've heard the weather's going to be nice again.'

He hangs up. Doyle checks the time on his phone and sees that it's four in the morning. He weighs up the good news against the bad. The good news is that the killer doesn't know where Tabitha is, and so she's safe for the moment. The bad news is that someone is about to die in her place.

And he has no idea who.

TWENTY-THREE

She has never spent the night with a geek before.

Dorks, yes. An abundance of them. Even a few downright freaks.

But nothing compares to Gonzo for sheer strangeness. He's in a world of his own there. And it seems to be a world that doesn't sit comfortably anywhere in this corner of the universe.

She's not sure she can pin it on any particular facet of his personality. He's just generally . . . well, odd.

The staring, for example. He does a lot of that. And she's convinced that, half the time, he's not even aware he's doing it. She can be in the middle of something totally mundane – washing up a mug, say – and she'll turn around, and there he'll be. Just standing there, looking at her. And instead of wigging out she'll remain the polite guest and say something like, 'Are you okay?' And it's as if that causes him to snap out of some kind of trance, and he'll say, 'What? Oh, yeah,' and he'll look around the room as if trying to work out what fantastic forces caused him to be transported there.

She went straight to bed last night. Would have done so anyway, what with all that had happened. She felt mentally and physically drained. But even if she'd had the energy of a nuclear reactor she would have escaped to the bedroom. Just to be away from His Weirdness.

Sleeping was a different matter. The bedroom just wasn't

conducive to rest. She could put up with all the posters from movies such as *Terminator*, *The Matrix*, and *Alien*. She could even live with all those huge plants crowding around her bed like some flesh-starved triffids. What she couldn't get out of her head, though, was Gonzo's vagueness about his changing of the sheets. It kind of left her with the impression that he hadn't changed them in weeks. Maybe even months.

She wasn't about to put it to the test. There was no way she was going to permit her skin to come into contact with . . . well, whatever had been allowed to permeate or encrust those sheets.

Instead, she changed into pajamas, spread her old clothes across the bed and pillow, then lay on top of those, covering herself over with her night robe. In that situation, and with the thoughts and images rushing through her head, sleep was fitful. At one point she came awake crying out Helena's name.

And so this morning she is tired and cranky. There is nothing in the refrigerator – not even any milk. For breakfast she had to make do with toast and peanut butter washed down with black coffee, and she never takes her coffee black. Gonzo munched his way through an overflowing bowl of Coco Pops. Also without milk. Said he prefers it that way, the weirdo.

Small talk is a no-no. She tried it a few times, and it just got too bizarre. Like when she said to him, 'So, do your parents live in New York?' and he replied with, 'Depends on what you mean by parents.' Or, making breakfast, when she asked him if he wanted coffee, and he started telling her about the effects of that beverage on his bowels. Oh yeah, and why does he keep asking her which brand of corn chips she prefers?

She spoke with Doyle about it an hour ago. This was after she'd phoned Mrs Serafinowicz. She stuck to the story. Told Bridget she was fine, there was nothing to worry about, she just needed to get away from that building for a day or two, blah,

blah, blah. Then, when Doyle called, she said what she really thought. Took the phone into the bedroom and let rip. Told him this wasn't working. That it was like being cooped up in a mental asylum, and that she would sooner take her chances with a homicidal maniac than go stir-crazy with this nut-job.

Doyle calmed her down, as she knew he would. He has a gift for that. He only has to open his mouth for her to feel instantly more secure, more serene.

Unlike the freak who's sitting across from her at the table right now, staring at her while she skim-reads a magazine article on the success of Microsoft. Yes, he has a gift too, she thinks. The gift of turning me into a fucking nervous wreck.

Why couldn't Doyle stay with me? If he's so worried about my safety, why didn't he abandon whatever personal plans he had last night, and spend the night with me? If he had stayed . . . If he had held me in his arms . . .

'Is there anything I can do, you know, to make you happy?'

She wants to keep staring at the magazine. Pretend she didn't hear that. If this is his idea of coming on to her . . .

'What?' she says. 'What was that?'

Directly challenged like this, he suddenly looks like he wished he hadn't said anything.

'What I mean is . . . What I'm trying to say is . . . If there's anything . . . that I can do. You know?'

She closes the magazine. Which is crap, anyway. Written by geeks to be read by other geeks.

'Actually, yes. There is something you can do for me. You can make me happy in bed.'

He flushes the color of his hair. His head is like a tomato with spectacles.

'What? I, uhm . . . What?'

'The sheets, Gonzo. They need changing. If I have to stay

here another night, then it has to be with clean sheets. Do you have any?'

Gonzo looks around him, as if he is thinking they ought to be in plain sight.

'I, uh, no. I don't think so.'

'Is there a laundry room in this place?'

'Sure. In the basement.'

'Okay, good. We're getting somewhere. Then what you need to do is strip the sheets from the bed, take them down to the laundry room, and get them clean and dry.'

He looks at her as though the notion is an alien concept to him.

'I . . . I can't do that.'

'What do you mean, you can't do it? How hard can it be? You've done it before, haven't you? Please tell me these sheets have been cleaned at some point since you bought them.'

'No. I mean yes, they have been cleaned. But I can't. Not now. Detective Doyle said that we can't leave the apartment. I have to be with you, at all times.'

'He meant the apartment *building*, Gonzo. I'm not asking you to head across to New Jersey. Just the basement. For half an hour. Okay?'

He scratches his head. 'I don't know. I think I should give Detective Doyle a call first.'

She loses it then. 'Jesus Christ, Gonzo. Will you just go wash the fucking sheets before I throw the whole bed out of the fucking window?'

Gonzo stands slowly, uncertainly. 'Last night Detective Doyle called you a lady. Ladies don't talk like that.'

'You're right,' she says. 'I should have said please. Now please go wash the fucking sheets. Okay?'

★

Doyle's shift won't start until four in the afternoon. Which is killing him. Wandering around the apartment like this, trying to find chores to occupy his mind, trying not to get in Rachel's way, is just not working. He finds he's constantly checking his cellphone to make sure he hasn't missed a call. He feels like a man whose wife is about to give birth.

He needs the distraction of work. He will be kept busy in the aftermath of the Helena Colquitt killing. He will follow the procedure, the routine. He will talk to the people he is supposed to talk to, put the questions he is supposed to ask, write the reports he is meant to write.

All of which will be hard given that he suspects none of it is worth jack shit.

What will keep him going on this seemingly fruitless task is the possibility that somewhere, buried deep perhaps, is a clue to the unraveling of these apparently random killings. Okay, Helena wasn't the intended victim. But the killer thought she was. So why? Why did he think that? And why target Tabitha anyway? What links her to the other victims?

And the more important question right now: do any of those victims provide pointers to the next one?

He believes the killer when he says that he isn't going after Doyle's family. For one thing, the man hasn't lied to him once so far. He's provided Doyle with uncertainty, ambiguity, clues which are open to interpretation. But no downright lies. And deep down, Doyle knows that his own family doesn't fit the pattern of killings. He has no idea what that pattern is, but for some reason he knows that Rachel and Amy aren't part of it.

So how does he know that? What is he missing?

Laden with a plastic basket containing a mountain of washing that threatens to landslide and bury him at any moment, Gonzo has to wrestle with the basement door to get it to open. He snakes his arm round the door jamb, feathers it up and down the rough wall in search of the light switch. He finds it, clicks it on.

Nothing. The bulb must be dead.

He exhales. Steps gingerly through the doorway. Tries to make his feeble eyes gain mastery over the dimness in here.

The blow to the side of his head sends him reeling across the room. He bounces off the wall, hears his glasses clatter to the floor. He puts his hands up to fend off his attacker, but it's a pathetic defense. Another cruise missile pilots its way between his hands and zeros in on his cheek. When it slams home, it feels as though it detaches his head from his shoulders, leaving his body to crumple to the floor. His gargantuan brain, capable of composing complex pieces of software without going anywhere near a computer, scurries for the panic button and allows his survival instincts to take the helm. He tries to push himself up from the floor, because that's the only message he's getting.

And then something soft and warm is pulled over his head. Musty cloth presses tightly against his mouth and nose. He tries to suck oxygen through the weave, but it won't come quickly enough. The claustrophobia and the pain make him want to vomit, but he swallows it back, knowing that he could drown in his own sick. He feels an asthma attack coming on. He's going to die. He knows he is going to die.

Everything turns to black.

She had hoped for at least an hour of peace and solitude, maybe even longer given the amount of washing she made him take downstairs – Jesus, does he actually wear those clothes? An hour without the staring, without the randomness. Time to reflect. To think about Helena, her parents, her life. To decide what to do with her future when she gets out of this damned city.

So when there's a rap on the door barely ten minutes after Gonzo left the apartment, she is not amused. Can't he even manage a simple task like—

Oh.

She doesn't recognize the man standing there in the hallway when she opens the door. But he's tall, he's good-looking and he's holding up a leather wallet containing a police badge.

'What are you doing?' he says. 'Didn't Detective Doyle tell you not to open the door to anyone?'

'I . . . I'm sorry. I thought it was . . . Who are you, exactly?'

'Detective Todd Morton. I work with Cal Doyle in the Eighth Precinct. He sent me to get you. We don't have much time.'

She stares at him. Keeps hold of the door, just in case.

'What do you mean, not much time? Time for what?'

'I hate to tell you this, but we think the killer's on to you. He knows where you are. We need to move you out. We've already got Gonzo in a car downstairs.'

'He knows? How could he know? Detective Doyle said I was safe here.'

The man sighs. She thinks he looks embarrassed.

'We think he must have been tipped off somehow. It's the only way. Maybe Gonzo . . . We don't know.'

'Gonzo? No. Not him. He couldn't . . . I mean . . .'

'Whatever, we're taking you to separate places. Just to be on the safe side. From now on this stays with you and the police. Nobody else will know. We're organizing a twenty-four hour guard for you. Detective Doyle has offered to do the first watch.'

She feels her heart skip a little. Doyle? Spend a whole day with her?

'Where are we going?'

He smiles. 'Didn't I say? Your place. I'm going to take you back to the apartment Mrs Serafinowicz put you in. Right now it's as safe as anywhere else, especially with police protection. Are you okay with that?'

She scans him up and down again. He looks like he could be a cop. He knows too much for him not to be a cop. He knows about Cal Doyle, Gonzo, and Bridget Serafinowicz. He even knows that Bridget put me up in a vacant apartment after Helena was killed. How could he know all that and not be a cop?

But still . . .

'I think I should call Detective Doyle. You mind if I do that first? Just to check with him?'

Another sigh. Exasperation this time. 'All right. But can you make it quick?'

She turns away from him. Starts toward the phone. Realizes then that she doesn't know Doyle's number. Gonzo has it, but she doesn't. She turns back, and sees that the detective is craning to look along the hallway outside the apartment. His hand is tucked under his jacket, as if in readiness to pull his gun.

She thinks, This is no bullshit. He's really expecting trouble.

'I . . . I don't have his phone number.'

The man looks at her in disbelief. He digs a phone out of his pocket and starts thumbing buttons on it.

'What do you want? His home number? Wait, he's probably on his way to your apartment by now. I think I got his cell number here somewhere, but we got to be real fast.' He pauses, glances up the hallway again, slips his hand back under his jacket.

Shit. This is for real. He could have killed me several times over by now if he'd wanted to.

'Never mind,' she says. 'Let me grab my stuff. Thirty seconds, okay?'

She runs for the bedroom, almost tripping over in her eagerness not to waste any more of Detective Morton's time.

★

In the car, he asks her lots of questions about her life, and invents a life for himself in response to her own gentle probing. He gives himself a wife and two kids. Twins, in fact – Jesus, they can be a handful. Plus a dog which he never wanted to get in the first place, and which is tearing apart what little furniture they have, that little scamp. Which, by the way, is his name: Scamp.

He enjoys weaving this alternate world on the fly. Relishes the challenge of throwing in each new deceit whilst avoiding becoming caught in any contradictions.

But it's obvious she doesn't suspect a thing. Each additional fragment of his fantasy is swallowed whole. She's building up an image of a solid, dependable cop just doing his bit to help out the poor victimized civilian. And each city block he takes her closer to her apartment only serves to reassure her that there is nothing wrong with this picture.

When they finally pull up in front of her building and he takes her bag and leads her up to the front door and invites her to open up, he senses the relief in her. The absolute trust she now feels for him simply radiates from her.

And when he follows her up the staircase, he has to smile at what he has accomplished today.

Because the clues were there, if she chose to see them.

Didn't he tell her the killer was on his way? How much clearer could he have been?

And then there was his name. Detective Todd Morton, was how he introduced himself.

Todd, from the German word *Tod*. And Morton, from the French word *mort*. Both meaning death.

Detective Death.

What a cool name.

TWENTY-FOUR

Bridget Serafinowicz sets down her bags of shopping with a groan. Her knees hurt, her ankles hurt, her shoulders hurt. Why does growing old have to be so painful? Why do our bodies have to go through this goddamn-awful process of becoming ever more decrepit? If we have to die, why can't we stay healthy and fit until we do? It should be a simple case of turning the light off one night, never to wake up again. Not this. This is just torture.

But it shouldn't be like it was for Helena either. Not violent. Life should not be ripped away from people like that.

Her stomach clenches as she thinks about what happened upstairs. Here, in her building. So close.

The reporters were here again this morning. Ringing her buzzer, trying to cajole her into granting them an interview. The vultures. She ignored them. Stayed inside until they got bored of doing their highly speculative pieces to camera and finally drifted away to sniff out more ghoulish and sensational stories.

She came out then, when it was safe. Went to lunch with her friends Golda and Phyllis, just as she always does on a Saturday. But it wasn't the same. They were far too keen to hear the details of what exactly took place, then far too quick to cast them aside in favor of their own baseless imaginings. Bridget found the whole experience so distasteful she couldn't finish her tuna sandwich.

The shopping helped. Again, something she has always done

after lunch on a Saturday. She found it comforting to adhere to her routine, even though she had been tempted not to bother today. Being amongst all those people, none of whom had an inkling about what she had gone through, made the events seem somehow more distant, more unreal.

But it *was* real. Coming home again has emphasized that. It's as though the building has been tainted with an aura of horrific violence.

She starts unloading the bags. While she puts the grocery items away she thinks about Tabitha. That poor girl. She doesn't deserve such misery. So much death . . .

She wishes Tabitha were back here with her. She would comfort her. She would put things right for her. She would do all the things she would have done for her own daughter, if she'd been fortunate enough to have one.

She hopes Tabitha doesn't leave because of this, but she suspects she will. And when she does it will be heartbreaking. Life will seem so much emptier without her.

Bridget opens the last of her bags and smiles at the contents. A teddy bear, from the Build-A-Bear Workshop on Fifth Avenue. Dressed up as the Statue of Liberty, no less. Something to help convince Tabitha that New York has a friendly face too. That it's not such a bad place really. That she should seriously think about giving it another chance.

Bridget locks up her apartment and forces her complaining bones up the stairs to the second floor. She takes the master key from her pocket and opens up Apartment 2B. She will make it look nice again. Even though Tabitha was in it for only a brief period and won't have created much mess, she will make it perfect again. She will tidy and clean and polish, and she will make the bed and place the bear carefully on the pillow. For when she comes back.

She goes inside. Closes the door behind her.

But still her screams are heard right along the hallway.

Mrs Li is back in her apartment so fast she can't remember the journey. Like she traveled faster than thought itself.

And in her apartment she is screaming at her husband and pointing back the way she came and trying to make the uncomprehending fool appreciate that while she is prepared to change light bulbs in the dark, and do a lot of other things besides, the nature of which she is not about to go into just now but which they need to discuss at some point, she is absolutely not willing to tackle apparitions of the type she has just encountered in the basement. She draws the line at that one. And so what is he going to do about it? Huh? Huh?

She is almost surprised when her husband shuts off the television and gets up from his chair. He looks solemn, concerned. It seems as though he is finally going to take decisive action for once. He assumes the bearing of a tribal chief, about to take part in a duel to the death to defend his loved ones. She experiences a sense of pride swelling in her bosom.

Her bosom deflates when she sees him walk in the wrong direction, toward the bedroom.

She starts to yell at him again. She works herself up into a frenzy, throwing at him every sharp spear of insult she can think of. She threatens to leave him. Worse, she threatens to tell all their friends how bad he is in bed.

She clams up when he returns from the bedroom. She is silent because she has seen that he is holding an industrial-sized flashlight. Not like the puny plastic one he gave her earlier. This one is muscular. It looks capable of lighting up a whole football stadium. A part of her wants to know why he couldn't be bothered to dig it out for her before she went down to the basement, but she suppresses it. Instead, she watches while her husband steps into the kitchen area and takes the large meat cleaver from its hook on the wall.

Now she knows he means business. There is a boldness to him, a meanness even, that she has not seen in a long time. And as she follows him out of the apartment she experiences a tingling she thought was lost to her forever.

Together they descend the staircase to the basement. At the door to the laundry room they pause. Mr Li pushes open the door and flicks on his flashlight. A cone of light punches through to the far wall. As he plays it over the interior of the room, long fingers of shadow angle and stretch away from them. Mrs Li taps her husband on the shoulder and points in the direction of the washing machine. They start toward it.

Something crunches underfoot. Mr Li flicks the beam downward. He shifts his boot, and the light glints off the myriad fragments of glass from a pair of crushed spectacles. He gives his wife a puzzled glance, then presses on into the room.

Mr Li finds the mountain of washing and keeps the beam focused on it, as steadily as he can manage. There is no movement from the bundle. No sound either. Mrs Li is beginning to wonder if her imagination was playing tricks on her. She believes that her husband will bury his meat cleaver in her skull if that turns out to be the case.

Mr Li steps closer and closer. He lifts his foot and presses it gingerly into the pile. Mrs Li holds her breath. She almost expects a hand to dart out and grab her husband by the ankle. In which event she is out of here again.

Mr Li tries once more. This time he aims a swift strong kick into the center of the mass. His foot strikes something solid and there is a muffled cry. He leaps away, calls his wife to come closer. She has no desire to go anywhere near that thing, whatever it is, but her man is insistent. She is almost crying when he hands her the flashlight and tells her to keep it trained on their target.

Her hand shakes, but she does as she is told. Soft murmurs of fear bubble from her lips as she watches her husband start to pull off the sheets and garments forming the pile. Each time he yanks something away, he takes a leap backward, his cleaver at the ready to strike down whatever is lurking here. Mrs Li thinks she is going to pee herself any moment now.

And then it comes into view. It's a man. His arms and legs are tied with cord, and there is a cloth bag over his head. Duct tape is wound tightly around the bag at the point where the man's mouth should be.

Mrs Li's fear suddenly changes its focus. This man could be suffocating here.

She cries at her husband to remove the bag. He looks at her, then back at the trussed figure. Keeping his cleaver at the ready, he reaches down with his other hand and snatches at the bag.

When Mrs Li sees what caused her to worry so much, what caused her to rant and curse, what caused her almost to have a heart attack, she wants to seize the cleaver from her open-mouthed husband and separate the red-headed lunatic's head from his scrawny shoulders.

The first call comes in just as Doyle is preparing to leave for work.

'Hello?'

'D-Detective Doyle? It's me. G-G-Gonzo.'

'Gonzo? What is it? What's wrong?'

'You promise you won't be m-mad?'

'Gonzo, I'm not promising anything. Just tell me what the fuck this is about.'

'I . . . the girl. Tabitha. Sh-she's gone.'

'Gone? What do you mean, gone? Gone where?'

'I don't know. I was downstairs. It wasn't my fault. When I got back up here—'

'Gonzo. Stay there, okay? I'm coming right over.'

'O-okay, but it wasn't—'

Doyle doesn't wait to hear the excuses. He ends the call and then grabs his jacket. In the hallway he meets Rachel coming the other way.

'Gotta go,' he says.

She raises an eyebrow. 'Who's your date?'

Doyle doesn't answer. He stops only long enough to grant his wife a peck on the cheek, and then he's out of the apartment and clattering down the staircase. When he gets outside, he races for his car and jumps behind the wheel.

That's when he gets the second call.

The voice says, 'Cal? It's Jay. I know you're not on duty yet, but I thought you should hear this.'

Doyle feels the dread build in the pit of his stomach.

'Hear what, Jay?'

Holden pauses. 'This is fucking crazy, man. I can't even believe this myself. But with all the weird stuff you've been saying about a serial killer . . .'

'Spit it out, Jay.'

Another pause. 'He came back. Whoever whacked Helena Colquitt, he came back and got the other one.'

Doyle's mouth is suddenly very dry. He finds it a struggle to get his words out.

'The other one? What do you mean?'

But he knows precisely what he means. He just can't bring himself to accept it.

'The roomie. Tabitha Peyton. He came back, got her too. Weird thing is, he used exactly the same MO. She's in the bathtub, legs over the side. Exactly the same. Crazy.'

Doyle stares out of his grimy windshield. This conversation is too surreal. It can't be happening. He saw Tabitha last night. He spoke to her this morning. She was safe. She was alive. How could things have gone so drastically wrong in the space of a couple of hours?

'Cal? You there, man?'

Doyle hears his own voice speaking. He thinks it sounds surprisingly calm and level. And yet it seems detached from him, as though he is listening to somebody else.

'Thanks for letting me know, Jay. I'll come straight over.'

He hangs up and continues to stare out into the street. Ahead, a woman is walking toward him with her dog. Nice day for a walk, he thinks. This is what spring is made for. Walking. Enjoying the first signs of sun, of growth. Of life.

And then it hits him. A wave of grief and rage.

He says one word. *No.*

But it's not a simple quiet utterance. It's a long drawn-out syllable that is hurled from his mouth with a force that feels capable of shattering his windshield.

Outside, the woman turns her dog and quickens her pace in the opposite direction.

It takes a frustratingly long time to get there.

He is not in a police sedan, with its lights and sirens and air of authority. He is in his own rust-bucket of a car, and all he has at his disposal is a car horn; and everybody else on the streets, many of whom have much more imposing vehicles and much more impressive car horns, simply blare back at him and flip him the finger and mouth words such as 'asshole'.

But he gets there.

He gets there just as they are lifting Tabitha's lifeless and naked corpse from the bathtub. It becomes real then. She is dead.

Despite the frequent but unconvincing arguments that have been running through his head about there being some mistake, Tabitha Peyton is most assuredly no longer in the land of the living.

You'll be safe. I promise.

That's what he told her in the coffee shop. That he would protect her. And she believed him. She trusted him unreservedly. And he let her down.

'You believe this shit?'

Jay Holden. At Doyle's side.

'I mean, that the guy has the balls to kill one girl, then come back the next day and kill the other one?'

Doyle says nothing. He is too numb. It seems too much of an effort even to think, let alone speak.

Holden doesn't let up. He grabs Doyle by the upper arm and turns him so that they are face to face. Holden's expression is more serious than any that Doyle has seen on him before. And when Holden speaks again, it is in a low rumble.

'You know something, don't you? Me, I don't know shit. I'm just a simple cop. This is all fucked up and I don't know why. These girls dying like this. The shrink and the other vics. Maybe they're connected and maybe they're not. I have no idea. But you know, don't you, Cal?'

Doyle maintains eye contact with Holden. He neither confirms nor denies Holden's suspicion. But he knows that Holden isn't stupid. It doesn't take a detective to work out that Doyle has a deeper interest in this case than is normal.

Holden nods. As though he has just heard Doyle's thoughts.

'When you want to talk, you know where to find me.'

And then he walks away.

Doyle feels his legs itching to take him in Holden's direction. God, if he could only tell him. If he could share this burden with somebody else. Anybody. How much of a release would that be?

And then another voice breaks into his thoughts. A voice much less welcome.

'Hey, Doyle! Good to see you again.'

Doyle turns to see Folger, with the usual stupid grin on his face. Behind him, Kravitz stands silently.

Folger continues: 'You called in for a look at the babe? Another stunner, huh? Better even than the first one, in my book. You think they were rug munchers? I think they musta been. There's not a trace of rug left on either of 'em.'

His laugh is raucous and unaccompanied. He tries to nudge his partner in the ribs, but succeeds in reaching only as high as his solar plexus. Kravitz recoils, slightly winded, but also looking faintly embarrassed and irritated.

Doyle shakes his head in apparent pity. 'Folger, get a life.'

He turns away, but Folger decides he hasn't finished.

'Get a life! That's rich! You hear that? Get a life. From the guy who has people dropping dead all around him. From the guy who doesn't get cases any more serious than traffic offenses. From the guy who's so fucked up he thinks all the crimes in the city are the work of one evil mastermind. This is no comic book, Doyle. There ain't no such person as Lex Luther. Get a life. Jesus, what a joke.'

Doyle knows he should keep on walking. He should maintain his cool and leave all this behind. Doesn't matter what they think. Doesn't matter what they might say about him when he's gone.

Like hell it doesn't.

He does an about-turn and strolls back to Folger. The Homicide detective stands his ground, but Doyle knows it's only because he's given himself no choice. You can't throw out a pile of shit like that and then take refuge behind your partner when it starts flying back at you.

'Nah,' says Doyle. 'That ain't the joke. You wanna know

what the real joke is? It's when people say that short people make up for it with big dicks. It's just not true. I know that because I spoke with a hooker named Alicia.'

Doyle hears a collective intake of breath from around the room. It's been rumored for a while that, through sheer desperation, Folger has been getting it on with a fat old prostitute, but nobody has had the temerity to raise the topic in his presence.

Until now. And Doyle isn't keeping his voice down as he reveals all.

'Alicia told me yours is the tiniest she's seen in her whole life, and she's gonna be fifty this year. That's a lot of dicks to compare against. She did say you've got stamina, though. Said you were grunting and gasping in that bedroom for over an hour. Until she got tired of waiting and helped you climb up onto the bed.'

The room erupts. Folger erupts too, but it's with uncontrollable fury rather than laughter. When he lashes out, Doyle is ready for it. He's expecting it. In fact, he wants it.

He swats away Folger's telegraphed punch as though it's a mere inconvenience, and then he responds in the way he has been planning all along. Grabbing Folger hard by the throat, he pushes him backward. Only by a couple of feet. Just enough to send him ass over tit into the bathtub.

'Holy shit!' somebody says.

Folger pulls himself up in the water and starts to drag himself out of the tub.

'Oh, you did it now, Doyle. Your career is over. It was nothing anyway, but now you are so finished. You are fucked, boy.'

He steps onto the floor, water pooling around him. He stretches out a finger, then slowly circles his arm so that the finger takes in everyone in the room. 'You all saw that, right? You saw him assault a fellow officer.' His finger finally lands on

Kravitz. 'You saw it too, right? For the report. You saw what he did.'

Doyle sees Kravitz look down on his partner. And what he realizes is that the man is looking down not just through altitude, but through attitude too.

'Yeah, I saw it. I also saw you throw the first punch. You want that in the report too?'

That's when Doyle decides it's time to go. He takes one last look at the face of Tabitha Peyton, then walks out the door. Nobody in that room is going to report him for standing up for himself. If anyone's career is over, it's Folger's. At the very least, there's probably a divorce about to take place between the Homicide cops.

He trudges down the staircase. He should feel better after putting Folger in his place, but he doesn't. Folger is an irrelevance. The face at the forefront of his mind right now is not Folger's but Tabitha's. Tabitha's beautiful, innocent face, now reflecting the peace she once craved. Maybe she was right to feel so disenchanted with this city. It finally claimed her, didn't it? And there was nothing he could do to prevent it. Nothing he could do to turn her life around and provide her with the opportunity to discover happiness.

When he hits the street outside, his heart is filled with darkness. There is the potential for murder in that heart.

And he's not sure he wants it to go away.

TWENTY-FIVE

He pounds on the door. Which in itself is a favor, because what he really wants to do is kick it right down.

When it opens a crack, Doyle slams his palms on it and sends Gonzo reeling across the living room.

'What the fuck happened, Gonzo? You were supposed to be looking after her. How could you take your eye off the ball like that?'

Gonzo's jaw moves up and down, but nothing comes out. It's like someone has pressed his mute button.

It's only then that Doyle notices the absurdly large, white-framed spectacles that Gonzo is sporting. Only then that he sees the swelling on Gonzo's cheek, distorting his face into that of a hamster with a peanut in its jowls. Only then that the truth dawns on him. He lowers his voice to a more respectable level.

'Oh shit. Tell me what happened.'

'I . . . I don't know, Detective. I went down to the laundry room. I didn't want to, but Tabitha insisted. She wanted clean sheets. So I went. I thought it would be okay if I wasn't going out of the building. Only the light wasn't working down there, and all the windows are boarded up. I couldn't see a thing. And then somebody hit me. They put a bag over my head and tied me up. I was down there for hours. I'm sorry, Detective. I did my best. I really did.'

Doyle stares at the pitiful wreck before him. He knows that Gonzo is absolutely right. There's nothing more he could have done. He's not a cop. He doesn't know how to fight. He's just a kid. A kid with really bad glasses. What the hell was I thinking?

Except that I didn't think it would come to this. There wasn't supposed to be any fighting. The killer was never supposed to find Tabitha. How did he do that? How does he always manage to stay one step ahead?

'You think she's okay, Detective? You think you'll be able to find her?'

Doyle hears the optimism, and is saddened that he has to quash it. 'We found her, Gonzo. She's dead.'

Gonzo tilts his head, blinks. 'Tabitha? Our Tabitha? The one who stayed here last night?' He steadies himself on the back of a chair, then gently lowers himself onto the seat. 'How could that be?'

Doyle has no answer.

Gonzo suddenly straightens in his chair. 'I didn't tell anyone. I swear. I didn't tell anyone she was staying here.'

Doyle puts out a hand to calm him. 'It's okay. I know you didn't. Somehow the killer figured it out. I don't know how he did it, but he's damn smart. Did you pick up anything on him in the laundry room? His voice, his height, his clothes?'

'Nothing. I just walked in there, and bang! That was it.'

Doyle gestures toward Gonzo's face. 'You should get that looked at.'

'I'm okay. It's sore, but I'm okay. My glasses got broke, though. These are my old pair. I don't see so well out of them.'

'Get some new ones. Send me the bill.'

'You don't have to do that.'

'Yes. Yes, I do. I got you into this mess.'

'You couldn't have known. It wasn't your fault.'

'Gonzo! Stop being so fucking nice to me. It *is* my fault. It's all my fault. I shouldn't have brought her here. I shouldn't have asked you to watch over her. You could have been killed, do you understand that?'

'But I wasn't. I'm okay. I was glad to help out. I like you. And . . . and I liked Tabitha too.'

The purity of motive hits Doyle hard. There is no selfishness here, no hidden agenda.

'Yeah,' he answers. 'I liked her too.'

He moves to the window. Across the street, a low-rise school building in concrete and glass occupies most of the block, but he doesn't really take it in. Doesn't really see anything. It's just a meaningless geometric shape. His head is too crowded with other thoughts. He's been outsmarted. Again. The killer said this one would hurt, and it does. God, it hurts.

The others hurt too. Their names will be forever seared into his memory. Cindy Mellish. Lorna Bonnow. Sean Hanrahan. Andrew Vasey. Helena Colquitt. And now Tabitha Peyton. A roll call of lost souls. And all reaching out for Doyle. All calling to him from beyond the grave. And isn't there a note of blame in their plaintive cries?

He thinks it's time.

Time to do what he should have done at the very beginning of all this. Time to surrender.

He thought he could win. He was arrogant enough to think he had the intelligence to catch this evil bastard. But now, humiliating as it might be, he has to accept he was wrong.

The killer is laughing at him. Ridiculing his puny efforts. He could easily have killed Tabitha here, in Gonzo's apartment. Instead, he chose to make a statement. By taking Tabitha back to her apartment and killing her in the way he intended last night, he was saying, *I can do what I want and you can't stop me.*

And Doyle is starting to realize he's right about that. The killer does what he wants. He goes where he wants, murders who he wants. He's like a ghost. He can't be seen or touched or caught. But if he chooses to haunt you, then you're condemned. He will pass through your walls and he will whisper in your ear and you will do his bidding. And then you will die.

'Detective? Are you okay?'

Doyle turns his gaze on Gonzo. 'That attitude of yours? The way you just want to be of some value? Don't ever lose it, okay? No matter how many times life kicks you in the balls, stay just the way you are, Gonzo.'

He starts heading for the door.

Gonzo calls after him. 'Where are you going?'

Doyle pauses, just for a second.

'To catch a ghost.'

He should be proud. What he did with Tabitha Peyton today was practically a work of art. Nobody would have been expecting that. It was a stroke of genius. He should open some champagne.

And yet . . .

The kid. The geeky red-headed fuckwit with the stupid name. Gonzo.

What the hell was he doing there? Again! Seeing him outside Vasey's place not once but twice was disconcerting enough. But this!

Why would Doyle take the Peyton girl to him? He can't be a cop. Cops don't look like that. And they certainly put up a better fight than he did in that basement.

So what the fuck?

I should have killed him, he thinks. Yes, that would have been the best thing to do. It would have been so easy. I missed an opportunity. He's starting to get under my skin, and I can't let him interfere like this.

There are people who need my help.

Doyle works his shift. He spends most of it going through the reports on the various murders, over and over again. Hoping to catch something he's missed. Praying that he'll find something that will mean he doesn't have to go through with his decision. But it's fruitless. He knew it would be. He's looked at all the paperwork before, dozens of times. Other than the link between Vasey, Hanrahan and Cindy Mellish, there is nothing. And even then it could be that Hanrahan and the girl were killed simply as pointers to Vasey as the next victim. There may be no more of a connection than that. There is nothing to suggest that any of the other victims were linked in any way to Vasey.

So that's it, then. He is left with no choice.

He gets up from his desk. Steps toward the door. He passes Holden's desk. Holden is typing at a keyboard. He has pulled overtime on the murders of the two girls. He looks up at Doyle.

'You wanna talk?'

Doyle considers the offer. He wishes Holden hadn't asked. It would be so easy to say yes.

'Tomorrow,' he says. 'We'll talk tomorrow.'

Holden nods slowly and returns to his typing. Doyle moves out into the hallway and enters a storeroom. He opens a wall cabinet and takes down what he needs. He's supposed to sign it out but he doesn't bother. He drops the item into his pocket and returns to his desk.

Then he waits.

It's almost one-thirty in the morning when he gets home. He'll be back on duty at eight. It's a tough switch-over. Doyle knows a number of detectives who don't even bother going home, especially if they live way out in the sticks. Some of them grab what sleep they can on a cot in the station house. Some even go partying between the shifts. Family man that he is now, Doyle always goes home. He goes home and he slips into a warm bed with his warm wife and he sinks instantly into a deep and reinvigorating slumber.

But not tonight.

Tonight his brain has no plans for winding down. It has too much to consider. Too much to worry about.

His future, for instance. Or, to be more precise, whether he has one.

So, instead of going to bed, he switches on a lamp and fetches a cold beer from the kitchen and makes himself comfortable on the sofa. And then he raises his beer bottle in a farewell toast to his career.

Because it's over. One way or another, his life as a cop is over.

Maybe his liberty too. And his marriage.

Hell, his whole life is over.

Fuck it.

He takes a long swig of beer. God, that feels good. Enjoy it while it lasts, Doyle. It could be a while before you have the opportunity to get good and drunk again.

He drains the bottle. Goes to the kitchen again. Comes back with a trio of bottles. Already open, because he doesn't plan to waste any time.

He's halfway through the second when his cellphone rings. He's not surprised. He's been expecting this.

'Talk,' he says. 'Tell me what a good job you did.'

'Hello, Cal. You answered quickly. What's the matter? Can't sleep? Now why would that be?'

'Don't fuck with me. I've had it. Say what you gotta say, and then fuck off. I'm tired of this shit.'

'Don't be like that, Cal. You knew it would be painful. I told you it would. You didn't really think you could keep Tabitha hidden from me for long, did you?'

'You didn't have to do that to her. She did nothing wrong. She never did anything to hurt you.'

'And I never said she did. Jesus, Cal, you still don't get it, do you?'

'Get what?'

'You don't understand what's happening. Brain power. That's what's missing here. Find it, Cal. Use it.'

'You finished? I need another beer.'

'Depends on what you mean by finished. Tabitha's death was a hell of a showpiece, but she wasn't the finale. There will be others. But if you mean am I finished giving you help, well that's up to you, buddy. Like I told you, I'm not going to sneak anything in. You want my help now, you'll have to ask for it. So what's it going to be?'

'I need to think about it.'

'So think about it. I'll give you one hour, and then I'll call you back. It'll be up to you then. You decide if you want my help or not. Either way, somebody else is set to die in the next twenty-four hours. Maybe you'll get lucky this time. This could be your chance to shine, Cal. What have you got to lose?'

When the call ends, Doyle almost laughs. What have I got to lose? Everything, that's what.

Tabitha wasn't the finale, the caller said.

Well, she was for Doyle. He can't have another death on his conscience.

He's in a lose-lose situation now. If he continues to play along with his mysterious caller's little game, then there's every likelihood another innocent life will be lost. Experience has taught him that he's not a strong enough player to prevent that outcome.

And the alternatives?

Well, he could do what he did before: cut the bastard out. Refuse to take his calls. The sonofabitch hated that. Couldn't handle not having an audience, someone to play with.

But it didn't prevent further deaths. All it did was reduce Doyle's chances of catching the killer from infinitesimally small down to nil.

So there's only one move left to make.

He has to pass on everything he knows to the Department. Let them handle this. Give them a half-decent chance of stopping this insane genius. A person whose existence they're not even aware of right now.

They'll throw the book at Doyle, of course. That's a given. Probably throw the whole fucking library. He's left them no choice. Maybe if he'd gone to them much earlier he could have gotten away with a mild disciplinary charge. But not now. He's covered up too much, for too long. Some people on the force are already looking for ways to kick him out. They've been just itching for him to step out of line. Well there you go, guys. I'm so far off the line I can no longer even see the fucking line. Go ahead, string me up.

And if, by some miracle, the PD displays even an ounce of sympathy for his plight, that'll go straight out the window once they hear what else he's been up to. The killer knows things about Doyle. Lots of things. Things even his own wife doesn't know. And if he chooses to divulge that information – as he undoubtedly will once it becomes apparent that the cops have heard all about the calls he has been making – then Doyle can forget about any mercy pleas.

Unless, of course, the killer has been bluffing all along. Maybe he's been exaggerating the extent of his inside information.

Not that it matters now. With or without any revelations the killer is able to make, Doyle's ass is toast. It's only a matter of degree now. Severely burnt or completely carbonized.

'You coming to bed?'

Rachel, standing in the doorway. Wearing just a long T that barely covers her modesty. She peers at him through half-closed eyes. Her hair looks as though it's just been hit by a blast of wind.

'Soon. I need to unwind first.'

He hopes she'll go back to bed, but instead she comes over to join him on the sofa. She tucks her legs beneath her and rests her chin on his shoulder.

'You okay?'

What to say? Yeah, I'm fine, but tomorrow they'll be carting my ass to jail?

'Yeah, just thinking.'

She laughs through her nostrils, and he feels the warmth of her breath on his neck.

'That's not like you. Does it hurt?'

He feels he should laugh back, to let her know it's nothing serious. But he can't do it.

'I'm not sure I can be a cop anymore.'

She raises her head. 'What? What brought this on?'

'Dunno. Things have changed. I've changed. The job doesn't mean what it used to.'

She strokes a finger across his cheek. It's gentle, soothing.

'Are you in trouble?'

He shrugs. 'Aren't I always? Seems I can't do anything to stay outta trouble these days.'

'Is it the phone calls?'

He looks at her, and she says, 'I heard your phone again, a few minutes ago. I know there's something going on, and I know you can't talk about it, and it's killing me. Worse than that, I think it's killing you too. Tell me one thing, Cal. Tell me it's going to end soon. Tell me this isn't going to carry on for the rest of our lives.'

It's an easy one to answer. 'It's not going to carry on. It's nearly over. I promise.'

Yeah, it's nearly over. Everything he ever worked for is nearly over.

'Then . . . maybe things won't seem so bad once it's out of the way.'

He holds back a reply to that one. Swallows it down with a mouthful of beer.

She leans closer, kisses him on the cheek. 'Come to bed.'

He nods. 'Soon.'

She gets up from the sofa again. He watches the gentle gyration of her hips as she walks to the door.

'Rach?' he calls. She looks over her shoulder at him. Her heavy eyelids lend her expression a dreamy, seductive quality.

'I love you,' he says. 'You know that, don't you?'

'Come to bed,' she answers, and there is a promise there that lingers in the air even after she has gone.

He aches to follow that promise and catch it. And when, instead, he chugs from his beer bottle, he finds it a poor substitute that tastes bitter on his tongue.

But he drinks it anyway. He drains all the bottles in front of him and tries to summon up the energy to go fetch some more, but finds that he can only stare into nothingness and listen to the silence.

When his phone finally rings again, he checks neither the time nor the caller ID. He knows who this is from, and that it will be precisely one hour since his last call. He experiences a sense of finality as he presses the answer button.

'Hello again, Cal. Time's up, pal. What's it to be? You want my help or not?'

'I want your help,' says Doyle.

'You sure? I don't want to twist your arm or anything.'

'Just say what you gotta say.'

'All right, Cal. I'm glad you've seen sense. Here we go . . .'

As the music fades in, Doyle tunes out. He doesn't even listen to what the man is telling him. Just lets him say his piece. Doesn't interrupt. Doesn't give him any reaction. Nothing for the pond life to feed off. And when the monologue is over, Doyle hangs up without even a word.

He stares into space for a few moments longer. Then he reaches for the item he brought home from the station house. A digital voice recorder, still wired up to his cellphone. He switches it off. At the start of his shift he will hand it over to the Lieutenant.

And with it, he'll be handing over his life.

TWENTY-SIX

Sunday morning. Doyle is wending his way to work again. The traffic is light, and it's going to be another beautiful spring day. It feels to Doyle as though the fingers of sunlight reaching to him through his windshield should be accompanied by a heavenly choir. He wonders if he's being told he should be driving to church instead. To seek some forgiveness. To discover if, even at this late stage, there's any hope of salvation for him.

Waiting at a stop signal, he glances at the voice recorder sitting on the passenger seat next to him. It also seems to be sending him messages. Trying to entice him. As if it's saying, *Go on, you know you want to*. Falling prey to temptation he picks it up and switches it on. And that's why I don't go to church anymore, he thinks. The priests always said I was weak. But why the hell not? What've I got to lose? Might as well hear what the Lieutenant's about to hear before he tosses my ass in the slammer and swallows the key.

The music first. Something modern. Doyle knows this song. He's not good on titles, but the band playing this one sings it time and time again.

Why does it always rain on me?

First clue? Has to be. But it means nothing to Doyle.

Then the killer's voice breaks in. That damn silky voice that will haunt Doyle forever.

'Certainly raining a lot on you lately, huh, Cal? If it carries on like this, you'll need to get yourself a hat. Protect that brain. It's the only thing that's going to get you out of this mess.'

The caller pauses for a moment, raising the music's volume and then lowering it before he speaks again.

Sonofabitch thinks he's a damn DJ now.

'I don't want you making any mistakes on this one, Cal. You don't have a good record so far. It must be breaking you up inside. How do you cope with that? All those mistakes? It must affect your behavior, your relationships. Maybe I should ask your wife. She of all people must sense something is wrong.'

He pauses again while he gives Doyle another blast of the song.

'What's the matter, buddy? Nothing you want to say to me? I understand. You must have a lot on your mind right now. As if all these people dying wasn't enough. You've got the distractions too, right? All that small stuff that just gets in the way. The little irritations that you could do without. It's all raining down on you, right, Cal?'

The chorus once more. Repeating the title: *Why does it always rain on me?*

'It's okay. You don't need to say anything. Save your energy for what's to come. Just remember that I'm here to help when you need me. Speak to you soon, my friend. Oh, and by the way, you have until eight o'clock tonight. Eight p.m. Get it right this time, Cal. I'm rooting for you, buddy.'

The call ends then. Doyle shuts off the recorder. What the hell was that all about? There were clues in there? Rain? What fucking rain?

It angers him that he cannot read anything of value into what he's just heard. Is he really that stupid? Granted, he's no chess grandmaster, but can't he at least do something with what he's just been given?

Fuck it.

Why am I stressing over this, anyhow? Makes no difference. Not my problem anymore. Let the PD figure it out. Let them decide what to do with me, too.

When he gets to the squadroom, he keeps his hands in his pockets, turning the voice recorder over and over. His mouth is dry. He tries licking his lips, but his tongue rasps on the parched skin. Through the windows looking into the Lieutenant's office, there is no sign of Cesario.

Doyle turns to LeBlanc, who is biting into a soggy egg and bacon muffin. 'The boss not in yet?'

LeBlanc wipes yolk from his mouth with a napkin. 'He's at the Big House for a meeting. Could be there for a coupla hours.'

Doyle nods his thanks and moves to his desk. Great, he thinks. It's like pissing your pants and then being told you have to sit in them for the rest of the day.

He does some paperwork, makes some phone calls, answers a few more calls, but he feels he may as well not be there for all the impact he's making. If all the cops were as absent from the planet as he is today, the crooks could go wild.

At just after ten-fifteen his desk-phone rings again. What is it with you people? Don't you know it's a Sunday? A day of rest, folks. Go cut your lawns or visit your aged aunts or jog around the park. Just stop bothering me when I'm on the verge of jumping off the cliff that was my life.

He answers it anyway. Reels off the usual, 'Eighth Precinct. Detective Doyle.'

'Detective Doyle? It's Mrs Sachs here. I hope you don't mind my bothering you like this, it being a Sunday morning and all.'

Out of the corner of his eye, Doyle catches sight of Lieutenant Cesario entering the room and moving across to his office. He feels his heart start to knock on his rib cage as if to say, *You're on, Doyle. Time for your swan song.*

All he needs to do now is get rid of Mrs Sachs.

'Hello, Mrs Sachs. How are you today?'

'How am I? I don't know how I am. I'm either deliriously happy or crushingly disappointed. What should I be, Detective? Tell me how I should feel.'

Doyle watches Cesario take his coat off and sit in his chair. He for one doesn't look overjoyed. Doyle wonders if he's getting heat from upstairs over the roommate murders. Well, Lou, maybe I can help you out on that score.

'I'm sorry, Mrs Sachs. I don't understand what it is you're asking me.'

'Well, you spoke with Mr Repp, didn't you?'

Doyle recalls his visit to Repp, and it almost causes him to smile.

'Yes, I spoke with him.'

'Then I guess what he said to me yesterday must be with your permission. So I should be happy, am I right?'

'Mrs Sachs, what did Repp say to you, exactly?'

'That my Patricia is willing to come home. That she's in some financial trouble, and that if I'm willing to provide the money for her to pay off her bills, she will come back home to me. That's what he told me, and that's what I would love to believe. Only . . .'

Her voice cuts off, and Doyle is convinced she is choking back a tear. It's what she would love to believe. But deep down, she knows she is being fleeced. She knows her daughter is dead.

'Mrs Sachs, can I assume from what you've just said that Repp is willing to act as the courier here? That he is offering to take the cash to your daughter and then bring her back?'

'Yes. That's what he told me.'

'And how much money did he say your daughter owes?'

'Just over four hundred thousand dollars. It's not the money. The money I can raise. But . . .'

Son of a bitch, thinks Doyle. You wouldn't listen, would you, Repp? I gave you fair warning, but you wouldn't listen. You're still gonna take the old lady's money and then you're gonna disappear. Well, we'll see about that.

'Mrs Sachs, let me look into this, okay? Give me some time to check it out. Meanwhile, keep tight hold of your money. Don't give Repp a penny till I clear it. Okay?'

'All right. Yes. Thank you. I'll wait, but . . . I don't want to lose her, Detective. If she really is willing to come home . . .'

'Just give me until tomorrow, please. One more day to check this story out. Your daughter has been gone since 2001. One more day isn't going to make a difference.'

There's a pause, and then: 'You're right. I can wait another day. When you're my age, the days fly past like they're minutes. I'll wait. Thank you, Detective. You've been good to me.'

'Goodbye, Mrs Sachs.'

He almost slams the phone down. What the hell does Repp think he's playing at? Does he think this is a game? Does he think he can just ignore what I said and carry on doing things his way? What a shit. What a lousy, stinking . . .

What am I doing?

Why am I getting so caught up in this? Five minutes from now I won't even be a cop. Repp will be in somebody else's caseload. Why am I letting him get to me like this?

Why? Because I care, that's why. I care about people like Mrs Sachs and all the other victims who deserve to have somebody on their side, fighting their corner. It's why I became a cop.

And that's what I'll miss. See, I was wrong. When I sat here complaining about working the small cases instead of the high-profile ones, I had it all wrong. It's the Mrs Sachses of this world that make the job worthwhile.

And I'm gonna throw it all away.

Doyle looks again into Cesario's office. This is one of the hardest decisions he's ever had to make, but he knows he can't back out now.

He gets up from his desk. Slips his hand into his pocket and grasps the digital recorder. Starts dragging leaden feet toward the Lieutenant's room.

In the scheme of things, with all these corpses piling up around him, Mrs Sachs's problems are peanuts. Yes, he'd happily smash Repp's face in right now if he had the chance, but let's get things in perspective. People are dying and will continue to die if nothing is done. On that scale, Repp is way down the list. He's an irrelevance. An irritant. A . . .

Doyle stops in his tracks.

What was it the caller said on the phone?

As if all these people dying wasn't enough. You've got the distractions too, right? All that small stuff that just gets in the way. The little irritations that you could do without. It's all raining down on you, right, Cal?

Doyle stands there in the middle of the squadroom, his eyes darting but seeing nothing as he replays the phone call in his mind.

Shit!

He looks up. He sees Cesario raise his head and catch sight of him, then give him a look of inquiry.

Doyle feels himself being tugged toward Cesario's office. He takes a step forward.

And before he can stop himself he is spinning on his heels and heading out of the squadroom. He looks straight ahead, blinkered to the other detectives. He marches out into the hallway and then down the stairs, taking them two at a time. Taking them so fast he runs the danger of tripping and sending himself hurtling through the air. But he's oblivious to the risk. He just needs to know. He needs to find out.

He breezes past the sergeant's desk, through the wooden front doors and out onto the sidewalk. He takes out his cellphone and speed-dials a number.

A single question burns in his mind. To anyone else it would sound trivial, but to Doyle it's the most important question in the world. And he knows who will have the answer.

'Hello?'

'Hi, hon, it's me.' He tries to sound casual, to keep the tremor of urgency out of his voice.

'Cal, what's wrong?'

So much for not panicking his wife.

'Nothing's wrong. I just need to speak with you.'

'You're okay? I mean, the way you were talking last night—'

'Forget about that. A touch of the blues, that's all. Today's another day.'

'Okay, so good. I'm glad. Because you had me worried.'

'I know. Forget about it. Seriously.'

'Okay. So, then, why the call?'

Any other husband might be irritated by the question, the tone of suspicion. But then other husbands probably call home more often than Doyle does. He admits he has only himself to blame. When he has his work head on, home and family tend to get pushed out. It has caused friction between him and Rachel before, and he has promised her that he will try harder. This should be one of those calls, making up for his failings in the past. Unfortunately it isn't.

'Well, this is gonna sound kinda weird. But things are pretty quiet down here today and, well, we're doing a quiz.'

'A quiz? You're doing a quiz? In the station house? Things are so slow that you have time to do a quiz? All the criminals in your precinct have decided to take the day off?'

'Yeah. And I got this question. If we get this right, our team wins.'

'Callum Doyle! Are you expecting me to help you cheat?'

'One team point. That's all we need. And it all rides on this question. Please, hon. You gotta help me out here.'

He hears a sigh, but he knows she can't resist quiz questions. 'Shoot.'

'It's a music question, okay? Britpop, I think, so right up your street. I recorded a few seconds of it. Ready?'

'Go ahead.'

He takes out the digital recorder and holds it in front of the phone. He presses the play button. The music comes across loud and clear. Just before the killer's voice breaks in, Doyle shuts it off and puts the phone back to his ear.

'Did you hear that?'

'Yeah. "Why does it always rain on me?" The title's in the lyrics, Cal.'

'I know, I know. But I can't remember who sang it. I need to know the band.'

'That's easy,' she says. And she tells him. Goes on to say, 'Ask me another.' But he's not listening. She said what he thought she would say. What he hoped she would say.

It's from an album called 'The Man Who'.

The band's name is *Travis*.

The person who is supposed to die at eight o'clock this evening is Travis Repp.

TWENTY-SEVEN

Nothing has changed. It's still the case that people have died. More people are about to die. It's just that now he has a little more information about the next intended victim. The conclusion? He should still hand what he's got over to the Lieutenant.

Everything has changed. He was about to go under. Now he's been thrown a lifeline. He can catch the killer. He can set up a trap at Repp's place and catch the killer. The conclusion? He should save his career and his liberty and maybe even come out of this a hero.

What a di-fucking-lemma.

Because if he opts to go it alone, and he gets it wrong . . .

Again . . .

Well, it doesn't bear thinking about.

And yes, he could still be wrong. He got it wrong before, when he believed that Paddy Gilligan was about to take a hit.

Yes, Doyle, but that's because you didn't do your homework. You made assumptions. You didn't even bother to check out the fucking song, you moron. 'Hanrahan's Last'. How easy would that have been if you'd checked the song?

So the lesson is?

The lesson is I have to be sure. I have to be certain beyond all doubt that the next vic is Repp.

And I have about nine and a half hours to do it.

★

Back in the squadroom, he bumps into Cesario coming the other way.

'You wanted to see me?' says Cesario.

'Uh, no. It can wait.'

'You getting anywhere with that theory of yours about those DOAs being connected?'

Doyle fingers the recorder in his pocket again.

'No. Other than the shrink, I can't find anything.'

Cesario nods, like it's the outcome he expected. 'Actually, I'm kinda glad. The last thing I need right now is a serial killer on the loose. It's bad enough that the city's murder rate has shot up lately without it all being the work of some mysterious homicidal maniac. Worth a shot, though, huh?'

He slaps Doyle on the arm and heads out of the room.

Doyle feels like a kid who's just lost a major football game and been told he did his best. The patronizing tone in Cesario's voice was that obvious.

He shakes his head and moves to his desk. Sits down and stares at the mound of files in front of him. One manila folder for each of the deceased. His lie to Cesario was only a partial one. Of course there's a link between the victims: they were all killed by the same man. But beyond that there has to be another connecting thread of which he is as yet unaware. Doyle refuses to believe they were targeted at random. There has to be a reason. And the reason has to be in these files.

But he's been through them. Time after time. He's found nothing. It's another quiz question: *What do the following have in common?* But this isn't one he can pass on to Rachel. He has to solve this one for himself. He has to locate the thread so that he can tie it to Repp. Only then can he be certain that he's figured out the identity of the next victim.

A few days ago he was convinced he had it. It all looked as though Vasey was the focal point. Both Cindy Mellish and Sean

Hanrahan consulted Vasey, and then Vasey himself became a victim. But then it all fell to pieces. None of the other victims were ever clients of Vasey. So maybe the only association there was that Mellish and Hanrahan were murdered partly as a way of signposting the way to Vasey as the next victim.

Or is that just what the killer wanted him to think?

Did he want Doyle to think that this was all there was to it, when in fact there was something more concrete in the apparent relationship?

Okay, so hold that thought. Let's explore this a little more.

Mellish and Hanrahan consulted Vasey. Lorna Bonnow and Tabitha Peyton never did. Or, at least, they don't appear on Vasey's official client lists. Which in itself is not definitive because Cindy Mellish isn't on those lists either. The other two victims – the doorman of Vasey's building and Helena Colquitt – can be disregarded as collateral damage.

Let's assume for the moment that Lorna and Tabitha didn't consult Vasey.

However . . .

Maybe they did go to see a shrink!

Tabitha Peyton was a wreck. Beautiful, intelligent, delightful – yes, all those. But a wreck too. She lost both her parents. It drove her to drink, to meaningless relationships, and almost to self-destruction. Wouldn't it also have driven her to seek professional psychological help at some point?

It's a possibility. Doyle regrets now that he didn't ask her directly when he had the opportunity, but at the time he had already dismissed the Vasey hypothesis.

And what about the nurse, Lorna Bonnow? Did she ever see a shrink?

Doyle decides it's time to abandon his desk.

★

The husband or the lover. It's almost a coin-toss.

He opts for the boyfriend, partly for the reason that he lives here in Manhattan, but primarily because Doyle suspects that if Lorna was in the habit of divulging her deepest darkest secrets, it was more likely to be to her clandestine lover than to the partner on whom she was cheating.

Doyle's immediate impression of Alex Podolski is that he is one of those guys who spends a lot of time in front of the mirror. His long hair is shiny and immaculate. He wears a canary-yellow T-shirt that is tight enough to ripple with the underlying muscles. And he seems to have cultivated a manner of looking sidelong at people when he addresses them, presumably because he has decided that it's his most striking pose.

Podolski invites Doyle inside, and glides with the grace of a panther across his living room. Doyle follows him in with the refinement of a bull elephant. He notices how the walls are festooned with martial arts equipment: curved swords, nunchucks and various wooden sticks, poles and spears.

'Quite a collection,' Doyle says.

'Thanks. Amazing what you can find on eBay. I just finished placing an order for a *fukiya*. That's a Japanese blowgun that fires poison darts.'

Doyle figures he's supposed to sound impressed. 'This all for show, or do you put it to use?'

Podolski smiles. 'It's for show. Although I might change my mind if I ever find the bastard who killed Lorna. Not that I'll need it. My hands should be enough. I'm a karate black belt.'

Again I should be impressed, thinks Doyle.

Podolski looks him up and down, assessing him. 'You do any martial arts yourself?'

'A few years ago,' Doyle lies.

'What? Kung Fu? Taekwondo?'

'Karaoke,' Doyle says. 'Had to give it up after injury, though. Kept straining my throat, you know?'

Podolski stares at him, obviously trying to figure out whether Doyle is mocking or joshing.

Get uppity with me, Bruce Lee, and I'll put you on your ass, thinks Doyle.

Podolski smiles. 'I'll take that as a no. You should try it. Get back into shape.'

'That's okay. I get enough exercise chasing after assholes all day. Speaking of which . . .'

He pauses, lets his gaze linger on Podolski. He sees the man's eyes narrow. At least, he sees one of them narrow, given the way Podolski is maintaining his sidelong photoshoot pose.

For someone who should be supremely confident of his abilities, he's a touchy bastard, thinks Doyle.

'. . . we're still trying to catch Lorna's killer,' he continues, and notices how Podolski relaxes his shoulders. But only slightly.

Doyle says, 'You mind if I ask you a few things about her?'

Podolski hesitates. 'What did you say your name was again?'

'Detective Callum Doyle.'

'And the precinct?'

'The Eighth. Why do you ask?' But he knows precisely why.

Podolski tightens up again. Doyle sees the muscles twitch in his jaw.

'Lorna got a call, on the night she was killed. It's what made her go outside. The guy on the phone said he was a detective from the Eighth Precinct. Said his name was Boyle or Doyle – something like that.'

Doyle tries to remain unruffled. 'Yeah, we know. To be honest, it's the only reason I got involved in this case. Officially it belongs to Detective Lopez at the Twenty-Seventh Precinct. He told me the caller tried to pass himself off as me. I want to know why. It could be we've crossed paths before.'

Podolski considers this, then nods. 'Okay, what can I tell you?'

Here we go, thinks Doyle. It's a long shot, but . . .

'We're looking into Lorna's past. In case there's something there. Anything you can tell us could be useful, no matter how insignificant it might seem. Okay?'

'Sure.'

'So what I want to know is whether Lorna ever suffered some kind of trauma. Some event in her life that may have drastically affected her state of mind. Do you understand what I'm getting at?'

'I think so.'

'So was there anything like that? She ever mention anything to you about some terrible thing that happened to her? Doesn't have to be recent. Coulda been years ago.'

It's gonna be a no, thinks Doyle. Podolski is about to shoot this theory down in flames. At best, he's gonna say that they never talked about personal shit. They screwed, and that's as far as it went. Maybe I should have opted for the husband rather than this self-obsessed jerk-off.

'Well, there was the baby.'

Doyle struggles to keep his voice level. 'The baby?'

'Yeah. Lorna and her husband, they were trying for a baby for years. Finally she got pregnant. Went full-term, but something went wrong. It was stillborn.'

'When was this?'

'About two years ago. Before I knew her, in case you got any funny ideas about me being the father.'

The thought hadn't crossed Doyle's mind. 'She told you this?'

'Yeah. That's how we were. We were open with each other. She was crazy about me.'

Thinks Doyle, Well, who wouldn't be? What with your fighting prowess and your shiny locks and your remarkable profile and—

'And I was crazy about her too, you want the truth.'

Doyle detects for the first time a note of genuine emotion in Podolski's voice. Nice save, man. Maybe you're not such a prick after all.

'It musta hit her hard.'

'Yeah,' says Podolski, nodding. It seems to Doyle then that Podolski has finally dropped his shield. His body language has changed. He's no longer out to impress with the macho bullshit. He's just being himself. Alone and frightened and grief-stricken.

Then Podolski adds, 'They went through a bad time, both her and her husband. In fact, I think he was worse, the way she told it.'

Okay, thinks Doyle. The million-dollar question.

'Did she talk to someone about it? I mean, at the time. A psychologist, someone like that?'

'I dunno. I guess so. I mean, you'd think that must be routine, right? When you go through something like that?'

Absolutely, Doyle thinks. Routine. The hospital would have provided counseling. No doubt about it. Lorna Bonnow must have talked to a shrink.

It's something. Doyle doesn't know what, but it's something. It fits a pattern.

'Thanks,' he says. 'That's been useful.'

Podolski seems surprised. 'It has? That's all you want to know?'

'For now.'

He walks to the door, but turns just before he leaves.

'I'm sorry for your loss,' he says. And means it.

The first thing he does when he gets back to the squadroom is to make a phone call to the husband.

'Just a quick question or two, Mr Bonnow, if that's all right. I understand that you and your wife lost a baby a couple of years ago.'

Bonnow pauses before answering. 'What's that got to do with anything?'

'Maybe nothing. We're just trying to make sure we look into every possible reason for your wife's death.'

'I don't understand. How on earth could the loss of our baby lead to my wife's murder?'

'I'm not saying it did. We just want to talk to people who she had any prolonged contact with. That includes the people she worked with, but also anybody else, such as the people at the hospital where your wife gave birth.'

'Oh. I see. That's pretty . . . well, that's very thorough. I didn't think . . . I thought the police had given up on my wife, ya know? That other detective – Lopez – he didn't give me much hope that you would ever catch this lunatic.'

'Well, I have to tell you, Mr Bonnow, we're working some long shots here. But we're not giving up just yet.'

'Oh. Okay. That's good. What do you want to know?'

'The hospital. Which one was it?'

'Mount Sinai.'

'Mount Sinai? Here in Manhattan?'

'Yeah. Lorna thought she could get better care over there. I was against it. I was worried we'd get stuck on the Brooklyn Bridge with her pushing out a baby, ya know?'

'Okay. And after the birth, I assume you were offered counseling to help you deal with it?'

'Yes.'

'Was that also at Mount Sinai?'

'Yes it was.'

'You saw a psychologist, is that right?'

'Yes.'

'Do you happen to remember his name?'

Doyle hears an expulsion of breath.

'It was two years ago. I can't remember things from that long ago.'

'Try, Mr Bonnow, please.'

The line goes quiet.

Say Vasey, thinks Doyle. Please say his name was Vasey.

'The only thing I remember about him . . .'

'Yes?'

'Is that he was Indian.'

The disappointment pushes Doyle's eyes closed. 'Indian?'

'Yes. To be frank with you, I could hardly tell what he was saying. The whole thing was a complete waste of time, ya know?'

Doyle is starting to believe that this conversation is a waste of time too.

'All right. Thank you, Mr Bonnow. That gives me something to look into.'

'So you'll keep looking, right? You haven't given up?'

'No. We haven't given up. We won't give up until your wife's killer is locked up, I promise you.'

'Thank you.'

Doyle hangs up the phone and sighs.

An Indian.

A shrink yes, but certainly not Vasey. Not even under a different name. This is not what Doyle had hoped to hear.

But he can't give up. It's all he has to go on. It's still possible that there is a connection between Vasey and this Indian doctor.

Doyle slides a telephone directory across and looks up the number for Mount Sinai Hospital on Fifth Avenue. He calls the switchboard, asks for the records department. When he gets put through, he explains who he is and what he wants, which is the name of the psychologist who counseled the Bonnows about two years ago. In response, they tell him that their records office has only a skeleton staff on Sundays, and that it would take them at least a day to find the information he is requesting. They also inform him that they would need to see a court order before they could release that data.

Doyle hangs up. So much for that.

He can't wait a day, and he can't ask for a court order.

Sighing again, he leaves his desk and goes to fetch the print-outs of Vasey's client records. He limits himself to the past five years, but it's still a forest's worth of paper. He sits down with them, starts to work his way through them yet again, this time looking for any mentions of an Indian psychologist or Mount Sinai Hospital.

The process eats hungrily into the time he has left.

And he finds nothing.

TWENTY-EIGHT

'So, have you come to apologize?'

Anna Friedrich lounges back in her expensive white leather sofa and crosses her impossibly long legs. Doyle tries not to let himself be distracted by those legs, but it's difficult when they're so naked and exposed. Not that she's indecent in any way. She is wearing a baggy woolen sweater and a band of black material that at least has pretensions of being a skirt. But those legs do tend to dominate the view. He thinks it must be like being an umpire at a tennis match for nudists. How the hell can you be expected to keep score?

'Apologize for what, Ms Friedrich?'

'For the way you treated Andrew? For the way you tried to label him as a criminal?'

'We were doing our job. You know better than most that we had to ask him those questions.'

'There are ways of asking.'

'He was linked with two murder victims. It was important that we got to the truth.'

'Yes, well, you didn't, did you? Because if you had, Andrew would still be alive.'

Doyle didn't come here for an argument. To curtail it, he drags his gaze away from Anna Friedrich and her legs, and sets it free to wander around the room. In response, the room shouts money back at him. Doyle doesn't think he could even afford the wallpaper: it would probably cost less to paper the room in hundred-dollar bills. There's enough scarce hardwood in the furniture here to make conservationists weep. And the carpet is so plush it makes him feel as though he has bath sponges tied to his feet.

'Your boyfriend working today?'

'Yes. In Saudi Arabia.'

'Boy, that's some commute.'

She doesn't smile. 'He's in the oil business. He's over there a lot.'

'Shaking it with the sheikhs, huh? I bet it's hot out there right now.'

'Detective, do you really want to get into a discussion about climates, or is there another purpose to your visit here this afternoon?'

'Actually I came to ask you about your ex-husband.'

'Why? Are you still trying to pin the earlier murders on him?'

'No. But I do want to find out who killed him.'

'Really? Then I suggest your time would be better spent elsewhere. I have already been interviewed by the police. Several times, in fact. I have told them everything I can.'

'Everything?'

'Everything. No, Andrew did not have any enemies. No, he was never threatened to my knowledge. No, he did not have any financial worries. No, he did not tell me of any meetings arranged at his apartment on the night of his murder. No, he—'

'Did he know any Indians?'

She stares at him. 'What?'

'Did he know any Indian people? I'm thinking psychologists here. Indian psychologists.'

She continues to stare. 'Are you trying to be funny, Detective?

Throwing out random questions like that just to prove a point? What's next? Are you going to ask me if he ever ate pistachio ice cream on a Friday? If you've come here just to piss me off, then I should warn you—'

'Actually I'm serious.'

She is silent for a moment while she searches Doyle's face.

'You're serious?'

'Deadly.'

'You really want to know if Andrew knew any Indian psychologists?'

'Yes.'

Another pause. 'All right. Well, then, I guess the answer is probably yes.'

'Only probably?'

'Andrew was a renowned and well-connected psychotherapist. He attended many conferences and worked with many people. My guess is that he probably had professional dealings with people who were from India.'

'But nobody specific that you can think of? No close friends that you were ever introduced to?'

'No. Not that I can recall.'

Damn, thinks Doyle.

'Okay, I got another one for you. Mount Sinai Hospital. Did your husband ever do any work there?'

'No. I don't know. Why are you—'

'What about Indian doctors at Mount Sinai?'

'Enough! Detective Doyle, what the hell are you doing here? I am on the edge of picking up my phone and calling your superiors. What the fuck is this?'

Doyle thinks he should go now. This is getting him nowhere. What's stopping him is that he has more questions in his pocket. The problem is, Anna Friedrich isn't going to supply him with answers. Not as things stand. She's a lawyer. She knows how cops work. With most people, Doyle could get away with claiming that he's merely pursuing something that cropped up during the investigation. But that won't wash with this lady. She's too smart and too savvy for that.

'I . . . I'm trying to make a connection.'

'Well you're going the wrong way about it, Detective. You really think this is the way to establish a rapport with me?'

Doyle almost cracks a smile. 'Uh, no. I don't mean a connection between us. I mean between the victims.'

Friedrich waves a hand as if to say, *Whatever*. But Doyle can tell she is faintly embarrassed by her misunderstanding.

'I thought we already discussed your fanciful connection. In your interrogation room. Back when Andrew was still alive and you still had someone you could harass.'

'Yeah. Yeah, I know. But . . . but I still think there's something.'

'We've been through this. The only concrete thing you had was that the murdered ex-cop was once a client of Andrew's for a very brief time. And before you say anything, I still don't believe that the Mellish girl ever even met Andrew, let alone had some kind of secret liaisons with him. He told me he didn't know her, and I believe him. So that's it. That's all you have. And what it doesn't do is get you any closer to finding my ex-husband's murderer. So now, if you wouldn't mind . . .'

She uncrosses her legs, starts to rise. She's about to show him the door.

'That's not all,' he says, and he surprises himself by how loudly and firmly he says it.

'What?'

'It's not all I have. I think there's more to it.'

She lowers herself onto the sofa again. 'What do you mean?'

Doyle says nothing.

'Detective? What do you mean, there's more to it?'

Go now, Doyle tells himself. Get out of here. Before you say something that will land you in deep shit. This woman's a lawyer. A good lawyer. One false move with her and she'll have you licking her shoes.

But he finds himself unable to get up from his chair.

He says, 'I think it goes wider than most people think. Beyond the three victims you've just mentioned.'

She shakes her head, clearly mystified. 'What are you talking about?'

'There have been other murders recently. You may have read about them or heard about them on the news. All over the city. Totally different MOs. Nothing to tie them together. Nothing obvious, anyhow.'

'Okay, so all the more reason for you to get one off the books by finding my husband's killer, wouldn't you say?'

'That's not what I mean. I think there's someone . . . someone out there.'

'Someone out . . . Who? Detective, you're making absolutely no—'

And then the lightning bolt strikes. He sees it in her face, the way her mouth drops open.

'You've got to be shitting me. A serial killer? You're talking about a serial killer?'

Doyle's nod is a subtle one. He almost can't believe it himself when it's stated so clearly, so baldly.

She says, 'Let me be clear about this. The NYPD is now of the opinion that a number of murders recently committed in this city were the work of one person, and my ex-husband was one of his victims. Have I got that right?'

'Uhm, not exactly.'

'Not exactly? How not exactly?'

'It's not the official line of the NYPD that these murders are the work of a serial killer.'

'Okay, I get the picture. They don't want to panic the city. But *unofficially*. That's what the police now believe.'

In response, Doyle puts out his hand and waggles it from side to side, a pained look on his face.

She says, 'Jesus Christ, Detective. This is like talking to Lassie. A little help here, if you please. You want a crayon so that you can draw me a picture?'

'It's not what the NYPD believes. It's what I believe.'

'You. Just you?'

'Just me.'

The room goes silent. Doyle is not sure which way this will go. He suspects she is probably wishing for her ex-husband to be back in the room. Someone who knows about people who are one sandwich short of a picnic.

She says, 'Why? Why do you believe that?'

He shrugs. 'A hunch. A feeling.'

'Uh-huh. Tell me, do you hear voices in your head at night? Can you tell what dogs are saying when they bark? What do your police buddies think about this hunch of yours?'

Doyle casts his mind back to when Cesario slapped him on the arm and said it was worth a shot.

'Not a lot.'

Friedrich smacks her lips. 'Great. So you're flying solo. You're ignoring the advice of your Department, refusing to follow their example, and instead you're following up your own half-baked theories. Actually, scratch that. Theory is too grand a term for this. You're relying on intuition. You're clutching at straws, scrabbling for a connection that isn't there. Hence all the bizarre questions about Indian psychologists and hospitals. You want there to be a link so that you can tell yourself you're right. It doesn't matter how insignificant that common thread is, as long as it exists. It doesn't matter that it won't help you solve any of these murders. You just want to prove something. Isn't that right, Detective?'

'No. That's not right.' But she has wounded his confidence. Of course there's a link. The victims were all killed by the same man. But what if that's all there is to it? What if there's no rhyme or reason? What if the victims were selected purely on the basis of a pin stuck in a telephone directory?

No, he thinks. I refuse to believe that. There has to be something, and maybe Anna Friedrich is the only person who can tell me what it is.

'I think you should go now,' she says, and once more she gets to her feet.

'Just give me a few more minutes of your time. Please. I just have one or two more questions.'

'What about?'

'About your marriage to Dr Vasey. About why you split up.'

'Are you serious? You really expect me to start talking about highly personal stuff like my marriage breakdown on the basis of your gut feeling? Forget it, Detective. You're asking too much. I can't help you. Now if you don't mind . . .'

She puts her arm out, gesturing to the door, requesting him to leave.

He gets up, but instead of heading for the door he moves directly to Friedrich and looks her in the eye.

'I am not wrong. He is out there. He has killed several times already and he will kill again. Look at what's happened. Ask yourself why the city has recently seen a number of unsolved, apparently motiveless murders. Ask yourself why the police don't seem to have made any progress on catching your husband's killer. Could it be because they're looking in the wrong places? Could it be because maybe I'm right about this? And if I have it ass backwards, so what? What harm could it do to answer a couple of lousy questions? Indulge me. Lunatic that I seem, let me have what I want so that you can get me out of your hair. Please.'

She maintains the eye contact, reading him. He lets her in. Lets her see that this isn't some bullshit game he's playing.

She glides away and sits down.

'Take a seat, Detective. What do you want to know?'

He accepts the invitation without hesitation, in case she changes her mind.

'Your marriage to Dr Vasey didn't work out. I'm not asking for all the details, but can you give me a rough idea of what went wrong?'

'Nothing dramatic, if that's what you're wondering. No third party or anything like that. We were just too wrapped up in our careers. Both ambitious. Both wanting to succeed. Neither of us had any time for the other. It wasn't really a marriage.'

'So you dissolved it. Was that by mutual consent?'

'Not really.'

'So whose idea was it? Yours?'

'One of us had to do it. We couldn't have carried on as we were.'

'How did Andrew take it?'

'Hard.'

'He was devastated?'

'Well, I wouldn't go that far. He was upset. But he was still in control. It didn't stand in the way of his work.'

'Are you sure? I mean, could he have been worse than he seemed?'

'No. If anything, he seemed worse than he was.'

'I don't understand.'

'Andrew had a flair for melodrama. He liked to throw tantrums. He turned on emotions like a tap when it suited him. I knew him well enough to tell when it was real and when it was phony.'

'So you don't think he was as badly affected by your split-up as he claimed?'

'No, I don't believe he was. I think he had already accepted we were doomed as a couple. I just don't think he liked the idea of me calling the shots.'

Shit, thinks Doyle. This doesn't fit. Square pegs and round holes.

'Then you don't think he would have needed to seek counseling?'

Her eyebrows shoot up. A pair of arrowheads aimed at the sky. 'Detective, have you forgotten what Andrew did for a living?'

'Yeah, I know, but don't shrinks see other shrinks when their heads are messed up? Or do they just do it themselves?'

She laughs. 'You know, I'm not sure about that one. What I do know is that Andrew would never have consulted another therapist. He was too concerned about his reputation ever to consider such a thing.'

Damn.

'Okay,' he says. 'Thank you. I appreciate your honesty.'

He stands up, ready to leave now.

'You didn't get what you wanted to hear, did you?'

'Not exactly.'

'I'm sorry. Maybe . . . well, maybe it's telling you something.'

'Yeah. Maybe.'

He takes the long walk to the door.

She catches up with him. Says, 'This means a lot to you, doesn't it?'

'You don't know how much.'

'Then I wish you luck.'

He nods. And then he leaves, wishing he could rely a little less on luck and a lot more on certainty.

TWENTY-NINE

A song by the Black Eyed Peas comes on the car radio. Doyle turns it up and hums along.

He's parked on West 13th Street. Travis Repp lives on the first floor of a three-story apartment building. The stoop of the building is separated from the sidewalk by a gated fence that encloses a small, well-kept garden containing lots of shrubs. Doyle got the address from a copy of Repp's application for a private investigator's license.

He checks the clock on the dash. Six-thirty. An hour and a half before the killer is due to strike, but Doyle is taking no chances. He wants to see everyone who enters and leaves that building from now on. Hell, he wants to check out anyone who so much as glances at that building. He's gonna catch this son of a bitch.

He's going to catch him here because Repp is the next victim.

We know that, don't we, Doyle?

Don't we?

The name of the band is Travis. The killer talked about people who are distractions or irritants. Well, there's no bigger irritant than Travis Repp. Who else could it be?

But on the other hand . . .

Doesn't it seem just a little bit too easy?

The caller knew that Doyle would check out the song. He

knew that Doyle had failed to do so properly before, and that it had cost a life, so there was no doubt that he would check it out fully this time.

So why would he make it so easy?

And this idea of psychologists linking all the victims together. Isn't it just a little bit tenuous? They all saw a shrink. All except Vasey, who, it seems, didn't consult a shrink. But he is one, so that's okay. That ties it all up in a nice pink bow.

Yeah, like hell it does. For one thing, what about Repp? Did he ever have a need for therapy?

Doyle doesn't know the answer. He knows next to nothing about Repp, let alone why he's been selected as the killer's next target.

A car slows as it passes Doyle, then pulls into the curb just outside Repp's building. Doyle sinks down low in his seat and watches as the driver gets out. It's Travis Repp. He doesn't even glance in Doyle's direction. Just goes straight into his building and closes the door.

'It's okay, man,' Doyle mutters. 'I'm watching your back. Scumbag that you are, I'm gonna keep you alive.'

A song from the cast of Glee comes on the radio. Doyle turns it right down again.

Almost seven-forty. Doyle is getting antsy. The only sign of anything possibly happening was half an hour ago when another car pulled up in front of Repp's, and a suited guy got out and pushed through the iron gate. But he was quickly joined by the car's passenger – a woman who was yelling after her partner – and it became clear to Doyle that they were just a bickering couple who lived in the same building. Since that brief flurry of excitement, nobody has ventured anywhere near Repp's place. Nobody has given it the once-over. Nobody has pulled up in a car and sat there waiting. Other than Doyle himself, that is – a fact which is starting to make him distinctly uncomfortable.

He has given himself a deadline. Five minutes to eight. At that time, he will march up to Repp's building and sound his buzzer and demand to come in. He will enter on the pretext of wanting to talk about the scam that Repp is running. In reality, he will be there to save Repp's life. Even if it means revealing his presence to the killer, Doyle knows he can't stay out here on the street when there's a man in there who is about to die.

And if the killer shows, great. Who knows? Maybe he's already inside the place. He could have been waiting in there all day, just waiting to pounce as the clock strikes eight. Go for it, thinks Doyle. Give me the chance to plug you, you piece of shit.

There's a complication, of course. It has nagged at Doyle several times, but so far he has refused to think about it too hard. What if the killer decides to go quietly? What if he puts his hands up and surrenders and invites Doyle to take him in, giving him the opportunity to spill everything he knows about Doyle? How prepared is Doyle to let that happen?

Because if he's not, his only other option might be to take the life of a man who is no longer a threat. Sure, he deserves to die. No doubt about it. For Tabitha and all the others, he should take a bullet. Doyle could repeat that to himself any number of times after he fired his gun. But would that be enough to make it right?

Doyle shakes his head. He can't worry about such things. He has to just let it play out, and worry about the consequences later.

But he would so like to take that man off this earth. He has never felt so strongly about eliminating someone before now. With him gone, the whole city would breathe a sigh of relief. There would be one less cause of misery in the world.

As if the victims hadn't suffered enough already. Tabitha, especially, when she lost her parents. But also Hanrahan, with his partner being killed in that shoot-out. Look what that did to him. And then there was . . .

Wait a minute!

Doyle tenses up so much he feels as though all his ligaments should snap. Ants crawl along his scalp. His mind has already worked something out, but he's not sure what it is yet.

Okay, start with Cindy Mellish, the bookstore girl. She was dumped by her boyfriend, and it really messed up her head. Ditto Lorna Bonnow when she lost her baby. And Vasey . . .

Yes! It fits.

Vasey was kicked to the curb by the delectable Anna Friedrich. She revealed as much to Doyle only hours ago.

Loss. Could this be about loss?

Could it be that it's not about the fact that these people were connected with psychologists, but about what drove them to seek help in the first place? Is that what this is?

Doyle runs the notion through his head again and again. It feels right. Only . . .

Repp. What's his loss? His failing business? Some girlfriend or wife in his past?

Doyle once more curses the fact that he knows zilch about Repp. Doesn't know whether there's a Repp-shaped hole in this puzzle or not.

Slow it down, Doyle. Think it through some more.

They all suffered some kind of loss. A deep loss that affected them profoundly. At least in most cases. According to his wife, Vasey claimed to be devastated, but probably wasn't. But maybe that doesn't matter. It's what the killer believed that matters.

So what did they do because of this loss? They went to see a shrink. Yeah, but . . .

Maybe that's not it.

They were suffering, or claimed to be suffering. Tabitha was hurting so badly she even decided to commit suicide. Pretty ironic when you think about it, the way she was planning to end it all.

Oh sweet Jesus.

Surely not?

Doyle's heart hammers against his chest. His brain feels as though it could burst with the blood that is surging through it.

He takes out his cellphone and selects a number from his contact list.

'Eighth Precinct. Detective Holden.'

'Jay? It's Cal. Can you do something for me?'

'No, is the answer that jumps to my lips. And that's even before I've heard what it is you want. That's what you've done to our relationship, man. I hope you're satisfied.'

Doyle ignores the sarcasm. 'I need some numbers.'

'Yeah? How about six-six-six? There's something not totally right about you lately, like you're possessed or something.'

'Seriously, man. Some phone numbers. Can you get them for me?'

'Whose numbers?'

Doyle reels off the list.

'Uh-huh,' says Holden. 'Pardon me for asking, but why can't this wait till tomorrow, when you can come in and get them your own self?'

'Because it can't. I need to follow something up. Please, Jay.'

Holden sighs. 'This is your stupid theory again, right? You need to let this go, Cal. Really. People are starting to talk.'

'The numbers, Jay. Please.'

Another sigh. 'I'll call you back.'

'I'll hold.'

'Cal, what the fuck are you— Oh, forget it.'

The line goes quiet. Doyle's right leg shakes up and down while he waits. A fast beat. It does this when he's anxious.

Holden comes back on the phone and starts reading out the numbers. Doyle scrawls them in his notebook, then utters a quick thank you and hangs up before Holden can ask him any more questions.

He taps in the first number on his list and presses the call button.

'Hello?'

'Mr Podolski? It's Detective Doyle here. I was at your apartment this morning?'

'Yeah, yeah. What's up? You get the bastard?'

'Not yet. I just need to ask you a coupla more questions about Lorna. You mind?'

'No. Go ahead.'

'Lorna told you about the baby, right? And she said it hit her hard. Her and her husband.'

'Yeah. She came to terms with it eventually, but he never did.'

'Okay, but before she came to terms with it. She was bad, right?'

'Well, yeah. I mean, who wouldn't be?'

'How bad? Did she tell you?'

'Bad. Real bad. I don't know what you want me to say.'

'Bad enough to want to kill herself?'

'What?'

'When she told you about this part of her life, losing the baby and all, did she ever say that she got so depressed she thought about committing suicide?'

Come on, thinks Doyle. Tell me I'm onto something here.

'Well, yeah. She did say that. How did you know?'

Bingo, thinks Doyle. But only if . . .

'What did she say, exactly? Do you remember?'

'She said . . . she said it hit her when she was leaving the hospital. Like a wave of grief. She was walking out of the hospital

306

with her husband. They were heading back to their car, and they had to cross the street. And then this ambulance came screaming along, and she . . .'

'Go on.'

'She . . . she said she wanted to jump out. In front of the ambulance. She wanted to just step out and let it mow her down, that's how messed up she was. Look, is this necessary? I don't like talking about this stuff. I'm not sure that Lorna would have—'

'It's useful, believe me. I'm not playing with you, Alex. I need to know these things.'

'Well, okay. If it helps.'

'It does. Thank you. I'll be in touch, okay?'

'Okay. But—'

Doyle hangs up. He almost cannot believe what he's just heard. It's coming together too smoothly.

He tries to control his breathing. It's too early to be counting chickens.

He looks at the next number on his list. Taps it in with trembling fingers.

'Hello.'

'Josh Whiteley?'

'Yeah, who's this?'

'This is Detective Doyle from the Eighth Precinct. I'm one of the officers working on the homicide of Cindy Mellish. I just need to ask you one or two questions. That okay with you, Josh?'

'I don't know. I mean, I thought you guys were done with me. It wasn't me, you know. I had nothing to do with it.'

'I know, Josh, I know. All I want is for you to fill in a little background detail for me.'

'All right. What do you wanna know?'

'About when you broke it off with Cindy. You told the other detectives she didn't take it too well, is that right?'

Whiteley snorts a laugh. 'That has to be the understatement of the year, man. She flipped. Kept following me around, telling me how much she *needed* me. I mean, it was getting *embarrassing*, you know?'

'She was crazy about you?'

'She was crazy, period. I mean, I liked her and all, but I needed some space, you know? Every time I turned around the girl was there, sucking up my oxygen. She—' Whiteley breaks off, as if realizing how this is starting to sound. 'But this was a long time ago, man. She was out of my life way before—'

'I know, Josh. Trust me, I'm not looking to jam you up here. I'm just trying to get a handle on her state of mind. You cool with that?'

'I guess.'

'Good. So Cindy refused to let go. She was desperate. She would have done anything to make you change your mind, right?'

'Yeah. That about sums it up.'

'So did she resort to emotional blackmail of any kind?'

'How do you mean?'

'I mean like threatening to hurt herself if you didn't take her back?'

There it is, thinks Doyle. The big question. Come on, Josh. I need a big fat *yes* here.

'Yeah, she did that.'

Doyle punches the air. He has to stop himself from releasing a cry of triumph. It would sound a little disrespectful given the topic under discussion.

'How, Josh? What exactly did she say she would do?'

'Like, all kinds. Taking an overdose. Jumping off a building. Like I said, she was nuts.'

No, no, no. Wrong answer, Josh. Think again.

'Anything else? Did she make any other specific threats to self-harm?'

'Well, yeah. But it was lame. She was just trying to get to me.'

'How, Josh? Why was it lame?'

'One night, she called me up. Said she was going to cut her wrists.'

Doyle hears his phone creak as his grip on it tightens.

'Go on. What happened?'

'I told her to go ahead and do it then. I mean, I don't want to sound unfeeling or anything, but she was seriously bugging me. What you have to understand is—'

'I understand, Josh. Tell me what she did. Did she cut herself?'

'No. What I mean is, not really. The next day she showed up with a coupla scratches on her arm. I've had worse from my cat. When she showed them to me, I just laughed. I know I shouldn't have – I mean, the crazy bitch probably needed help – but, well . . .'

Doyle knows that Josh Whiteley is waiting to hear more words that will help him feel good about himself, but Doyle is past caring about his welfare. He presents him with some prime bullshit instead: 'Josh, you've been a great help. Knowing something about how Cindy's mind worked could help us figure out what happened to her.'

'Okay. Just as long as you don't think it was me. I'm in the clear, right?'

Doyle ends the call without answering the question. Let the kid stew if he can't be concerned about anyone but himself.

And then he allows himself to start believing.

Another box has been ticked. It all seems so simple now. So fucking obvious. How the hell could he not see this earlier?

There is one more number on his list. He enters it on his

cellphone. This will be the litmus test. The confirmation of what he already knows to be true.

His call is answered, and he launches straight into it. Time is not his to waste.

'Miss Friedrich, it's Detective Doyle again. I have another question for you.'

The rush of his words causes her to hesitate. Then: 'All right. Go on.'

'You need to bear with me. It might sound a little off-base.'

'Detective, I think we've already established your level of eccentricity. Whatever you ask now won't surprise me.'

'You told me that Dr Vasey wasn't as badly disturbed by the break-up of your relationship as he claimed. Is that right?'

'That's what I believe, yes.'

'Not affected enough to cause him extreme mental distress or to make him seek counseling.'

'That's right. I think I'd come to know him well enough to determine when he was just being theatrical.'

'Okay, but he did *claim* that he was devastated? Whatever he actually felt about you, he tried to make you feel that you were ruining his life?'

'Yes, but as I say—'

'What form did that take?'

'Excuse me?'

'What words did he use? What did he say to try to make you feel bad?'

'Well, I . . . I don't recall exactly. He ranted and raved, that's all I remember. I was used to him doing that, so I tended to tune him out. Is it important?'

'It could be. Let me help you. Did he ever threaten to harm himself?'

The silence is long enough to give Doyle his answer. When she speaks again, she is subdued.

'How did you know that?'

'Then he did?'

'Yes. Yes, he did. He threatened to commit suicide.'

Praise the Lord, thinks Doyle, but decides not to say.

'How? How was he going to kill himself?'

'He . . . he said he was going to string himself up. Hang himself. But it was bluster. I knew he had no intention of doing anything like that.'

'No. But he said it anyway?'

'Yes. That's what he said. But I don't . . . Detective Doyle, I'm starting to find this just a little bit too creepy. What's going on here?'

'I don't know. Not fully. And what I do think could be wrong.'

'But you're not wrong, are you? You know something. You're not as crazy as the other cops believe, are you?'

'Maybe. We'll see. Watch this space.'

'Oh, I'll be watching. Prove them wrong, Detective. And prove to me you're not the asshole I thought you were.'

'Tall order. I'll see what I can do.'

When he gets off the phone, he brings all the pieces together in his mind. Watches them slot neatly into place.

It was thinking about Tabitha that provided him with the first clue. How she decided to commit suicide by jumping into the East River, and then the irony of her being killed by drowning. It led him to think about the other victims, and in particular what Sean Hanrahan's wife had said about him being on a sure route to the graveyard. Vasey's case files also contained notes about discussions with Hanrahan regarding possible thoughts of suicide. It was a natural thing to ask him about. He had lost his partner. He was depressed and drinking heavily. The signs were all there of a cop who might be on the verge of killing himself.

And how would Hanrahan have committed the act? Why, the same way most other suicidal cops do it: by eating his gun. And how did he finally meet his end? That's right – a gun blast to the head.

It could have all been coincidental, of course.

But not anymore. Not after what Doyle has just heard in those phone conversations.

Cindy Mellish, the bookstore girl. Loses her boyfriend and makes a feeble attempt at cutting her wrists. How does she die? By having first her wrists, and then the rest of her, sliced wide open.

Lorna Bonnow, the nurse. Lost a baby and felt like throwing herself in front of a moving vehicle. Dies when a car mashes her into pulp.

And then Vasey. Threatens to hang himself. Ends up with someone doing it for him, and in spectacular fashion.

That's the connection. Has to be. The killer's warped view of helping people is not limited to contacting Doyle and giving him pointers to the next victim.

It's also about helping people to die.

Doesn't matter how serious they were about it. If they said it, they must have meant it. And the killer sees it as his moral duty to provide them with the assistance they need to fulfill their destinies.

Son of a bitch.

That's why Tabitha had to be drowned. When the perp found her at Gonzo's apartment he could have shot her, stabbed her, smothered her or finished her off using any one of countless other methods. But he chose drowning. Or rather, there was no choice to be made. Death by drowning was the fate she had already ear-marked for herself.

But what of Repp? Where does he fit into this? What fate did he unknowingly select?

Doyle wishes he knew. But there's no time left in which to find out.

He consults the dash clock again. It's after seven-fifty. In a few minutes Doyle will have to enter Repp's house. In a few minutes more he may have to confront a serial killer.

He feels uneasy. He tells himself it's only natural, given what may be about to occur. But he knows there's something more.

He still believes it was too easy, working out that Repp is next. But what else could the clues mean?

The digital recorder is still in Doyle's pocket. He takes it out and switches it on. He listens again to the music and then the killer's voice.

'Certainly raining a lot on you lately, huh, Cal? If it carries on like this, you'll need to get yourself a hat. Protect that brain. It's the only thing that's going to get you out of this mess.

'I don't want you making any mistakes on this one, Cal. You don't have a good record so far. It must be breaking you up inside. How do you cope with that? All those mistakes? It must affect your behavior, your relationships. Maybe I should ask your wife. She of all people must sense something is wrong.

'What's the matter, buddy? Nothing you want to say to me? I understand. You must have a lot on your mind right now. As if all these people dying wasn't enough. You've got the distractions too, right? All that small stuff that just gets in the way. The little irritations that you could do without. It's all raining down on you, right, Cal?'

Those references to the distractions, the small stuff getting in the way. Who else could that be but Repp? And then the music. Definitely by Travis. From the album 'The Man Who'. Rachel was certain about that.

And yet . . .

The earlier stuff. Was that just meaningless preamble? That advice about protecting his brain with a hat was pretty random. And then the next bit about mistakes and his wife . . .

Oh fuck.

Fucking hell.

Doyle fires up the engine. Slams the lever into drive. Powers the car away from the curb.

Because it's not Repp. He got it wrong.

Horribly, horribly wrong.

THIRTY

'You fucking idiot!'

This from Doyle. Yelling at himself as he drives. Not caring a jot whether anyone sees him yelling at himself as he drives.

'I told you it was too easy to be Repp. Why would he make it so fucking easy?'

He drives like he has no concept of either danger or courtesy. He squeezes his car through spaces that don't look big enough, nearly taking the wing mirrors off several vehicles. He spends most of the journey with his hand firmly glued to the car horn.

It should be a drive of only a few minutes, but it seems to be taking him an age to get there. Every time he glances at the clock another minute of his precious time has been eaten away. Doubts keep assaulting his mind. They tell him he's not going to make it. But he has to make it. Even if he were to put in a call to Central they couldn't get a car there any faster.

And even if he had oodles of time – and bang, there goes yet another minute on this fucking hyperactive clock – what would he tell the cops? That he'd just figured out what that phone call meant – the one from the killer? Or maybe he could just make up an emergency to get the sector cars to respond and then explain it all later, perhaps while the killer is busy telling the cops all about his special relationship with Doyle, and what he knows about his past deeds. Wouldn't that be a neat ending?

At the intersection with Second Avenue, the lights go to red. Doyle grits his teeth and floors the gas pedal. He leans into the car horn again as he weaves past a truck and then screeches around the corner. He can't stop now. He can't fail. If he does, another life is lost and the killer is once again at large.

That can't be allowed to happen. Not again.

He flits the car from lane to lane, ignoring the protests of the drivers he cuts up. Powers right onto Ninth Street. Tries to do the same when he gets to Stuyvesant, but overlooks the fact that Stuyvesant is about the only freaking street in this part of the city that doesn't stick to the standard grid layout, and which therefore has an angle of intersection much less than ninety degrees. Doyle has to fight with the car as it slews to the left, missing a collision with a parked vehicle opposite by a fraction of an inch.

There are no parking spaces left on this short street that are big enough to take his car. At least not lengthways. Doyle drives forward between two sedans, feeling the jolt as his car bumps onto the sidewalk. A man who was about to walk that way jumps back in fear for his life, then starts gesticulating wildly at Doyle.

Doyle ignores him. He's more interested in his clock, which tells him it's one minute to eight. He prays that the killer's watch is slow.

He practically falls out of the car, slamming the door behind him before he races up the steps in front of the house. It all looks so quiet here, so tranquil. A spark of optimism arcs inside him.

But when he tries the door and finds that it's unlocked, when he steps inside and his nostrils are assailed by the stench, his hopefulness shudders and dies.

The killer is here.

It was Rachel who gave him the vital information. Only he didn't realize it. It wasn't the fact that the song was by Travis. It was the name of the album: 'The Man Who'. Taken from the title of a well-known book.

All that crap the killer said in his call. It wasn't nonsense at all. It carried every key word he needed.

The stuff about needing a hat. And then his mistakes, and his wife.

Put it all together and you're back to the book again.

The Man Who Mistook his Wife for a Hat.

And why is that important? Because of who wrote it.

Oliver Sacks.

The next victim is Mrs Olivia Sachs.

Very clever. Ingenious, even. Especially with that leaving open of the trap for the unwary: the fairly obvious link to Repp. A trap which Doyle was careless enough to fall straight into. Hell, he practically dived in there at the first opportunity.

But now he knows better.

Repp hasn't been the only 'distraction' from the murders. Mrs Sachs has been a distraction too. And, of course, she fits the pattern. Only too well.

What was it she said about the time she got the phone call from her daughter in the burning South Tower?

I said to God, let it be me in that building. I'm old, I've had a good life, let it be me who has to walk into that wall of fire. Anything to save my baby.

And that was it. That was enough to seal her fate. Perhaps she told that story a thousand times, to a thousand different people. But somehow it reached the ears of the killer. He latched onto it. And now he plans to grant the wish of Mrs Sachs to be reunited with her daughter.

Doyle knows this beyond doubt.

Because what he can smell in this hallway is gasoline.

★

Some things you can't prepare for.

You can draw your weapon and you can kick open the door and you can hope for the best.

It doesn't always pan out as you'd like.

Mrs Sachs stands in the center of her tastefully decorated parlor. She is drenched from head to toe, and there is a massive puddle around her feet. The pungent odor of gasoline is over-powering. Lying on its side on the floor is a gasoline canister.

Mrs Sachs doesn't move. Her head is bowed, her shoulders slumped. She seems already resigned to her fate. Her frail, be-draggled form is a pitiful sight.

Standing next to her is a man in a gray suit. He ticks all the tall, dark and handsome boxes, like he should be on the cover of a cheap romance novel. Doyle has never seen him before. Has no idea who he is.

What he does know is that, much though he'd like to, he can't shoot the sonofabitch.

Because the bastard is holding a cigarette lighter in his out-stretched hand. And it's lit.

'Freeze, motherfucker!' yells Doyle. Because it's the kind of thing he's been trained to do. You don't ask nicely and you don't ask twice. You hit 'em fast and hard, and you don't give them time to think.

Except that Doyle doesn't know what his next move should be.

He can't shoot this guy. Can't hit him. Can't arrest him. Can't even get anywhere near him. That flame is only a couple of feet away from Mrs Sachs. With all the fumes in here, it's a wonder she hasn't already gone up like a firework.

The man clearly knows he has the upper hand. There is no fear in his eyes. No indication that he senses the game is up.

Knowing this, the man smiles and reaches under his jacket.

'I said freeze! Do it, motherfucker, or you're a dead man.'

But there is no stopping this man. When his hand reappears, it is clutching a gun of his own. A gun which he slowly brings to bear on Doyle.

'Drop the gun! Drop it or I'll shoot, goddamnit!'

Doyle hears the way his voice has gone up an octave. He's starting to panic. His finger is tightening on the trigger of his Glock, but he knows he cannot fire.

The man's smile broadens. 'I tell you what,' he says. 'Why don't you drop *your* gun instead?'

The man's gun is now level with Doyle's. It's a standoff. Or at least it would be if it didn't seem as though everything was stacked in the killer's favor. One of them can shoot, the other can't. Life is unfair like that sometimes.

The man takes a step toward Doyle. 'Come on, be a good little boy. Put down your weapon and I might think about letting you live.'

Doyle is itching to start blasting away. His pupils are immense, his muscles taut. His every fiber has been dedicated to the task of taking out this sick fuck. He is so close to the release point that what he sees before him now is not a human but a target. His mind has already dehumanized the figure, readying Doyle to send out the bullets.

But all the while there is that little warning light, suspended in the air. A small spike of heat, just waiting for gravity to suck it down into that pool of liquid death.

Doyle feels the need to blurt something out. Anything.

'She doesn't need your help.'

The man cocks his head slightly. His lips twitch.

'What did you say?'

'Mrs Sachs. She doesn't need your help. You've made a mistake.'

'You don't know what you're talking about.'

'Mrs Sachs doesn't want to die. All she said was that she wished she could have taken her daughter's place if it meant saving her life. That's not the same as her wanting to die now. If you kill her, you won't be helping her.'

Another twitch, but his smile is fading. 'Shut up. You're just trying to stop me. It's too late for that. It's decided. The call for help has gone out. I have to . . . I have to do what's necessary.'

'Sure you do. But this isn't necessary. You want to help people, don't you? Well, this isn't helping. Think about it. Mrs Sachs doesn't want this, so how are you doing her a favor?'

'She said she wanted to burn.'

'Yes, but only if it meant saving her daughter. That doesn't apply now. Killing Mrs Sachs will serve no purpose. Her daughter is dead.'

As Doyle says this, he is sure he sees a sudden tremor in Mrs Sachs. As though his declaration about her daughter has cut her like a knife. It pains him that he is piling more misery onto her after all she's been through.

The man turns his head a touch. Looks dispassionately at the sodden bag of bones that is Mrs Sachs.

Come on, thinks Doyle. Dig deep. Find your humanity.

The man returns his gaze to Doyle. It is still the gaze of a madman.

'Enough talking,' he says. 'I have a mission. Drop the gun. I'm giving you five seconds.'

'Forget it, asshole. You ain't walking out of here.'

'Five,' says the man. 'Four . . .'

'Don't make me do this,' says Doyle, when in truth he doesn't know what he will do. He is out of options. He either kills the guy and watches Mrs Sachs become a raging inferno, or he puts the gun down and hopes it will buy him some time to think of another approach.

'Three . . .'

The man takes another fractional step toward Doyle, but still he holds the lighter directly above the pool of gasoline.

'Two . . .'

Doyle wants to scream, to run, to shoot, to surrender, all at once. He feels all the different pressures straining him in a thousand directions.

And then it happens. The unexpected. Something he didn't figure was a part of this equation.

Mrs Sachs moves.

She moves faster than he would have thought possible. A sudden launching from the position she has steadfastly maintained since Doyle arrived.

Seeing the surprise on Doyle's face, the killer starts to twist his own head toward Mrs Sachs. But he is too late. She flings her arms wide and jumps onto his back like some rabid starving animal. Her hands cross over in front of his neck and her skeletal fingers sink into him for purchase.

The noise is that of a gas hob igniting, but multiplied many times over. A front of hot air punches Doyle in the face. The center of the room is now filled with a huge fireball that starts to spin and dance and scream.

Doyle keeps shifting his aim, searching for a clear shot. But the burning mass moves too fast. Through the dazzling flames he can make out the arms of the killer, clawing at the demon on his back. But still she clings on, and the man's piercing screams send spears of ice through Doyle's veins.

In what is perhaps a last-ditch, unthinking attempt to survive, the killer suddenly starts pumping his legs. He runs straight at a glass-fronted cabinet, twisting to his left just before he collides.

The whole front of the cabinet implodes, and as the man rebounds in a shower of glass fragments, Mrs Sachs finally becomes detached from him and thuds to the floor. As the man continues to spin and career off walls and furniture, Doyle holsters his gun and races to the window. With a roar of effort he yanks down one of the heavy drapes.

He knows what his training is urging him to do now. It could almost be a question from a police exam: *You have two victims – one almost certainly dead, the other still with a chance of surviving. Which one do you help first?*

Doyle heads straight for the body of Mrs Sachs.

He throws the curtain over her and pats it down until he is certain the flames are out, then runs back out into the hallway. Next to a copper umbrella stand, a fire extinguisher is attached to the wall. Doyle rips it away and heads back into the parlor. He sees that the man has dropped to the wooden floor and is just sitting there, blazing away. Doyle is reminded of some newsreel footage he saw once of a Tibetan monk who sat cross-legged and immolated himself in protest at something or other.

Doyle tackles the flaming gasoline puddle in the center of the floor first, blasting it with the extinguisher more times than it needs. Then, slowly, he crosses the room to the remaining pyre. He takes aim with the extinguisher. Waits a few seconds. Waits a few more seconds. Then puts out the fire.

He looks down at the charred, sizzling mass. Wrinkles his nose at the smell of roasting flesh. Wonders why people do what they do.

Stepping back to Mrs Sachs, he chooses to leave her covered. It seems more fitting somehow. He wants to remember her as she was when he first met her. Aged, frail, but still with a spark of life. Still capable of flirting with him.

And then he thinks about what he said just minutes ago.

About the emphatic way in which he asserted that her daughter was dead. That was the trigger. That was what made her realize that her life was no longer worth living. And it was what saved his own.

And all the other victims. Dead not because of what they did or what they desired, but because of what they said.

Such is the power of words.

THIRTY-ONE

Of course, he tells them everything.

When they arrive in droves – the cops, the medics, the fire department – he tells them all he knows.

He tells them how he got a phone call from Mrs Sachs, saying that she wanted to talk with him about her problems with Repp, and that when he got to her house he was confronted by this madman, who had forced Mrs Sachs to make the call and who was now intending to kill both her and Doyle. He tells them how the guy was screaming that this was to teach Doyle to stop poking his nose in where it didn't belong.

They ask Doyle what the perp meant by that. He tells them he doesn't know. It doesn't make any sense.

And when he has said all this he has to swallow down the sour taste it leaves in his mouth.

In the hours that follow, the bodies are examined. Partly melted credit cards are found in the man's wallet. Enough to identify him.

His name is John Everett.

The investigating detectives search Everett's house in Queens, and what do you know? They find detailed notes on a number of people who have been murdered in the city recently. Notes about where they lived, their likes and dislikes, their personal habits, their daily schedules, and so on. Especially noteworthy is information on how these people indicated their desire to end their miserable existence.

Well, well, well, the detectives say. Isn't it funny the way things pan out sometimes? Turns out that Detective Doyle's theory wasn't so wacky after all. And if Doyle hadn't kept plugging away at it, maybe the killer would never have showed himself like he did.

So what the cops get is an instant clearance of several unexplained homicides and a perp they don't even need to prosecute, seeing as how he's been burnt to a cinder. Everyone in the NYPD is happy.

Everyone, that is, except Callum Doyle.

He's tempted to let it go. As time passes and the evidence against Everett continues to stack up, Doyle is sorely tempted to accept that the cases are solved and that he should move on with his life.

The investigators find a pair of shoes in Everett's bedroom that match up with footprints left on Vasey's wooden floor. They find a leather biker's jacket with a tag missing from one of the sleeve zips, the tag having been found in the bathroom where Helena Colquitt was drowned. Fingerprints found on the SUV used to kill Lorna Bonnow match those found all over Everett's house. The shotgun used to kill Hanrahan is also found at Everett's place. And when photographs of Everett start to appear in the media, several people come forward to say that they saw him near the scenes of crime, one of those helpful citizens being the owner of *Peppe's Pizza Piazza,* who says he served Everett not long before Helena Colquitt was murdered.

There seems no doubt about it. The evidence is too overwhelming. Everett murdered all those people. Case closed.

Well . . . maybe it's still open a crack. For Doyle, at least.

For one thing, how did Everett get to know so much about

his victims? Has anyone even tried to explain that? Some of those details were intimate, personal things. How did he find them out? Hanrahan wouldn't have gone around telling everyone he met that he was thinking of swallowing his piece. Tabitha said that she told only Mrs Serafinowicz and Doyle that she considered suicide. Vasey was too worried about his reputation to have gone blabbing that he threatened to hang himself in a pathetic effort to win back his wife.

How did Everett discover all this information about his victims? Did he know them? Did he work with them in some way?

And then of course, there's the glaring omission from Everett's otherwise detailed notes.

Doyle himself.

The man on the phone knew a heck of a lot about Doyle. The names of his wife and child. Where he was born. Being abandoned by his father. His phone numbers. Even that he was working on a case involving Mrs Sachs.

So where's all that in the notes? Doyle doesn't get so much as a mention.

In a way he's glad, because it would have meant answering a lot of awkward questions. But still, it seems curious that he's not in there.

All these things he could probably overlook. With a little effort he could dismiss them with a remark such as, 'I guess I'll never know.' And, over time, he would come to forget the unexplained and just be happy that he, Callum Doyle, was responsible for stopping a serial killer.

He could do all this were it not for one problem. The gnawing problem that keeps him awake at nights:

The voice of Everett that he heard in Mrs Sachs's home is not the same voice he heard delivering clues to him over the telephone.

He has tried telling himself he must be imagining things, that he is looking for demons that cannot possibly be there. Voices sound different on the phone. At Mrs Sachs's house the adrenalin was free-flowing: the way Everett spoke then was probably nothing like his usual speaking voice, and Doyle was not exactly calm enough at the time to analyze the guy's speech patterns. So he tells himself he should forget it. He's chasing shadows.

But Doyle doesn't always believe what he tells himself. The voices were different. He'd bet his life on it.

So what does that mean?

Everett was the killer. Doyle believes that much. But if Everett wasn't giving Doyle all those clues, then who was? And why? The caller never claimed to be the murderer; Doyle simply made the assumption that he was. It was a natural enough inference: the man knew so much about those already deceased and those about to die. Who else but the killer could know those things?

Someone did. He knew many things about many people.

So how?

Thinks Doyle, I don't have a fucking clue.

Three days after the death of Everett, Doyle is on a job that involves a trip to One Police Plaza. Before he leaves, he takes the elevator up to the eleventh floor. As he steps through the doors he bumps into Lonnie Adelman. The CCS detective is carrying a huge wad of documents under one arm, and his characteristically flushed face is that of a man who has just done a hundred-meter sprint to catch a bus, rather than that of someone who has merely walked along a corridor.

'Cal! Hey, man, how's it going? Nice work on the serial killer thing. Seems like I can't read a newspaper these days without seeing your ugly mug staring out at me. You got the paparazzi following you around yet?'

Doyle shrugs. 'I got lucky. Right place at the right time. The press are making it into more than it was. To be honest, I'm not sure all this coverage is good for me.'

'Sure it is. And you deserve it too. Luck, my ass. From what I heard, you're the only one who had the balls to push the serial killer angle.' He drops his voice to a conspiratorial whisper. 'Frankly, if it wasn't for you, the white shirts would still be scratching their heads and crying over their COMPSTAT figures.'

Doyle feels his face becoming as red as Adelman's. 'Maybe. Anyhow, that's why I dropped by. To give my thanks to you and to Gonzo. That work you did on that laptop I brought in really—'

Adelman stops him with a raised finger. 'And now you're giving me too much information. That was a favor for a buddy. A favor I'm not sure I want anyone else to know about, if that's all right with you.'

Doyle smiles. 'It stays between us. Just know that I'm grateful, okay? To you and the kid. Is he around, by the way?'

'The Brain? Actually no. He called in sick a few days ago. Something about a bang to the head. I guess he has to look after his most precious organ, right?'

While Adelman laughs, puzzlement creases Doyle's brow. He knows better than Adelman about the bang to Gonzo's head, and didn't think it looked serious enough to take time off work. But that's not the only thing bothering him.

'I'm sorry, what did you call him?'

'What, the Brain? You don't think it suits him?'

Doyle feels his stomach clench. A snatch of conversation jumps back into his mind.

Forget about what your heart tells you to do. It's the Brain that's important here. You don't need anything more than that.

And then another one:

Brain power. That's what's missing here. Find it, Cal. Use it.

And then yet another:

Protect that Brain. It's the only thing that's going to get you out of this mess.

Brain. With a capital B. Not the organ but a person. Gonzo.

Nah, thinks Doyle. Now you're getting ridiculous. How could he possibly have anything to do with this?

It would explain a lot of things, though, wouldn't it, Doyle?

'You okay, Cal?'

'Uh . . . yeah. Just thinking about Gonzo. Weird kid, ain't he? That voice of his . . .'

Adelman laughs again. 'I know what you mean. Sounds a little like . . .'

Marge Simpson, thinks Doyle. Say Marge Simpson.

'Cary Grant,' says Adelman. 'Doesn't go with his image at all, does it? Talk to him on the phone and you'd swear he looked like a movie star or a corporate executive. Maybe he should go into the voice-over business. He could even—'

But Doyle is already diving into the nearest elevator. 'I gotta go, Lonnie. Thanks again.'

He doesn't hear what Adelman calls to him after that. Doesn't hear what the other occupants of the elevator are saying to each other. He hears only one voice: that of his mysterious phone caller. And the only picture in his head is that of Gonzo.

He finds it impossible to marry the two together.

And that's what makes it the neatest trick of all. Cleverer than any of the clues given to him about the victims.

It fooled him completely.

He can hear the music from the hallway. A heavy, pounding bass that must drive the neighbors crazy. Doyle stands outside the door to Apartment 32 and pauses. He still doesn't fully understand what's been going on. Doesn't know who Gonzo is anymore, or what he's capable of.

329

What he does know is that he mustn't underestimate the man inside this apartment. He's not what he seems. Not by a long way.

And so Doyle slides his Glock from its holster and mentally prepares himself to use it on the nerdy kid he thought had become a friend.

Slowly, he raises his left hand. The hand containing the key he has just persuaded the building superintendent to hand over. As quietly as he can, he inserts the key into the lock. When it's fully home, he takes a deep breath. In one fluid movement he twists the key, pushes open the door and steps inside.

His heart seems to stop beating when a voice screams at him, then revs up again when he realizes it's just the rock group on the hi-fi. Most of the words are indecipherable. The only one he can make out is 'hellfire'.

The place looks deserted, but he wishes the so-called music wasn't depriving him of one of his senses.

And then a shape looms into view. Entering the room from the kitchen area. A male. Holding something in his hand.

Doyle swings his gun onto the target. When he sees Doyle and the gun aimed at his chest, the figure jumps and releases what he's holding. The plate of waffles crashes to the floor, almost unheard above the music.

Doyle and the other occupant of the room stare at each other. In unison they yell the same question:

'Who the fuck are you?'

It's not Gonzo. Not even in disguise could this be Gonzo. He's about forty pounds heavier, has a center parting in his lank brown hair, sports a wispy attempt at a moustache, and wears a T-shirt that says 'Life, but not as we know it'. Another heavy-metal-loving nerd, to be sure, but definitely not Gonzo.

'Turn the music down,' Doyle shouts.

'What?'

Doyle gestures toward the sound system. 'The music. Shut it off.'

The young man holds his palms up as if pleading not to be shot. Not taking his eyes off Doyle and his gun, he sidles over to the hi-fi rack and powers off the amplifier.

The silence that greets Doyle is eerie after the cacophony.

'Who are you?' he asks.

'M-Michael.'

'Michael what?'

'Michael Rowson.'

'What are you doing here?'

'I . . . I live here.'

'What do you mean, you live here? Since when?'

'I . . . I've lived here for about a year.'

Doyle glances at the doors to the bedroom and the bathroom. 'Where is he?'

'Who? What? Are you sure you're in the right place?'

'Turn around.'

'What?'

Doyle reaches into his pocket and takes out his wallet. He flips it open to display his gold shield.

'I'm a cop, Michael. Now turn around and put your hands on the wall.'

Michael does as he is told. Doyle frisks him, but finds nothing.

'Don't move a muscle.'

While Michael strains to maintain his position, Doyle checks out the other rooms. Still nothing. It's as if Gonzo never existed.

'All right, Michael, start talking. What the fuck is going on here?'

'Can I lower my arms now?'

'No. Not until I get an explanation. You don't live here, Michael. I've been here. I've been in this room. You weren't here. There was no sign of you. So cut the bullshit before I get really pissed.'

Michael pauses, thinking something over. 'All right. I think I know what this is about. But I didn't do nothing. I mean nothing illegal, okay? I was just . . . finding stuff out. That's not a crime, is it?'

'Michael, what the fuck are you talking about?'

'The hackers' convention. In Seattle. I've been there for a week. Isn't that . . . isn't that why you're here? Did somebody rat on me?'

Doyle senses he's telling the truth. He really does live here, and Gonzo doesn't. Which means that he doesn't know where the hell Gonzo is. Unless . . .

'Michael, do you know a kid called Gonzo?'

'Gonzo? What's he got to do with this?'

'You know him?'

'Sure I know him. He's the one who told me about this apartment when I was looking for a place. I asked him to water my plants while I was away. Wait a minute – is that what this is? Has Gonzo done something wrong?'

'Listen to me, Michael. This is important. Do you know Gonzo's address?'

'Are you kidding me?'

'Why would I be kidding you? Do you know it or don't you?'

'Sure I do.' He nods down at Doyle's shoes. Doyle looks down too, wondering what the hell he's supposed to see. And then it dawns on him.

'Downstairs?'

Michael nods. 'Apartment 22.'

Doyle continues to stare at the carpet, as if doing so could allow him to see straight into Gonzo's apartment. And then he's heading for the door.

'Hey,' Michael calls after him. 'Can I lower my arms now?'

Doyle takes the stairs two at a time. He wonders how thin the ceilings are here. Gonzo must have heard the music being abruptly cut off. Did he hear any of the yelling too? Does he know that Doyle is here?

As Doyle reaches door 22, another question occurs to him. Why did Gonzo go to all the trouble of using Michael's apartment when Doyle asked him to look after Tabitha? Why not simply use his own?

When Doyle leaps at the door and kicks it open, he gets his answer.

There are no sofas or armchairs here. No dining table or bookcases. No television. No normality. Gonzo could not have invited anyone in here without revealing that he was not simply the amusing social misfit or the endearing eccentric. He has gone way beyond that.

A better description might be 'unhinged'.

Because this place is like a shrine. A shrine to technology.

Arranged in a large circle is a set of desks. There are over a dozen of them. And on each desk there is a computer, facing inwards. All of the monitors are blank, but the computer towers hum softly and their tiny lights wink at Doyle. He gets the strange feeling that they're talking about him.

He pushes the door closed behind him. Keeping his gun at the ready, he steps through a narrow gap in the circle of desks. When he reaches the center of the arena, he turns slowly, looking at all these computers. Wondering what they're for.

And then he hears it.

It's behind him.

The silky-smooth voice of his helper.

'Hello again, Cal.'

THIRTY-TWO

Doyle whirls. He raises his gun. Lines up its sights with the bridge of Gonzo's spectacles.

Okay, he thinks. What are you going to do now, Doyle? Put bullet holes in a damn machine?

The image on the monitor smiles. 'Sorry, Cal. Did I scare you?' He pauses for a second, and when he next speaks, his words are in the high-pitched squawk of the Gonzo that Doyle has come to know and like: 'Would you prefer it if I talked like this? Is that better, Detective?'

Doyle doesn't know why, but he keeps his gun trained on the screen. He's never trusted computers.

'Where are you, Gonzo?'

Gonzo shifts back to his normal voice, the one that Doyle still finds hard to believe belongs to this man. It feels like he's watching a ventriloquist act. Any second now the real perp will appear with his hand up Gonzo's ass.

'I think I'll stick with this voice, if you don't mind. The other one gets pretty tiring after a while. You don't know how much of a struggle it was to maintain it in front of Tabitha for all that time. I had to keep the conversations to a minimum. Which is a shame, because she was so pretty and intelligent, it would have been nice to have a serious chat with her.'

'I said, where are you?'

'Not there, Cal. Not at the apartment, if that's what's worry-ing you. No, I'm long gone from there. I knew you'd figure out my part in all this eventually. Took you a while, but I'd say you were above average as far as the cops of this city go. I know that's not saying much, but you can take it as a compliment if you like.'

This new Gonzo is so calm, so self-assured. Nothing like the gauche young man he now seems to have discarded, like a snake shedding its skin.

'How'd you do it, Gonzo? How'd you pull it off?'

'Pull what off?'

'The homicides. How'd you get Everett to kill all those people for you?'

Gonzo puts a finger to his chest and raises his eyebrows in surprise. '*Moi?* No, you've got it all wrong. He didn't do it for *me*. He did it for himself. He did it because it was his way of helping people. I told you what it was all about in our phone con-versations. Helping. Everett helped his victims, I helped you. It's what makes the world go around.'

'You helped Everett too, though, didn't you?'

Gonzo shrugs. 'I guess I can't stop myself. It must be in my genes.'

'Why? What was he to you? How'd you even know he'd be willing to do this shit?'

Gonzo smiles. 'Take a look behind you, Cal.'

Doyle whirls again. Another monitor has come alive. The image is dark and fuzzy. Doyle moves toward it, squinting to make sense of it.

He sees a bed, with someone lying in it. An old woman. There are tubes snaking out of her. A hospital?

'I don't—' Doyle begins, but then there's movement on the screen. A figure of a man comes into shot. He moves away from the camera and over to the bed. He leans over the old woman, takes her hand, says something to her. When he's done talking, he walks around the bed, pulling the sheets out from below the mattress and then tucking them back in again. Smoothing them down. Getting them all nice and neat. When he walks away from the bed, there is sadness on his face and in the slump of his shoulders.

The man is Everett.

He disappears from view. The light goes out and the picture turns black.

'Nice movie,' says Doyle, 'although a little Ingmar Bergman for my tastes. You got anything more upbeat?'

Gonzo says, 'If it's drama you want . . .'

The same monitor flares back into life. Same image of the old lady. Everett appears again, does the same walk, the same talk. Circles the bed again, untucks, tucks. Gingerly slides the pillow from beneath the lady's head, plumps it up a little, places it over her face . . .

What?

Doyle finds himself being drawn closer to the monitor. He cannot believe what he's seeing. Thinks, I'm watching a murder. As it happened. Jesus Christ!

The picture fades again.

Doyle turns. 'The woman. Who the hell was she?'

'His mother. She had cancer. Terminal. Everett's view was that he was doing her a favor. It's how he got started.'

'Where was that? A hospital?'

'Not a hospital. Everett's house. He was her carer.'

'His house? He filmed this shit? Jesus. How did you—'

'Watch. There's more.'

Doyle turns once again. We're back in the room. No old lady this time. Instead, an attractive young one, sitting on the bed. Everett is on the bed too, next to her. They have drinks in their hands. The girl appears to be enjoying herself. She sways gently as she giggles.

And then she keels over.

Collapses unconscious on the bed. A little something extra in her drink, Doyle guesses.

Everett leans over her and examines her face. He puts two fingers to her neck to check her pulse. Then he gets up from the bed and moves out of shot.

A minute later he's back again, a tumbler of water and a medicine bottle in his hands. He puts them down on the nightstand while he sits the girl up. She's limp and unresponsive. He slaps her face a couple of times and she comes round just a little. Just enough to sit there unaided and stare blankly at him.

He takes the bottle and shakes a couple of tablets into his hand. He pops them into the girl's mouth, then picks up the tumbler and puts it to her lips. He has to tip her backwards to make it go down. He repeats the maneuver. More tablets, more water. Then again. The girl just sits there, taking it. Not aware of what's happening to her. Not knowing she's being murdered.

Everett loses his patience. He picks up the bottle again, but instead of shaking a couple of pills out onto his hand, he simply puts the bottle to her lips and tries to pour its contents down her throat. He grabs her by the hair, pulls back her head, forces the whole fucking bottle into her mouth . . .

The screen goes blank, and Doyle is glad of it. When he faces the disembodied head of Gonzo again, he can feel himself trembling.

'She was the second,' says Gonzo.

'Don't tell me. She once took an overdose. Or maybe she just thought about it. Because that seems to be enough for you sick motherfuckers. The slightest excuse. That's all you need. How'd you find her, anyway?'

'I didn't. This was way before Everett even knew I existed. There were two others like this before I came on the scene. He established the pattern himself. I just made it easier for him to continue.'

'Then how did you know he was doing this stuff? How'd you get hold of the home movie?'

Gonzo laughs. 'You really haven't figured it out yet, have you? I'm amazed. It's really quite simple.'

Doyle waits for the explanation, but Gonzo isn't forthcoming. The two stare at each other, even though they are not physically in the same room. Doyle has to keep reminding himself that he's alone here. Just him and numerous boxes formed from metal and plastic. And yet he's never felt so much the focus of attention.

The voice that breaks the silence also breaks his heart. It shouldn't be heard here. Not amongst all this death and violence.

'Whatcha doin', hon?' is all the voice says.

It's the voice of Rachel. Doyle's wife.

A different monitor this time. Doyle races over to it. He sees a close-up image of Rachel, staring right back at him. It's like she's been abducted from the real world and converted to a stream of bits that has been imprisoned in this machine.

'Rachel!' he says. 'RACHEL!'

Gonzo says, 'She can't hear you, Cal.'

Rachel turns her head slightly. She's listening to another voice. That's when Doyle realizes she wasn't talking to him. She was talking to their daughter.

He doesn't quite catch what Amy says, but Rachel replies with, 'No, don't wear that one. Wear the blue one.'

When Amy responds with a whine, Rachel rolls her eyes and moves away from the camera. Doyle watches her go. Watches her walk right out of the room. He knows that room.

It's their living room.

It's where he lives. He's looking straight into their apartment. How the hell can he—

And then he figures it out. It's the point of view. It tells him exactly where the camera is in his home. It's where the computer sits on its desk.

The computer with a webcam.

The realization stuns Doyle. He never knew such things were possible.

'You've taken control of our computer. You can see everything we do in that room. You can hear everything we say. That's . . . that's how you know so much about me. And those movies of Everett. You got those in the same way, didn't you?'

'That's right, Cal. He kept a computer in the spare bedroom where he looked after his poor sick mother. It's how I found him. It's how I found all of them.'

'All of them?'

Gonzo smiles again, and another voice cuts in. Doyle turns to see Cindy Mellish in profile. She's in her nightdress, and she's talking on the phone. She's crying as she tells her ex-boyfriend how she's planning to cut her wrists.

Three desks along, another monitor flashes on. Lorna Bonnow. Sitting up in bed with her lover. Telling him the story that Alex later told Doyle, about how she wanted to jump out in front of that ambulance.

From behind Doyle, another voice. Doyle looks round to see Vasey. He's sitting in his office chair, listening and nodding. The voice he's listening to belongs to Sean Hanrahan, and he's talking about how close he came to putting his service weapon in his mouth.

On yet another monitor, Vasey again. At his desk, but on the phone this time. He's pleading with his wife. Telling her how he doesn't think he can manage without her. Doesn't know what he might do when he gets home. He's even thought about ending his own life . . .

Then there's Tabitha. Curled up on a sofa. Tears running down her cheeks. Sitting alongside her, stroking her hand, is old Mrs Serafinowicz. Tabitha is telling her about her trip to the Brooklyn Bridge.

And to top it all, there's a moment of fame in the collection for poor old Mrs Sachs too. Not her image. Not even her voice. What makes this hardest of all to watch is that it's Doyle himself, telling his wife the story of the sad, wizened lady who once made the mistake of wishing she could swap places with her terrified daughter. It's Doyle himself who is sounding the death knell for Mrs Sachs.

The recorded clips are brief – just enough to capture the moment each victim orally signed their death warrants – and they are on a loop. Each time they repeat, the volume level increases. Doyle finds himself rotating slowly on the spot, his gaze skipping from screen to screen as the words overlap and the sound builds. This is how he did it, he thinks. This is how he infiltrated lives. He's the ultimate voyeur. He sees all, hears all. You don't even need your own computer. You just have to know someone who does. That's why Lorna Bonnow and Sean Hanrahan and even Mrs Sachs weren't safe.

Incredible.

While Doyle tries to absorb all this, tries to cope with the enormity of it all, the volume from all the computer speakers continues to mount, the calls for execution being hammered into him, until all he wants to do is put his hands to his ears to drown out the cacophony.

And then it stops. The computer screens turn to black again. All the dead withdraw into oblivion. The only face remaining is Gonzo's.

Doyle says, 'Why would Everett be interested in these people? What were they to him?'

'Everett was mad as a hatter. The only thing he wanted to do was kill people while telling himself he was doing them a service. I gave him that opportunity. I just called him up, the same way I called you. Told him I knew all about what he'd done to his mother and those girls. He was terrified at first. I think he believed I was God or the Devil or something. I used some fancy words – told him I would help him to pursue his calling, or something like that – and he jumped at the chance.'

'So,' Doyle says, 'this is what you've been doing with your life. Spying on people, searching for victims to feed to your pet serial killer.'

Gonzo shrugs. 'Beats television. Have you seen the crap they put out there these days? Having said that, most of what you guys get up to is pretty damned dull, you know. Sorry to be insulting, Cal, but what you do behind closed doors doesn't exactly light any fires, you know what I mean? Except, that is, when you talked about Mrs Sachs.'

Doyle decides not to join in with Gonzo's laughter at his own joke.

'So why bother? If it didn't look like I was going to be one of your precious victims, why bother with watching me?'

'Why? Because you were valuable in a different way.'

'How so?'

'You were a cop. A detective, no less. That meant I could get you involved. That's why I found Everett a victim in your precinct. It's why I got him to write your phone number on Cindy Mellish's wrist. I thought the message would eventually get back to you, even if you weren't initially assigned to the case.'

'Still doesn't explain why you picked me. I'm sure you've

found lots of detectives on your little box of tricks. You could have picked any one of them.'

'True. But not all of them know Lonnie Adelman.'

It takes a second for Doyle to realize what Gonzo is telling him.

'The diary.'

'Yes, the diary. Who else were you going to take that laptop to but your computer expert buddy Lonnie? That was my way in. I knew Lonnie would pass the computer on to me. The plan was I would contact you directly after that. I wasn't even sure it would be face to face. I thought maybe a quick phone call, using my fake voice. That's why I used my real voice when I first called you at home. 'Course, what I didn't expect was that Lonnie would actually bring you into my room to introduce you. Jeez, that was a panic moment. I couldn't use that ridiculous voice in front of him, and I couldn't use my normal voice in front of you. Luckily, Lonnie didn't hang around long enough to hear me speak.'

It strikes Doyle that it was mighty convenient that Cindy Mellish kept something in her diary that linked her to Vasey. But then he gets a follow-up strike that is even more of a haymaker.

'You altered the diary, didn't you? Vasey was telling the truth. He never met Cindy Mellish.'

'Well done, Cal. You're learning. I'd told you the diary was important, so I had to give you something. What better than a clue to a future victim?'

Doyle has to struggle to prevent a sense of admiration creeping into his thoughts. It's hard not to marvel at the sheer ingenuity of all this, let alone the technical wizardry. He has to remind himself just how evil and twisted this bespectacled clown actually is.

'So then we met, and you got a taste for putting yourself so close to the investigation. You just couldn't keep away after that.'

'Yeah, that was fun. Being right next to you, with you having no idea what I was doing. It got kind of addictive. Meant I had to stick with the stupid voice, though.'

Another thought occurs to Doyle. 'I got a phone call from the helper. When you and I were sitting in my car that time.'

'Oh, Jesus, Cal. Now you're letting yourself down again. You ever heard of speed-dialing? A simple press of a button on the phone in my pocket, that's all. You weren't taking calls from me at the time, so I knew you wouldn't answer it. And even if you changed your mind, all I had to do was hang up again.'

'Yeah, well you can wipe the smug smile off your face, Gonzo. You ain't so perfect. You killed the wrong girl, remember?'

Annoyance flares in Gonzo's eyes, and he raises his voice. 'I didn't kill anyone. Everett did it. The mistake was his. I gave him all the data he needed. I told him where she ordered her pizzas. I told him about her love for Harleys. I even told him what time she ran her bath, so that all he had to do was turn up and push her in the darn thing.'

'Your data was insufficient, and not for the first time either. It's why you were so surprised when I couldn't find Cindy Mellish's computer in her bedroom. You didn't think to check it after you got all the information you needed on her, and so you didn't know her mother had moved it. Same applies to Tabitha Peyton. You told Everett she was the only one who lived in that apartment. You told him that because you were relying on information you got before Tabitha's computer broke down. Admit it, Gonzo. You're not perfect, and neither is your system. You fucked up.'

'NO!'

There's an expression on Gonzo's face that Doyle has seen many times before on others. It's the look of fear and desperation that stems from not being in control. Technology is what gives Gonzo his power. He has nothing else. No looks, no physical strength, no charisma. He's the kind of guy who would have been bullied mercilessly in his childhood. He would have been the butt of all the jokes, the victim of all the pranks. With his computers he has a way to get back at the world. Tell him it's flawed and you might as well be belittling his manhood.

And then, slowly, Gonzo regains his composure. He re-affixes his malformed smile and wags a warning finger at Doyle.

'Very good, Cal. You almost had me there with your feeble attempt at psychological manipulation. Can you take it as well as you dish it out? How about if I remind you of your part in all this? The things you knew and chose to keep to yourself? The mistakes you made in not reading all the clues I gave you? You don't get to walk away from this, Cal. There's blood on your hands.'

'I can live with the choices I made.'

'Can you? Really? Maybe I did make a mistake with Tabitha. There, I said it. But you know what? You know what the funniest thing of all is? You fixed it for me. It was you, Cal. You delivered her right to my door. I didn't have to lift a finger. Don't you think that's priceless?'

Doyle's gun is at his side now, but he can feel his fingers tightening around it. He so wants to start blasting away at the cackling maniac in front of him. It wouldn't solve anything, but boy would it make him feel good.

Gonzo continues to revel. 'All I had to do was call Everett to come get her. I told him how to break into the apartment building and I told him about this red-headed nerdy kid she was staying with. We never met, you see. To him I was merely a voice on the phone, just like I was with you. Before I went down to the basement I called him again. I told him this was his big chance to go in and take the girl. He wasn't supposed to attack me, the moron. Although I suppose he did make me look more innocent.'

Doyle realizes now why Tabitha was abducted rather than drowned in the apartment upstairs. It wasn't simply a case of Gonzo or the killer making a statement; it was to prevent the police from crawling all over this building and looking into Gonzo as a possible suspect. It was all about keeping him out of the picture – something with which Doyle was only too happy to comply.

'You know why I did that?'

Gonzo appears confused. 'Did what?'

'Brought Tabitha to you. You know why? Because I trusted you, Gonzo. Maybe you're not used to that, people trusting you. But that's what it was. Sure, I made a mistake. A huge mistake. It's something I'll regret for as long as I live. But given the same circumstances again, I'd do exactly the same thing. Sometimes you have to accept people for what they appear to be. Otherwise, you'd never trust anyone. You'd never love anyone. Your life would stay empty. I don't want to live that way.'

Gonzo pushes his tongue into his cheek while he mulls this over. When he responds, he seems almost human again.

'Yeah, well, it's not always so easy.'

He doesn't elaborate, but Doyle can tell there's a lifetime of bad experiences behind those words.

'Nobody's saying it is. You said this was all about trying to help people. So maybe I can help you. Maybe—'

'No, Cal! Don't even go there, all right? This isn't an AA meeting. I don't need your pity.'

'I was just trying to—'

'Yeah, I know what you were trying to do. Don't patronize me, okay?'

'All right,' says Doyle. 'Level playing field. Man to man. Explain this to me.'

'Explain what?'

'Why you did this. What's this really about, Gonzo? With all that intelligence you got up there, why did you choose to do this instead of using it to really help people?'

'Why did I choose to go to the dark side, you mean?'

'If you like.'

'I did it . . . to prove a point.'

'The point being?'

'The point being that the NYPD is even more short-sighted than I am. The point being, Detective, that they can't even see past their own fucking noses when it comes to solving crime. So what if I can't do a mile-and-a-half run? So what if I have bad eyes and asthma? Where do brains figure into all this? Doesn't that count for anything?'

Doyle's eyes widen. 'You applied? To the PD?'

'Yes I applied. Didn't even get as far as the Police Academy doors. I tried to tell them what a mistake they were making. I told them how valuable I could be to them. But would they listen? No. All they were interested in was turning lunks like you into assholes in uniform.'

'Gonzo, you work for the NYPD. They need the kind of expertise only people like you can give them.'

'I'M NOT A COP! I wanted to be a cop. I wanted to make detective. I wanted to show the world that there's more than one way to catch criminals. And if the NYPD had let me, I would have become the best damn cop this city has ever seen. Their mistake, Cal. Big, big mistake.'

For a moment Doyle is dumbfounded. A sulk. That's what this is. On a grand scale. A child lashing out after one too many rejections. An 'I'll show you' gesture of the worst kind.

'So do you think you've made your point?'

'Oh, I think so, don't you? Look at how you floundered when you didn't have me to help you. You needed me, Cal. You needed my information. Without me you were nothing. Those murders would still be taking place now if it wasn't for me. You didn't solve those murders at all. It was me. Jesus, the rest of the NYPD didn't even know they were connected – that's how dumb they are. That's why they should have accepted me, Cal. Their loss.'

Acceptance. That's the crux of it. A sad and lonely misfit craving some kind of acceptance. And then the deadly ramifications when he doesn't get it.

'It wasn't the right way to do it, Gonzo. There are better ways. You could have told us about Everett from day one. And we would have looked up to you for that.'

'Sure you would. Or maybe you would have taken all the credit and then locked me up for computer crime. I know how you guys work. You don't want to be made to look stupid by some kid fresh out of college. Well now I've shown you. I'm not a jerk. I can do things you can't. Now you know.'

'Yes, I know. But nobody else does, Gonzo. This bomb you dropped has limited impact. Was it worth it?'

Gonzo laughs, but there's no humor there. Instead, he sounds almost weary.

'Yet again, you disappoint me, Cal. It doesn't matter what *they* know. I was doing it for me, not them. I was proving the point to myself.'

'And now that you've done that, what's next? Where do you go from here?'

'What's next? I told you a million times, buddy. It's all about helping. Now it's my turn.'

Gonzo raises his arm so that it comes into shot on the monitor. In his hand he is carrying a Glock pistol.

Doyle levels his own sidearm, and feels foolish when he realizes he's drawing down on a computer.

'What are you doing, Gonzo? Where did you get the gun?'

'I work at 1PP, Cal. The building is full of these things.

Somewhere there's an embarrassed cop who still hasn't admitted losing his weapon.'

'Put it down, Gonzo. It doesn't have to be like this.'

'It does, Cal. You know it does.'

Around Doyle, all the monitors come on again. All showing the same image of Gonzo lifting the gun and pressing its muzzle to his temple.

'Gonzo!'

For the last time, Gonzo slips back into his high-pitched geek voice.

'So long, Detective. I enjoyed working with you.'

The explosion, blasting out from every computer speaker in the room, is deafening.

On the monitors, the side of Gonzo's head erupts. His eyes cross as a geyser of blood spurts from his skull, and then he slumps forward, out of sight.

Then, one by one, the monitors go back to sleep. One by one, the lights on the computer towers blink and die. The whirring fans wind down and their noise fades.

All is silent.

On his way out of the room, something catches Doyle's eye. It's taped to the inside of the door. A little memento. He takes it down and slips it into his pocket.

And then he leaves.

THIRTY-THREE

Three days later. Doyle at home, enjoying the peace and tranquility. Enjoying life with his family.

Tucked up in bed, Amy asks, 'You catch any bad guys today, Daddy?'

Doyle strokes her forehead, pushing strands of hair off her face. 'Not today, hon. Today was pretty slow.'

'Then tomorrow you'll have to catch lots more. Hundreds of them. Or maybe even dozens.'

Doyle smiles. 'I guess I will. It's gonna be a busy day.'

'I'm gonna be busy too. I hafta draw two pictures for Miss Olefski.'

'Mrs Lefty?'

'No, Daddy! Miss Olefski. My teacher.'

'Oh! I thought you said Mrs Lefty. Like maybe she has only one hand. And the other arm has a big crab claw at the end of it. And she has a big hump on her back. And one of her eyes has a—'

'Daddy, stop it!' says Amy, even though she can't stop giggling. 'I'm gonna tell Miss Olefski what you said about her.'

Doyle puts his hand to his mouth as though he's terrified at the prospect. 'Oh, no. Please don't do that.'

'All right, I won't. I'm not a tattle-snail, are I?'

'No you're not a tattle-snail.' He pauses for a moment. 'Hey, I got something for you.'

'You have? What is it?'

'It's been in my pocket for days. I keep meaning to give it to you. Here . . .'

He slips his hand into his pocket and takes out the object he found taped to Gonzo's apartment door. It's the button. The one with 'Captain Awesome' written on it. The one he pinned on Gonzo.

He says, 'Shall I put it back in your shiny box?'

'You don't have to. You can keep it if you want.'

'Can I? I'd like that. Thank you. It means a lot to me.'

'That's okay. Can you turn out the light now? I'm tired.'

Doyle gives her a goodnight kiss and then switches off the light. As he leaves, he closes his fingers tightly around the button, then drops it back into his pocket.

In the living room, Rachel is at the computer again, working on her photographs. As he strolls over to her, music starts playing over the computer speakers.

'Why Does It Always Rain On Me?' by Travis.

Doyle stops in his tracks. Rachel turns to face him.

'What's the matter? You look like you've just seen a ghost.'

A ghost? Yeah, something like that.

'What? No. It was just . . . the music. Took me by surprise. After me asking about it the other day.'

'Actually, that's what made me dig it out. I haven't listened to this in ages. You don't mind, do you?'

'No.' Although he does mind. He could happily live the rest of his life without ever hearing this song again.

Doyle steps closer to Rachel. Standing behind her, he looks at what she's working at on the computer. He sees the same image he saw a couple of weeks back: the old black man sitting on the stoop of his apartment building.

'Whatcha doing?' he asks.

'A local magazine saw my photo. They want to use it on their cover. Only they don't want any product placement.'

Doyle leans closer. 'What product placement?'

Rachel grabs the mouse and makes a few clicks. Another window opens alongside the first. The same man on the stoop again.

'Spot the difference,' says Rachel.

He sees it then. In the original photograph, there's a can of Dr Pepper on the step at the man's feet. In the new image, it's gone. Not a trace of it ever being there.

'The soda can,' says Doyle. 'Where'd it go?'

'I took it out.'

'You can do that?'

'I can do anything I want. The wonders of technology. I can turn him into the President, or Mickey Mouse. The media do it all the time. The newspapers take people out of photographs and they put others in. Foreign governments put their dead leaders in situations that make it seem they must still be alive.'

'I guess so. That private eye I was telling you about? He musta done something like this to fake a photo of Mrs Sachs's daughter.'

'See? Happens all the time. Never believe what you see on an image that's been through a computer.'

A call of 'Daddy' comes from Amy's bedroom.

'I'll get it,' says Rachel. She gets up from the chair.

Doyle continues to stare at the computer screen.

Never believe what you see . . .

'By the way,' Rachel says. 'You might need to get your pal Lonnie to come and look at that machine. Amy says it's been doing funny things when she's talking to Ellie on it. She says it keeps showing her pictures of a weird guy with red hair and glasses. I haven't seen it myself, but that's what she says.'

And then she's gone to tend to Amy.

Slowly, Doyle raises his eyes and looks straight into the webcam.

'Gonzo? Are you out there, man?'

He expects no response. Expects just to feel stupid for talking to an inanimate object and waiting for it to talk back.

But a response is what he gets.

The screen darkens. The photographs Rachel was working on disappear.

When the monitor brightens again, it shows Doyle a view into an empty room. A study, with lots of bookshelves. Doyle doesn't recognize it.

He wonders whose room this is. Wonders, too, how many other supposedly private places in the world are being observed right now. If Gonzo could do it, then so can others.

Movement on the screen. A figure enters the room, walks across it and sits in front of the computer.

No, thinks Doyle. It can't be.

It's one face he thought he would never see again. A face that is being shown to him in order to taunt him, to make him realize that he doesn't always get things right. To make him feel humble.

And he does. Humble and sad and guilt-ridden.

Because the person staring back at him, now somewhat older than in the photographs he has seen, is Patricia Sachs, long-lost daughter of Olivia Sachs.